P9-DXI-328

Ace Books by Sharon Shinn

ARCHANGEL
JOVAH'S ANGEL
THE ALLELUIA FILES
ANGELICA
ANGEL-SEEKER

WRAPT IN CRYSTAL
THE SHAPE-CHANGER'S WIFE
HEART OF GOLD
SUMMERS AT CASTLE AUBURN
JENNA STARBORN

THE
ALLELUIA
FILES

SHARON SHINN

ACE BOOKS, NEW YORK

This is a work of fiction. Names, characters, places, and incidents either are the product of the author's imagination or are used fictitiously, and any resemblance to actual persons, living or dead, business establishments, events, or locales is entirely coincidental.

For Susie,
for when she has time to read

THE ALLELUIA FILES

An Ace Book / published by arrangement with
the author

PRINTING HISTORY
Ace trade edition / April 1998
Ace mass-market edition / May 1999

For information address: The Berkley Publishing Group,
a division of Penguin Group (USA) Inc.,
375 Hudson Street, New York, New York 10014.

ISBN: 0-441-00620-5

ACE®
Ace Books are published by The Berkley Publishing Group,
a division of Penguin Group (USA) Inc.,
375 Hudson Street, New York, New York 10014.
ACE and the "A" design are trademarks
belonging to Penguin Group (USA), Inc.

PRINTED IN THE UNITED STATES OF AMERICA

10   9   8   7

CHARACTERS

The Jacobites

Jacob Fairman, their martyred leader
Conran Atwell, their current leader
Rinalda Linise, another martyr, the
  mother of twins
Tamar, a young woman
Zeke, a young man

Peter
Jani
Duncan
Horace } Jacobites still
Sal   active
Wyman
Loa

The Angels & Their Families

Bael, Archangel and leader of the
  host at the Eyrie
Mariah, Bael's angelica
Omar, Bael's son
Mercy, leader of the host at Cedar
  Hills
Jared, leader of the host of
  Monteverde
Catherine, Jared's sister
Lucinda, who resides on Angel
  Rock
Gretchen, her aunt

The Edori

Maurice, captain of *The Wayward*
Reuben sia Havita, his first mate

Joe
Rico } sailors aboard
Michael   *The Wayward*

The Gentry

Christian Avalone, a wealthy
  Semorran merchant
Isaiah Lesh, a Manadavvi landholder

Ben Harth, another Manadavvi
  landholder
Simon Davilet, an importer of
  technology
Isabella Cartera, a Bethel landowner
Richard Stephalo, a Bethel
  landowner
Annalee Stephalo, his daughter

Others

Ezra, a former priest
Jecoliah, oracle at Mount Sinai
Emmie } servants at the Manor
Jackson   on Angel Rock
Celia and Hammet Zephyr,
  proprietors of the Gablefront Inn
  on Angel Rock
Jasper, steward at the Berman
  House, a hotel in Semorrah
Jenny, a servant at the Berman
  House
Gene, chief ostler at Cartabella, the
  home of Isabella Cartera

Arla
Caley } residents of Chahiela
Maretta

Alina } Students at the
George   Augustine School

Figures from the Past

Delilah, Archangel one hundred
  years ago
Alleluia, briefly Archangel during
  Delilah's time, then oracle at
  Mount Sinai
Deborah, oracle at Mount Sinai after
  Alleluia
Caleb Augustus, Alleluia's husband
Michael, Archangel before Bael
Joel, Archangel before Michael

Samaria

CHAPTER ONE

It was full dark when Tamar and Zeke entered the city, and still they moved with the caution of thieves. They had arrived within view of Breven at about noon and camped out far from the main road till dusk brought a welcome coolness and a measure of safety. Even so, it was worth their lives to cross the city line. But it had seemed, on balance, even more dangerous to stay in Luminaux.

They had assumed the guise of a young Jansai merchant's son and his submissive sister. This allowed Tamar, at least, to layer her face and body in the traditional scarves without which no respectable Jansai woman left her house. Zeke—pretending to be one of the arrogant gypsy traders—could not cover his face without arousing suspicion, but he had wrapped his head in one of the flowing white cloths the Jansai used to protect themselves from the unrelenting desert sun. And he had made sure its long edges draped themselves over his shoulders and halfway down his bare arms. Just glancing at the two of them, no stranger would notice that these travelers bore no glowing Kiss in their right arms. No one would halt them in the road, demanding their names, their identities, their suspect affiliations.

"What street are we on? Did you see?" Zeke murmured to Tamar as they passed yet another unmarked intersection. They had entered Breven from the west and had to pass through the less savory parts of town before they reached their destination in the business district close to the port.

"There are no signs till we're near the wharf. We just keep walking toward the ocean."

"But what if we're walking in the wrong direction?"

Tamar throttled a moment's extreme irritation. They had been on the road more than a week, moving by night from town to city, dodging Jansai, angels, and the merely curious. Zeke's company, never exactly to her taste, had grated on her more and more as the days dragged by. There was nothing he was not afraid of, no worry he failed to articulate. *A fine revolutionary,* she thought scornfully. Though perhaps she did him an injustice. She had not witnessed her parents' slaughter at the hands of religious zealots, as he had; her mother and father had perished the same way, years earlier, but she had been weeks old, not an impressionable fifteen. Perhaps she, too, would be fearful and nervous if she had seen what Zeke had.

"Conran told us," she said, lifting her hand in its billowing sleeve to gesture at the glowing horizon. "Most of the city business is done on the streets nearest the water. Ahead of us, there? You see lights? He told us that things are easier to find once you're in the business district."

"But it's so dark," he complained.

"You'll wish it was this dark when we get to the port," she said. "Once we're under a streetlight, it'll be that much easier to tell who we are. Or who we aren't."

"No one can see *your* face," he said.

She almost stopped dead in the street, but the last thing she wanted was to start an argument with Zeke, do anything that might attract attention. "What does that mean?" she demanded, keeping her voice low. There appeared to be few others abroad at this hour, in this neighborhood, but still. No need to create a scene. "We've only traveled five hundred miles in the past seven days to get here, to this city this night, but if you're afraid—if you don't think you can go through with it—"

"I didn't *say* that!" he responded sharply, his voice as quiet and intense as hers. "I think I have a right to be afraid. I think you're a fool not to be. If anybody in this city—*anybody*—recognizes us, we're dead, both of us, no questions asked, no news returned to our friends, no prayers said for our souls—"

"Since you have no use for the god, I don't see why you'd care if some priest prayed over you—"

"Well, when I'm dead I want someone to know it, even if it's just Conran and the others."

"They'd figure it out soon enough," was her grim reply. "Those who are still alive themselves."

It was such a shocking thing to say that she was not surprised when he did not answer, and they kept on their uncertain course toward the city lights. Well, but it was true. Luminaux, for so long the haven of the Jacobites, had become in the past few months no safer than any other city in Samaria. Since Archangel Bael had loosed his Jansai fanatics on the Blue City, not one of the cultists was safe. Oh, the Luminauzi had tried to protect the Jacobites, offering them shelter in secret rooms and false cellars, while formally protesting the invasion of the Archangel's soldiers. But the Luminauzi were a civil, not a military force; they were the artists and intellectuals and politicians of Samaria. They didn't know how to repel armed Jansai bursting through their doors at three in the morning. They couldn't save the screaming men and women dragged from their attics and hidden passageways by the Archangel's warriors. The Jacobites who could, fought back (and, trained to terrorism, sometimes won these brief desperate skirmishes). Those who could not perished. Those who could run scattered from the city in all directions.

They were to meet again in Ileah in two months' time, those who were alive, who could make it that far, who escaped the notice of the mercenary Jansai and ordinary Samarian citizens who didn't mind turning in a Jacobite for a tidy reward. Meet again and decide, then, how to carry on their mission.

"Have you ever thought," Zeke asked unexpectedly, breaking the long silence, "of setting sail for Ysral instead?"

"Instead of fighting here? Instead of bringing the truth to a whole world that does not want to see and can only blindly believe in lies so old and impossible that only a child could fall for them? Instead of doing what I know is right—what my parents died for—what *your* parents died for? Instead of—"

"I suppose not," he said on a sigh.

"No," she said. "Never."

"Well, I have."

"Now's your chance," she said. "Breven's your port. Catch an Edori boat tonight, be in Ysral in two weeks. You'll never be in danger again."

"Well, I've thought of it," he said defiantly. "I'm tired of running, and hiding, and always being afraid. And if we're all killed—if all the Jacobites are dead—who will be left to carry on the fight? Maybe in a generation or two, when the whole world is wiser, Samaria will be willing to listen to us—"

Under her layers of loose cloth, Tamar hunched her shoulders as if to shrug off his touch. The same old tired argument. *We cannot reason with them; we cannot make a difference; let us withdraw and try again next year, next decade, next century.* Cowardice, she called it, and usually to the person's face, but it still was not the time to be starting spectacular arguments with Zeke.

"Do what you want," she said. "There must be an Edori ship in port. You'll never have a better chance."

"And what about you?" he said.

"What about me?" she said, but she knew the answer. This whole venture had been her idea—destination, date, and disguise—and she absolutely could not complete it without his help. It was rare enough for a Jansai woman to be out on the streets at night, even properly attired and accompanied by a male member of her family; not one would be out alone. Without Zeke's protection, nominal as it was, Tamar could not pretend to this role. And if she was not a Jansai woman here in Breven . . . well, she would have to be an ordinary Samarian. Farewell, veils; good-bye, flowing garments that covered her from throat to toe. Only Jansai women dressed this way in the desert, where, even in early spring, the temperature could ascend to astonishing degrees of heat.

It was not her face that was so recognizable; indeed, there might be only half a dozen people, besides her immediate friends, who would know her on sight. But the fact that she bore no Kiss in her right arm—that would set her apart instantly. That would identify her at once for who she was. Jacobite. Cultist. Anarchist. The breed singled out by Bael for his special vengeance.

"I can't leave you alone in Breven," he said.

She wondered if, all along, this had been his plan; if this was why he had agreed to accompany her in the first place. She had spoken truly: he would never have a better chance to get to Ysral, for the Edori ships docked there every day, and the Edori were famous for taking on Jacobite refugees. Of course, boarding a ship from that well-patrolled dock was even more dangerous than crossing the desert on foot.

"You can," she said, "if you wait till we leave the priest's house."

"Won't you be afraid? If you're by yourself?"

She smiled in the dark. Zeke wasn't a half-bad fighter, and if they were ever unlucky enough to fall into hand-to-hand combat here on the Breven streets, he would no doubt make a handy battle partner. But if they were that unlucky, they were completely doomed, because they would never escape these streets alive after engaging in a brawl like that. She wouldn't miss his company, that was certain; and her survival skills were no doubt good enough to see her back across the desert alone.

"Once I've got the Kiss," she said, "I won't be afraid. If you'll stay with me that long, you can go, and luck to you."

"Well, I haven't decided for sure," he said, but his voice was rushed with relief. "But I've been thinking about it."

"You've got to go where your heart dictates," she said. "Mine will take me to Ileah. If yours says Ysral, then go. I won't stop you."

He did not immediately reply, and she let the silence lengthen between them. In any case, the less talking now, the better. They had moved past the huts of the poor on the outer perimeter of the city through the wealthy, quiet neighborhoods where the streets were lined with massive, shuttered, secretive homes. Now, nearing the wharf, they entered the busy nighttime world of Breven's business district. Glowing circles of light puddled at the base of the streetlights on every corner; the occasional truck growled by, clanking with its metal cargo. Voices muttered from behind shut doors or called to each other across the width of the pavement. Footfalls produced by invisible travelers sounded staccato and menacing in the dark. From farther away came ocean sounds: the groaning of ships pulling against anchor, the slap and trickle of waves against the wooden dock. The air was heavy with the damp, scented exhalation of the sea.

"We're getting closer," Tamar breathed, and laid her hand on Zeke's arm. Not that she was afraid, certainly not; but any Jansai woman would cling to her brother if she was abroad on a night like this.

"What was the street again?" he murmured.

"Saturlin. We're supposed to find the Exchange Building and turn right, and Saturlin is a few blocks off that."

"The Exchange Building? What's that?"

"The tall one with the eagle on top. You must have seen it in picture books."

"Oh. That one. If we—"

But "Ssh," she whispered, and pulled him back to the shelter

of the brick building they were passing. They could just fit into
the narrow niche provided by the glass door; the awning over
the lintel covered both of them in shadow. Zeke mouthed a word
at her—"What?"—but she shook her head, and in a few moments he heard it, too. First the rumble of the motor (big transport, from that sound alone), then the laughter carrying eerily
far over the city streets. Minutes later the vehicle passed them,
a huge, open truck carrying a load of Jansai soldiers in its cargo
space. There was a jumble of talk and laughter, indistinguishable
words, then the sudden splintering crash of glass as one of the
Jansai threw a bottle over the side. Tamar felt Zeke flinch beside
her, but the truck was gone. No one had seen them.

"Wonder what they're doing here," Zeke whispered.

"Looking for Jacobites. If you try to find an Edori boat tonight, be especially careful."

"There might be more."

"I'd count on it."

With renewed caution, they continued forward, crossing
streets in the middle of the block to avoid the lamplights, sticking as close to the buildings as their bones allowed, communi-
cating with hand signals so they could more closely monitor the
sounds around them. They saw no more transport trucks. The
few foot travelers they passed walked as stealthily as they did,
on the other side of the street, and did not accost them.

The Exchange Building was not hard to find, for it was one
of the newest and tallest in the business district of Breven. Even
in the unreliable street lighting, it was a glittering black, for it
had been hewn from a cold, dense granite alive with crushed
quartz crystals. On the edge of the roof, twenty stories up,
perched a ferocious bird of prey, carved from the same black
rock. Its wings were half-extended and its face was twisted in
a perpetual snarl; it clutched a strand of beads in one claw and
a round globe in the other. The Jansai motto, Tamar remembered
now, meant to signify trade and barter around the world. For at
one time the Jansai were Samaria's most legendary merchants.
Now they were the continent's most fearsome soldiers.

Well, they had always been fearsome, always had a history
of violence and brutality. But not until the past twenty years
had their savagery been yoked and bent to the will of the Archangel.

Tamar touched Zeke on the shoulder and pointed to the right.

He nodded and followed her. Across the street, two men were engaged in a heated argument that was punctuated unexpectedly by harsh laughter. This whole block was lit with a ring of lamps, so that it was almost impossible to slink back into welcome darkness. Tamar kept her hand in the crook of Zeke's arm and tried not to look like she was hurrying.

Cross the street; escape the floodlights of the Exchange Building. Pick up the pace a little, hurrying into the shadows. Here, the salty, fishy smell of the ocean was especially strong, and the wind pressed her garments tightly to her chest and thighs. Another streetlight, another stretch of pavement to cross. Back into darkness. One more block safely negotiated.

Zeke saw the street sign before she did. "Saturlin," he breathed, and crowded her toward the right. Saturlin was more of a cobblestoned alley than a true street, so narrow that most of its traffic surely came on foot. But it had the advantage of sporting absolutely no streetlights—which was also a disadvantage, because it was nearly impossible to make out distinguishing characteristics of any of the low buildings they slowly felt their way past.

"How will we know it?" Zeke asked, his voice edgy. "Do you have a street number? A name?"

"Eighth house on the left," she murmured. "With red shutters."

"Red shutters! I can scarcely see the windows, let alone the color of the paint—"

"There. Two buildings up. There's a light on in the window and it looks to me—well, there are shutters. They might be red. Let's get closer."

They crept nearer, arriving at the uninviting wood door reinforced with three bands of bronze. Faint light did indeed filter down from the second-story window, and as it passed through the slatted frame it seemed to cast a rosy glow on the peeling paint of its shutters.

"Six, seven, eight . . . Well, I think this is it," Tamar said.

"*Think?* And if it isn't? What will you say to whoever answers the door?"

"Oh, be quiet," she said impatiently, and rapped on the door as loudly as she dared. The silence of Saturlin, which had seemed comprehensive, instantly grew more complete; it was as if the house itself held its breath while the residents inside looked up wide-eyed and apprehensive. Midnight visitors must be a rarity, then. Tamar knocked again, just as forcefully.

She was not prepared to have the door flung open or to find a giant of a man glowering down at her from the threshold. She took a step backward, stumbling into Zeke, and found herself gulping once from nervousness.

"Well?" the large man demanded. "Who are you? What do you want? Why do you come to my door at midnight?"

"I came—we're looking for a priest named Ezra," she began, but before she could say another word, the big man grabbed her arm and jerked her inside. Zeke, scrambling after, barely made it inside before the door slammed shut behind him.

"Ezra!" the man repeated in a fierce whisper threaded with both amazement and fear. "No one comes here asking for him! No one! Who are you? What do you want? Tell me at once or I'll call the watch on you."

Tamar shook herself free, feeling calmer now. This was the right house, sure enough, and it was unlikely this man would be turning anyone over to the Jansai authorities. "My name is Tamar. I was told about Ezra by a friend of mine named Conran Atwell. This was the place I was directed to go."

"Well, and Conran Atwell had best keep his directions to himself." The big man scowled. Now that she got a chance to look at him, he was not quite the giant he had seemed at first, but large enough. It was his burly figure, wild beard, and rough mane of dark hair that made him seem so overpowering. "I don't like strangers who come calling in the dead of night."

"We won't take up more of your time than we can help," Tamar said. "Can you direct us to Ezra?"

"No, I cannot, and I would not if I could!"

"Are you Ezra?" she pursued coolly. The big man stared down at her.

"And if I was, why would I tell you that? The priest Ezra is no more. That should be enough for you—*and* for Conran Atwell."

"I need to see him," Tamar said, unheeding. "I need his help. I know he is here—or that he's you—and I won't go until I've had a chance to talk with him."

"You'll go soon enough if I throw you out on the street," he threatened her.

"I don't think you can afford an altercation on your doorstep," she said. "Or you would not have been so alarmed when we arrived."

"What man can afford a brawl in Breven?" he muttered, but he was eyeing her sideways in an effort to judge her nerve and her tenacity. She could not tell how much of the bluster was real, how much she assumed, but she had quickly lost her fear of him. Conran had assured her that Ezra would help her ("though you may have to ask him more than once"), and Conran had never lied to her. And she had come this far. . . .

"I only want one thing from you. I won't stay a minute longer than I have to. I won't ask for shelter, or food, or any other aid. I just want Ezra's . . . services."

"And what can you afford to pay him?" the big man asked bitterly. "Nothing, am I right? You Jacobites are all alike. All guts and glory and not a penny among you."

Zeke had smothered a gasp when their host named their party, and the older man threw the younger one a look of scorn. "Well, who else but Jacobites would come to an ex-priest in the middle of the night, asking for the only service a priest can provide? Besides, if Conran Atwell wasn't named Conran Atwell, he'd be named Jacob Fairman, for he's the most thorough anarchist I ever met in all my life."

"I have money," Tamar said quietly. "Not much, but some. Would fifty gold coins be enough for you?"

It stopped the big man in his rantings, and even Zeke stood stock-still with surprise. *If he'd known how much I was carrying on me, he probably would have robbed me this side of Breven,* she thought cynically. Samaria had only recently changed over from a system of gold coins to paper currency. Most of the merchants were enthusiastic about the new money, but the more wary elements of society still preferred cold, hard metal. For one thing, the exchequers at the Exchange Building had to be keeping track of how much money they printed, and that meant they could trace the bills from hand to hand—or so the suspicious believed. But gold was an anonymous bounty, and it never devalued, and you could melt it down to create something just as precious as its barter weight. No one would turn down an offer of gold—particularly not when the number in the offer was so high.

"It might be," the big man said, giving her a long hard speculative look. "If I could see this money. If I had it in advance."

Bargain, bargain, bargain, part of her brain said, but another part, the part that had trusted Conran this far, merely wanted to strike the deal and get it over with. "Are you Ezra?" she demanded.

"I'm Ezra."

"Then you can have the money now."

And she slipped her knapsack from her shoulder and knelt right there in the cramped foyer, and she pulled out her gold. She had taken a narrow piece of red velvet and sewed it into a sleeve, and slipped in the coins one at a time; then she had tied strings between each coin and coiled the whole thing as tight as it would go. Thus no clink of money would give her away—to Zeke, to anybody—as she traveled.

"Shall I show you every coin?" she asked as she used her pocket dagger to slit each bit of string.

"Every last one," said Ezra.

So she used the tip of her blade to rip out the hem at the top of the sleeve and poured out the gold in a glorious tumble onto the cold floor. She could feel both Zeke and Ezra staring. Nobody walked around carrying a ransom like this, not in Breven, not anywhere.

"Very well," Ezra said. "Tell me what you want."

She came fluidly to her feet. "I want you to install a Kiss in my arm."

"You're a Jacobite. You have no need for a Kiss that will bring you to the attention of Jovah. You do not even believe Jovah is your god."

"I have a need for a Kiss that will help me masquerade as someone other than a Jacobite."

"So you fear for your life, and you compromise your principles to save your skin."

"As do you, as does everyone."

Ezra's eyes narrowed at that, for he clearly wondered what Conran had told her, but he did not reply directly. Instead, he jerked his head in Zeke's direction. "And him? Does he also want the Kiss? And does he have his own fifty gold pieces, or does he think you shall pay his way?"

"I would think fifty gold pieces would buy Kisses for ten of my friends," she said, "but you must ask him."

"No," Zeke said, speaking for the first time since they had

leaped inside the door. "I don't want a Kiss in my arm. I have no need of one—I am going to Ysral."

"Well, and good luck on that venture," Ezra growled. "Twice this past week Edori ships have put into port and been boarded by Jansai warriors. I'd guess they searched every cargo hold and lifeboat, looking for prey just like yourself."

Zeke's chin went up. It was clear to Tamar that he did not care for the ex-priest. "I'll be careful," he said. "I got us this far safely."

Ezra was fitting the coins back into their velvet carrier. When he was done, he knotted it at the top and slid the whole package into a voluminous trouser pocket. "Doesn't matter to me what you do or whether you make it," he said. "I'll do what I'm paid for, and then you're both out of here."

Tamar nodded. "Then let's get to it."

Ezra led them up a shadowy stairwell to a suite of rooms on the second floor. Tamar looked around critically as they entered. The stone walls were badly mortared, and the electric light was dim and insufficient for the space, which was furnished with chairs, tables, and other oddments that appeared to have been salvaged from a junk heap. The whole building gave the impression of being ancient, ill-built, and poorly kept, like some of the older structures in Luminaux that had undergone inadequate renovation after the advent of electricity. But Breven, she knew, had had few permanent buildings along its wharf until the past century, so this place was very likely less than a hundred years old. It had just been carelessly put together and was no doubt cheap as dirt.

But what other residence could an ex-priest afford?

Ezra gestured toward a tattered black chair set awry in one corner of the room. "Sit there," he instructed Tamar. "I'll be back in a few minutes."

"She's already paid you," Zeke said loudly, swinging around to watch Ezra as he headed for the door. "So you'd better be back."

The big man briefly broke stride, then left the room without turning back to reply. Settling herself on the chair, Tamar silently shook her head. No matter what, she was at the priest's mercy now. Zeke's posturing served no purpose.

But Zeke turned back to her, satisfied with his empty threat. "Tamar," he said, coming over to crouch beside her, "where in the world did you get that much money? And why didn't you tell me you had it?''

She elected to leave the second question unanswered. ''Conran gave it to me.''

''And where did *he* get it?''

''He said it was a legacy. That my mother left it.''

''Your mother? Who—why—none of the Jacobites have that kind of money!''

Tamar was silent a moment. Only a handful of the remaining Jacobites had ever known her mother and father, and none of them had bothered to sit and tell her warm, sweet remembrances of her martyred parents. That they had died for the cause, she knew, in the first bloody uprising nearly thirty years ago, the event that had taken the life of Jacob Fairman and the other early fanatics. That she was their only child she also knew, and their names had been given to her as Lianna and Rolf. But what they looked like, how they had met, what had drawn them to the fiery radical Jacob Fairman—no one had ever bothered to tell her that. Once or twice she had suspected that her mother was a daughter of the Manadavvi, the wealthy elite class living in the rich province of Gaza, and that would certainly account for the inheritance of fifty coins. Or perhaps not. The few affluent individuals who had joined the Jacobites had usually dumped all their jewels and assets into the community coffers, always woefully low. For a young woman to have the foresight to set aside a dowry for her daughter was singular in the extreme. So perhaps Conran had lied about the money.

''Well, that's what he told me. Frankly, I don't care where he got it. It'll buy me my Kiss.''

Zeke gave a minatory look at the door through which Ezra had left. ''Maybe it will,'' he said darkly. ''If we can trust him. What do you know about him, anyway?''

She shrugged. ''He was a priest for twenty-five years and now he's not. Conran was not specific. My guess is that he was caught in some kind of illegal pursuit, so the oracles stripped him of his position.''

''Installing Kisses in rebels?''

''Conran says not. Not until after he was defrocked, anyway.''

''So you're not the first who's come to him.''

''No, but I don't think there have been many others.''

"Is he a Jacobite?"

"I'm not sure," she said. "He'd almost have to be, to be a friend of Conran's. But if he was a priest for twenty-five years—well, wouldn't he have to believe in Jovah?"

"Maybe he converted. Maybe he came to see the truth."

"Maybe he thinks they're all fools—angels, priests, *and* Jacobites," Ezra said from the doorway. He was carrying a small leather briefcase that was so covered in scratched, layered dust that it appeared to be written on in mysterious hieroglyphics.

Zeke swung around to challenge him. "So you don't believe in the god Jovah, who sends sun and rain, and listens to the prayers of the angels, and guards our souls when we die?"

"No, and I don't believe that there's some great electronic brain orbiting over our heads on some thousand-year-old spaceship, either. Although, to tell you the truth, I couldn't really decide which theory is more preposterous."

"Then why did you spend half your life as a priest?" Zeke demanded.

"Because it paid well. Now shut up. Go sit on the other side of the room, you're annoying me."

Zeke stiffened and seemed to be considering a protest, but then he stalked away and flung himself onto a dilapidated couch next to the window. Ezra pulled up a chair on Tamar's right side and opened his briefcase on his knees. She could not see inside; she was not sure she wanted to.

"Will this hurt?" she asked.

"Not at first. I'll numb your arm before I start. When it wears off, it'll hurt like a knife wound for a day or two." He snorted. "We always tell parents, 'Oh, it's painless, the baby doesn't feel a thing,' but of course that's a lie. Hurts like hell. The baby just can't say so, and none of the adults can remember what it felt like to be Kissed by the god."

"How long will it take?"

"About half an hour. If you sit still and stay quiet."

She nodded instead of replying, to show him she could be silent. He drew a wide, flat jar from his briefcase and pried it open, then stirred the contents with his finger. She frowned briefly as a faint odor drifted past her.

"Hold out your arm," he demanded, and she extended her right hand. She had already rolled her sleeve up all the way to her shoulder, for the Kiss would be inserted just under her bi-

ceps. He smeared a dollop of white paste on her arm where the
Kiss would go.

"Manna-root salve," she murmured.

The ex-priest looked at her sharply. "Manna root is one of
the ingredients, but how do you know that?" he asked. "Only
the priests use it. It's too rare for ordinary men and women to
play with."

She shrugged against his grip. "There was an Edori woman
I knew in Luminaux. She had some. Apparently the Edori use
it all the time. It's not so rare in Ysral."

Ezra grunted. "Maybe not. They say the angelicas used to
know how to pray for manna seed to fall from heaven, but
they've forgotten or lost the prayers that used to coax it from
Jovah's hands. But the Edori remember prayers none of the rest
of us ever learned."

"I thought you didn't believe in prayers to Jovah."

"I believe in the results I see."

They sat for a while in silence as the salve went to work.
First it felt cool against her arm, then it caused a shivering tingle,
and then the whole area went dead. After about five minutes
Ezra poked at her arm with a needle.

"Feel that?"

"No."

"All right. Look away if the sight of blood offends you."

But it was her own blood, her own body, and so she watched.
Working with an unexpected delicacy for a man with such big
hands, Ezra retrieved a small, wickedly thin knife from his briefcase and made one quick incision in her arm. She felt a certain
pressure but no pain, even as the blood quickly welled up along
the cut. Only when the droplets slid down her skin, past the
numbed area, did she feel their sticky warmth.

Ezra was pulling another treasure from his case. "Ever see
one of these?" he asked. "Not attached to a person, I mean."

He handed her a strange contraption that looked like nothing
so much as an opal-backed spider, only bigger than any spider
she'd ever seen. With her left hand, she took it, and held it up
to the insufficient light. The top portion was smooth, beautiful,
gemlike, an extremely hard glass filled with opaque shadows.
The bottom half consisted of a tangle of metallic black wires,
stiff but bendable.

"A Kiss," she said. "How does it work?"

He snorted again. "Depends on what you believe, I guess. The faithful say that the Kiss is a product of Jovah's, fashioned by his hand, and that the blood of a man—or woman—animates it. The Jacobites believe that it is some kind of electronic link to this spaceship they're always talking about. And that human warmth or movement or what have you switches it on and allows the computer to track them around the planet till they die."

"The second explanation sounds infinitely more reasonable to me," Zeke called from across the room.

"Be quiet," Ezra said, not even looking at him. "As for the mechanics of it—" He took the object back from Tamar and proceeded to separate the trailing wires. "These are inserted into the incision and graft themselves to the bone over a period of three days. You can remove or reposition a Kiss for up to seventy-two hours, but after that, there's no digging it out of a person's arm without breaking through the bone itself. Or cutting his arm off." He grinned wolfishly. "Which is something I have known to be done. Here, now, brace your hand against the edge of my chair. And hold very still."

"Can I talk?"

"I would imagine nothing could stop you," he said, but absently. With one hand, he was holding the Kiss; with the other, he was prying apart the edges of her slit skin. He seemed to do no more than lay the wires against the cut and wait. Through the deadened nerve endings, she almost believed she could feel those narrow metal fingers shiver with a slowly quickening life of their own, sink through the layers of muscle and vein to seek out the sturdy anchor of the bone. Ezra applied some pressure to the crystal top of the Kiss, edging it back and forth to attain some perfect placement, then was still again.

"Does it light up?" Tamar asked.

"Does what light up? The Kiss? Not that I've ever seen."

"I've heard it said that when true lovers meet for the first time, the colors in their Kisses go wild."

His face wore a disdainful look. "Romantic tales told by lovelorn girls," he said. "The idea makes no sense."

"Well, it would make sense if Jovah was a computer," Tamar argued. "If he had his reasons for wanting to mate certain men and women. The lights and colors could be—not an emotional reaction, but an engineered, scientific one."

"Ridiculous," Ezra said. "It doesn't happen."

"So how many of these Kisses have you installed over your life?" she wanted to know next.

"Uncountable," he replied. "Thousands."

"And where did you get the Kisses?"

He responded with a short dog's-bark laugh. "When I was first ordained, I was presented with this case of instruments and a box of one hundred Kisses. When I had used up every last one, I returned to the oracle on Mount Sinai, and she gave me one hundred more. And so I continued for as long as I was a priest."

"Where do the oracles get the Kisses?"

"I did not ask. Perhaps they construct the items themselves. Perhaps there are storerooms of them buried in each of the retreats. Perhaps Jovah sends them as requested. I never cared."

"And how many Kisses do you have left from that final box of one hundred?"

This time the laugh was fainter. "Five."

"Then I am glad I came to you when I did."

"And this night of all nights. You are never completely safe in Breven, but today and tomorrow and the next day you might be considered a little less at risk."

Tamar's voice was scornful. "That is why we chose to come tonight, of course. Do you think we are complete fools? With the Gloria to be sung tomorrow morning, all the angels and most of their Jansai servants will be on the Plain of Sharon. We do not have to worry about them."

"Well, I would still worry a little bit," he said. He lifted his hand cautiously from the Kiss, but it stayed grounded in her arm. He nodded. "Good. It looks like it has rooted. I'm going to smear some more cream around your incision and bind the whole thing."

"And how do I care for it while the wound heals?"

"It shouldn't take more than a couple of days to heal. The cut is shallow, and the manna root is a marvelous salve—and, here, you can take this jar of ointment. I've got more. But remember, the Kiss itself will not be absolutely implanted in your arm until the three days are up. Keep the area dry and cover it with a bandage daily to keep it free from dirt and dust. After that, you should have to give it no more care than you give your fingernails or your teeth."

"And if something goes wrong? If it hasn't—rooted?"

He gave her that lupine grin again. "Then come back. I'll fix it."

"You know I can't do that."

"I wouldn't trouble myself. In the twenty-five years I installed Kisses, day in and day out, only twice did a Kiss fall awry. And in both those cases, the problem lay with the person receiving the Kiss—both young children who scratched and clawed at the alien marble in their arms. That's the reason we always preferred to graft the Kiss to infants—they don't like it any better, but there's less they can do about it."

"And when the salve wears off? Will it hurt?"

"Like any wound. It will improve every day."

"Then we're all done here?"

"You're done."

Tamar rolled her sleeve back down, glad that its full folds hid the bulky bandage. She had hoped she would be able to walk out of Ezra's place boldly, flashing her badge of citizenship, but apparently she had three more dreary days to wait before she could pass as an ordinary woman of Samaria. Well, she had waited twenty-eight years. She could wait three more days.

"Ready, Zeke?" she asked, coming to her feet. Ezra, rising to his considerable height beside her, forestalled her with a gesture.

"And where do you plan to go once you've left here?" he asked. "No respectable inn would take you at this hour of the night."

"We can go to the wharf," Zeke said, crossing the room to join them. "I need to look for passage to Ysral."

"Not at midnight," Ezra said. "That's when the patrols are most zealous."

"Do you have a suggestion?" Tamar asked quietly.

He gestured around the room where they were standing. "It's not luxury, but you can spend the night here," he said. "Leave at dawn. It's safer."

"I have no more money to pay you for such a great favor," she said.

Ezra shrugged. "Included in the fee."

"Then we accept your offer," Tamar said before Zeke could come up with any protests. Though she suspected he was as glad as she was to find a haven for the night.

Ezra nodded once, sharply, and turned to leave the room. Even this gesture of altruism did not incline him to easy friendship. "Don't disturb me when you leave in the morning," he said. "Just take the stairs and go out. The door will lock itself behind you."

"If we are not to see you again, let me thank you now," Tamar said, her voice slipping into the slight singsong of formal gratitude. "For the use of the room, and for the great service you did me tonight. Even though I offered you money, you could have refused, and you did not. I am in your debt."

He waved off the speech, though he did not look entirely ill-pleased. "Best be careful on the streets as you leave, Gloria or no Gloria," he said. "Be especially wary on the wharf. The Jansai love nothing so much as Jacobite meat for breakfast, especially when that Jacobite is on the verge of escaping."

"We'll be careful," Tamar said, holding out her left hand. Almost reluctantly, the big man took it.

"Jovah keep you," he said, "if you care for that blessing."

She smiled, and responded with the Jacobite's traditional farewell: "May your friends guard your back, may the seasons be kind, may you never weary in your faith, till we find the Alleluia Files at last."

CHAPTER TWO

Zeke and Tamar were up at first light. They quickly dressed and ate from their dwindling supply of rations. Tamar wasted a few minutes investigating the Kiss on her arm. During the night the numbing agent had evaporated, and she had woken to a deep, insistent ache—not unbearable, but not easy to overlook, either. She carefully untied the bandage Ezra had applied and was pleased to see no bleeding or swelling around the incision. Manna root was an excellent salve indeed.

The Kiss itself looked different in the light of day—more vibrant, more concentrated. *More sentient,* Tamar thought, though that was a concept that belonged more to the angels than to a properly educated atheist like herself. If it indeed represented an electronic link to the computer that orbited overhead, then it might perhaps have animated somehow as it connected to her flesh, but it did not grow more alive. It was a mechanism, a thing, constructed by men for the edification of a machine.

Still, the faintest milky glow seemed to swirl dreamily in its crystal depths.

She spread a little of the manna ointment around the incision but, contrary to Ezra's instructions, did not rebandage her arm. When she donned her Jansai veils and garments again, she left her arms bare so the Kiss would show. It might not be completely anchored in her bone yet, but she would be careful not to bump or bruise it; this was a badge she could not wait even one more day to show.

"Are you finally ready?" Zeke asked impatiently as she finished tying her headdress in place.

"Ready. Let's go."

They moved quietly down the steps and let themselves out on the street, closing the door behind them. Tamar tugged on the handle till she felt the lock fall home, then she turned to survey the close alley. Not much more welcoming in spring sunlight. They needed to get to the more publicly traveled areas.

"I've been thinking," she said. "Instead of canvassing the wharf, it might be safer to go to the marketplaces or the cafés and see if we can find an Edori captain off his ship. Make arrangements there. He might be able to help you get safely on board."

"Makes sense," Zeke said. "But how will we recognize a sea captain?"

She grinned. "Well, I'd guess any Edori we run into in Breven will be a sailor, whether or not he's a captain. That's a start. And of course we'll recognize any Edori we see."

"True enough," Zeke said. "Let's go look."

It *was* true; though rare on the Samarian continent these days, Edori were instantly recognizable anywhere. Dark-haired, dark-eyed, mahogany-skinned, Edori all possessed a certain resemblance that would have set them apart from ordinary Samarians even if their genial, welcoming dispositions did not. Tamar had not met many Edori, for most of them had emigrated to Ysral over the past hundred years, but all of them had amazed her with their fearlessness, joyousness, and genuine interest in the world around them. She could not believe centuries of oppression had not bred such common delights from them. It had only taken a trio of decades to turn the whole lot of the Jacobites grim.

Breven by day was a very different proposition than it had been by shadowy night. For one thing (Gloria or no Gloria), there were hundreds of people abroad, cramming the sidewalks and filling the pitted roads with vehicles of all descriptions. Most of those they passed were Jansai—as distinctive as the Edori, but mainly by virtue of their loose, flowing clothing and predilection for gaudy jewelry. But the whole range of Samarian society could be found on these streets, for Breven was a trading capital second only to Luminaux. In the past fifty years it had even eclipsed Semorrah, the inland city that had been the business heart of Samaria for centuries. Thus Zeke and Tamar passed elegant Manadavvi from Gaza, middle-class burghers from Bethel, ordinary farmers from southern Jordana—and, finally, a solitary Edori man standing outside a shop window and looking in with an expression of wonder.

He was gazing at a confection of lace and satin, a woman's garment that Tamar would never have expected to see in a Breven market, and she nodded at Zeke to let him know she could handle the opening conversational gambit. Accordingly, she came to a halt beside the spellbound traveler and let loose a lilting laugh of complicity.

"I'm not sure what I'd say to a man who brought that home to *me*," she observed. "But at least I'd know what was on his mind!"

The Edori turned to her instantly, his waist-length braid whipping over his shoulder. A quick grin lightened his dark face. "Well, if a man wanted to bring a woman a gift he'd be sure she'd like, this might not be the one," he replied. "Is what I was thinking."

"Are you shopping for a wife—a lover?" she asked, remembering belatedly that the Edori were said to never marry. "Or merely courting?"

Still smiling, he put both hands before him, palms outward, as if pushing away trouble. "A man like me's got no business courting," he said.

"And why would that be?"

"I'm a wanderer by nature. The ocean is my lover, or so the women say."

"Oh, a sailor," she said, nodding sagely. "And how long will you be in port?"

He glanced up at the sun, measuring time, and laughed. "Another two hours, it looks like. I should be back on board already. But facing two weeks of nothing but wave and wind, a man likes to take a few more minutes to feel his feet on solid ground."

"Cargo boat?" she asked. "Or merely pleasure?"

He laughed again. "Well, despite what you'll hear any sailor say, there's a pleasure merely to be on board ship, crossing the ocean again and again. But we're a cargo boat. We trade mostly in spices, gold, and electronics."

"Passengers?" she asked, and suddenly her voice was very low.

His face immediately grew sober, but not a muscle in his body changed position. Anyone watching them would have noticed nothing tense in either of their postures. "From time to time," he said. "But it's a rarity."

"Would it be possible," she said slowly, "for you to tell me the conditions?"

"Are you the one who desires passage?"

"No. My friend. The man across the street who's eating the tangerine. He wishes to set sail for Ysral immediately."

"It's not my decision," the Edori said regretfully. "My captain's on board already, and it's his boat. His choice. I'd be willing to ask him. One man isn't much of a burden."

"He can pay a little, though not much," Tamar said. "But he can work to help pay his way."

"It's not the gold. It's the getting out of Breven harbor. Let me ask. I'll see what the captain says."

"You said you're sailing in two hours. Will you come meet us somewhere? What shall we do?"

The Edori thought swiftly. "The ship's called *The Wayward*. She's docked on the southern edge of the port, facing the Varnet Building. Do you know it?"

She shook her head. "Describe it."

"White marble. Sixteen stories. Everything else around it is squat and dark, so you cannot miss it."

"All right."

"If the captain has agreed to take your friend, an hour and a half from now we'll throw a red blanket over the railing that you can see from shore. I'll bring the dinghy to the dock and pick him up. He must be watching for the blanket, for that will be the moment I leave the ship, and it will only take me ten minutes to make it to shore. I will only stay dockside long enough to pick up a passenger. If he is not there, I will return to my ship immediately. Is that clear?"

"Perfectly clear. I know thanks are inadequate—"

Now he smiled again, the rich, happy smile of the Edori. "We, too, know what it is like to be persecuted by the Jansai," he said. "We are all brothers under the skin. We will help anyone who asks. No thanks are needed."

"But I am glad to give them. And my friend will be profuse in his gratitude."

"Your friend—his name is?"

"Zeke. Ezekiel."

"I am Reuben sia Havita. I hope he is with us as we sail."

And then casually, so as not to seem too eager or too afraid, they parted, the Edori heading purposefully toward the wharf, Tamar crossing the street and meandering forward a block until she caught up with Zeke.

"Well?" he asked urgently, his voice low.

"He's willing, but he has to check with his master. We need to be at the harbor in a little more than an hour. They'll signal from the ship."

"What's the cost?"

"He quoted none."

"That's ridiculous!" Zeke replied, his voice rising. "No one would do such a service for free!"

Tamar glanced around, but no one appeared to be eavesdropping. "Sshh," she hissed. "I told them you'd be willing to work for your passage. And it wouldn't hurt you to bring your own food."

"We don't have much left."

"We have some time. Let's see what we can find in the market."

Accordingly, they made their way to the open-air bazaars that could be found in any sizable Samarian city, and began shopping. It was spring, so there were few fresh fruits to be found, but they wanted dried food anyway, rations that could be packed and carried and eaten at leisure. Zeke, preparing for a longer trip, bought more than Tamar did, but she, too, was looking at a journey. They had little money left between them—they had started out with very little, except Tamar's secret cache—so they bartered with the merchants and bought as dearly as they could.

"It's time to head toward the dock," Zeke said for the hundredth time, when there were still plenty of minutes to spare, but Tamar could not entirely blame him for being nervous. So she said, "All right," and stowed a package of wrapped apricots in her backpack, and they headed toward the southern edge of town on streets that paralleled the sea. Not until they had glimpsed the Varnet Building did they cut east toward the wharf. Just in case anyone was watching them. Just in case anyone was curious.

They took a roundabout route through the shops and office buildings that were just now, at about nine in the morning, opening their doors for business. Tamar could not resist casting a longing eye at some of the fashions on display in the broad windows—though she had seen things just as fine in Lumi-naux—and anyway, she had neither the money nor the idle vanity to see herself attired in such frivolous shoes and gowns. No self-respecting Jacobite did.

When Zeke got distracted, it was at the doorway leading into an electronics shop, and what stopped him was the sound of singing pouring from some hidden source. He was not the only one to be swayed by the music. A crowd of perhaps twenty people had come to an almost absentminded halt in the street and on the sidewalks immediately outside the store, and they were all listening with rapt, bemused expressions.

"What is it?" Tamar whispered, but Zeke shook his head without replying. She stood still and listened more intently. There were two singers performing in matchless harmony, a man and a woman whose voices rose and fell in a complex, shifting pattern of melody and descant. Their voices were passionate beyond description, beyond the ability of their bodies to contain them; it seemed as if their notes must shatter their hearts and then explode the wiring of whatever fabulous circuitry had carried the music so improbably to this street corner in Breven.

It was the climax of the song, of course; within moments the duet reached its conclusion to the sound of thundering applause, likewise broadcast over the shop speakers to the spellbound audience in the street. It was a moment before Tamar thought to draw breath. She noticed others near her similarly gathering their wits and inhaling long drafts of air.

"What was that?" she demanded quietly of Zeke. "One of those new recordings?"

He shook his head. "The Gloria," he said. "They seem to be carrying a live broadcast. You have just heard the angels singing, probably for the first time in your life."

Tamar stiffened. There was no skill, no superiority she was willing to cede to the angels. "It was not so fine," she lied. "But why are they still singing the Gloria? I thought it began at dawn."

"A little after," he said. "And continues all day, or so I've heard. What incredible music."

"Was that Bael that we just heard singing? Bael and the angelica?"

Zeke shrugged. "I don't know. I wouldn't recognize his voice if he stopped me on the street and called my name. But they all have voices like that. Voices to turn you into a believer."

She would have scolded him furiously for such a heretical remark, except that any of twenty people could have overheard her—and she herself had just witnessed the music that had so moved him. "Well, I'm glad you got a chance to listen to a few notes," she said briskly. "But we can't stand here loitering."

"We've got time," he said. "Just a few more minutes."

She stared at him in true irritation, but before she could remonstrate, the voice of a new singer came lilting over the speakers. It quite literally turned Tamar in her tracks to face the open doorway, as if by such a minute adjustment in her stance she could more closely audit the music being performed five hundred miles away on the Plain of Sharon. This performer was a young woman singing completely a cappella, and her voice was so sweet and so true that it seemed elemental, unrehearsed, like starlight or autumn or sea. The verses melted into each other, wealth poured into wealth; the very air Tamar breathed seemed gilded by the singer's richness. When the liquid silken outpouring of song came to a wistful conclusion, the silence was so empty that Tamar almost staggered forward into it. She put her hand out to steady herself against the wall of the shop. Her blood pounded suddenly into the back of her head; her eyes shut against a momentary dizziness. Suddenly her arm ached with a sharp and fire-edged pain.

"Zeke," she said brusquely. "We must go. Now."

"I know," he said, and reluctantly started forward again, threading his way through the unmoving crowd. Tamar had to force her feet to follow him, for they had turned heavy and difficult. She still trailed one hand along the marble wall of the building to aid her balance. She closed her eyes briefly and shook her head. She must have lost more blood last night than she had realized; shame on Ezra for not warning her about the aftereffects this morning.

"That's odd," Zeke said, a few paces later, by which time she had more or less recovered.

"What? That they broadcast the Gloria like that? I didn't know it was possible."

"It's the first year they've tried it. But that's not what I meant. Your arm. Look at it."

"What about my—" she began, and then faltered. The Kiss, which had seemed more alive this morning, now positively blazed with an iridescent flame. Colors sparked in its nacreous depths, faded, and grew calm as she watched. "Jovah guard me," she said faintly.

"He won't," Zeke replied automatically. "What was that all about? It's almost completely dull again now."

"I have no idea," she said. "Maybe it's some part of that—bonding process Ezra talked about last night."

"It looks like it would be hot. Is it hot?"

"No," she said, but she touched it anyway, to find a fugitive warmth just now fading from the glass surface. Perhaps that surge of heat she had felt moments ago was not her imagination after all. "No," she said again.

"Strange," he said. "Maybe you should ask someone what it means."

"Certainly. The first angel I come across, perhaps—or, no, a Jansai warrior. There are plenty of them here. 'Excuse me, kind sir, but I'm a Jacobite in hiding and I've just had a Kiss installed in my arm, and I wondered if you could explain to me—' "

"Well, you could ask somebody less suspicious. Someday."

"I'll do that. Meanwhile, you have a ship to board."

By now, they were only a block over from the wharf, and in the spaces between buildings, they could spot the array of ships clustered along the harbor. The smaller vessels—the sailboats, the fishing boats, the shuttles—were crowded up to the wooden dock, masts and sails and banners creating a tangle of shapes and colors against the sky. Farther out, stately and patient, were the big ships too heavy for the shallow waters at the harbor's edge.

"What's this ship's name? Do you see her?" Zeke asked anxiously. Once clear of the bewildering effect of angel song, he had reverted to his normal fretful personality.

"*The Wayward.* I think she's a midsized ship, because the Edori don't have huge cargo boats, but he said he'd have to send the dinghy in. So she must be out a ways. . . . Yes, I think that's her. Straight out through those two buildings, do you see?"

"No, I—oh, yes. Yes, I do. But there's no red rug on the railing."

"Be patient. I think we have a few more minutes to wait. He didn't want to come to shore until the last possible moment."

The Edori ships were all easy to spot, for they were smaller, sleeker, and in general less showy than the Jansai vessels. Tamar had heard that they were also faster, usually outrunning the Jansai, who practiced piracy on the high seas. *The Wayward* had little decoration to distinguish it, except the name painted in flowing red letters on the bow and the flag of the Edori nation flying from its mast. Like the Jansai, the Edori had made a bird their mascot, but theirs was a white falcon winging its way diagonally across an onyx background. *Freedom.* All the Edori had ever wanted.

"How many more minutes?" Zeke wanted to know.

"I don't know. Ten, maybe. Fifteen. How quickly can you get to the dock from here? He said it would take him ten minutes to reach the dock from the ship."

"I could make it in three."

"Walking casually, so you would not draw attention?"

"Well, five, then. It's only a hundred yards away."

"Do you want me to stay here or come with you? Which would be less noticeable?"

"Come with me. No, stay here. It would look odd if someone saw us walking together and then I boarded the boat and you did not. And you'd better take off that Jansai disguise as soon as I'm gone."

"I know. I will. Is there anything else you need? Anything else I can tell you? Any messages I can carry back for you when I meet the others again in Ileah?"

"Tell them I'm in Ysral, and to look for me if they ever go there. Tell them I'm safe and happy. That it's what I wanted."

There had been a girl in Luminaux whom Zeke had been involved with—a pretty girl with red-blond hair and a mild disposition. As far as Tamar knew, she had escaped the Jansai depredations. "Anyone in particular I should tell?"

"No. Conran. Anyone who asks."

She had lost so many friends in the past few months that it was hard to lose one more, even one as unrewarding as Zeke. She was finding it difficult to say good-bye. He was one of hers, part of her circle; and that circle grew smaller every day. "Take care of yourself," she said, putting her hand on his arm. "Find new friends, and safety. Don't lose your faith. Never forget us."

"There's the signal," he said, and unexpectedly bent down to kiss her on the mouth. "Good luck to you, too. Watch me to the ship, and I'll wave as we pull away to freedom. I won't forget. We'll meet each other again."

"Till then," she said. "Till we find the Alleluia Files."

He gave her a smile of rare, genuine excitement, and turned to hike at a brisk but reasonable pace toward the dock. She faded back into the shadow of the Varnet Building, watching as she had promised. She almost lost him once or twice in the press of people on the wharf, but then she caught sight of his tall, thin figure again, weaving through the crowd. And—the waters of the harbor were crowded, of course—but surely that was the dinghy that had cast off from *The Wayward* the instant the red blanket billowed over the rail? It picked its way past the sail-boats and the outbound barges, taking a quiet, determined course for the dock.

"Free and safe," she murmured, still watching. Zeke was on the dock; the shuttle craft was twenty yards away. "As you always wanted."

And then four idle men in close conversation at the edge of the water turned with one motion and formed a phalanx around Zeke. Even from this distance, Tamar could see the astonishment on his face, succeeded quickly by comprehension and terror. Two of them grabbed his arms; one of them spoke to him in measured tones, informing him of his crimes; the fourth one pointed toward the water and shouted. But the dinghy had already reversed itself, heading rapidly back toward its mother ship, and there didn't seem to be a patrol boat in the waters. The Edori appeared to be safe.

Not so Zeke. As she slumped against the wall, dizzier now than she had been at the angels' singing, Tamar watched him struggle and protest and grow frantic with fear. One of the Jansai hit him, and he fell backward, kept upright only by the men who held his arms. Two of the other Jansai laughed. On their jackets, Tamar could see the sapphire crescent moon that was the badge of the Archangel Bael.

"Zeke," she whispered. She had pressed one hand against her mouth, one against her stomach; she was afraid she would either start screaming or retching. She felt like a traitor, allowing him to go alone to an undetermined hell, but there was nothing she could do now to succor him. If Ezra had betrayed them, there was nothing she could do to save herself. She pressed her back as tightly as it would go against the cool white surface of the Varnet Building, and felt herself shiver in the meandering, dispassionate spring air.

CHAPTER THREE

Jared tilted his head toward the sun and shut his eyes, hoping that if he merely concentrated on the music, and did not look at the performers, he would be able to appreciate the singing as he should. Both Bael and his angelica, Mariah, had exceptional voices, and their duets at the Gloria were generally considered outstanding; but Jared couldn't stand either of them, and so it was hard to like their music. And at two hours for a standard mass, he had a long, hard wait ahead of him if he didn't find some way to make the time pass pleasantly.

It was cool this year, this far north, and the weak spring sunlight did little to warm his cheeks, but it was still a welcome sunlight for all that. Gaza had experienced a long, bleak winter, and no matter how often Jared flew aloft to pray for sunshine, the clouds had always returned, full-bodied and sullen as a rejected mistress. But the Gloria signaled the start of true spring, the promise of gentle days, budding greenery, clear skies. It could not come soon enough for Jared.

Mariah's thin soprano broke free of Bael's powerful bass, and Jared opened his eyes again, his concentration broken. The years had been kinder to the Archangel than to his wife; every now and then on the highest notes, her voice showed the strain of age, a tendency to grow sharp, almost screechy. Nobody else had commented on it, at least in Jared's hearing, but surely they had noticed. Well, she had been angelica for nineteen years, and she had been past thirty when she assumed that role, so perhaps he should not judge too harshly. It was a difficult task, this annual performance of the Gloria on the Plain of Sharon. Mariah still accomplished it with adequate grace.

For a moment Jared studied the singer and the angel waiting
motionlessly beside her. As always, they looked to him like
prophets culled from the ancient pages of the Librera. Bael—
with his pewter hair, full beard, flowing blue robes, and broad
silver wings—looked as if at any moment he would fling out
his arms and speak pronouncements handed to him directly from
Jovah. Mariah seemed no less possessed. Reed-thin, black-
haired, dramatically dressed in a slim red sheath, she delivered
her solo with passionate, writhing conviction. Her eyes were
shut tightly, her hands were clenched and drawn up to her heart,
and she produced every note as if it were the word of the god
himself.

Jared sighed infinitesimally and looked away. He should not
mock them, not even silently and to himself, but their blind zeal
had stirred up no end of trouble during the past two decades,
and he for one would be glad to see their tenure ended next
year. But who was to follow them? That was a troubling question indeed. Even when the oracles asked Jovah that question
directly, the god did not reply. No successor had been named,
so no successor had been groomed, and for the first time in more
than seven centuries, Samarians blankly faced a future in which
they had no idea who would be their spiritual and political
leader.

Jared had no doubt that Bael was willing to continue his rule
for another twenty years, and it worried him that some of the
other angels might agree to such a solution. Surely a council of
angels, river merchants, Jansai, and Manadavvi would be con-
vened to consider their alternatives if such an eventuality
arose—if Jovah never spoke—but Bael was a powerful man
with a horde of influential friends. If he wanted to keep the job,
failing divine intervention, it might be impossible to wrest it
away from him.

Jared's eyes wandered from Mariah's contortions to the face
of the young man standing just behind her. Well, not so young
as all that—at thirty-five, three years older than Jared and far
more ambitious. Bael's son by a liaison outside his marriage,
Omar was an intense, intelligent, and highly focused individual.
It had been the tragedy of Bael's life that his only child had
been born human, not angelic. Omar's tragedy, too. For nobody
doubted that Omar would have been willing to take his father's
place as Archangel if mortals had been allowed to ascend to that

position. As it was, Omar would appear to be out of luck.

Even had Omar been angelic, such a bequest would have been unprecedented. In the annals of Samarian history, the title of Archangel had never gone from parent to child. In fact, most often it rotated between the three angel holds in Gaza, Bethel, and Jordana—Jovah's way, most likely, of making sure no one family consolidated power too great even for the god to balance. But then, it was unprecedented that Jovah had waited so long to choose his next Archangel.

Jared knew that he himself was considered a contender for the post of Archangel. As leader of the host in Monteverde, the angel hold in Gaza, he held a position of some authority and respect. And the Archangel before Bael had come from Cedar Hills, the hold in Jordana. Bael himself was from the Eyrie in Bethel. Thus, it was Monteverde's turn to produce the next leader. But Jared felt he was unlikely material. He lacked the single-minded dedication to power that Bael had evinced for all nineteen years of his reign; he lacked the desire to bend others to his will. It was hard for him to work up a real rage, or even an unshakable conviction. And, at least to judge by Bael, an Archangel must be able to do all that and more.

Now, suddenly, Bael's voice was joined to his angelica's again, and the two voices rose in scrolling harmony. This time when Jared closed his eyes, it was in a moment's pure pleasure; ah, that was a nice turn, that shifting melody, that leaping octave. When Bael's voice broke free of Mariah's to commence with the second male solo, Jared allowed himself to simply enjoy a few moments of excellent music. Despite his opinion of the man, Jared had to admit that Bael could sing.

It was another half hour before the mass concluded, and during that time Jared had found his thoughts drifting off again and again. Everyone else seemed rapt and overawed by the performance, but Jared could only pay attention for isolated measures. Still, he politely joined the wild applause, and nodded when an Eyrie angel murmured in his ear, "What a voice the man has! Surely Jovah listens!"

"He listens to us all. Or so we hope," he answered piously, and earned a puzzled look. He gave the angel a lazy grin and turned to find Mercy standing beside him.

"Where exactly do we fall on the schedule?" she wanted to know. "Do we sing next? Last? Did you bother to ask?"

"No, I thought you would," he said, giving the answer that he knew would annoy her most. She bridled, and he couldn't help laughing. He reached out a careless hand to squeeze her shoulder. Small, brown, and compact, she stood more than a head shorter than he; only her wings, just now folded primly back, gave her any stature.

"You're such an easy target," he said. "We sing fourth. I did inquire."

She frowned at him, but it was impossible for Mercy to remain angry at anyone. "You're such a trial to me," she said. "I suppose you haven't practiced your part, either, since I was in Monteverde three weeks ago."

"Well, once or twice. Do you think it would be inappropriate if I just glanced over the music once more—?"

"I think I'll do a solo, thank you very much," she said. "I've been rehearsing one, just in case."

"Hush," he said. "Omar is about to sing. You don't want to distract him."

She gave him another expressive look—whether it was to signify her low opinion of him or Omar was unclear—but instantly fell silent and turned to listen. It was a comfort to Jared to know that Mercy had even less love for Bael and his family than he did. Which was odd in itself since Mercy, true to her name, cared for almost everybody. She had led the host at Cedar Hills for fifteen years, since her father died on her twenty-sixth birthday, and she had managed it well. Although she had never married, she had had three daughters, and more or less mothered everyone else who fell into her sphere, even Jared. He could not resist the impulse to tease her, but he liked her more than he liked anybody else he knew. Most people did.

Omar had a rich, brooding baritone that just now was driving back the tentative sunlight over the Plain. Jared had heard tales of the girls who swooned over the sound of that melancholy voice, but frankly, it had never appealed to him. This might be a man you would want to sing at a loved one's funeral, but on a joyous occasion such as the Gloria, his voice seemed wholly out of place. Or perhaps it was merely the selection, a plaintive, mournful plea for guidance and salvation. Jared thought he actually heard someone behind him weeping.

"A little too affected for my taste," he whispered in Mercy's ear. She nodded emphatically but put a finger to her lips to silence him. He grinned again, then stifled a yawn.

The next singer, however, was more to his taste, a young angel from Mercy's hold singing a dizzyingly accomplished aria to the accompaniment of a flute. She was good enough to put him on his mettle, and so it was with a certain enthusiasm that he guided Mercy through the crowd to the central clearing where the other performers had stood. There was quite a throng gathered on the Plain this year, and the angels from the three holds stood at the heart of it. Around them, in widening circles, stood the Jansai, the Manadavvi, the rich river merchants, the corporate farmers, the lesser gentry of Samaria, and the curious, ordinary folk who made this one great annual pilgrimage to bask in the reflected glory of the realm.

"How many people would you guess?" he asked Mercy in a low voice as they waited for the audience to settle. "Six thousand? Eight?"

"Hundreds of thousands," she replied. "Or did you forget? They're broadcasting the Gloria this year."

He glanced quickly around, for he had somehow overlooked the significance of the banks of microphones and strings of black cable. Well, for the past ten years the Gloria had been recorded through just such equipment, and sales of these recordings had been phenomenally successful, and so he had forgotten that this year the event would be carried live to any citizen who had a receiver.

"Now, *that* makes me a little nervous," he said.

"Nothing makes you nervous," she retorted.

The crowd had grown quiet, almost (or so it seemed to Jared) eager. He might not be Archangel material, but he did have his virtues: and one of them was a voice to please the heavens. He nodded twice at Mercy, to give her the beat, and they both burst into song at the same instant.

It was the Margallet Duet in D major, one of the most demanding and breath-stealing compositions in the sacred canon, a short but rigorous piece. Jared felt as if his whole body was singing it, his toenails, his wristbones, his scalp. The music rushed from his heart, driven by the same ecstatic beat; he was not aware of breathing in or alchemizing oxygen into song. He merely became the music, body and soul, and beside him, Mercy did the same.

He was almost surprised when the song came to its abrupt,

delirious conclusion. He took a quick step forward to avoid top-
pling over; it was as if some great contrary pressure had suddenly ceased to be exerted. The crowd was still clapping and
calling out praises before he had completely recovered himself,
but he looked down at Mercy with a smile.

"Good enough for you?" he asked.

"I think you did practice."

"Not at all. I'm a natural."

"Nobody's a natural at Margallet. That was fun."

"Let's do it again next year," he said, and they both waved
once more to the audience. As they moved from the center circle
their place was taken by a young angel who looked to be in her
mid-twenties. Her blond hair fell in a simple, straight cut to her
shoulders; her wings were lacquer white. In the direct sunlight,
poised and still, she looked like an ormolu statue of an angel.

"Who's that?" Jared asked Mercy in surprise. "How can
there be an angel in all of Samaria that I don't recognize?"

She had to stand on tiptoe to see over the crowd. "Who—
oh, that's Lucinda. She came with Gretchen Delmere."

"Lucinda? What kind of name is that for an angel? Gretchen
Delmere? Who are these people?"

Mercy shook her head. "I forget how young you are. But I
would have thought you'd have heard this story sometime. Lucinda is the daughter of Rinalda Linise. Or don't you know who
she is?"

Jared found his lips forming the name Rinalda Linise, but he
did not speak the words aloud, for Lucinda had started singing.
Thought dried up; he turned to listening marble. She sang with
a lucid, rainwater purity that blended with the air, the sunlight,
the dance of butterflies around them; *this,* it was suddenly clear,
was the fresh scent of spring. Neither the notes nor the lyrics
registered with him. He had no idea if her song was gay or
pensive, if she prayed for rain or peace or thunderbolts. But she
sang, and the whole world became music.

When she stopped, there was dead silence for a few moments
as angels and mortals shook themselves back to a state of common comprehension. The applause that followed was so long
and so sustained that Bael might be supposed to be jealous.
Jared saw Mariah approach her and speak in her ear, shouting
over the noise of the clapping and calling, but the girl blushed
and shook her head. Keeping her eyes down and hurrying as

best she could through her admirers, Lucinda quitted the center circle and disappeared into the crowd.

"You *must* tell me more about her," Jared exclaimed, turning back to Mercy, but her attention had been caught by an angel from Bethel, and she was deep in another conversation. Then Jared was accosted by a woman from Luminaux, whom he only vaguely remembered meeting, and by the time he was free of her, Mercy had drifted off.

The Gloria was falling into its more relaxed state, one that would endure for the remainder of the day. As soon as Bael and Mariah had sounded their final "amen," the official business of the day was done; all the rest of the performances were less for the glory of the god than for the entertainment of the masses. So as soon as the Archangel ended his piece, the vendors opened their booths for commerce, and the melee began.

It was said you could buy anything your heart desired on the blue streets of Luminaux, but it was almost as true on the Plain of Sharon the morning of the Gloria. Of course, there was every imaginable food item available—several thousand people had to eat, after all—but in recent years the Gloria had become a souvenir hunter's dream. Shirts embroidered with angel motifs, oil portraits of Bael, miniature reproductions of all three angel holds, posters printed with the list of all Archangels from Uriel to the present, cookbooks featuring Mariah's and Mercy's favorite recipes—all this and more could be had for a handful of coins or a few of the crisp new paper bills.

Naturally, you could buy recordings of Glorias from the past decade as well as other music. Highly prized were copies of the sacred music brought with the first settlers to Samaria seven hundred and fifty years ago. These recordings, until recently, had only been available on the original silver disks that could be played nowhere except on special equipment built into the Eyrie and Monteverde. But sound—recording it and sending it where someone wanted it to go—was the new frontier in technology, and some clever fellow had discovered how to copy the settlers' music onto the bulky black disks Samarians used today. Jared had been told the quality was quite good, and sales had been brisk. Particularly popular were the tracks laid down by Hagar, the first angelica, whose voice Jared had never heard matched. Although, frankly, he would have plunked down a few

dollars for a recording of the solo Lucinda had just performed.
Well, perhaps it would be available.

Jared wandered through the merchants' booths, idly looking
over the merchandise and eating a meat pie. With half an ear
he listened to the music still coming from the center of the plain;
it would go on all day. It sounded like the angels had finished
singing, and now the amateurs were lifting their earnest voices
to Jovah. As the day wore on, livelier groups would present
their music, and listening would become more fun; but the unspoken rule seemed to be that no one should sing anything lighthearted before the hour of noon.

He paused at a small family-run booth and stared meditatively
at the items for sale, predominantly items of clothing embroidered with the blue crescent moon that was Bael's standard.
Vests, shirts, scarves, reticules, all bore the sapphire sliver,
sometimes one big scythe of it across the whole broad back of
a blouse, sometimes hundreds of tiny moons duplicated in a
random pattern across an entire bolt of silk. He wondered if
Bael knew what license the vendors were taking with his personal monogram, which he wore in sapphire jewels on silver
bracelets around each wrist.

Jared glanced down at his own bracelets, plain gold bands set
with emeralds, each cluster of three gems arranged to form a
simple leaf. All angels wore such bracelets, to mark their lineage
and their hold; angels from the Eyrie wore sapphires, those from
Monteverde wore emeralds, those from Cedar Hills wore rubies.
Jared had seen some of Bael's Jansai wearing the crescent
badge, but this was going a little too far.

He looked up, debating a stern reprimand, but the merchant
was busy totaling up a sale and looked quite happy about it.
Jared hesitated, shrugged, and moved down to the next booth.
Ah, glass sculpture featuring representations of angels in flight,
in prayer, in dramatic poses. Hardly, one would think, an im-
provement over the merchandise in the last booth.

"Shopping for home decor, I see," said a man's voice behind
him. "I cannot wait to see which exquisite piece you choose."

Jared turned, a grin already on his face. "I am guided by
your taste, Christian," he invited. "Choose for me."

Christian obligingly stepped forward and began examining
the statuary. "Well, of course, this is a nice effort—I particularly like the agony in the angel's face. What is she praying for,

do you suppose? It cannot be something so mundane as rain or sunlight.''

"She is asking the god for enlightenment," the young shopkeeper said, suddenly entering their conversation. He was enthusiastic and sincere, and most probably was the artist as well. "See? She looks to the heavens, but her hands are spread toward the earth. She knows that despite her wings, she will live a mortal life, grow old and die, and she asks Jovah to help her reconcile that with her divine nature."

"Ah," said Christian, and gave the glass angel a friendly pat on the head. "Sort of a universal theme, then."

"Could I show you anything else? We can customize our pieces, you know. See, she wears tiny bracelets around each wrist—I can set them with whatever gems you desire. Well, gem chips.''

"They would have to be chips," Jared agreed.

"Let us think it over." Christian nodded to the artist, taking Jared by the arm. "We have a little more shopping to do."

"Good prices!" the young man called after them. "And remember the customizing!"

"Jovah defend me," Jared said when they were a few paces away. "And the sad thing is, I'm sure he does a tremendous business."

"A guardian angel for every room," said Christian. "Does he do silver and bronze in addition to crystal?"

"If we asked, I'm sure he would. He customizes, you know."

"Well, if I ever need to buy you a gift—"

"Which, thank the god, I cannot imagine you ever will—"

"I'll know just what to get you."

"So!" Jared exclaimed. "Before you had a chance to torment me, had you been enjoying the Gloria? I looked for you last night, by the way, but could not find you."

Christian pointed behind them, in the general direction of the hotels set up toward the northern edge of the plain. Less than fifty years ago, Archangel Joel had finally given permission for a few wealthy business investors to build permanent structures on the Plain of Sharon to act as housing units for those who attended the Gloria. Up till that point, everyone who journeyed in for the event stayed in progressively more elaborate tents and pavilions, so that setup and teardown could take all week. It had seemed foolish to build hotels that would only be used for two or three days a year, but the Manadavvi and the river merchants—and even the angels—were getting used to their comfort and did not relish camping out on the night before the most important social event of the year.

The hotels, of course, were an instant success, usually completely reserved more than a year in advance; Jared could not imagine attending a Gloria under any less civilized conditions. And the hotel owners had almost as instantly come up with ways to increase their revenues, by sponsoring summer music festivals and autumn merchandise fairs on the broad grounds of the plain. Jared assumed that within a few decades the plain would become so booked with other major events that there would hardly be a day open for the Gloria itself.

"I wasn't staying with the rest of the Semorran contingent," Christian was saying. "I was a guest of Isaiah Lesh."

Jared's eyebrows rose, though it was hardly a surprise. Christian Avalone was the most influential, and probably the most wealthy, of the Semorran merchants; the fact that Jared liked him personally didn't make him any less of a politician, his finger always on the fluctuating pulse of the Samarian market. And Isaiah Lesh was the patriarch of the oldest Manadavvi clan in Samaria. The two men had much in common, not the least of which was a complete and utter fascination with power. Christian was the younger of the two, a sleek, attractive, charming, and possibly dangerous man in his early forties; Isaiah, well manicured and faultlessly civil, was at least fifteen years older. But they had been allies for years—and not always friendly to the angels.

"So you stayed up talking late into the night," Jared said lightly as they strolled forward. They continued to glance into the booths they passed and silently pointed out anything of particularly gaudy interest. "Let me guess. And one of your topics was the inadequacies of the angels and how you could make them see reason."

"Certainly Bael's name came up once or twice, but I wouldn't say we were dwelling on his flaws. I like that picture of Mariah, don't you? The grimace seems particularly dead-on."

"Perhaps she posed for it. Was it the new tax that irked you, or the ban on technological imports?"

Christian waved a hand dismissively. "Old news. Old topics."

"But still very real grievances."

"We'll bring them up at the next council meeting. Again. Eventually Bael will come round to our way of thinking. Or you will."

"*I* will?"

"Or Mercy. Or whoever is named Archangel," Christian added.

Jared couldn't help grinning. "Then you'd better start cultivating Mercy, because it's unlikely to be me."

"No, not if ambition has anything to do with it," Christian agreed. "Though there's no one I'd prefer to see—"

Jared chopped a hand through the air to cut off the discussion. "So, no new complaints? Just the same old grumbling?"

"You know the story," Christian said mildly. "The Manadavvi and the river merchants are never content. We always must be complaining about something. But in the end, we're compliant."

Jared let it go. As Christian said, unrest among the power enclaves was constant, even in the historical context; as far back as Archangel Gabriel's time, these two groups had been trying to wrest power from the angels. Jared made it a point to stay on good terms with Isaiah and his brethren, and let Bael fight the real battles. But he made sure he was never less than fully apprised of what the Manadavvi did and thought at all times.

Christian had come to a stop in front of another booth and picked up another portrait. This one was done in charcoal and showed a certain aptitude for art as well as a familiarity with its subject. "Now this I'm half-inclined to buy," the merchant said. "It's good, don't you think?"

Jared looked over his shoulder. "She'd kill you," he said. "Mercy isn't one to encourage these sorts of excesses."

"But it's caught her look, don't you think? I've seen that expression on her face a hundred times."

"Ten dollars," the artist said quickly, standing up and coming over to wait on them. "Or one gold piece."

"I can't resist," Christian murmured, and pulled a wad of bills from his pocket. Jared rolled his eyes but forbore to make another comment. He waited while the young man carefully inserted the portrait in a protective cardboard jacket, and then he and Christian continued down the broad aisle of booths.

"She'll see it when she comes to Semorrah," Jared warned him. "You'd better hide it away somewhere."

"Nonsense, she never comes to visit. You don't either, now that I think of it."

"Name the day. I'm always glad to sample the sophistication of the city. Monteverde is lovely and calm, but every once in a while it's a little tame."

"How about—two and a half weeks from today?" Christian suggested, so smoothly that Jared wondered if somehow this invitation had been the point of the entire conversation. "Can you get free?"

"Mercy will tell you that I'm always too willing to get free," Jared responded. "I'll be there. Perhaps I can stay a day or two."

"I'll tell the boys to expect a debauch," Christian said. His two young sons had always been rigorously polite every time Jared had met them, but then, he had only seen them for a few minutes at a time under the direst of social pressures. Christian's wife had died shortly after the youngest one was born, and Jared didn't imagine that Christian had much time to provide a warm and nurturing home for them.

Before Jared could reply, Christian's attention was claimed by a group of Castelana merchants strolling by in the opposite direction. Jared greeted everyone pleasantly enough—he knew them all, of course—then slipped away, looking for more congenial company.

He found it quickly enough, in the form of three young Manadavvi women who gaily caught his arms and persuaded him to eat lunch with them. Since the Manadavvi land fell in the province of Gaza, Jared was a frequent guest in the wealthy households, and knew all the sons and daughters. Particularly the daughters. Not one of the great Manadavvi families didn't hope the leader of the Monteverde host would take a fancy to his oldest girl and bring her home to his hold. It wasn't just that there was no honor higher for a mortal than to marry an angel— think of the power such a wife might wield! What father would not want to see his daughter so advantageously situated?

From their hands, Jared passed back to the merchants, and, by easy stages, back to the angels. It was late in the afternoon when he finally caught up again with Mercy, who was, for a wonder, sitting alone at an impromptu café draped with a bright yellow awning.

"Can I sit with you, or are you enjoying your solitude?" Jared demanded. Not waiting for an answer, he pulled up one of the wrought-iron chairs, turned it around backward, and seated himself. Resting his arms on the back, he stretched his wings out behind him as far as they could go.

"I'm enjoying my solitude, but I'd rather have your company," she said. "Are you hungry? Do you want to order something?"

Jared made a slight gagging noise. "I don't think I'll eat again till I'm seventy. I've had more pies and cookies and cheese pastries—"

"I know," she said. "But one day a year won't hurt you."

"So have you had fun?" he asked. "Who have you seen?"

They talked idly for a while, trading gossip and information. Mercy was even more surprised than Jared had been that Christian had been so cozy with Isaiah Lesh.

"I don't care for that much." She frowned. "And did you see where the Jansai pitched their tents?"

Hotels or no hotels, the nomadic Jansai always brought their own accommodations. Always had, always would. "I didn't notice."

"Clear across the Plain. As far from the main strip as they could get."

"So?"

"So is there a rift between the merchants and the Jansai? They've always been allies. What are they divided over?"

Jared shrugged. "The trade with Ysral, would be my guess. The Jansai want to control the flow of goods into Samaria, but the Edori are welcome at more and more ports—"

"There's plenty of room for Jansai and Edori boats at any harbor."

"Well, then—who knows? Does it matter?"

Mercy shook her head with a great deal of irritation. "Why are you such a care-for-nobody?"

"I'm not!"

"You are. You're such a bright young man. You have so many gifts. But you—nothing matters to you. You let everything slide by. What does it take to stir you up? What does it take to catch your attention?"

"Well, a spat between the Jansai and the river merchants isn't it," he said, amused. "How can it possibly matter? If it's important, we'll find out about it. If not—why worry?"

She leaned forward, suddenly intense. "You should be Archangel, you know," she said. "You're the only logical choice. Everyone should know it. Jovah should know it. *You* should know it, and you should be at the oracles' doors day and night demanding that they petition the god on your behalf. It is not good for Bael or the merchants or Samaria for us not to know who the next Archangel will be. And do you care? Do you worry? This is your life! Your duty! And yet you spend your days flirting with Manadavvi girls too silly to remember their own names."

"In the first place, why should I be Archangel? Why not you?"

"I'm too old."

"Just about Bael's age when he ascended."

"And I have daughters and other responsibilities and I don't want it. But you—"

"Why me? Why not Jonas or Sara? No law I ever heard said the Archangel had to be leader of the hold."

She brushed all this aside. "Because you're a natural leader, or you would be if you asserted yourself. Because you're a brilliant thinker when you remember you have a brain. Because you have a highly developed moral sense and an ease with people that makes you courteous but nobody's fool. Because you look the part."

He burst out laughing. "Well, thank you for that, I suppose, but I don't think it's on Jovah's list of qualifications."

She sighed. "And all you do is laugh at me, and go on your usual indolent way."

He reached out a hand and gave her shoulder a slight squeeze. "Jovah's will be done," he said gently. "It is up to the god to name the one he would exalt. If I spent my nights ranting at the doors of Mount Egypt or Mount Sinai, the oracles would have no more news for me than they do now. Let it go. Trust your god."

She sighed again and spread her hands apart, signifying resignation. Jared dropped his arm. "So tell me about the rest of your day," he said. "Who else did you talk to?"

"I spent five minutes with Gretchen Delmere. I wanted to

talk to her longer, but someone snatched her away from me."

"*That's* what I wanted to ask you about!" he exclaimed. "That girl—Lucinda? Who is she? What's her story?"

Mercy instantly grew grave. "A sad one. It goes back, oh, twenty-five or thirty years. When the Jacobites were first becoming a nuisance."

Jared rapidly cast his mind back to that chapter of Samarian history. Well, "nuisance" might not be the right word. Jacob Fairman had begun a town-to-town campaign to evangelize for his concept of Jovah—not a god but a machine, a spaceship, left over from the time of the first settlers' arrival. According to Fairman, this spaceship, which ceaselessly orbited overhead, was endowed with wondrous equipment and abilities. It had huge stores of grain which it could release when the angels prayed for food; it had miraculous chemicals which it could shoot into the atmosphere when the angels prayed for rain. It was equipped with fearsome weaponry which could unleash tremendous destruction when the angels prayed for a thunderbolt to strike the earth—or when mortals displeased the god, and he punished them with his fury.

The threat of Jovah's wrath, of course, was the reason the Gloria was sung on an annual basis. It had been written in the Librera, the holy book, that every year at the spring equinox people from all over Samaria must gather and sing to the glory of the god. By coming together in harmony, they were proving to the god that they lived together in peace. If they failed to perform the Gloria on the scheduled day, the god would strike the mountain range on the edge of the Plain of Sharon. If, three days later, they still had not sung, he would strike the river Galilee, which was the border between Bethel and Jordana. If even this failed to convince them to sing, he would loose a thunderbolt that would destroy the world.

It had happened once, nearly two hundred and fifty years ago, in the time of the Archangel Gabriel. The Gloria had been delayed, and the god had struck down the Galo mountain that used to anchor the southernmost edge of the Plain. There was still, under two and half centuries of creeping undergrowth, a huge black circle of rock where the thunderbolt had fallen. Never since that time had the date been missed.

But Jacob Fairman had not been impressed by this evidence. Certainly the lightning had struck, he said, but it had been tossed

down by a warship, not by the god's pointing finger. Every
sacred mystery he could explain away through science. The
magical Kisses every believer wore in his arm? Electronic links
to the ship's main computer! The ability of angel prayer to call
forth sunshine or lure down rain? The ship's response to preset
aural stimuli. Nothing stumped him. Nothing silenced him, either. And a small, growing group of Samarians began to listen
to him, to believe him, to question the very foundation of Samarian society.

Of course, he was outlawed and his words were banned, but
he only went underground, and his adherents grew. Many believed Archangel Michael had had no choice but to execute
him—Fairman and a handful of his followers—for political
treason and religious heresy.

It hadn't stopped the Jacobites, however, though for many
years they had seemed dormant. Bael, from the time he had been
instated as Archangel, had vigorously suppressed them, and
everyone had thought he had eradicated their influence. But five
years ago there had been an unexpected resurgence in Jacobite
fervor. Bael had quelled it in the most ruthless manner possible,
aided willingly by his Jansai troops. It would not have been
Jared's way (had he been in Bael's position), but he had to admit
it had been effective.

Although recently there had been more rumors. . . .

Jared shook his head. "This girl is too young to be one of
the original cultists. She could hardly have been born in Jacob
Fairman's lifetime."

"That's just it." Mercy sighed. "That's when she was born."

"Tell me."

"It was, as I say, almost thirty years ago. Jacob Fairman's
adherents were turning up in the oddest places. In Luminaux."

"I would have expected that," he murmured.

"In Castelana. In some of the Manadavvi households. In Cedar Hills."

Now Jared sat up straighter. "In *Cedar Hills*? Impossible!"

Mercy nodded. "There was a girl. Rinalda. She was the
daughter of angels, but she was mortal herself. Well, she was
the great-granddaughter of the Archangel Delilah, so perhaps
someone should have expected her to have passionate and rebellious blood. She had three sisters, all of them angels. Perhaps
this led her to believe that life was unfair. Perhaps it led her to

seek other avenues of excitement. Who knows? In any case, she had left Cedar Hills to seek her fortune in the world. And somehow met up with Fairman and his—heretics.''

"Did you know her?"

"A little. I was more than ten years younger, and I had spent most my life at the Eyrie. I didn't know everyone at Cedar Hills well. And she had little patience with angels at that time. Or ever.''

"So what happened?"

"So she fell in with the Jacobites and became quite a convert, and traveled with them from town to town proselytizing. Apparently, she was quite charismatic, too—as you might expect! A woman from the angel holds denying the existence of the god! Who wouldn't believe her? She drew crowds wherever she went.

"Naturally, Michael couldn't allow this to continue, so she was found and brought back to Cedar Hills. Against her will, of course. They say she tried over and over to escape. No one was supposed to bring her news of the Jacobites, but apparently someone did, because she always seemed to know when there was some particularly bloody confrontation. And she knew when Jacob Fairman was killed. And it made her nearly mad.

"But by then,'' she continued, speaking a little more slowly, ''she had another problem. For, although she had hidden it for quite a while, eventually it became obvious that she was pregnant. And would soon bear a child.''

"Whose child?" Jared asked sharply. "Fairman's? A Jacobite's?''

"Well, she had already been a prisoner for eight months before anyone noticed her condition, and it was another four months before her delivery. So it was clear that, whoever had sired her child, he most likely lived at the hold.''

Jared spoke carefully. "Was she—did she say—had she been assaulted while she was prisoner there?''

"I don't think so,'' Mercy said. "Rinalda was not the type to keep such an abuse to herself, had it been so. I think she took a lover, and it helped make her wretched days more bearable. But she never named him. Not though Michael threatened her with the wrath of Jovah himself.''

"And when the baby was born? What then?''

"When the baby was born, it was clear that whoever her lover was, he was angelic. For she bore an angel child. And only an angel can bear or sire another angel.''

Jared took a quick breath. "Lucinda?"

Mercy nodded. "And Lucinda's sister. A mortal girl."

Jared stared. "Twins? One angelic, the other not? I have never heard of such a thing."

"Nor had anyone else. The consternation at the birth was almost equaled by the amazement. For although there is always rejoicing when an angel is born, Michael found it hard to credit that any of his flock had actually consorted with the Jacobite prisoner."

"Still. She had lived there most of her life, after all," Jared said. "They must have known her for years. It was not as if she was some rebel farmer's daughter who had been brought in and incarcerated."

"True. Yet Michael was furious and demanded that whoever was responsible step forward and admit his guilt. No one did, of course, and as I say, Rinalda never named him. She was made to suffer, though. They instantly took Lucinda away from her, to be properly raised by someone more suitable to oversee an angel's upbringing."

"What happened to Rinalda and the other girl?"

Mercy was silent a moment. "Died," she said quietly at last. "How?"

"She managed to escape. Taking the baby with her. It was less than three weeks after she'd given birth, and she wasn't strong. And it was winter—the worst winter southern Jordana had seen in this century. Two days later a Jansai caravan found her on the side of the road, frozen to death, the baby girl in her arms. Also dead. I don't remember the last time I have felt so sad."

"I don't wonder. What a miserable tale."

"The day after that," Mercy went on, as if he hadn't spoken, "the angel David killed himself. Flew as high as he could go over the Heldora Mountains, folded his wings to his sides, and let himself fall. You cannot imagine the shock we all felt. He had been such a beloved and warmhearted boy. Everyone assumed, of course, that he had been Rinalda's lover. We never had any proof. But I see no other way to read the story."

"And this is the heritage of that lovely girl! No wonder she sings with such an unearthly voice."

"I don't know how much of her own story she knows. So few people remember it these days—and, of course, Gretchen has kept her far from Cedar Hills for most of her life."

"Yes, tell me about this Gretchen and where in the world Lucinda has been all these years. I don't believe I've ever laid eyes on either of them."

"Gretchen was David's sister—mortal, of course, but brought up in the hold just like he was and used to angel ways. About three years after David and Rinalda died, she went to Michael and offered to raise Lucinda herself. He objected at first, because he saw no reason an angel should be raised anywhere except one of the holds, but she finally convinced him. She had always been a fairly earnest young woman, and David's death made her almost grim. Quite formidable. In the end, Michael agreed. And she took Lucinda away with her to Angel Rock and there, as far as I know, they have lived ever since."

"Angel Rock! That dreary place!"

"Yes, it is not where I would have chosen to grow up myself. But she does not appear to have taken any particular harm from it. She looks reasonably refined and you have to admit her voice is amazing."

"Yes, but those are fairly external signs. To be brought up by a joyless maiden aunt on some tiny island in the middle of the ocean—it makes even my careless blood run cold."

"No, I don't envy her her life," Mercy agreed. "I invited Gretchen to come to Cedar Hills for a few days, and bring Lucinda. I hope she accepts. I think it would do them both good to be around more ordinary company for a while. And I plan to tell Gretchen that I'd be happy to keep Lucinda for a few weeks—or a year or as long as she cares to stay. I think it's time that girl had a few normal hours in her life."

"I wonder why this aunt Gretchen spirited her away like that," Jared commented. "I would have thought she would have considered Cedar Hills the best place for the girl."

"Maybe she was afraid Lucinda would always be treated strangely because she had such an odd history. Or maybe she was angry at Michael because he allowed such a series of disasters to happen, right under his nose. Or maybe—and sometimes I've thought this was the true reason—she was afraid of Rinalda's tainted blood. That rebel streak. She wanted to get the girl as far from the mother's influences as possible. Who knows?

Maybe she was right. There are no Jacobites on Angel Rock.''

"Let me know if she comes to you at Cedar Hills. I'd like to get to know her. I'll come down and visit.''

"I'll be glad to have you.''

After a few more idle remarks, they rose to their feet and went their separate ways, back to the friends and obligations of their separate holds. It occurred to Jared as he wound his way through the still-lively crowd that he had promised to make two visits in the next few weeks, although neither journey had been in his mind when he first came to the Plain. Not that it mattered; Christian and Mercy were two of his oldest friends. Visits to them could be nothing but enjoyable.

CHAPTER FOUR

Lucinda moved through the Gloria with a sense of inexhaustible wonder. She had never seen so many people gathered together in one place in her life. Perhaps two dozen souls all told lived on the island they called Angel Rock, and it was rare even half of them were in the same room simultaneously. To be confronted with thousands of new faces all at once was confusing and bewildering.

And wonderful. She couldn't remember the last time she'd been so excited. Well, she could, though. The day, a little over two years ago, when a cruise ship carrying a hundred passengers from Luminaux to Ysral had foundered off the edge of Angel Rock, and all one hundred had come to stay on the island. The three small inns that served as the main commercial center of the island could not easily accommodate all guests, but they did what they could. Men and children were bunked in the taprooms and the parlors, while the women were allotted the beds and couches and floors of the bedchambers. Two young girls had shared Lucinda's room with her, and they stayed up late into the night, talking excitedly about the adventure at sea and life back in Samaria. These unexpected guests had stayed for a week, and Lucinda had spent that whole time walking around in a state of rapt, awestruck delight. The shortage of food, the complete lack of privacy, the problems with the plumbing— none of these had bothered her in the least, though they had seemed about ready to drive Aunt Gretchen mad.

That was the time she began pestering her aunt to bring her to Samaria for a visit. *Can we go for my birthday? Can we go to visit your relatives? Can we go for the Gloria? Can we go, can we go, can we go?* Gretchen seldom talked about Samaria.

Most of what Lucinda knew about the place she had learned
from visitors who docked for a day or two at Angel Rock, to
replenish food and fuel, to rest after a bad storm, to leave a mate
who had fallen ill. But nothing had prepared her for this pageantry.

She was not sure her aunt ever would have heeded her pleas,
except that one day an invitation came from the Archangel himself, asking them to attend the Gloria. She remembered that
Gretchen had read the letter with an odd mixture of alarm and
resignation, then sighed before she handed it to Lucinda.

"I would have thought he would have forgotten all about us
by now," was Gretchen's comment. "I suppose we have that
Jonas to thank for this."

"Jonas?" Lucinda asked absently, quickly scanning the letter.
Her heart had started a galloping rhythm in her chest; it took
all her energy to keep her voice calm. Gretchen hated any display of emotion. "Oh, that young angel who was here last
month."

"Yes, who was just supposed to stay overnight and ended up
staying for three days because you flirted with him so much."

Lucinda looked up. "I didn't *flirt* with him," she said mildly.

"Well, whatever you call it, when you sit up all night playing
melodies on your harpsichord and singing harmony together."

"He had a nice voice," Lucinda said.

"Well, you can be sure he flew back to Bael and told him
just how fine *your* voice is, and that's why the Archangel has
invited you not only to come to the Gloria, but to sing."

"He says that? Where?"

"On the second page. He adds that if you aren't familiar with
any of the sacred music, or aren't comfortable singing in front
of a large group of people, he certainly won't pressure you."

"Oh no! I would like it very much!"

"It's his way of telling me," Gretchen said, taking the letter
back and reading it for a second time, "that he wonders if I
have raised you right, taught you all the things you need to
know. It's his way of finding out if I have been a fit guardian
for you."

"Why wouldn't you have been? And why would he care?"
Lucinda asked, puzzled. Gretchen merely sniffed and refused to
answer.

"But he can't fault me for your voice or your musical training," her aunt went on with a certain grim satisfaction. "That he'll see right away."

"He will? Then does that mean—oh, Aunt Gretchen, can we go to the Gloria? Can we really?"

"We don't have a choice about it," Gretchen replied, but her voice, and her expression, softened as she looked at Lucinda's joyous face. "You don't gainsay the Archangel. But you're happy about it, aren't you? Well, then. Maybe it's worth going."

They had spent the next few weeks in a frenzy of preparation, cleaning and repairing their best clothes, practicing the music Lucinda would sing at the Gloria, hiring neighbors to care for the inn while they were gone, contracting with a ship owner to carry them to Breven.

This should have been easy, since there were ships in and out of Angel Rock on a daily basis. But many of them were Edori vessels, and Gretchen had an advanced and unshakable distaste for the Edori which she had never satisfactorily explained to Lucinda. "They're heathens," she told her niece once. "They don't live like civilized folk." Another time she spoke contemptuously of the Edori's heretical religion, similar to the Samarians' true belief in Jovah but radically different in that the Edori did not recognize Jovah as the one supreme god. Still another time, she mentioned that the Edori did not believe in marriage and recognized no bond to another living soul. Lucinda let most of this roll once through her head and then melt away, as she did with so many of her aunt's pronouncements. The truth was, Lucinda had decided, Gretchen lived by a set of rigid standards that she was afraid to relax for herself, and so she viewed with profound distrust anyone who was gaily able to contravene her own narrow definition of correctness.

So—although Gretchen had overcome her dislike of the Edori enough to trade with them on a regular basis—she would not accept a berth on one of their ships. Which was unfortunate, since most of the ships that put into the small harbor at Angel Rock were Edori.

It had not always been that way—or, at least, Angel Rock had not been intended as a haven for Edori. Until the last century it had not even been inhabited. The ocean that lay between Samaria and Ysral was too vast for an angel to cross in one day, and so angels had never been able to fly the distance to the smaller continent. It had been Edori who had first navigated

the unmarked sea to discover Ysral, whose existence had long
been rumored. Edori had settled Ysral and made it their homeland, and so many of them emigrated there that within fifty years
of its discovery, almost no Edori were left on the central continent of Samaria.

Once the Edori established themselves on Ysral—and once
they began ferrying back boatloads of exotic fruits and marvelous grains—it became only a matter of time before the Jansai
and other Samarian entrepreneurs opened up their own trade
routes to Ysral. And once ordinary Samarians were traveling
between continents, it became imperative for angels to find some
way to negotiate the waters so that they, too, could freely move
between civilized lands. They could journey by boat, of course,
though it was beneath their dignity. They preferred to fly.

And so exploratory teams of Jansai were sent out to locate
suitable islands along the route to Ysral where an angel could
rest along the way. Angel Rock, which was almost midway
between the two continents, proved to be perfect. It was large
enough to support a small community that would cater to the
traveling angels, and hospitable enough to make that community
a pleasant place to live.

It was never expected to be more than an outpost, a single
utilitarian dorm with one or two misanthropic overseers who did
not mind their solitary existence, but it had grown to be something a little more lively. Angel traffic was heavier than first
anticipated; Edori ships put in there constantly, Jansai traders
less regularly, and commercial liners from Luminaux or one of
the Manadavvi ports even less frequently. But it had become a
point of pride among the residents of the island to be able to
offer good food, quality accommodations, and passable entertainment to their visitors, and so the reputation of the island had
become quite high. High enough to draw world-weary tourists
every once in a while, who stayed for the summer season, swam
in the sun-warmed ocean, bargained with the Edori for incredible goods, and generally considered the island a luxurious retreat from the stresses of their lives.

So it had not been, for Lucinda, a particularly lonely existence. But that did not keep her from desiring, with all her heart,
to travel to Samaria and sing at the Gloria. It took so long for
Gretchen to find a ship she was willing to cruise on that, more
than once, Lucinda considered offering to fly them both to the

continent. But she knew better than that. Gretchen was afraid to fly. They would go by boat or they would not go.

At last a Manadavvi pleasure ship came through, and the captain willingly agreed to take two passengers as far as the port of Lisle on the edge of Gaza. Were they willing to leave in the morning? They were. Providentially, one of their guests that evening was an angel who would be flying back to the Eyrie in the morning. With him, Gretchen sent a letter to Bael informing the Archangel that she and her niece would arrive at Lisle in nine days. Would he have someone meet them there to escort them to the Plain of Sharon?

The voyage itself was much more boring than Lucinda had expected. She was not allowed near any of the interesting parts of the ship (the engine room, the galley, the captain's bridge), and the area of the upper deck where she was permitted to stroll was greatly restricted. She did enjoy standing at the stern and watching the aquamarine water curl away into a sculpted white wake as the ship made its stately way through the ocean. And she struck up a few conversations with the other travelers on board, though she had always found Manadavvi to be haughty and unsociable, and these were no different. And Aunt Gretchen, predictably, was seasick. So Lucinda had very little to do and no one to talk to.

But, oh! how different it was in Lisle, in Gaza, on the Plain of Sharon! And what color, what music, what splendor there was at the Gloria!

Within minutes after singing her piece, Lucinda had managed to evade her aunt's eye and melt into the crowd. Since they had arrived at the hotel on the Plain, it had become easier and easier to slip away from Gretchen, who had become increasingly distracted by all the people gathered for the event. This despite the fact that Gretchen had tried to keep a tighter hold on Lucinda than usual. But here, at the Gloria, it was impossible to keep track of anyone.

The first thing Lucinda did when she got free of the angels was buy a stick of candy-coated ice cream. She had seen dozens of others eating these confections and she had practically ached with desire. When she learned that not only did the ice cream come in a variety of flavors, but the candy coating did as well, she was struck dumb. She had not even imagined such luxury in her life.

The ice-cream vendor smiled at her. It was early in the day and he was not yet irritated with the crowds. "There's strawberry ice cream covered with white chocolate, strawberry ice cream covered with dark chocolate, chocolate ice cream covered with orange candy, chocolate ice cream covered with mint, cherry ice cream covered with peppermint—"

"Strawberry and white chocolate," Lucinda said very quickly, before she could hear another choice and change her mind. She handed over a silver coin (Gretchen had given her a handful and said gruffly, "I suppose you'll want to buy a few things"), and moved down through the bazaar. Nothing in the world could compare to this.

She knew her meager hoard of coins wouldn't buy much, but she didn't care about souvenirs anyway; it was enough for her to be able to stare and absorb. The scarves, gloves, blouses, skirts, shoes, rings, bracelets, hats, belts, statues, paintings, mugs, dolls, and other treasures formed a fabulous array, gorgeous and dizzying, and she moved from booth to booth content just to look. She bought two more ice creams (different flavors) and kept moving down the aisles.

She did have trouble negotiating the crowds because of her wings. She was not used to having to hold them so tightly to her body to keep them from being trampled on or knocked against, and more than once she cried out sharply when someone's unwary foot came down hard on a trailing wing feather. Everyone was profuse with apologies, and she knew it was her own fault; she saw other angels moving easily about, seeming none the worse for wear. But then, they had had practice living among throngs of people.

Of course, she didn't know a soul here, so she was pleased when total strangers made a point of stopping her more than once as she browsed. They didn't say much, and kept their voices extremely respectful—"Beautiful song, angela!" "I enjoyed your solo so much!" "Jovah is sure to have heard your voice, angela, you sing like the god's own chosen child"—and she wished she could have more extended conversations with one or two of them. And she wondered why they called her "angela." No one on the island did so.

Eventually, she got a chance to ask. She had come to a stop

before a booth that sold musical recordings, and she was fingering the black disks when a smooth voice spoke in her ear. "Are you considering buying a mass, angela? I'd recommend one of the ancient recordings over the modern ones. Our singers have their virtues, but none of them approach Hagar's brilliance."

She turned with a ready smile, for she had recognized the voice. She had met Bael's son Omar two nights ago at a dinner so huge she had been tempted to count the plates to see how many sat at the table. They had exchanged only a few words, but he had seemed pleasant enough then. And now she was eager to talk to anyone.

"I cannot buy one," she said. "I have no equipment to play it on. But wouldn't I love to have a handful of these!"

"The equipment is not expensive. Perhaps your aunt will buy one for you to take back with you. I would think music would hardly be considered a luxury in such a lonely place as Angel Rock."

"It's not so lonely," she said, smiling again. "And as for music, I have always been willing to make my own."

"And a fine job you do with it. I enjoyed your piece very much, angela."

"Thank you," she said. "But why does everyone call me angela?"

He looked amused. "I suppose they would not on the island. It is a term of courtesy—angela, angelo—bestowed upon angels. And the Archangel's spouse, of course. If you want to be very polite, that is how you always address an angel. And the angelica."

She shook her head. "There is so much to remember. We don't have this many rules on Angel Rock."

"Well, rules multiply in direct proportion to the number of human beings gathered together in one place. I suppose, on Angel Rock, you would need no more than one or two laws to satisfy everyone. But here on Samaria—" He laughed softly. "We cannot have nearly enough."

She was not sure how to reply to that and was relieved when he continued after a very brief pause. "So how are you enjoying your visit to the mainland? This is your first trip back since you were very small, as I understand it?"

"Yes. I can't even remember having been here before, though

Aunt Gretchen says I was three when we left. But I love it! It's so exciting! So much to do and see and find out—''

"So you aren't feeling a little overwhelmed by all the splendor?''

"Not at all!'' she replied sunnily. "I just wish it would go on for days and days.''

"Well, most of us feel that one day is about all the revelry we can stand. But I'm glad you're enjoying it. Would you feel up to having a light meal with my father and me? He sent me over to fetch you, in fact—if you have no other obligations.''

One can't gainsay the Archangel, she heard Gretchen's voice in her ear, but it wouldn't have occurred to her in any case. "I'd be delighted,'' she said. "Where is he?''

Omar led her to an open-air café set up under a red-striped tent. Bael and Mariah were already seated at a white wrought-iron table set with low stools that allowed angel wings to be comfortably folded in place. Bael's silver wings, in fact, lay behind him in a pleated cascade over the grass that formed the café's floor. Lucinda stepped carefully to avoid treading on them.

"Lucinda! My girl! Come sit with us, angela, please do!'' Bael addressed her in a booming voice that seemed designed more for prophetic utterances than simple social conversation. She settled herself across from him; Omar sat to her left, facing Mariah. "We're so pleased you could join us for a little luncheon. Are you quite starved?''

She laughed guiltily. "Actually, I've been eating ice cream for the past hour. We have nothing like that on the island. I just love it.''

"I hope you haven't made yourself sick,'' Mariah said in a quick, worried voice. "That ice cream is so sweet and rich. I can only eat a few bites before my stomach—well.''

"Oh, I feel fine,'' Lucinda said blithely. "But I'm not too hungry right now. Maybe I'll have something to drink.''

"Sir!'' Bael called out, summoning the waiter. "The young lady would like something to drink!''

In a few minutes they were all settled with their iced juices and their trays of cheese and breadsticks, and Bael was able to refocus his attention on his guest. He leaned slightly forward across the table, fixing her with dark blue eyes that seemed capable of staring at hell without wavering.

"So! Are you enjoying your first Gloria?" he demanded in that rolling voice.

She was getting just a little tired of this question. "Very much. The music was amazing. I was just spellbound during your performance. Angelo." Belatedly she nodded at Mariah. "Angela."

Bael waved this off. "My angelica and I have sung at nineteen consecutive Glorias. We are expected to be brilliant. But your voice took us all by surprise. Tell me, who have your teachers been?"

"My aunt Gretchen, mostly. From the time I was very small, she taught me—oh, everything. Scales and breathing exercises and basic harmony until I was old enough to start learning real music."

Mariah leaned over and spoke in her husband's ear, although everyone at the table could hear her. "Strange. I don't recall that Gretchen had a particularly exceptional voice."

"Adequate merely," he replied, again as if no one else could overhear. "But as long as she understands music, her voice is of little consequence." He addressed Lucinda again. "And what is your repertoire? You performed the solo quite impressively, but can you sing the masses as well?"

"Oh—of course—maybe a hundred of them," she said. "I haven't counted."

"A *hundred*?" Bael repeated. "All by memory?"

"I was taught that it was impolite to sing with the score in front of you. As if you didn't care enough about the music to learn it."

To her left, Omar laughed softly. "And Gretchen Delmere was always certainly an expert on politeness."

"Well. A hundred masses. That is certainly a remarkable number," Bael said. "I take it that you actually can read music—that you did not learn these merely by listening to a recording and memorizing?"

Aunt Gretchen had been right; Bael wanted to make sure she had had the proper instruction and made it clear he didn't believe she could have. "I can read music," she said.

"She has no equipment to play a recording on," Omar said. "So she told me. Which makes her accomplishment even more amazing."

Lucinda looked at him. She was not enjoying this part of the conversation, though she was making an effort to hide it. More of Aunt Gretchen's politeness. "Is it such a high number, then?" she asked him. "How many do you know?"

He laughed aloud. "Maybe a dozen quite well, and fifty or so well enough to remember them if I practice," he said. "Those serve me adequately on the occasions I am called upon to perform."

"So your musical background is sufficient," Bael went on, addressing Lucinda again. "And your deportment seems satisfactory. I assume you have been taught the other basics—literature, history, rudimentary mathematics?"

"Well, I suppose you could quiz me," she answered with a smile. "Otherwise, how will you be sure I really do know what you think I should?"

There was a short pause while everyone else at the table assimilated the fact that they had been rude and that she was not so unsophisticated that she did not realize it. Bael, however, if he was nonplussed, did not show it. He reached across the table to pat her hand.

"There, now," he said, in a voice too loud to be as soothing as he intended. "You mustn't be offended. You seem a rare, exotic creature to us, and we only want to get to know you."

"I don't seem exotic to me," she replied, but she managed to smile. "You're the ones whose lives seem strange."

"As they are," Omar murmured. "As they are."

"But then, tell us more of life upon this island," Mariah said in her high nervous voice. "Is it really just you and your aunt living there? No one else?"

"Oh, no. There are twenty-two other people there right now. And Hammet is expecting his brother and cousin to come out any day now, because the inn has grown so much he needs help to maintain it. Actually, Hammet has talked about building another hotel—more of a luxury place, you know, because we *have* been getting more tourists during the summer months— and then he'd probably have to hire five more workers. So we could be growing pretty rapidly in the next few months."

"And exactly how do you—well, how do you entertain yourself? Out on an island with twenty-two other people?" the angelica asked.

Lucinda grinned. "Mostly I work. There's only me and Aunt Gretchen and Emmie and Jackson, and the hotel has eight rooms. So I clean, and do laundry, and work in the garden, and sew, and trade with the merchants who put into port, and help in the kitchen and—'' She laughed. ''If it needs to be done, I can do it. There's never time to sit and be bored.''

''And do you have any friends there, child?''

''Child'' did not seem like the right word for someone who was nearly thirty, but Lucinda let it slide. ''Twenty-two friends,'' she said with a smile. ''How many do you have?''

That stopped Mariah; indeed, it stopped the whole table, although Omar was silently laughing. Lucinda just let the reply hang there, too stubborn to soften it with another comment. She might be a wide-eyed miss from the desolate island, but she had dealt with her fair share of unscrupulous shipowners and wily Jansai, and she knew how to hold her own in any transaction.

''Mariah counts all the people of Samaria as her allies and friends,'' Bael said finally. ''And here comes one of them now. This is another I would like to have you meet.''

He was gazing beyond her, so Lucinda quickly turned her head to see a middle-aged, dark-haired woman making her way slowly through the crowd. She was dressed very simply in a white robe and sandals, and she held the arm of a young girl walking beside her as if she needed physical support.

''Jecoliah,'' the angelica said in that voice she still appeared to think was a whisper. ''I did not know she was here.''

''I saw her briefly last night,'' Bael replied. ''Omar, could you direct her to our table?''

''Certainly, Father,'' the young man said, and came smoothly to his feet. In a few moments he was leading the white-robed woman to their table and helping her seat herself on his own stool. Then he and the girl with Jecoliah stood a few paces behind her, patiently waiting.

''Jecoliah,'' Bael said, his deep voice raised even a little more than usual, as if he spoke to a deaf woman. ''We are pleased to see you here. Are you enjoying the Gloria?''

''Very much,'' she said. ''Are you?''

Bael missed the humor in the reply, for he went right on speaking, but Lucinda could not help a private grin. ''Indeed, I am. Jecoliah, I wanted to introduce you to one of our young guests. Her name is Lucinda, and she has come in for the week from Angel Rock. Lucinda, this is Jecoliah, the oracle of Mount Sinai.''

Jecoliah peered in Lucinda's direction out of friendly, cloudy eyes, and Lucinda realized that the older woman was not deaf, after all, but nearly blind. "You must be David's daughter," she said instantly. "I am indeed pleased to meet you. You look something like him, though he was darker than you are. But you have his eyes."

Jecoliah was the first person in Samaria who had mentioned her father's name, and Lucinda immediately liked her. She was delighted when, at that very moment, someone called out to Bael, and the Archangel and his wife left the table. Omar slipped quietly into Mariah's deserted seat.

"I know nothing about my father except what my aunt has told me," Lucinda said. "And she does not talk about him much."

"Well, he was young, which made him rash, and he was in love, which made him ill-advised," Jecoliah said with a sigh. "But other than that he was sweet-tempered and good-natured, and you couldn't find a soul to say an unkind word about him. He was a good man."

"The oracle speaks, and thus every word is true," Omar murmured.

Lucinda ignored him. "Forgive my asking," she said to the other woman, "but I am not certain what an oracle is. Or does."

Omar smiled, but Jecoliah merely nodded. "You would have no knowledge of us, there on Angel Rock. There are three of us, one in each province, and we serve as mediators with the god. We can speak to him—not directly, not by voice—but through special screens that allow us to ask him questions and receive his written reply." Jecoliah smiled. "I do not see well at all—that is why I have one of my acolytes lead me around as if I were an old woman—but I can see well enough to read the script of Jovah's hand."

Lucinda was fascinated. Gretchen had never talked about oracles. "And what sorts of questions do you ask the god?"

"Lately, who will be Archangel, but he has not replied," Omar said.

"No, but he will," Jecoliah said calmly. "He always does. And we ask him who will be angelica or angelico to the Archangel. And we report to him events that transpire so that he can interpret them for us—perhaps not for this generation, but for the next one and the one that follows. We tell the god the details of Samaria, and he tells us how to live."

It sounded complex and mysterious to Lucinda, and she decided not to pursue it further. "Did you know my mother as well as my father?" she asked.

Jecoliah shook her head. "Very little. Only well enough to see what everyone saw, that she was passionate and hard to hold. And to be angry that her life ended as wretchedly as it did."

"Old tales. Old wounds," Omar murmured, but there was a warning note in his voice. Lucinda looked directly at him.

"I know the story of how my mother lived and died," she said. "Don't be afraid of what she'll tell me."

He smiled at her with a certain rue, and she liked him better than she had for the last twenty minutes. "Any tale of pain and betrayal stirs the emotions when it's told, whether for the first time or the hundredth," he said. "I've no doubt you'll hear it more than once during your sojourn in Samaria. Just remember that it was long ago, and no one suffers anymore, and nothing you feel can change it."

"And you remember that I am not a child," she said softly.

He nodded. "Then we will deal well enough together."

Lucinda stayed another ten minutes talking to the oracle and the Archangel's son, but that last exchange with Omar lingered in her mind more than the rest of the conversation. She felt uncharacteristically broody as she left the table and continued wandering through the fairgrounds, or maybe it was just that she was getting tired. The week had been a long one, after all, and this day had started before dawn and been packed with events. So she was actually relieved when she spotted Gretchen's thin, tall form moving stiffly through the crowds, obviously on the lookout for someone, most likely herself. And she was more surprised than excited to learn that she and her aunt had been invited to spend a few days at the angel hold in Jordana, and that Gretchen had accepted.

The trip to Cedar Hills took three days, though Lucinda and any of the other angels could have completed it in less than half that time. But they moderated their pace to accommodate the caravan that traveled below them on the paved highways of Samaria.

When Lucinda learned how her aunt and the other mortals from Cedar Hills were to be transported, she almost decided to ride with them. She had never seen anything like the huge, rumbling vehicles with their great exposed engines and long hollow bodies designed to carry human cargo over great distances. These particular vehicles, so the angel Jonas informed her as they waited for the journey to begin, were luxury accommodations. They were specially fitted on the interior with padded seats and comfortable footrests and both heating and cooling systems to keep the air temperature bearable.

"And this is the *only* way to travel, if you're not going to fly," he said. "The Jansai transport trucks—Jovah save me. They're open-air vehicles, nothing to shield passengers from the wind or the sun or the rain, and they're noisier than the river falling over the Gabriel Dam. They'll take you over the ground three times faster than you could go on horseback, but it's a miserable way to achieve speed."

"And those are your only choices? The Jansai trucks and these?"

Jonas bobbed his head from side to side in an equivocating way. He was a good-looking, friendly young angel whom she knew from his past visits to Angel Rock (when she was flirting with him), and he seemed willing to tell her every bit of information she didn't know.

"Well, there are the public buses, and they fall somewhere in between in terms of comfort. But they take days and days and *days* to cross a hundred miles, because they stop at every little town along the way. Now, a few Luminaux engineers have been working on designs for smaller vehicles—cars that might carry only three or four passengers at a time—but the concept has been pretty much derided as inefficient. And Bael has not been a friend to locomotive advances. He has resisted funding any new scientific projects, and he discourages the universities from developing much new technology. So nobody's done much toward modifying passenger vehicles. But maybe next year, or the next year, with a new Archangel in place—"

She'd already heard that phrase more times than she could count. *When the new Archangel is installed . . . When Bael's replacement is found . . .* Since no one knew who the new Archangel would be, everyone was free to indulge in the most optimistic hopes about what that person would accomplish.

"So, you think the new Archangel will be more of a friend to technology?"

"Depends on who's chosen. For myself, I don't care much, but there are a lot of people who do. There are many who'd like to see the Augustine University back in Samaria—or who'd like a chance to see what the Augustine researchers have come up with lately."

"What's the Augustine University?"

"Well, it used to be the most advanced scientific research institute and teaching facility on the continent. Based right at the foot of Mount Sinai. Started by a man called Caleb Augustus and an Edori named Daniel sia Calasinsa. It flourished during Delilah's day, and for twenty or thirty years after that. Credit them with virtually all the electronic amenities we have today. But, like Bael, Archangel Joel was no fan of technology, and he tried more than once to shut the school down. Eventually, the professors just moved the whole place to Ysral. Where only the Edori are benefiting from the new marvels of science."

"So they're the ones who built these trucks and buses?"

"The prototypes. The early models."

"And what is it that Bael has against science?"

Jonas smiled. "You must know your history better than that."

"Samaria was founded by settlers escaping a brutal war on a planet far from here," she recited in a childlike singsong. "Technological advances had brought this world to the brink of destruction with weapons so powerful they could not be withstood. Our forefathers prayed to Jovah, and he took them in his hands and carried them to Samaria, where he instructed them to live in harmony all their lives."

"Very good!" he applauded. "So Bael's fear, theoretically, is that if we encourage any scientific advancement, we will eventually build whatever weapons these other ancestors discovered, and destroy ourselves and the whole planet. He's not the only Archangel to have felt that way, of course. That's why we as a society have not crept very far down the road of progress in the last hundred years."

"Maybe it's a slow road."

"Maybe we have no incentives to make it a faster one."

They might have continued debating for the next half hour, but at that point the rumble of the big engines grew to a deafening level and the big buses shuddered to life. Around them, the air was suddenly patterned with a massive interleaving of angel wings as the contingent from Cedar Hills took flight. Jonas and Lucinda flung themselves aloft and began the long journey southward.

Lucinda loved to fly. It was something of a guilty pleasure, because Gretchen hated to see her take wing, constantly fearing that she would meet with an errant breeze and go cartwheeling down into the beautiful, treacherous acres of the sea. Early on, she had promised her aunt that she would never fly so far away that she couldn't see the green-and-tan contours of Angel Rock—which had severely limited the scope of her travels. The idea of flying for hundreds of miles, without pausing, without circling back, made her giddy with anticipation.

She drove her wings down sharply, repeatedly, gaining altitude as fast as she could, till she was far above the ground, the trucks, the other angels. She saw Jonas glance up at her and rise a few yards, but nowhere near her level. A few of the other angels also turned their faces up to her, calculating her speed and her distance. They seemed to be smiling.

This high up, the air was frigid and full of devious, sometimes dangerous currents. The cold did not bother her; like all angels, her body was built to withstand the icy temperatures at high altitudes, and indeed, she was often uncomfortable in a warm room. As for the malice of the wind, well, that was an adversary she had faced time without number; she had had no other real opponent in the past twenty-eight years, and so she had sharpened all her skills on it.

Now came a sudden uprush of air, swift and powerful; she pulled her wings closer to her body and let herself glide on its back. It stopped abruptly and she fell, loving the breathtaking drop, the sensation of speed in the moments before she spread her wings again and eased herself from side to side to slow her descent. For a few minutes she coasted, then she arced upward again, higher than before. She flew forward as fast as she could for as long as she could stand the pace, outdistancing both the trucks on the ground and the angels in the air. Then, once more, she folded her wings to her sides and plummeted toward the earth in a dizzying, blinding drop. Unfurling her wings with a snap, she felt the shock of arrested motion along every nerve and bone in her body. She hovered for a moment in place, and laughed out loud.

A few minutes later Jonas caught up with her. Lucinda had

rarely had an opportunity to fly beside someone; she liked this camaraderie, and waved at him gaily.

"How far are we going today?" she called over to him. "Do you want to race me to the next resting point?"

"I don't think so," he called back. "I've come to tell you to display a little more decorum. You're causing much concern behind you."

She glanced back, but faces were invisible from here. "My aunt?"

"I would guess she's already dead from fear. No, Mercy herself asked me to try and calm you down. This is not at all the kind of behavior we expected from the demure young girl from Angel Rock."

Lucinda grinned. "There wasn't much else to do for fun when I was growing up. Of course, I had to make sure I was somewhere Aunt Gretchen couldn't see me. Don't tell me you can't take a dive like that."

"Well, I can, but I don't like to. The few times I've been accidentally cast down by the wind, I have merely prayed to come out alive."

"You should try it when there's nothing below you but ocean."

"Thank you, I think not."

She laughed at him, but she settled down. It surprised her to learn that the other angels were so much more sedate—she would have thought anyone with wings would have practiced the same acrobatics—but it was not in her to deliberately upset anyone who seemed to have her interests at heart. So she dropped to a lower altitude, slowed into a more regular pace, and in this unremarkable fashion covered the rest of the miles of the trip.

They spent two nights on the road in hotels only slightly grander than their own on Angel Rock. Gretchen noted this fact with some smugness; she prowled the corridors of each inn, jealously on the lookout for amenities she had not thought of or could not offer. The two of them shared a room both nights, and Gretchen talked more than usual, almost exclusively of the personalities they had encountered, both at the Gloria and on this trip. She mentioned names of people Lucinda could not remember and did not think she'd met. It seemed to her Gretchen was reminding herself of the life she had once lived, briefly and completely immersing herself in it one more time, either to regret it forever once she left or to reassure herself that she was better off now. It was hard for Lucinda to tell. In any case, she wasn't required to make many replies to Gretchen's ruminations, and so she listened sleepily and drifted quietly into dreams.

On the third day, they arrived at Cedar Hills. The angel hold was an open, inviting place, a charming muddle of short buildings and tall ones, residences and shops, pathways and garden plots and sudden sprays of fountains. Angels and mortals mingled together on the streets and in the restaurants, and to Lucinda's eye, at least, they all seemed happy and industrious.

Mercy showed Lucinda and Gretchen to their quarters, a suite of rooms in a long, low building that seemed to be some kind of dormitory. "This is where most of the unattached angels sleep," Mercy told them. "We have other quarters for the residents with families, but this is generally quieter, since there aren't children screaming up and down the hallways. My rooms are in that red building—over there—and most of the grand functions are held in that big white building we saw as we came in."

"This is lovely," Lucinda said, looking out the window at the open square. In the fresh spring sunlight, everything appeared newly washed and cheerful.

Mercy smiled at her. "You like it? I confess to a certain partiality myself. I was brought up at the Eyrie, of course, and it has a majesty that Cedar Hills doesn't possess—but that was the point of Cedar Hills. When they built it, they wanted it to be accessible to everyone, a place no one would hesitate to come with a grievance or a problem. It's much newer than the Eyrie and Monteverde, of course, since it was built—oh, in Gabriel's time. Two hundred and fifty years ago. So it hasn't seen quite the wear and tear of the other holds!"

Gretchen was looking about her with a face so full of emotions it was hard to sort them out. Unlike Mercy, Gretchen had been raised at Cedar Hills and, until she took her niece away twenty-five years ago, had rarely left it. Lucinda watched her, wondering what she was thinking. Was she glad to be back or sorry? She had abandoned so much and missed so much and could never recapture any of those lost years. For almost the first time in her life, Lucinda wondered what passion had driven

Gretchen to leave a home she loved, carrying a small child in her arms, and retreat to the most isolated spot in their entire world. The question made her feel a little cold, despite the sunlight. She put her hand lightly on her aunt's arm.

"Come on," she said. "Let's unpack our stuff and then get some lunch. You can show me everything."

"What I remember," Gretchen said, but she allowed herself to be turned toward the closets. Mercy watched them a moment, a thoughtful expression on her face, before she turned and left them alone in the room.

The next two weeks passed in a companionable haze. There was never a minute's boredom at Cedar Hills or, if you wanted companionship, a lonely moment. Every meal was communal; every activity could be shared; and visitors to the compound arrived nearly every minute. It was a cornucopia of souls.

Lucinda spent most of her time with the other angels. In particular, she enjoyed flying aloft with the others to sing to Jovah. Although Gretchen had doggedly taught Lucinda every one of the prayers used to address the god, Lucinda had only rarely asked him for rain or sun or wind. At Angel Rock, they pretty much took what the god would send.

But she enjoyed flying straight into a pelting rainstorm, coming to a fluttering pause beside another angel, and raising her voice in harmony to beg the god for sunshine. And she was delighted when, an hour or two later, she could actually feel the shifting pressure of the air around her as the clouds unraveled and the rain trickled to a halt. She accompanied Jonas on three weather intercessions over various parts of Jordana, and she loved the experience every time.

She participated in the impromptu concerts that somehow seemed to happen every night after dinner, and she learned the singing games that required great feats of memory and vocal range. She flew to Luminaux one day with Jonas and two other angels, and walked the blue streets of that elegant city with awe and reverence. Surely there was no place in the whole world as beautiful as this.

During the two weeks of their visit, Mercy planned two formal dinners, one to honor the angel Jared of Monteverde, and one to honor the Archangel's son Omar, both of whom had dropped by for quick visits. Lucinda had not met Jared at the

Gloria, though he had been pointed out to her, and during this visit she had only a five-minute conversation with him.

"Are you enjoying your stay here?" he inquired as they loitered in the foyer leading to the dining hall. He posed the question in a careless, casual voice—but then, everything about him seemed careless and casual. He was a tall man, but he slouched against the door frame as if his height offered him no particular advantages; he was good-looking, with strong, regular features and long, curling black hair, but he did not appear to have paid much attention to his clothes or his styling. Only his gray eyes, lively and alert, gave much clue to the quickness behind the indolence.

"Very much! There's so much to see and everyone has been so friendly. We went to Luminaux the other day. I've never imagined such a gorgeous place."

"No, Luminaux is quite unmatched," he agreed. "Although for sheer architectural whimsy, you should take a trip to Semorrah. The city isn't as livable, but the design is fantastic."

She laughed. "I don't think we'll be here long enough for me to visit all the major tourist attractions. Though what I've seen so far—"

"Makes you want to stay?" he suggested.

"Makes me want to come back," she amended. "I think I'd miss my home if I were gone for long."

"Not what I'd expect to hear from someone who grew up in your particular home," he commented. "Then again, perhaps I underrate it. I've never been to Angel Rock."

"Have you never been to Ysral, then?"

He nodded. "Half a dozen times. But I've taken my rest on one of the Jansai boats traveling between continents. The seas are so crowded with merchantmen traders these days that you don't really have to worry about finding a place to halt for the night."

"Our loss, then," she said, smiling.

He smiled back. "Well, next time I go I'll be sure to stop by. Now that I know how friendly the natives are."

And that was all they said to each other. Yet there was something about him that appealed to her deeply, prompting her to ask Mercy about him the next time she had a chance.

The small, brown-haired angel laughed and shook her head. "I adore Jared, I truly do, but I despair of him, too. There's a man whom the god has blessed with every gift, and all he does is idle his time away."

"What gifts?" Lucinda said cautiously.

Mercy snorted. "Besides the obvious one of physical beauty? Intelligence. Integrity. The ability to deal with all kinds of men—and women. You should see the mortal girls fawn over him. Not that he seems to care. He's had his liaisons, of course, but never anything serious. If nothing else, I wish he would find a few months of happiness with some little angel-seeker and produce a child or two. Then maybe there would be something in the next generation to look forward to."

"Maybe he's just waiting to fall in love," Lucinda said.

Mercy made that graceless sound again. "Angels seldom do," she said. "The Archangel always marries according to the god's will, but not even he considers the bond exclusive. Most angels spread their affections fairly far and wide—and a good thing it is, too! The more lovers they take, the more often they produce angel children, and that is something that seems rarer every day. Well, I don't despair of Jared yet. He'll surprise us all someday. In some way. I'm sure of it."

Omar, when he came to Cedar Hills, put more energy into getting to know the visitor from Angel Rock. Lucinda was not sure she was glad to see him, since she had felt some mistrust of him by the time they parted on the Plain of Sharon, but here in Jordana he appeared to make a special effort to please.

"How long are you staying?" he asked her one afternoon as they strolled through the shops of Cedar Hills, eating ice cream. "I'd like to bring you back to the Eyrie for a few days. It's something you really should see—the oldest of the angel holds, and the most beautiful. It's built right into the mountaintop, and the stone is this sort of glowing rosy color, and when you're inside it, it feels like you're wrapped in warmth. I can't explain it very well, obviously."

"I'd like to see it," she said. "And Semorrah. Jared said that was worth visiting."

"He was right. And the Gabriel Dam, and Monteverde, and even Breven, though it's not as pretty a place as the other cities. But the shipyards are fabulous."

"I don't know how much longer we'll be here," she said. And then, because she wasn't sure how well she would enjoy a tour in Omar's company, she added without enthusiasm, "I'll ask my aunt if we can take a journey."

But Gretchen, when approached, was adamant: They had to leave the very next day. This was news to Lucinda, and she received it with mixed emotions. Much as she was enjoying Samaria, the constant barrage of people and events was beginning to wear on her. And she missed Angel Rock with an intensity that surprised her. But to leave the very next morning—!

"Couldn't we wait a day or two? Omar said—"

"No," Gretchen said firmly. "Mercy says we'll find any number of boats that can take us home, all docked at Port Clara. We can get there in a couple of hours. So, hurry now, better start your packing. Make sure you don't leave anything behind."

Something had upset her, that much was clear, and Mercy seemed just as mystified as Lucinda. "I hope it's not something I've said, some courtesy I've omitted," the older angel said to Lucinda. "She seemed perfectly happy yesterday."

Mercy had sought her out in her rooms that evening, and sat by the bed watching Lucinda pack. "Oh, I don't think it has anything to do with you," Lucinda said. "Aunt Gretchen is very moody. The smallest thing can make her mad for days. It may be that she's remembered something at the inn that she wants to get done. It may be that somebody said something to make her feel she'd trespassed too long on your hospitality. It may be—she might have remembered something from twenty-five years ago, and it made her sad, and she can't stand to be here another minute. With Aunt Gretchen, it's pretty hard to know."

Mercy watched her with shadowed eyes. "You must have had a difficult time of it," she said. "Growing up as you did, with an embittered woman on a desolate island. I feel like I've done wrong by you. You were born at this hold, and it's my hold. I should have come after you much sooner."

"I didn't need coming after," Lucinda said serenely. "I've always been quite happy where I was. And Aunt Gretchen loves me. She's difficult and contrary and I sometimes think she's ruled by fear, but she loves me. I haven't felt the need of others to care for me."

"Still. If you get too lonely. If you just want a change. For any reason at all. Will you come back and visit me? There will always be room for you."

Lucinda crossed the floor and kissed the older woman on the cheek. "I will," she said. "Thank you for the offer."

The next morning, they were on the road before nine. Lucinda had elected to ride with Gretchen in the van that Mercy had specially ordered for their use. It was not nearly as much fun as flying, but Gretchen had looked so frail and alone as she climbed into the big, empty vehicle that Lucinda didn't have the heart to abandon her. The ride was fairly bumpy, and too noisy to make conversation easily, so they traveled in a silence that suited them both.

Lucinda looked out her windows, watching the gentle green countryside roll by, and wondered when she would actually make it to Samaria again. Somehow, this trip seemed like the one big event of her life, the splash of bright color to which she would compare all other days, sighing with fondness and regret. She seemed destined for a quiet life, half-lonely and half-full of wonder, and that had always been enough for her; but she could not help being a little sorry that her period of glory was ending so quickly. She made herself smile and toss the rueful thoughts away, but she continued watching out the window.

Port Clara was even smaller than Lisle, and there were only Edori boats docked there this morning. Lucinda felt a small lift of hope—surely this would delay their journey by a day or two—but she had underestimated the strength of Gretchen's desire to leave Samaria. She marched up to the first sea captain she found on the wharf and bargained for passage to Angel Rock. Then she hurried back to where Lucinda was patiently waiting with their luggage.

"We leave within the hour," she said. "Best buy anything you think you might need for the journey."

Lucinda squinted out into the harbor. "Which ship?" she asked.

Gretchen pointed. "The one there at the end. It's called *The Wayward*."

CHAPTER FIVE

B_{ack} in Luminaux, Tamar found everything changed. None of her Jacobite friends were there; all their houses and apartments had been rented to others or left empty till new residents could be found. She was afraid to approach the sympathetic merchants and artisans she had relied on for help in the past. After her experience with Ezra, she believed anyone could betray her. If he had betrayed her. She couldn't be sure. But who else? And could not anyone else, anyone at all, whisper her name to the angels or the Jansai? So she avoided the familiar streets, rented a room in a district she did not know, and took a job cooking at one of the city's hundreds of cafés. She needed the money. She needed the food. She needed to buy time to think.

The trip from Breven had been accomplished easily enough, although her nerves were so unsteady that every minute had been harrowing. If Ezra *had* betrayed them, she was lost; she walked through the city streets with a spotlight on her head. He could describe her height, hair color, clothing, the rubbed red newness of the wound around her Kiss. . . . She must disguise herself.

So she had spent a careful half hour at the market, buying materials, and she had used one of the filthy public rest rooms to do what she could to alter her appearance. An application of dye made her bright blond hair several shades darker, and a few cuts with a razor made it short, spiky, severe. Sapphire eye shadow turned her green eyes a murky aquamarine. Heeled sandals added inches, new clothes changed her style. She gazed in the mirror and forced herself to stand upright, straighten her shoulders, assume a commanding expression that said *I belong here,* a posture and an attitude that no fugitive would attempt. She powdered the scarlet skin around the Kiss, dulling it to the flesh tone of the rest of her arm. She surveyed herself again. She did not much resemble the woman who had walked in.

She had very little money left, but she did not want to chance sneaking out of the city at night. Nothing could look more suspicious, not if they were searching for her. Her best course was a bold one: buying a ticket on one of the commercial buses that traveled between Breven and the rest of Samaria.

At the station—which was merely a heavy, striped tarp draped over a huge expanse of concrete—she found she had just enough money left to book a seat on a bus heading for Luminaux. That suited her; it was too early to go to the rendezvous at Ileah, and at least she was familiar with the Blue City. Even better, the bus would be leaving in half an hour. She found an empty bench and waited almost motionlessly for her route to be called.

The scent of sea air wafted in through the open walls, cutting a welcome edge through the overpowering odor of fuel. The grumble of many simultaneous motors was giving her a headache, but there was nowhere to sit to avoid the sound and the smell of the buses; they were parked on all four sides of the tent. Mute and miserable, Tamar endured.

At last, the thirty interminable minutes crawled by and the call went out: *All aboard for Luminaux! All for Luminaux!* She knew a moment's panic as she rose to her feet, clutching the little bag she had carried with her across the desert. What if they were waiting for her, Jansai soldiers disguised as weary travelers? What if they were cruelly allowing her to gain the border of freedom, laughing to themselves, watching as she tossed her head and strode with a carefree woman's walk right to the very doorway of the bus? What if they were to take her—*now*? No, not until she truly thought she was safe, not till the bus had rumbled to life, shouldered its way down the crowded city streets, attained the open road beyond the city limits. Would they take her then? Would they stop the bus, haul her off screaming and fighting, bludgeon her to death there on the side of the road? Or, worse, take her to the Archangel's hold to await who knew what sort of peril?

No one she knew had ever returned once the Jansai had gotten hold of them. Some of the Jacobites did not believe that could possibly mean the worst—torture and murder—they optimistically spoke of comfortable prisons and deportation to Ysral. As if a jail could be comfortable. As if any Jacobite, shipped off to Ysral, would not find a way to return to his friends in Samaria and tell them what had happened. No, Tamar was a realist. Anyone who fell into the Jansai's hands, or the Archangel's, was dead.

Like Zeke.

She would not think of Zeke.

If she had walked with him to the harbor, she would be dead, too. She would not think of that, either.

The bus shuddered deeply and rolled into reverse with excruciating slowness. Righting itself, it plowed forward through the city streets with a blind assurance that sent pedestrians, vendor carts, and smaller vehicles scurrying out of its way. They had cleared the narrow, cramped streets of the inner city and were bowling past the closed, watchful houses of the wealthy Jansai. They were at the city limits. They were on open road, gold desert sand stretching limitlessly on either side of them. They were ten miles from Breven. She was free.

The bus was a local, she discovered soon enough, making stops at virtually every small town between Breven and Luminaux; consequently, it would take three days to cover the miles between the cities. Well, on foot or by horse it would have taken much longer, so she shouldn't complain, but she was afraid hunger would do her in before they had covered half the distance. She had bought a little food before she left Breven, but it was not nearly enough. Like most Jacobites, she was lean to begin with, and her body had few reserves. But then again, like most Jacobites, she was familiar with hunger. She knew how to wait it out.

But by the third day, she began to get light-headed. As she sat on the bus, staring out the window, she suddenly felt her stomach drop away and her mind whirl into a dizzy spiral. The sensation was so physical that she clutched at her armrest, fearful of actually falling out of her seat. She closed her eyes, but her head kept spinning; she could almost feel the rush of wind against her cheeks. Again, her stomach seemed to plunge to her shoes; again, she felt as if she was tumbling down. And then, mercifully, the motion stopped.

She opened her eyes carefully to find everything about her

unchanged—the lush countryside serene outside her window, her seatmate drowsing peacefully beside her. *I must be getting sick,* she thought, *or closer to starvation than I thought. First thing I'll do when we get to Luminaux is buy a steak.*

And later that evening, five minutes after they'd pulled into the Blue City, that was precisely what she did. Mortimer's was run by a man who had always been sympathetic to the Jacobites, and the cook let her through the back door without a question.

But. "I'll feed you," said Sadie, the old woman who had been the chef here since before Tamar was born, "but you can't be hanging around here. They've come by a few times, looking."

"The Jansai?"

"Yes, and each time Mortimer showed them the whole place, top to bottom, before they were content to leave. So it's not safe here."

"Can I spend the night? I don't have anywhere to go."

Sadie pursed her lips. "I'll ask him," she said. "I don't know what he'll say."

But Mortimer sent back a message saying she was welcome to the bed in the cellar for a few days, but he couldn't promise to protect her if the Jansai came looking. That was as good a deal as Tamar expected, and she accepted quickly. She'd eaten the steak in about three minutes, and Sadie took pity on her and brought her a bowl of potatoes.

"I don't have any money," Tamar said.

Sadie shrugged. "When did you ever?"

"I'll help clean up."

"If you want." But the old woman was pleased.

It took Tamar two days to find a place to stay and a job at a small, well-respected restaurant. There was always work available in Luminaux if you were willing to do menial tasks. The city was filled with artisans and intellectuals who were not always keen on scrubbing floors and cleaning out stables. Tamar didn't mind dirty work—she'd been an ostler more than once, and prided herself on her ability to calm the edgiest-tempered horse—but this time she wanted a job with perks. Like food. At the restaurant, she could have all the scraps she wanted. So she was able to hoard her meager salary, paying out only what she needed for rent. And the single room in the dilapidated house on the edge of the city was a miser's dream, so most of

her money went into a sock that she hid under the bed. Saving
against the next journey.

It was still too soon to go to Ileah; the Jacobites were not
supposed to reconvene there for another month and a half. But
Tamar was guessing that the other rebels were also discovering
that there was little safety anywhere else and that they may as
well head for Ileah a few weeks early. In any case, she was
betting that she would not be the only one there if she arrived
before the rendezvous date.

But she could not go penniless and starving. So she worked
for two weeks, saving every copper. Meanwhile, she shopped
the bazaars, looking for bargains—sturdy shoes, comfortable
clothes, a new backpack. At the café, she ate everything she
could stuff into her mouth, putting on a few pounds against the
chance that her food would run out again. What she couldn't
eat, she took home if it could be dried and packaged for travel.
She had no end of nuts, raisins, apples, and crackers, everything
suitable for transport.

She did not go back to Mortimer's. She kept away from the
bars and the coffeehouses where her friends used to congregate.
She didn't try to track down the girl who had loved Zeke, who
had lived with her mother and father in a three-room apartment
over a used bookstore. There, the Jacobites had frequently gathered to debate philosophy and dream about their version of a
perfect world. Tamar may as well not have been in Luminaux
at all, for all the comfort it gave her.

One night, walking home from the restaurant, she took the
long way back to her room, through the center of town. Luminaux had been christened the Blue City because every building,
every statue, every flower, every cobblestone sported some
shade of that cerulean color. At night, the soft streetlights drew
the most subtle shades of cobalt, sapphire, and indigo from the
walls and the awnings; even the mist rising from the wet sidewalks seemed tinted with turquoise.

But color was not all that made Luminaux rich. On every
street corner, stooped old musicians crouched over their
scratched cellos, trios of young girls paused to sing exquisite
harmonies, painters set up their landscapes on easels and offered
to draw portraits on the spot. All night long, vendors sold meat
pies, licorice sticks, beer, and hot coffee. And that was just on
the streets. If you had the money for the entrance fee, you could

go into any one of hundreds of restaurants and taverns, try the food, listen to the music, watch the theater, or join the debate. Luminaux was a city not only of beauty, but of possibilities. Anything you wanted could be had there.

Except safety.

Tamar paused outside a darkened doorway and listened to a pair of trumpets weaving a silver melody. She had spent much of her life in Luminaux and never once walked into an establishment like this. Hadn't had the time, hadn't had the inclination. She had been too intent on changing the world, formulating plans, reading manifestos. And all it had netted her was the most solitary evening of her life, far from her friends (if her friends were still alive), far from realizing any of her dreams. Sometimes it seemed it would be easier to lay down all the burdens, philosophical and real, and stroll into a place like this and order a couple of bottles of wine. And drink both of them to the dregs.

She hunched her shoulders once against the chill of the spring evening, then put her feet in motion again and continued on home.

The question was how to get to Ileah, which was far from any commercial bus route—and an abandoned settlement at that. Seventy-five or a hundred years ago it had been an Edori sanctuary, one of the tracts of land put aside for exclusive use of the nomadic tribes who were being crowded out of existence by an exploding industrial population. But like all the other sanctuaries, it had been deserted when the Edori began their mass emigration to Ysral. Even while they lived in Ileah it had not been much of a city by anyone's standards. The Edori were gypsies, campers, itinerant folk who did not put much stock in permanent structures or municipal bylaws.

"It's got half a dozen tumbledown cottages, or maybe they were storerooms—whatever, a few ratty buildings and one working well," Conran had told them. It had been Conran's idea, of course, to meet in Ileah. Since Jacob Fairman's death a quarter century ago, Conran had been the de facto leader of the Jacobites. "It's far from the main highways, so it's virtually assured that no Jansai will wander through. I can't imagine that any travelers will stumble upon us, actually."

"How did you find it?" Jani had asked him, but Conran had merely smiled. It was a stupid question. If it had happened in

Samaria, if it existed in any of the three provinces, he would know about it. Conran knew everything.

He had drawn them a large communal map, insisted they all memorize it, and then destroyed it. No one had been allowed to copy it so that in case they were captured, they would not inadvertently lead their enemies to their friends. Tamar had studied the map for days. If she closed her eyes now, she could see the red line leading her from Luminaux to Ileah through the variegated terrain of Jordana.

But how to get there? She couldn't afford to buy a horse and she couldn't honestly rent one, since she was unlikely ever to return. If she walked, it would take her weeks, and she couldn't pay for the food she would need for a journey that lasted that long. Castelana, the nearest major city, was a hundred miles from Ileah; she could take a bus there and walk the rest of the way, she supposed. If she covered thirty miles a day on foot, the last leg of the trip would only take three days. It seemed her best option.

But then she got lucky, for the first time in the past six months. The woman who worked beside her in the kitchen took the opportunity one evening to share her problems with Tamar.

"It's a terrible thing not to trust your own daughter, but there it is," the woman said. "I know I've raised her right, and I know it's time she was trusted on her own, but I'm a mother and I worry."

"Troubles, Ellen?" Tamar asked absently. Ellen was motherly and fretful, and Tamar found her annoying but harmless. They had not become close, but they had managed to work together in passable harmony.

"My girl. Sophie. She's only seventeen. Edward has been courting her since the time she was fourteen, and I know they plan to marry. He wants to take her to Stockton to meet his mother—now, doesn't that just prove that he's a good boy and he's serious about my daughter? But they'll be four or five days on the road, and you know any innkeeper along the way will give them a single room if they ask for it, and I just don't know that I can trust the two of them to behave themselves."

If they've been courting for three years, they've had plenty of time to become lovers, Tamar wanted to say, but there was no reason to shred Ellen's comfortable illusions. Instead she closed her eyes briefly, recalling Conran's map of Samaria. "Stockton?'' she repeated. "Isn't that up around Semorrah?"

She knew it wasn't. "No, it's practically in the Caitana Mountains!" Ellen exclaimed. "I'm sure they're lovely people in Stockton, but you just can't expect them to be as civilized as the Luminauzi.''

"I have a friend in Stockton," Tamar said slowly. "I haven't visited her in at least two years.''

"Well, I wish you were going to visit her now."

Tamar pivoted to face Ellen and tried not to look too excited. "That's what I meant," she said in a mild voice. "If you think you could spare me from the kitchen for a couple of weeks. If it would ease your mind any. I'd be glad to go to Stockton with your daughter and her friend to play chaperon.''

Ellen's face lit up; she clapped her hands together and snugged them under her chin like a child at a magic show. "You would? Really, you would? Of course I can spare you! For something like this! And you could share a room with Sophie and the trip would cost you hardly anything, and then I could be sure she was properly watched after. Because you're a serious one, you are, and it's easy to tell you know what's right and proper. I'd feel so relieved if I knew you were with them.''

Tamar smiled. "When do they leave?"

"The day after tomorrow. If you can be ready that quickly? I'm sure they'd be willing to wait a day or two."

"I can be ready. I need to buy a few things, but I can get those this evening. What time do they depart? And how are they traveling?''

They were taking Edward's uncle's cart and team, though Ellen assured Tamar that it was far grander than an ordinary cart or she would not have countenanced Sophie traveling so far in it. Tamar nodded, but she was not deceived. A cart was a cart, whether or not someone had thought to install padded seats and an overhead tarp. It would be miserable in the rain, frigid in the cold, drafty in the wind, and bone wrenching every mile of the way. Still, it was transport, and Tamar was not about to sneer at any unexpected windfalls.

Accordingly, she speeded up her preparations to depart, paid off her landlord, packed up her bundles of dried food, and readied herself for the journey. Two days later she was saying hello to Sophie, farewell to Ellen, and good-bye forever to Luminaux. Her travel companions were much as she had pictured them.

Sophie was a little more luminous than she would have expected Ellen's daughter to be, but the dewy glow could have been produced by love or the mere fact of being seventeen, and would wear off within a couple of years. Edward looked to be sturdy, industrious, and two or three years the girl's senior. Tamar felt aeons older than either of them, but she greeted them as courteously as possible and threw her luggage into the back of the cart.

She was pleased to note that Ellen had not lied: The cart was outfitted with not only the cushioned seat that the driver could share with a passenger, but two padded benches facing each other in the rear of the wagon. As she'd expected, there was a light frame built into the back of the cart, over which a tarpaulin could be stretched if the weather turned bad. It wasn't luxury, but it wasn't contemptible either.

"Do you mind riding in the back of the wagon?" Sophie asked her anxiously before they had even climbed in for the first time. "It's just that Edward and I have so much to talk about, and I'd really rather sit next to him for the whole trip."

Tamar smiled. On the whole, she would prefer not having to make conversation with either of her fellow travelers. "The back suits me just fine," she said. "But you can tell Edward I'm willing to take a turn driving if he gets tired. I'm a pretty good hand with horses."

Edward, overhearing, looked doubtful. "They're my uncle's horses," he said. "I don't think he'd want me to trust them to just anybody."

Tamar shrugged. "I've worked at the Lamphouse and the Barmer," she said, naming two of the better-known stables in Luminaux. "And I used to drive passengers from the Exton Hotel to Port Clara in the hotel's carriage. You can trust me with horses. But I don't blame you for being cautious. You don't know me."

"She's a hard worker," Ellen put in, having audited all this from the sidelines. "Always shows up on time. You can trust her."

"Well, maybe," Edward said, making no promises. "Are you ready?"

Sophie quickly hugged her mother one last time. Tamar hopped into the back of the cart and made herself as comfortable as possible. In a few moments she was waving good-bye to

Ellen, to Luminaux, to the life she'd known best, and they were on the road to Stockton.

The first two days passed in utter and complete boredom, punctuated only by moments of severe discomfort, as the cart jounced briskly down the road toward Stockton. The road, at least these two days, was relatively good—paved and in excellent repair—since it was one of the country's major highways and accommodated a great deal of vehicular traffic. Of course, any time a truck or bus roared up behind them, Edward was forced to pull his wagon to the side of the road, and even then the horses neighed and strained against the traces. The fumes left behind by the big vehicles were noxious and enduring, and they were all coughing by noon of the first day.

But the weather held fine and the horses appeared to be in good condition, and she was on her way, so Tamar gave herself up to monotony and let the hours roll indifferently by.

The first night, they stopped in a town so small it had not been on Conran's map, but it did boast a couple of decent-looking inns. Edward chose one at random and bespoke two rooms. The three of them ate a somewhat awkward dinner together, Sophie making attempts at conversation with Tamar, who was not greatly interested.

"So, my mother tells me you have a friend in Stockton that you're going to visit. What's her name?"

"Elizabeth," Tamar replied.

"And where did you meet her? Did she used to live in Luminaux?"

Jovah save her, she was going to have to make up an entire history. "Yes. We were neighbors while I was in school. We were very close."

"Why did she move away?"

"To marry."

Edward looked up. "Really? Maybe I know her husband. I grew up in Stockton, you know."

Sweet god singing. Worse and worse. "His name is James Shelton. I don't know that he was raised there, though. I think he moved to Stockton to take a job."

Edward raised his eyebrows. "Not much commerce in Stockton. Unless he's in banking. There's a branch office of the Exchequer in Stockton, you know."

"Banking. I think that's it," Tamar said faintly.

"Do they have children?" Sophie asked.

"One. Born a couple of months ago. That's why I wanted to visit."

Sophie clapped her hands together (a gesture she must have copied from her mother). She appeared to be one of those un-fortunate women who became sloppily romantic at the very thought of holding an infant. "Oh, how wonderful! What did you buy her for a baby gift?"

"I didn't have time to get one. We left on such short notice—"

"Oh, but you have to bring them something! Their first baby!"

"I'll pick something up in Stockton. See what they need."

"No, no, you should have something in your hands when you arrive. Maybe if we have time tonight or tomorrow night, we can find something in one of these little towns along the way."

Tamar's protests were quickly overruled, and she inwardly seethed for the rest of the meal. As if she had any additional dollars to be throwing away on the fictional child of imaginary friends! She had best guard her tongue every minute for the rest of the journey.

The meal once over, they experienced another strained few minutes as they ascended the stairs to their rooms, side by side in the well-lit corridor. Tamar headed straight for her door and unlocked it, making no comment to Sophie. "I'll be right in," the girl said, and Tamar nodded. She closed the door behind her but left it unlocked, and true to her word, Sophie entered a few minutes later.

Tamar had already gotten herself ready for bed and climbed under the covers. Sophie moved moodily around the room, brushing out her long hair and sighing before the mirror.

"It's very hard to be seventeen," she burst out at last, setting down her brush and turning to face Tamar.

Oh, dear god, no, Tamar thought, but Sophie rushed on before Tamar could stop her. "No one realizes that I am a grown woman—that I know what I want and am perfectly capable of taking care of myself and making wise decisions. Everyone tells me, 'Oh, when you're older, you'll understand, you'll see why we didn't want you to do such and such. You'll thank us for making you do thus and so.' But they're basing everything on their own lives! On their own experiences! They don't realize that mine are so much different! My feelings are so much different than theirs.''

Tamar didn't quite have the heart to flounce over in bed and face the wall, but she did close her eyes. Sophie appeared not to notice. ''From the time I was quite young, I was very mature. I helped my mother with my younger sisters and brothers—and I worked, too! I know how to be responsible with money and I know how to hold together a household. Do you know how much it costs to feed five people for a week? I know, to the penny! And yet everyone says I am too young to marry. They even think I'm too young to fall in love.''

Don't ask my opinion, Tamar warned her silently. *Don't invite my comments. I'll tell you, I swear I will.*

''Don't you think it is one of a parent's duties to know when to let go?'' Sophie went on, unheeding. ''Don't you think a mother should realize when her daughter is old enough to be responsible?''

Tamar's eyes flew open. ''My mother and father were murdered when I was a baby,'' she said flatly. ''I was raised by friends of theirs who didn't have enough time to take care of their own children, so I was passed from hand to hand according to who had a free moment to spare that day. By the time I was ten, I was deciding where to live, what to eat, and who to trust. By the time I was seventeen, I had taken a lover, been abandoned by a lover, seen a friend kill herself, seen a friend kill another man. I think if you're seventeen, and you have a chance to be your mother's daughter for another year, or another minute, you should take that chance. Life on your own is not nearly as glorious as you might think. It is hard, it is bitter, and every minute of it wears you down. That's what I think.''

And in the absolute silence that followed, she closed her eyes again and turned on her side. Sophie did not say another word, but switched off the light and climbed into bed. Tamar fell instantly asleep.

So she was not surprised when, the next morning, all of the awkwardness of the previous day returned. On the front seat, Sophie sat as close to Edward as his grip on the reins would allow, whispering endearments or gossip in his ear. Tamar sat with one elbow on the back of her bench, watching the countryside roll back behind them. If her life had depended on it, she could not have come up with a single conciliatory thing to say.

Dinner that night was more relaxed, because they shared a table with a family of six traveling southward to Luminaux. Sophie, of course, instantly commandeered the baby, while Edward talked road conditions with the patriarch. Tamar concentrated on her food. When she was done, she excused herself and went up to her room.

Again, she was half-asleep before Sophie entered. The girl stood uncertainly in the middle of the room.

"I hope I didn't wake you up last night," she said. "I'm a restless sleeper, and my sisters have often complained that I talk through my dreams."

"Didn't hear a thing," Tamar said. "I fall asleep instantly and never wake up again till dawn. Don't worry about me."

"I'm glad to hear it," Sophie said. "I'll try to be quiet."

So of course Tamar simply had to turn over and feign sleep right away. Sophie waited a good half hour, sitting motionless on her own bed, before rising to her feet and tiptoeing from the room. The door made almost no sound as she closed it behind her. Tamar grinned in the dark and allowed herself to drift off to sleep.

After that, things went a little better. Edward seemed more at ease and Sophie simply glowed, radiant with the retained fire of passion. Tamar couldn't help envying her a little—youth, innocence, *and* happiness; it seemed unfair that someone should have all three—but it was no part of her plan to thwart the young lovers. She did not care what they did in the dark as long as, by daylight, they continued on toward Stockton.

The third day, Edward had even mellowed enough to ask Tamar if she was still interested in driving. No doubt he merely wanted an opportunity to put both arms around his beloved as they cuddled in the back of the wagon, but the offer suited Tamar just fine. Accordingly, she took a hand at the reins, and the next fifty miles passed a little more pleasantly.

"You drive well," Edward told her that night over dinner. "It's a little odd for a woman to be so used to handling a team."

Tamar grinned. "I can do a lot of odd things," she said. "I can drive a horse. I can shoe a horse. I can cook a meal for fifty. I can make a campfire, and I can repair an electrical line, if it isn't too far gone. I can drive a truck if I have to."

"You must have lived a strange life," Sophie said, her face shadowed by the memory of what Tamar had told her the other night.

Tamar looked at her and shrugged. "It was my life," she said. "It seemed natural to me. But I admit there are things about your life that appeal to me more."

It was on these terms of tentative goodwill that they continued the trip into Stockton. They arrived at the little town a few hours after noon on the fifth day of their trip, and Edward carefully negotiated the narrow streets.

"Where do you want me to let you off?" he asked. "Where does your friend live?"

Tamar had debated this point for most of the morning, and now she answered with partial honesty. "It doesn't matter," she said. "My friend lives a little outside of town, and I'll be traveling on to find her."

Sophie shot her a quick, troubled look. "We could take you to her farmhouse, or wherever she lives," she offered.

"No," Tamar said. "But thank you."

"We plan to leave for Luminaux again in four days," Edward said over his shoulder. "Where should we pick you up again?"

"I won't be ready to return that quickly," Tamar said gently. "So just go back without me."

Now Sophie looked even more troubled. "My mother will be unhappy," she said.

"I know. She'll think I lied to her. But I think you will be as responsible without me along as you have been with me."

"I meant—she likes you. She'll be sorry you're not coming back. Or do you plan to come back sometime?"

"Not anytime soon, I'm afraid. Tell her I'm sorry. She was always kind to me."

"Are you sure we can't take you to this friend's place?" Edward persisted. He had pulled the cart to a halt and now was turned on his seat to look back at her. Like Sophie, he looked grave and worried.

"I'm sure."

"Is there really someone you're going to?" Sophie asked.

Tamar smiled. "Yes, there's really a person and a place I'm going to," she said. "I'll be fine. Don't worry."

And before they could voice another concern, she had gathered up her belongings and hopped from the cart. It was not her wish to be rude, so she waved good-bye a few times as she began easing her way down the sidewalk. Edward merely nodded, but Sophie lifted her hand and waved dispiritedly, as if she was watching her best friend say farewell for the last time. It was a strange experience, Tamar found, to have virtual strangers anxious over her welfare. It was not quite as annoying as she would have expected.

There were several hours of daylight left, and she had no reason to dawdle in Stockton, so she set out immediately on foot. Ileah, she judged, was forty or fifty miles due south; she could not possibly make it there before nightfall, but she would get a good start. And she didn't need to be wasting any more money on hotel rooms. She could camp out for the night.

Accordingly, she settled into a steady pace, not too taxing, and headed southward. This side road was not nearly as good as the northeastern highway had been—indeed, it was little more than a trail, and it obviously saw very little use. Which was good for Tamar, excellent for the Jacobites. She was not much of a tracker, but she studied the dusty road, trying to determine if other travelers had passed this way recently, or if she would be the first to arrive at Ileah. She thought she discerned hoofprints in the dirt; soon enough, she would know.

She made a cold camp when it got too dark to see, and slept on a patch of grass that looked softer than it really was. Her bones hurt when she rose in the morning. She cleaned herself up as best she could and continued on. The morning sun was barely strong enough to chase away the chill she had acquired from sleeping on the ground, but by noon, walking had made her hot enough to wish for a cool breeze. She was remembering now why she had always hated traveling on foot.

But shortly after noon she was in sight of her destination. From a couple of miles away, she could see the poorly built stone cottages clumped together around what looked like a central green. At this distance, she could not see movement or hear noise—or even see smoke, which was odd. Ileah had never been wired for electricity, so any heat or power would have to come from fire. But there did not appear to be a single drift of smoke coming from any of the buildings, not even when she drew close enough to hail the settlement. Was it possible she was the first one here after all?

But no, she saw as soon as she came within sight of the green.

Other Jacobites had arrived early. And the Jansai had followed them.

There were maybe ten bodies strewn helter-skelter across the center park, heads at abrupt angles, arms outflung before them on the ground. Blood was everywhere, on their clothes, on the grass, rusty brown in the pale brown dirt. Tamar moved between them with a sleepwalker's unreality, bending down at each still form, checking for a pulse, checking for breath. None of them was living. She whispered their names as she moved between them—"Daniel, Dawn, Martha, Evan, Kate, Ruth"—because someone must mark their passing, and mark the site of their deaths. Not Jovah, of course—there was no god; he did not care who lived and died. But someone. The nameless deity the Edori worshiped. Someone. No one should die a death that went completely unrecorded.

Dazed, she moved through the rest of the sanctuary, searching for more of her friends. In one of the otherwise empty cottages, she found two more bodies. Almost all the other buildings were deserted.

But in the last hut she checked, she found another body. And when she put her hand to the red-stained chest, she felt the rib cage rise with breath. Her own lungs nearly collapsed from shock.

"Peter!" she cried, kneeling beside him on the dirt floor. "Peter, can you hear me? It's Tamar! Can you hear me? Oh, the false god save us, what can I do, what can I do . . . Peter, I'm going to clean you up and try to patch your wounds. Just lie still, I'll do what I can. . . ."

She flew back outside, to the dilapidated well in the center of the green. One of these early arrivals had pushed off the cover and found a usable bucket, and tied it to the stone edge of the well with a long rope. Tamar flung it down and heard it hit water, and hauled it up as fast as her hands could pull. The water was icy cold and would no doubt send an injured man into trauma, but it was all she had.

She spent the next two hours examining Peter, binding his wounds, rolling him onto a thin mat, and silently praying to a nonexistent god. Every time she caught herself asking for divine assistance, she clamped her mouth shut and forced her mind back to her task, but over and over again the words began cycling of their own accord through her brain. Conran had said once that it was easy to be an atheist in a kind world; it was when affairs were desperate that every man's inner strength was tested. She had never quite believed him before.

Peter appeared to have been both bludgeoned and stabbed; it was hard to tell whether the concussion or the wound had been worse. By the fact that the bleeding seemed to have stopped completely, Tamar judged that it had been many hours since the attackers had arrived. By the fact that Peter was still alive, she guessed that it had not been more than a day or two since they had passed through. Perhaps theirs were the horse tracks she thought she had seen on the road from Stockton.

On a normal day, she would have had nothing resembling medicine in her backpack, but she was still carrying the vial of manna-root salve that Ezra had given her. She spread the last of it on the dozen open cuts along Peter's neck and chest and arms, then bound everything up with the cleanest clothes she could find from the items in the cottage with him. Not sure if it was a good idea or a bad one, she trickled some water down his throat. If he didn't throw it all up, she would follow that later this evening with broth. She knew that a man could live days, sometimes a couple of weeks, without eating; she also knew the weaker he was, the more likely it was he would die.

Next a fire, because he was chilled straight through, and lying on the ground for a day or two had done him no good at all. She went outside again and dragged back branches and logs, enough to get a good blaze started. The cottage had been built to accommodate a central fire; there was a small circular hole in the middle of the roof. Or perhaps a century of neglect had caused the ceiling to cave in. In any case, the smoke could escape easily, and Peter could be brought as close to the flames as she dared.

After that, there was little she could do for him except allow his body to heal. She searched through the possessions the other Jacobites had left in one of the abandoned cabins till she found some cookware, then she put some dried meat into a pan of water and let this simmer over her fire. Dinner for the wounded man, if she could induce him to eat it. She didn't think she could swallow a bite herself.

It was afternoon before she had finished all these tasks, and she stepped outside the cabin for a moment to take a breath of air. And survey the scene before her. Twelve bodies in all. She did not think she could dig twelve graves, but the Jacobites were a clannish group; they would not mind lying side by side, body to body, whispering to each other through eternity of the atrocities they had seen in their lifetimes. A communal grave would do for them.

Accordingly, she next searched for a shovel among the boxes and backpacks and duffel bags that had been piled up in the cottage apparently chosen as a storage room. Someone had carried a fair collection of belongings on a small, wheeled cart (pulling it by hand, no doubt, since there didn't seem to be any sign of horses here; of course, the Jansai could have appropriated any animals they found). On the cart she found a shovel and an ax and an array of knives. Someone had come prepared for chopping out a new life in a primitive settlement.

On the west edge of Ileah, Tamar began to dig. The ground was still tough from winter frosts, and she found it harder going than she had expected. And nothing would be worse than stacking bodies in a grave and finding that it was too shallow. Doggedly, she continued, till her back ached and her arms trembled, and the light began to fail. Well, she would have to finish it tomorrow.

But she could not leave her friends all night to the vicious curiosity of night animals. One by one, she pulled the ten bodies from the green to the cabin where the other two had fallen, and she built a fire in the open doorway. Here they were as safe as she could make them.

From time to time she returned to check on Peter and to give him more water. Every once in a while, when she lifted his head, he would mutter feebly in an incomprehensible tongue. She wasn't sure; she thought that was encouraging. She spoke to him as she wiped his face and tilted water down his throat: *You're doing so well, I'm sure you'll be fine, one more drink, in the morning you'll be so much better . . . .* She didn't know who she was reassuring, the man on the pallet or herself.

In the evening, he did swallow a few spoonfuls of broth, and opened his mouth for more when she paused, afraid to overdo it. She was so heartened by this that, once he fell back into a troubled sleep, she made herself eat the rest of the soup. She was not hungry, but starving herself would serve no one. She must keep up her strength.

Although now she was as exhausted as, in the whole course

of her tumultuous existence, she could ever remember being. Every muscle in her body shook with fatigue, and her mind was dull with horror. She checked the fire burning at the corpses' door and then returned to the cottage she would share this night with Peter. Lying on a thin carpet of other people's belongings, she fell soundly asleep before she had time even to review the events of the day.

Cold woke her once in the middle of the night, and she got up to replenish both fires. Peter moaned once, softly. She gave him more water and checked his bandages. No blood appeared to be seeping through. Perhaps that was because he had no more blood left. She didn't know. She couldn't tell. She stumbled back to her bed and slept again.

In the morning, she divided her time between tending to Peter and digging the grave. She cooked an apple in her stew pot and mashed it up, spooning the sauce into her patient's mouth. He ate it; another good sign. Back outside, she dug deeper into the ground, until she hit what felt like bedrock. Then she moved outward, making the hole wider, big enough to hold another row of bodies, or two.

By noon, Peter was beginning to move choppily on his bed, and the grave was completed. She fed him more broth, and ate a substantial lunch before attempting her most woeful task yet. And then slowly, methodically, not letting herself think about it too much, she dragged one body after the other from the cabin to the grave, and buried her friends.

She was sweating and weeping as she heaved the last shovelful of dirt onto the fresh mound. She struggled for breath as she drove the spade in the dirt and leaned against it, all strength gone. She should say something; there should be a formal farewell. The dead should not have to leave this world until their names were spoken one last time.

She said all twelve names very slowly, paused to think, and then named them again, one by one. "Daniel. You could talk all night without stopping, and we laughed at you for your fierceness, but I wish I could take some of your fierceness right now into my heart. Dawn, you were well named, because when you walked into a room, it was as if sunrise repeated itself. Martha. You taught me how to skin game and cook it over an open fire, so that I would never go hungry and neither would anyone around me. Evan . . . I spoke to you maybe three times in my life, but each time you said a kind word. I will try to remember that kindness."

She pronounced six more names, six more eulogies. She paused to run her hand over her forehead. Her hair stuck to her damp face and then to her damp hands. Two to go. "Kate. You were the serious one. People said I was so solemn, but for you, everything was intense. Everything mattered. Everything was either right or wrong. I'll miss your certainty. And Ruth. A friend for any time, in joy or sorrow. Now a memory, for today and forever."

She folded her hands across the worn wooden handle of the shovel and leaned her forehead against her knuckles. And sobbed like she had not sobbed at any point in her life that she could remember.

By nightfall, Peter was thrashing about enough that Tamar was actually alarmed. She didn't want him to hurt himself or dislodge his bandages. He had opened his eyes several times, though he did not seem to recognize her, but he was conscious as he took his food and he watched her as she fed him. But sleep would not come to him again, or at least quiet sleep, and she was afraid.

To calm him, she began to sing. Music had been one of the many things most Jacobites disdained—because music was the medium through which the angels prayed to their mistaken god—and yet a few wayward melodies had found their way into Tamar's head and stayed there. Well, you could not live in Luminaux and be completely indifferent to music, and she had always found its power to be surprising and complex. The right song could enhance a mood or change it utterly; a few pensive bars mourned over by a violin could set her to dreaming, a riotous flare of woodwinds could send her dancing. It was not just the angels who could draw power from music.

What she sang now was a melody she had heard a few times in the streets of Luminaux, a sweet, wordless tune that had somehow gotten entangled in her ears and settled down for good at the back of her throat. From time to time over the past year, she had caught herself humming its wandering notes, and so it had stuck with her through repetition as well as charm. It was a lullaby or a love song, something gentle and romantic, and as she sang it now Peter settled and grew still.

There were no lyrics, so she made them up. "Sleep now, Peter, sleep my friend. Tamar watches over you. The stars turn over you. The earth turns under you. All will be well. . . ." Silly words, meaningless phrases, but they fit the melody and they seemed to give him peace. He grunted once more and clumsily turned to his side, and then he fell into a deep sleep.

Tamar was right behind him. The past few days—few weeks—of physical exertion and emotional turmoil had left her completely drained. She had no reserves of energy or mental agility left. Tomorrow . . . so much to do. She must look for food, hunt if she had time, search the unlikely spring bushes for bark and berries. Her own supplies were low and she hadn't found any extra food in the Jacobites' storeroom. Perhaps the Jansai had taken those provisions as well. Well, she knew how to set traps, and Ileah wasn't far from a mountain-fed stream; perhaps, if Peter was well enough, she could leave for the better part of the day to fish for food. She'd need a rod then, and some kind of fishhook. . . . Her thoughts darted more slowly from task to plan, and she drifted off to sleep.

Peter was better in the morning, but not exactly well. As she fed him another mashed apple, he looked her straight in the eye and said, "Tamar." She was so excited that she almost dropped the spoon, but when she cried out his name in response, he merely looked away, across the room. But it was a good sign; she knew it was a good sign. When he fell back asleep, she hurried outside and stood for a moment in the doorway, looking around.

The stream was west. Slightly east was wilder country, where she might expect to find rabbits and squirrels. She could set a couple traps first, look for the few edible plants that might be available at this time of year, come back to check quickly on Peter, then head off toward the river by noon. Even if she was gone five hours, he should be well enough. She would return in time to feed him once more before he slept again for the night.

Of course, she would need a rod, and if she had time, she might be able to fashion a bow—of course, she didn't have arrows—but there might be game birds, now that she thought of it, because she could hear wings overhead, and she turned quickly to see if it was grouse, pheasant, geese, or—

But it was huge. It was not a bird at all. It was man-sized, it had great monstrous wings, just now extended to a frightening breadth. *Jovah, dear Jovah, please god, if there was only a god . . .* The great wings tilted backward, the body straightened, swung toward the earth. A man, an *angel,* and he was on the ground not ten yards from her. He raised his hand as if to fling thunderbolts, and Tamar did not pause to think or even utter one more doomed prayer. She took off as fast as she could run, fleeing the false sanctuary of Ileah.

CHAPTER SIX

The month after the Gloria Jared spent mostly in transit. He did return to Monteverde for about ten days, making sure everything was well there, before heading off to Cedar Hills. But at Monteverde, as usual, his mother and sister had everything well in hand. They even pretended to be surprised to see him, which annoyed him, although it was supposed to shame him into being more attentive to the hold's needs.

"Why, Jared! It *is* Jared, isn't it?" his sister greeted him. "It's been so long since you've been here—but, no, you must be my brother after all. How nice to see you."

And she leaned forward to invite a kiss on her cheek. Catherine was eight years his senior, placid, ironic, and frighteningly efficient, and it was easier to admire her than to like her. Jared kissed her, dutifully but briefly, then turned to give his mother the same salute.

"We heard that your singing was wonderful at the Gloria," his mother said, greeting him more kindly than had Catherine. "Didn't you say Mercy would be singing with you?"

"Yes. The duet went quite well, or so everyone told me."

"So tell us about your adventures on the Plain of Sharon," Catherine invited, sinking to a low seat and gesturing for him to do the same. Almost unwillingly, he did.

"No adventures. I visited with Mercy and Christian, and avoided Bael and Mariah. Pretty much the same as always."

"Did that Gaelin girl catch up with you?" Catherine asked. "You know, what's her name, Zeb Gaelin's daughter. She was here asking about you a day or two before the Gloria, and she said she'd look for you there."

Jared felt a swift heat rise to his cheeks, not sure if it was anger or embarrassment. Beth Gaelin had made no secret of her infatuation with him over the past three years, and Catherine considered it infinitely amusing. Beth was a pretty enough girl, daughter of a Manadavvi lordling, with all the acceptable society manners. Jared admitted to a little ill-judged dalliance when he'd first met her, but it had been nothing serious. Nothing to inspire such devotion. She had become something of a nuisance ever since. He had been known to accept or decline invitations based on whether or not Beth would be present; that was how much he desired to avoid her.

"No," he said shortly. "If she was there, I didn't see her."

"Jared, dear," his mother said, "will you be staying for dinner? Or must you leave again right away? We get to see you so seldom, but I'm not complaining. I know how busy you are."

Ah, but trust his mother, in her sweetest voice, to drive the knife deeper than Catherine would ever bother. "I'll be here a week or two, or longer if you need me," he said with hard-won courtesy. "I do have plans to go to Cedar Hills."

"Oh, leave when you will," Catherine said breezily. "I don't think we ever really need you. But it would be nice to have dinner with you, for a change."

He forced a smile. "Count on it," he said.

But that had been the most unpleasant part of his quick stay back at his own hold. The first hour or so was always spent having his mother and sister remind him how carelessly he ran Monteverde. But after that, they were happy enough informing him of all the events that had transpired in his absence and how they had handled any small crisis, and the rest of the visit passed amiably. He had completely recovered his usual sunny disposition when, about ten days later, he took off for Cedar Hills.

It was a two-day flight, and he considered stopping for a day or two at Semorrah. But he wasn't sure how long Lucinda and her aunt would be staying at Cedar Hills, and he didn't want to miss them. Therefore, he broke his flight overnight at the river city of Castelana, and continued on into Jordana the following day.

"Though you needn't have hurried," Mercy told him privately once he'd arrived. "It's looking like Gretchen might never want to leave. She wanders around with a somewhat dazed expression on her face, half longing and half pain, or so it seems to me. Like she's ruing what she missed all these years."

"Maybe they'll move back, then," Jared said.

"It's crossed my mind. In a day or two I might suggest it to her."

"And then ask her why she left in the first place."

"I told you that."

"You told me your guesses. Not the same thing."

"So what do you think of Lucinda?"

"I've only exchanged a dozen words with her. But she's not exactly as I would have expected."

"In what way?"

He had not tried to put it into words for himself. "Less . . . naive," he said at last. "Not sophisticated, exactly, but self-assured even in a foreign and intimidating environment. She's not your giddy backwater farm girl. But still sort of fresh and unspoiled."

"If heredity counts for anything, she could be the most stub-born and strong-willed girl on the planet. Nobody's fool. And of course, Gretchen wasn't exactly a country bumpkin when she left here. She'd be bound to give the girl an education that was out of the ordinary."

"What happens to her next? She seems to think she's heading back to Angel Rock someday soon. Seems a pity to lose her forever to a place like that."

"I'm working on it. I'd like her to consider Cedar Hills her home."

Jared stayed in the southern continent for four days, flying down to Luminaux for three of them just because it was a pity to miss any chance to visit the Blue City. When he prepared to leave for Semorrah, Mercy showed a very faint disapproval.

"I saw you cozying up to Christian at the Gloria," she said. "What are the two of you hatching up now?"

"Nothing, as far as I know," he said, surprised. "Why would you say that?"

She shrugged irritably and toyed with the ruby bracelets on her arm. "Sometimes I think Christian's keeping bad company these days."

"Isaiah Lesh?" Jared asked. "They've been friends forever."

"Isaiah's a troublemaker."

"All the Manadavvi are. So far it's been minor trouble.

What's bothering you about Christian? He's one of your closest friends."

"He's spouting anti-Bael talk these days."

"He always has. So have you and I, when it comes to it."

"We don't like Bael. But we don't seek to oust him."

"Come, now," he protested. "Christian's a merchant. He knows supply and demand. He wouldn't waste his energy trying to get rid of someone who only has one more year of power."

Mercy spread her hands. "You talk to him. See what you think."

Jared gave her a solemn bow, but his eyes were laughing. "I'll report back to you, angela."

But her words had put him on guard, so that he noticed what he might otherwise have disregarded when he arrived in Semorrah: Christian was keeping very interesting company indeed.

Jared arrived at the river city a little before sunset and flew in lazily, as always, to enjoy the spectacular aerial view. Built on a tiny island in the middle of the Galilee River, Semorrah had been one of the mercantile centers of Samaria almost since the country was founded. The whole city was constructed of a glinting white stone, piled in layer after layer as building upon building crowded together on the narrow island. Not only was the architecture dense, it was imaginative, decorated with dizzying spires, whimsical arches, and friezes of great artistic complexity. By night, as the colorful lights of the city came up, Semorrah was startlingly beautiful to behold, a magical place of glitter and moon-white stone.

In past decades, despite its prominence, Semorrah had been a difficult city to get to. The rushing water of the Galilee had made it nearly impossible for engineers to build a bridge from the Bethel side of the river, while from Semorrah to the Jordana bank, only a famously unstable bridge had been constructed to span the water. But that was in the infancy of engineering, before the advent of the Gabriel Dam, before scientists had perfected their theories of relative weight and strength.

Fifty years ago Semorrah had become accessible, with broad, sturdy bridges crossing to it from both sides of the river. Traffic poured across these overpasses in such a steady stream that the merchants had had to hastily devise sensible restrictions, which included a ban on all motorized vehicles. The city was so small, with such narrow, crooked streets, that trucks and transports could not negotiate its lanes, and there was no possible way to enlarge them. So anyone wishing to bring cargo into the city had to unload his merchandise at one of the holding warehouses situated just outside Semorrah at the foot of each bridge, and from there it would be transported by horse cart to the appropriate location.

This reliance on such antiquated methods of transportation gave Semorrah a certain old-fashioned charm that heightened its already considerable tourist appeal. But Jared, and the merchants who traded there daily, were not blinded to the real Semorrah. It was a city of fast-paced, hard-hearted, completely ruthless, and thoroughly modern businessmen who never passed up an opportunity to make a dollar or undercut a competitor. It was a place where you had to know your facts, your assets, and your best friend's weakness to survive. And nobody survived the cutthroat Semorrah lifestyle better or with more suavity than Christian Avalone.

Which became evident within minutes of Jared's arrival at the home Christian had inherited from his father, a five-storied mansion overlooking the River Walk. A noiseless servant showed Jared instantly to a library, where Christian was having drinks with half a dozen other visitors.

"Good! You're here already. You're just in time for a glass of wine."

"Sounds good," Jared said, nodding to Ben Harth and casually assessing the rest of the company. "The flight made me thirsty."

"And it's excellent wine, since it came from Manadavvi country," Ben said in the deliberate, well-bred voice that was almost universal among the Manadavvi.

"Always my preferred vintage," Jared said, accepting a glass from Christian and sipping it cautiously. Truth to tell, he wasn't much of a drinker, wine or otherwise, but it was necessary to go through the motions in such a situation.

"I think you know everyone here," Christian went on, still speaking to the angel. True enough: two Manadavvi landowners, three well-connected Semorran merchants, one Castelana man, and a woman who was one of the biggest landholders in southern Bethel. "Although perhaps you haven't had much chance to get to know Solomon Davilet? He's just taken over his father's business in Castelana."

"I was just in Castelana a few days ago," Jared said easily, moving over to the merchant's side as Christian clearly wanted him to. "What's your particular field?"

"Electronics," said Solomon eagerly. "We were the company responsible for wiring the Plain of Sharon for sound so the Gloria could be broadcast across Samaria."

Which made him one of the cutting-edge corporate leaders in the country and no big fan of the technophobic Bael. "I saw the microphones," Jared said. "Did you have any way of gauging the success of the broadcast? How many people tuned in and so forth?"

"Well, we couldn't get numbers of listeners but we know how many stations were set up to receive the signal, since we had to do advance wiring at most of the individual receiver sites," the merchant replied. "But I can tell you this. There wasn't a city in Samaria of over one thousand souls that *didn't* have a broadcast hookup, and in places like Breven, there were maybe ten different sites."

"All commercial sites, though, right?" Jared asked idly, though the question was not idle at all. "I mean, you're still broadcasting business to business, aren't you, not going into private homes?"

"Mostly, but we have set up broadcast stations in a few individual homes and complexes," Solomon said.

"Complexes? Oh, Manadavvi compounds, you mean."

"Some of them. And, for instance, Luminauzi schools."

"But unless the Gloria were being performed every day, what would these people be listening to?"

"Well, that's just it. You'd need a broadcast center providing some sort of program for a certain number of hours a day and days a week. Actually, you might be better off setting up a small series of regional broadcast centers because of the difficulty of transmitting a clear signal over a long range. That's when technology goes hand in hand with artistry, don't you see?"

"Seems like it's a long way off," Jared observed.

Solomon smiled. Jared was suddenly and uncomfortably reminded of Bael; the smile was a fanatic's intense expression. "Not as long as you think," he said. "Not nearly as long."

Jared glanced around, but all the others appeared to be engrossed in their own conversations. Perhaps Christian expected Jared to learn something important from this young entrepreneur; perhaps he was trying to distance the angel from the other high rollers in the room. "So do you operate your own research and development divisions?" he asked. "Or how do you encourage new technology?"

"We have our own engineering staff, of course. But some of it we import, and then we fool around till we get a product that works for us."

"You import?" Jared repeated blankly.

Solomon nodded. "From Ysral."

"Ah," Jared said, nodding casually, though his whole body prickled with discovery. Definitely an ideological foe of Archangel Bael, as if he hadn't already realized it. "The Augustine school. Do you go there yourself to look over their new designs?"

"Studied there," Solomon said proudly. "I'm not a bad engineer myself. Well, my father has been interested in sound transmission since I was a child. It seemed like a good idea to get some firsthand knowledge if I was going to be carrying on the family business."

"So you must know the professors there. That gives you a little extra pull with them when you're looking at their products."

"Exactly. The arrangement has worked well for all of us."

From across the room, Jared could see Christian deep in conversation with Ben Harth, but watching the angel closely nonetheless. Surely Christian had expected Solomon to share just this block of information with the newest guest, though as a rule none of the merchants were particularly open about contraband imports when carrying on social discourse with an angel. What, then, had Christian told the others about Jared before he arrived? That he was safe to talk to? Or that he should be sounded out for any unorthodox opinions of his own? It was no secret that technology was trickling into Samaria despite Bael's best efforts, but before this, no one had walked up to Jared and explained precisely how it was done.

"Dinner, then," Christian said, raising his pleasant voice. "Is everyone hungry?"

They all offered quiet affirmatives and filed out, Jared in the rear. Christian fell back to accompany the angel from the room.

"I congratulate you on your unmoved countenance," the

merchant said when they were a few paces behind the other guests. "You show no shock at all."

"Am I supposed to?" Jared asked mildly. "I thought you invited me here because you enjoyed my company, not for my entertainment value for your other friends. Or were you hoping this little band of malcontents would be gone before I arrived?"

"No, indeed, I would have been happy had you arrived a few hours earlier. They're all leaving in the morning, so you won't have another good chance to talk to them."

"About what? Accelerating the technological pace at which Samaria is crawling through this century?"

"Exactly. I knew you would understand immediately."

"It's not my pace to modify if I would."

"But would you?" Christian murmured. "That's the question at hand. If you were in power. If you were Archangel."

"I'm not Archangel now. I have not been so named for the future. Winning me to your cause is most likely a futile gesture."

"Not if any reasonable man—or woman—is selected by the god," Christian said in a pious voice that rang oddly hollow. "You have friends, and you're persuasive. Where you show enthusiasm, others are likely to follow."

"And what makes you think I am a convert? Have I ever given you cause to think so?"

"You've given me cause to think you'll listen to reason. That's all we ask. It's only reasonable to see that our single hope of a secure future lies in advanced technology."

They were at the doorway to the dining room now; the others were seating themselves around the meticulously set table. Jared hung back a pace, lowering his voice still more.

"Our only hope of a secure future?" he said, his tones disbelieving. "What can you possibly mean?"

Christian had obligingly paused beside him. "It doesn't take a genius to see that if Ysral continues to develop a wide range of technology, and Samaria develops none—or continues to rely on the outdated pieces of equipment that Ysral agrees to share— that Samaria becomes the weaker, dependent nation and Ysral becomes dominant. What if that technology includes weapons, Jared? What if Ysral becomes a nation of warriors, and Samaria becomes a nation of victims?"

"The Edori are not at all warlike," the angel replied.

"There are more Samarians emigrating to Ysral every day," the merchant reminded him. "And Samarians, I regret to say, are not always the calm, peace-loving men we would wish them to be."

Jared shook his head. "You cannot sway me with a threat of war," he said. "War is the reason we abandoned technology to begin with, or have you forgotten your history? That is more likely to make me resist science than pursue it."

"I have other arguments," Christian said, laying a gentle hand on the angel's arm and urging him forward. "We can talk about them tomorrow. For tonight, let's just enjoy a convivial meal with like-minded friends."

The meal itself was much less strained than Jared was expecting. For one thing, no one talked treason. For another, the angel had been paired with Isabella Cartera, the Bethel landowner, and the beautiful widow was always pleasant company. She was Edori-dark, with rich brown hair and fathomless, lightless eyes, and it was possible to forget for hours at a time that she could outmaneuver any of the men in the room in a business deal. She used every natural charm to its fullest advantage, and then casually revealed how much cleverer she was than any of her allies or opponents.

"Christian kept promising us, 'My friend the angel will be here, my friend the angel will be here,' but of course we didn't believe he had any friends at all, let alone powerful ones," Isabella said in her molasses voice. "We were delighted when you showed up, of course, though it proved us all wrong."

Jared grinned. "How long have you all been cooped up here?" he asked.

"Two days. It was Ben Harth's idea. Some of us get together every few months and go over the basic trade agreements, trying to get better deals for ourselves, and we always go back home with the exact same percentages. It's what passes for a social life when your heart is ruled by money."

"Did you at least have time to go shopping while you were here?"

"Yes, Christian's little boys took me to all the newest boutiques. Christian actually owns one, did you know? Strictly for tourists. It's the most appalling place. He says it makes a fortune. I'm considering buying in with him."

"You should open a franchise on the Plain of Sharon. If you are truly interested in dreadful merchandise."

"I didn't make it to the Gloria this year, I'm afraid," she said. "I listened to you, though, on one of Solomon's little—receiver things. You were very impressive, but of course you always are."

So Isabella Cartera was one of the few private individuals who had been outfitted with Solomon's equipment. Apparently this nucleus of Samarian power mongers was more tightly knit than Jared would have supposed.

"Well, I have little to recommend me but my voice," he said.

"And your looks," she added promptly, reaching out a hand to catch hold of a lock of his hair. She drew it slowly through her fingers, stretching the curl to its fullest length, then lingeringly released it. "Although looks fade so fast, don't they? And it's not like you're the promising youth you once were."

She was at least ten years older than he was, so he took it for irony, but it may have been flirtation. "And I tried so hard *not* to be promising," he replied. "For my mellow, advanced years, I'm going to be dim-witted and difficult."

"Oh, I hope not," she said. "Surely you still have time to redeem those promises? We're all counting on it."

Not merely flirting with him; seducing him to the cause. Well, well, well. He smiled at her lazily. "Name the promises you'd like to see me keep," he said, "and I'll try to oblige."

He didn't know how she would have answered, but Ben Harth interrupted them with a snort. "Stop monopolizing the only woman at the table, Jared," said the Manadavvi. "Isn't it enough that you have all the silly young girls fawning over you, or do you have to have the attention of *every* woman in Samaria before you're happy?"

"I yield the prize," Jared said gracefully, ostentatiously turning his chair away from Isabella's. "So! Robert! Tell me how the markets are these days. Keep the terms simple, of course— I'm not the businessman you are."

The rest of the meal passed in a similar manner, though business topics did spike frequently through the congenial chatter the way talk of the weather would surface among any other group of people. Jared listened, but picked up no other significant details. Not that he needed to. He had a pretty fair idea of why these people were here—and why Christian wanted him to join them.

Although, as it happened, he underestimated both his host and his own potential in Christian's eyes. And that he discovered the following morning.

He had risen late, to find Christian already out of the house and most of the others departed. He had a light breakfast, entertained by Christian's two young sons, then strolled through the rooftop gardens overlooking the white city. He was admiring the angled architecture of the nearby mansions when he heard footsteps behind him, and he turned to find Christian approaching.

"How you can drink wine till midnight and be up with the sun is a mystery to me," the angel commented.

Christian laughed. "Old habit. I can't sleep past dawn or my blood riots in my veins. And I didn't drink that much wine."

"You'd be a fool to, in that band of cutthroats," Jared agreed. "I was afraid to take a swallow myself."

Christian laughed again and began a slow circuit of the perimeter path. Jared fell in step beside him. "They're old friends," he corrected. "And if I showed a moment's weakness, they'd carve up my body, divide my bank accounts, and forget they ever knew me."

"You weren't talking business the past two days," Jared said bluntly. "And my guess is the talk was even more ruthless."

"What do you think we were discussing, then?"

"Bael's inability to appreciate the—shall we call it, technological imperative?—and how you can speed his departure from his exalted position. And then, of course, you were also discussing the scientific advances you have made despite Bael's specific prohibitions."

"You sound angry," Christian murmured. "And surprised."

"A little angry," Jared admitted. "And not as surprised to learn how you spend your time as I am to find that you wanted me here to witness it."

"Now *that* shouldn't surprise you."

Jared halted and swung round to face the older man. "Don't cast me in the role of savior Archangel," he warned. "Even if the god named me as Bael's successor, what makes you think I'd take your part? Doesn't it occur to you that I might view this little convocation as heresy just as surely as Bael would?"

"No," Christian said sharply. "Because you're not another Bael. And if you think you are, or could be, you don't know what Bael is capable of."

Jared frowned and resumed walking. "He's narrow-minded and obstructive, and he's afraid of change," Jared said. "And I don't care for him personally. But if—"

"He's a fanatic, and he's dangerous," Christian interrupted. "It's not enough that he's tried to resist every scientific advance Solomon and Ben and Isabella and I could bring into the country. He commits murder in the name of ideology, and he breathes death on political rivals."

"Death and murder," Jared repeated. "Surely you're speaking metaphorically."

"I'm not," Christian said. "He's on a campaign right this minute to systematically eliminate the remaining Jacobites in Samaria—and I'd say he's made damn good headway."

"The Jacobites! Surely you can't expect him to tolerate *them* with any pretense of warmth."

"No, but I don't expect him to kill them."

"He doesn't."

"He does. A few weeks ago he loosed his Jansai troops on Luminaux with specific instructions to seek out and destroy any known Jacobites. And they managed to find a handful, but most of the rest of them had fled. And are even now being hunted down."

Jared could feel the muscles of his face contracting in a disbelieving scowl. "That's not true. Luminaux? Mercy said nothing of this, and I was just there."

"She might not know the extent of it. She might have thought the Jansai were merely rousting out the Jacobites, scattering them just to scare them. But there were deaths, my friend, and more than I think you'd like to count. And there are more deaths to come."

"What do you mean? If they're scattered—"

"Those who escaped the net in Luminaux agreed to meet in Ileah. Do you know it? It's an abandoned Edori sanctuary in Jordana. The Jansai plan to raid it once the camp is full."

Jared felt a rush of anger and impatience. "What's this about Ileah? How would Bael even know about something like that? You have to be fabricating all this."

"I'm not. Bael knows because he tortures captured Jacobites

before he has them killed. Some of his Jansai caught one in Breven as he was attempting to escape to Ysral, and he gave the interesting news about Ileah.''

Jared looked at his friend sharply. "And how do *you* know all this?"

"Because I torture captured angels."

"And the next question," said Jared slowly, "is why you care. So much. About Jacobites."

"Wanton destruction has never been my favorite pastime, despite the ruthlessness you might see me exhibit in my business dealings," Christian said lightly.

Jared shook his head. "You've got a more personal stake in it. You're friends with the Jacobites—or one of their believers."

There was a lengthy pause. Christian had come to a halt again and surveyed Jared with a long, sober look. Not glancing down at his hand, he reached out and snapped a thin new branch from one of the manicured bushes lining the walkway. "I've a deep and abiding interest in technology," the merchant said slowly. "It's led me to do a lot of research about scientific development in Samaria. Doing that, one can't help but come across continued references to the Jacobites' theories. And some of them make sense."

"You cannot be serious," Jared breathed.

Christian nodded toward a stone bench set to overlook the soaring architecture of Semorrah. They sat, Christian apparently at ease, Jared stiff and uncomfortable, his wings taut and quivering behind him. "What do you know about the Jacobite doctrine?" the merchant asked.

"That it states the god is a machine! That's all anyone needs to know!"

"The Jacobites believe that the entity we call Jovah is in reality a spaceship called *Jehovah,* which carried the original settlers here from their home planet more than seven hundred years ago. Now, you have to admit that the histories of Samaria—the Librera and all the old books that deal with colonization—are very vague on how we came to be here. The Librera says we were carried in Jovah's hands. Across countless miles of space. What hands? How far? Why couldn't there have been a spaceship called *Jehovah* that carried us this immense distance?"

"Because Jovah is not a spaceship. Jovah is a god."

"Stop thinking like a brainwashed angel for a moment, and use the intelligence I know you have," Christian said impatiently. "Just answer the speculation. Why couldn't we have come here in a spaceship?"

"What's a spaceship? A machine that can fly through who knows how many miles of space, carrying hundreds of people inside? That seems even more fantastic to me than the notion that a god could close his hands around his people and carry them from one place to the next. Why does it seem so plausible to you?"

"Because I have never seen a god, but I have seen trucks and transporters that can carry a hundred men over a thousand miles. I think with the right equipment and a little luck we could design vehicles that can fly through the air. And maybe through space."

"And so this—this vehicle has just stayed in the sky above us for all these years, all these *centuries,* and pretended to be a god?"

"I don't think the spaceship has pretended anything. I think it has responded to the words of humans. Say it is a machine. Open your mind to that possibility for a minute. Say it responds to oral commands. Music—what you call prayers. Say it has been programmed to respond one way when it hears one particular combination of notes, and another way when it hears a different combination. So one 'prayer' calls down sunshine and another calls down thunderbolts. Conceptually, it's very simple."

"And, technologically, it's impossible! You and your friends have just recently invented ways to carry sound from one city to the next. How can you expect anyone to have created a machine so complicated that it responds to such delicate and faraway commands?"

"The original settlers came from a place centuries more advanced than we are. If they could build a spaceship, they could build it to respond to aural cues."

"But how do you explain away the Gloria? It's the *god* who must hear the prayers sung every year, the god who wants proof that Samarians can live in harmony with each other. A machine wouldn't care about that."

"The Gloria is the easiest thing to explain away! Because it is so precisely orchestrated, don't you see? The prayers—the musical cues—must be sung on a specific date, at a specific time, from a specific place. If all the requirements are not exactly met, a specific doom is meted out. Jared, it's all mathematical! And machines function purely through math!''

"But there's so much else," Jared said, as if nothing Christian said had pierced his heart with a chill, as if the quick mind Christian admired hadn't begun a rapid, ruminative clicking as soon as the other man began making his case. "The Kiss, for instance—''

Christian balled his fist so the glowing globe embedded in his right arm showed in more visible detail. "You know the answer to that one," he said. "Electronic tracking devices so the machine can do head counts and genealogy charts.''

"And the oracles? The divine communications they receive from the god?''

"Have you visited an oracle lately?" Christian asked gently. "Taken a good look at those interfaces they use to ask the god questions? Those screens are built of glass and metal, but of a much higher caliber than anything we've come up with so far. Those interfaces were designed to send and receive electronic impulses. Why does a god need high technology? Unless he's a god that's a machine.''

Jared didn't answer. Christian waited a moment, then went on. "Are you familiar with something called the Alleluia Files?''

"I've heard the term. I don't know what it refers to.''

"But you know who Alleluia was.''

Jared nodded. "An insignificant interim Archangel who filled in for a few months while Delilah was injured.''

"But Alleluia went on to become an oracle of some distinction.''

Jared shrugged. "So?''

"The Jacobites believe that during the time Alleluia was Archangel, she discovered proof that *Jehovah* is a spaceship, and that she recorded this proof in some manner. Of course, she lived nearly a hundred years ago, before sound recording was theoretically possible—but her husband was Caleb Augustus, one of the founders of the Augustine school, and if anyone could have made a recording of someone's voice, he would have been the man. The problem is, no one has ever been able to find a copy of this recording—what the Jacobites have named the Alleluia Files—and so no one has been able to recover the proof.''

"What proof?" Jared demanded. "What did she discover?"

"According to the legend," Christian said slowly, "she found a way to transport herself to the actual spaceship. She stood on board it and conversed with the machine itself."

"Not possible," Jared said flatly.

"She was Archangel at the time," Christian continued, as if Jared had not spoken, "and so the story goes that this visit to the spaceship tested her faith to an extreme degree. And it was hard for her to give up her vision of Jovah as a god. But she was converted—which is why Alleluia is so central a figure to the Jacobite movement. If an Archangel can accept the truth, then cannot any man's eyes be opened?"

"A faux Archangel—a pretender," Jared said quickly. "She only held her position a few months. The god found her wanting—"

"So much so," Christian interrupted, "that he accepted her as oracle a few months later."

Jared braced his hands on his knees and looked down blankly at the swept stone between his feet. Every muscle of his body had tightened in protest; it had taken all his self-control not to slap his hands over his ears, not to jump to his feet and stalk away. The Jacobites were all crackpots and troublemakers, everybody knew that; it was folly to give a moment's credence to any of their lunatic theories. And yet Christian Avalone was one of the smartest men Jared knew. That he would even entertain such heretical thoughts, let alone use them to coolly explain away all of Jared's most basic beliefs . . .

"Why are you telling me this?" the angel asked at last. "What is it you want from me? Surely not to propose to Bael that he lend a thoughtful ear to the ravings of the Jacobites."

"I want you to look for the Alleluia Files," Christian said.

At this, Jared did come to his feet, and stood staring incredulously down at his friend. *"What?"*

More leisurely, Christian also rose. "When Alleluia was Archangel, there did exist two places in Samaria where she could have heard recorded sound. The angel holds. In the Eyrie and Monteverde, there were pieces of equipment that the original settlers had brought in, music machines that were duplicated no place else on the continent. I think perhaps Alleluia—or her husband—found a way to use those machines to make yet one more recording. And where better to hide it than in the middle of all those other recordings?''

Jared was shaking his head, not in refusal but in dismay. ''I can search at Monteverde, of course, and it probably won't be that hard to get a look at the Eyrie's music rooms, but—if I were to find this recording? What then? I don't know that I'd bring it to you, after all.''

''You would want to keep such a great secret to yourself?''

''*She* did, if what you say is true. She must have had her reasons.''

''And perhaps they're listed in one of the files. But you have incentives she did not for spreading the truth.''

''Those being?''

Christian spread his hands. ''That people are dying for that truth. Or that great falsehood, whichever it turns out to be. But if proof exists, we need to find it. And stop Bael in his malicious zeal. And go forward armed with knowledge.''

''And if there is no proof? If the files do not exist, or you cannot find them?''

Christian smiled. ''Then we find other ways to determine who exactly Jovah is.''

Jared left Semorrah in a profound state of shock. He could feel it drag at his wing tips, making his strokes slower and less efficient; he could feel it thickening the blood in his veins, making him grow chilly and uncomfortable in those high, familiar altitudes. It could not possibly be true, of course. The god was as he had always been, remote but real, as reliable a guide as the constellations overhead. No slick, persuasive argument could change Jovah's essential nature, could alchemize him from the divine to the mechanical.

But.

He would go to Monteverde, and he would look. That much he had promised. He should, by rights, go straight to Bael and repeat every word of the conversation, and he wondered why Christian was so sure he would not. Mercy would have—or maybe she would have. Mercy may have been reluctant, as Jared was, to see Christian condemned to sudden and complete ostracism, for Bael was not a man to let such a treason fester. Surely—even if Bael was murdering all the Jacobites he could scare up, which of course Jared doubted—surely Bael would not have someone as visible as Christian summarily executed.

But it made Jared uneasy to contemplate why Christian thought he was a safe confidant. It should have seemed like a mark of favor, but it did not. It made him feel gullible and easy to manipulate.

Unless Christian was telling the truth. Or believed that what he said was the truth. In which case, they were all on the downward slide into chaos.

At Monteverde, everything was peaceful. Here, there were no outrageous claims to make the normal world seem strange. His mother and his sister greeted him with their usual derisive affection. The petitioners gathered outside the principal receiving room, coming to ask for rain, for sun, for protection against the plagues. And of course, there were the usual Manadavvi visitors, here to ingratiate themselves with the angelic host or argue in the politest of terms about some tax they were quite sure was unnecessary. . . .

Jared managed to elude them all, at least for the first day of his return, and set about his task. If he was a highly controversial recording that no one should be allowed to find, where would he hide? Not in the obvious place, of course, but that's where he looked first: the music rooms.

Each of the three original holds had been designed with twenty or so of these chambers: completely soundproofed, acoustically perfect rooms fitted with the mysterious equipment that could play sacred music recorded by the first settlers of Samaria. Even today, those recordings outmatched anything later singers had been able to commit to disk; Hagar's sublime soprano was so superior that no one even attempted comparisons.

When Samaria was first settled, all three holds boasted such rooms; but in the time of Archangel Gabriel, one of the original holds was destroyed. Thus a whole set of those rooms had been wiped out at the Jordana hold called Windy Point, and until recently, there had been nothing like them at Cedar Hills. Certainly not in Alleluia's day. If those Alleluia Files were anywhere near a machine that could play them, they were here or at the Eyrie.

But they did not appear, after a whole day's searching, to be at Monteverde. Jared went through each room, one by one, checking every disk in the storage cabinet, opening each cover to verify that what was inside matched the label.

"What exactly are you looking for?" Catherine asked him a few hours after his search started. "You've been in every music room in the hold."

"Uriel's recording of the Marvina *Solo* in B-flat major," Jared replied without hesitation. "Have you seen it?"

"Well, not lately. Do you want me to help you look?"

Jared waved a hand. In fact, he had taken care to hide the recording in his room that morning, just in case anyone decided to be inquisitive. "Oh, no, that's all right. I'm enjoying coming across a few titles I'd forgotten we even had."

"Well, I'll ask around."

"Thanks."

He then spent a couple of hours in the archives, a musty, poorly organized warehouse that held, apparently, every outdated book, map, census, or tax roll ever compiled in Gaza. If he found anything in here, it would be through sheer luck or doggedness, and he knew before he started that he was not about to devote his life to this investigation. If Christian wanted to search for fugitive disks in Monteverde, let him come here and look for himself.

So he drew a blank that first day, but he wasn't surprised. If he had such volatile and inflammatory information on record, the last place he would hide it would be an angel hold where anyone could pick it up and listen to the contents. He would go to the Eyrie, because he had promised, but he didn't expect any better results there. If the Archangel Alleluia had not been a madwoman—and if she had actually had the adventure ascribed to her—she would have been clever enough to come up with some other hiding place.

Jared spread his wings and slowly sank to the dusty floor. And if she wasn't the mad one, perhaps Christian was. Murders and witch-hunts; could it really be true? Was Bael really hunting down and destroying the Jacobites? True, he had acquired the allegiance of a handful of Jansai warriors—an odd alliance in itself, since traditionally the Jansai, like the merchants and the Manadavvi, chafed against angelic dominance. And true, Jansai had never been above a little creative coercion in their long history of violence. But systematic extinction? Jared could not believe Bael capable of it.

One way to find out. He came decisively to his feet, brushing the dirt from his trousers and shaking out his wings. He would go to Ileah and see if there was any evidence of destruction. And then he would form some kind of idea of who to believe and what to do.

It was morning before Jared could get free of Monteverde. He had just emerged from the archive building when he was almost trampled by young Solomon Davilet, who was barreling down the path without glancing right or left. Jared jumped back, sweeping his wings behind him, and Solomon came to a quick halt.

"Jared! Just the man I was looking for! They said you were hiding somewhere, but I knew I'd find you."

Tenacious; a trait all successful businessmen shared. "Well, here I am," Jared said. "How can I help you?"

"I thought perhaps I was rude the other day," Solomon said earnestly. "At Christian's. When you asked about the transmitters. Of course I'd be glad to install a receiver in Monteverde. We're hoping to get some concerts and other events lined up. And we'd be happy to set up a receiver here. Wouldn't want to slight the holds in any way whatsoever."

"Of course not," Jared murmured. "But I don't know that a transmitter is something we would absolutely require—"

"It would put you right at the forefront of the new technology," Solomon said. "People would come from all over Gaza to hear the concerts. At least, we think they would. It would give you an incentive to draw visitors to the hold. And it would be good for us, too," he added as an afterthought.

Jared considered telling the young man that he had often wished for a way to *discourage* visitors from flocking to Monteverde, the most accessible of the angel domains, but he let it slide. It might be no bad thing to know exactly what the techno-revolutionaries were building next. Bael might squawk when he found out what Jared had invited into Monteverde, but he could explain it away, he thought. Or dismantle it, if it became all that troublesome.

"I appreciate your offer," he said. "I'd be glad to accept one of your receivers. Come have dinner with me and tell me where we should set it up and what's required. And what sorts of events we can expect to hear!"

So that had taken up most of the evening, and he had not

been able to avoid spending half an hour having drinks with a few of the Manadavvi who had, apparently, camped out in Monteverde for the season. It was late before he escaped them and pointless to take off at midnight looking for a plot of ground he wasn't sure he'd recognize by daylight, so he spent the night in his own room for a change. And in the morning, before anyone could stop him or inquire into his itinerary, he departed for central Jordana.

It was six hundred miles, more or less, to Ileah, too much terrain to cover in a day, so he broke his trip at a small town in northern Bethel. He'd had the forethought to consult a map before he left the Monteverde archives, so he had a fairly clear idea where Ileah should be. Accordingly, about ninety minutes east of Castelana, he sheered downward from flying altitude and continued at a low, cruising speed about a hundred feet over the land. Nothing much out here—not surprising, because a hundred years ago no one wanted to waste prime territory on an Edori sanctuary. But surely that was a cluster of stone buildings about two hundred yards ahead of him, and wasn't that smoke coming from one of them? He dropped lower and circled for a landing.

A few moments later he spotted a solitary figure standing before one of the tumbledown huts. A woman, apparently. He raised a hand in a friendly wave but she stood frozen, staring at him in something like terror. Seconds after his feet touched the ground, she took off in a frenzied run, clearly bent on escaping him. Jared drove his wings down hard to regain momentum, and followed in pursuit.

CHAPTER SEVEN

He had never seen anyone run so fast. With the slow, awkward downbeats required by low-terrain flying, Jared came after her, and he admired her speed. Just in case she had confused him with someone else, he called out to her a few times—"Hello, there! Don't be afraid! Wait for me!"—but as he had expected, she didn't even falter. Either she was afraid of angels, or she was afraid of everyone, because she kept racing away from him as fast as her feet would take her.

It wasn't fast enough. Several times Jared closed with her, coming near enough to touch, and he felt the faint shock spark from his wing tips to his shoulders as his feathers brushed her skin. The sensation jolted her, too; each time she redoubled her efforts, straining ahead with desperate determination. It was hopeless, of course. Angels had incredible strength and unmatched endurance, and even the fleetest human could not expect to outrun a flying angel. She either didn't know that or could not rationally accept it. She ran. She ran.

"I'm Jared!" he called to her, catching up again. "From Monteverde. Don't be afraid of me! I don't want to hurt you!"

Once she looked over her shoulder, and the expression on her face was of such stark panic that he actually missed a beat and lost a few inches' altitude. But he recovered quickly and came alongside her again. This was difficult, trying to match his pace to a human's stride; he either overshot his mark or fell back every time he tried to draw even.

"I need to talk to you!" he shouted down at her. "Stand still for a moment and let me ask you—"

Now she veered abruptly to one side; effortlessly, he followed. Their new course placed the sun behind him and threw the shadow of his wings over her fleeing form. He heard a single great sob escape her before she expended all her strength in one last burst of speed, and then she fell to the ground, gasping.

He landed lightly a few feet away and stepped toward her. "I'm Jared," he said again. "Please don't be afraid of me. I want—"

Instantly, she was on her feet again, stumbling forward. He was aloft again in seconds, but she had managed to gain a few yards. He was upon her again in minutes, of course, but he was beginning to get severely annoyed.

"I'm not going to hurt you, damn it!" he shouted. "Just stop! You can't outrun me! Just stop and talk to me!"

Once more she fell to the ground, fighting for breath, shuddering with exhaustion or terror. Once again, Jared landed a few feet away, and this time he made no move to come closer.

"Please don't be afraid of me," he said in as coaxing a voice as he could manage. "My name is Jared. I'm from the angel hold of Monteverde. I have no reason to hurt you."

From her hands and knees she stared over at him, and he noted that despite everything, she did not look a bit defeated. He had never seen such naked hostility on any face before. Certainly, he had never done anything to earn such a look in his life.

"Can you stand?" he asked, because he was tired of telling her not to be afraid. "Do you need help?"

"I can stand," she said in a voice full of loathing, and pushed herself upright. She continued to glare at him, completely unrepentant.

"I'm Jared," he tried again. "What's your name?"

She merely scowled and did not reply.

He gestured behind him. "And this place is Ileah, is it not?" Again, silence.

It appeared he had nothing to lose by full disclosure. "I was told I might find an encampment of Jacobites here," he said, watching her closely to see if that startled her. "Is that true?"

"You're too late," she said flatly. He noted idly that—despite her distress, despite her hatred—her voice was musical and sweet. Probably a singer of some sort. You could always tell. "They're all dead."

The harsh words landed against his ears like three separate

blows. From his automatic assessment of this new person, he was knocked into a state of grave disquiet. "All dead?" he repeated stupidly. "Are you sure?"

"I buried them myself," she said. "Do you want to dig up the grave?"

"No, I—how many? When were they killed?"

"Twelve dead. Maybe three days ago. It happened before I arrived."

"Do you know who did it?"

For the first time her expression changed. Her brows arched over her eyes with mocking dislike. "Angels?" she suggested.

Again, he had the sense of having been punched, this time in the stomach. "No," he said sharply. "Not possible."

She shrugged. "Then Jansai, I suppose."

"Do you have any guess as to why?"

"You're the one who named us Jacobites," she said. "Wouldn't you consider that reason enough?"

"No," he said again, just as quickly. "Even if you were."

"Isn't that why you're here," she asked, "looking for Jacobites?"

He passed a hand over his face. Suddenly he felt old, betrayed, inadequate, and unprepared. Was it really true? Had Jansai really murdered twelve Jacobites at this camp—and if so, had they acted on their own or at the Archangel's behest? Jansai, yes, he could believe them murderers, but not Bael, surely not the Archangel. . . . "In a manner of speaking," he said at last. "I came looking for information. I guess you've supplied it."

"Then you'll be going," she said. "Good-bye."

Now he was the one to feel a wave of hostility, and he glared right back at her. He couldn't help noticing a few physical details. Such as despite the fact that she had clearly lived a hard life, her features were as delicate and porcelain white as a Manadavvi's. And that the short, tousled hair was several shades darker than the pale blond brows, still raised questioningly over her green eyes. And that she had a Kiss in her right arm. And that she looked familiar to him, in the strangest way—not as if he had seen her before, but as if he would see her again, so often and so intimately that he would not be able to remember a time when she had been a stranger.

"Why do you have a Kiss?" he asked, the superfluous ques-

tion edging out all the other more important ones. "I thought
Jacobites didn't believe in Jovah."

She glanced down at her arm as if surprised to find what she
was wearing there. "It was part of my disguise," she said, looking back up at him. "I thought it would make me pass for one
of you."

"An angel?" he asked incredulously.

"No, a believer. I thought it would save me from persecution.
But apparently I was wrong."

"I'm not going to persecute you," he said automatically.
"But I wouldn't be counting on that disguise, if I were you. It
appears as if someone has betrayed you."

She nodded. "And I know who, I think. A man in Breven to
whom I went for help."

Jared frowned. "I don't think so," he said slowly. "I think
it was one of your own. Someone who got arrested in Breven
trying to escape to Ysral."

She sucked her breath in on a gasp of pain. She whispered
something—it may have been a name—but said nothing else.
"In any case," Jared went on, "if someone is looking for you,
he'll be looking for the Kiss, too."

She looked down at it again, this time with the same loathing
she had directed at the angel earlier. "Too late to try to get rid
of it now," she said. "I understand that once it's installed, it's
with you for life. But no one told me how sick it would make
me."

"Sick?" he repeated.

"Dizzy," she said. "Ever since I got it. Sometimes I feel like
I'm floating or falling. No one ever told me that would happen."

"Well, it doesn't, to most people," he said. "Are you sure
you don't have a fever? You look very pale."

He had come a step closer but she stopped him with her eyes.
"I'm not sick," she said clearly. "I don't have time for it."

"Well, maybe we can talk somewhere else," he said. "Can
we go back to Ileah?"

"What else did you want to talk about?" she asked. "The
Jacobites were here. The Jansai killed them—either for sport or
because someone told them to. Doesn't that about cover it?"

"But—are they *all* dead? All the Jacobites?"

Now her face showed scorn. "No, of course not! Do you
think there are only twelve Jacobites in the whole country? They

will find each other again, don't you worry, and they will once more strive to bring the message of truth to all men and women of Samaria.''

"I would think the message of truth is looking a little sorrier these days," he said grimly. "I might rethink my proselytizing if I were you."

"If we were weaker men and women, we might," she conceded. "But only cowards allow themselves to be defeated by violence and fear. If Bael is afraid of us, we must be making some progress. Now is not the time to lay down our arms."

"So you'd rather be a dead martyr than a live plotter?" he demanded. Fanatics made him furious. "Seems pretty short-sighted to me."

"That's because there's nothing you believe in enough to die for," she shot back.

He froze where he stood, anger battling with dismay—that it was true, that she had thought to say it. Well, no, there was nothing he could think of offhand for which he would lay down his life, but he had always thought that made him sane, not pitiful. "You could at least expend some effort guarding your life while you can," he said at last. "If the Jansai are patrolling this area looking for Jacobites, why don't you get as far away as possible?"

"I will, once Peter is well enough to travel."

"Peter?" he repeated quickly. He could see she instantly regretted the careless slip. "Who's Peter?" When she didn't answer, he began guessing. "Someone who survived the Jansai attack? Where is he—back at the camp? How badly is he hurt?"

"Why are you asking?" she flung at him. "Why do you care?"

He turned on his heel, back toward the cluster of huts that was Ileah. He didn't want to leave her here a few hundred yards down the road to Stockton, but something told him she wouldn't abandon her friend to an angel's questionable mercies. "Maybe I can help him," he said. "Let's go have a look."

He risked it; he took wing and returned to Ileah, hoping she would follow. He didn't even look back to make sure. Within a few minutes he had landed in the little village and stepped inside the only cabin with smoke coming from the roof. Yes, there was a sick man lying on a rough bed. Jared waited till his eyes adjusted, then knelt by the patient and did a quick examination.

His skin was hot, his color was high, and the bright eyes that crossed and recrossed the angel's face showed no signs of either fear or recognition. Jared inspected the bandage across the man's chest but didn't disturb it. This woman seemed competent and levelheaded enough to clean a wound and bind it properly. But the man definitely had a fever, and if he had had it for three days or more . . .

Running footsteps and then someone plunged through the door behind him. "Don't touch him," the girl panted. "He's sleeping."

Jared turned to face her. "He's got a high fever," he said bluntly. "Have you been able to feed him? Give him water?"

"A little. He doesn't have much appetite, but whatever he swallows he keeps down. He's getting better."

"Maybe," Jared said ominously. "But I don't think he'll make it without my help."

Again, she gave him that fixed scowl, but she couldn't quite bring herself to say she would sacrifice her friend to avoid accepting the angel's assistance. "How can *you* help him?" she asked at last.

"I can pray to the god for medicines that will heal him."

She surprised him with a harsh, forced laugh. "The god! The god that does not exist? Why would I want to accept any medicines from his imaginary hand?"

Again, he had to throttle his own anger. "Have you ever seen an angel pray to Jovah?" he asked quietly. "Have you ever seen an angel ask for sun—and seen the sun emerge from behind a veil of clouds? Whatever you believe about the god, whatever you believe about prayer, do not disparage it until you have seen it work."

"I do not believe in the god, and I have no faith in angels, either," she fired back at him. "Why should I trust anything you give me? It could be poison, for all I know."

"It will not be poison," he said. "It could save your friend's life. Now. Come outside and watch me pray to the god. Perhaps what you see and hear will convince you."

She did not want to, but he could tell she saw no easy way to refuse. She could not continue to mock him if she did not witness his failures—and maybe she was curious, too. Obviously, she had never had a chance to see an angel at his prayers; perhaps she wondered what such an act of blind devotion entailed. She followed him outside.

He took three running steps and threw himself aloft, climbing to cruising level. Normally, when he prayed, he flew as close to the ceiling of heaven as he could, to be near enough to Jovah to pour his song directly into the god's ear. But he wanted this Jacobite rebel to hear him, perhaps to be moved or even converted by the power of prayer.

When he started to sing, he felt like the whole world was listening, and he responded to the challenge. Maybe it was just that he had never had a skeptical audience before, and so he felt like he had something to prove; or maybe it was simply a peculiar combination of low altitude, high humidity, and the valley of central Jordana that created a setting of breathless acoustics. His own voice sounded new to him, welling up from some unfamiliar place in his chest; the words that he had sung countless times at hundreds of forgotten sites sounded fresh and powerful. He sang as if he offered Jovah the first prayer on the first Samarian morning, and he felt each note register separately on the god's merciful heart.

He was pleased with himself when, half an hour later, he touched down on the ground outside the wounded man's cabin. The girl, whom he had half expected to be inside, ignoring her angelic visitor, was standing outside waiting for him. She looked oddly disturbed, though she was making every effort to hide it.

"So?" she said when he came within earshot. "Where is this medicine the god is supposed to send?"

"It will arrive. It may take an hour or two—no longer. Be patient."

"And what does it look like? How will we know it?"

"It arrives in the form of small pellets. Jovah sends different drugs for different diseases. There are the pills that ward off plague and the pills that scare away fever. All kinds of medicines."

"How does he send it?"

"It falls from the sky."

She nodded in satisfaction. "Dropped from the storage hold of the spaceship. I see."

"It is not!" he denied, startled. "It is formed by Jovah's own hand, fashioned for the individual emergency—"

"If he sent blue pills when I was sick and yellow ones when you were sick and pink ones when Peter was sick, then I might think Jovah designed them for each separate crisis. But if he only has five or six different kinds of drugs, and that's what you get every time you pray, then I think this Jovah of yours has a limited stock, such as a machine might store, and he is not a god at all.''

He was so angry he could hardly stand still; but in the back of his mind, he was hearing Christian's voice. *Say the machine has been programmed to respond one way when it hears one combination of notes, and another way when it hears a different combination.* Jared thought of them as prayers; Christian called them aural cues. Could they be the same thing?

"I am sorry to learn you were unmoved by my prayer," he said stiffly to the girl, because he would not give her the satisfaction of knowing she had shaken him. "Perhaps you will be more impressed by the results."

"I heard you sing before," she said abruptly.

He focused on her. "I can't imagine when."

"At your Gloria. Over some piece of equipment in a shop in Breven.''

"There were a hundred singers performing that day. You could scarcely pick my voice out from all those other strangers.''

She gazed at him steadily a moment, and without another word began softly humming the closing bars of the Margallet duet. His part, not Mercy's. Usually a woman would hear and remember the soprano and alto lines, while a man would retain the music sung by the bass and tenor. Jared felt the skin on the nape of his neck dance with chill, and a frisson of excitement skittered over his Kiss.

"That's the piece," he admitted. "How do you know it?"

"I don't know it. I just heard it that one time."

"You must have liked it."

She turned away. "I have an ear for music. I can't help it."

And she ducked inside the cabin without looking at him again. Jared shook off his strange sense of premonition and settled himself outside to await the god's bounty.

It was not long in coming. Half an hour later the ground at his feet was pelted with a handful of hard cinnamon-colored tablets. He wished the girl had been outside to see them fall, but he knew even this miracle would not impress her. From a fabricated god, all gifts were suspect. Nonetheless, he gathered them up and carried them inside.

She was attempting to raise Peter to a half-seated position so she could pour a little water down his throat. Jared hastened forward to assist her, crouching on the floor and taking the injured man's weight against his own shoulder. She did not bother to thank him, but held the cup again to Peter's mouth and watched him drink. Silently, Jared handed her one of the pills. She slipped it into Peter's mouth and made him sip again. The sick man swallowed but twisted against their hold in protest. The girl signaled to Jared, and he lay Peter back against the pallet.

"How long before the drug takes effect?" she wanted to know.

"Maybe an hour. We can give him one every eight hours until they run out."

She held her hand out and he poured the rest of the red tablets into her palm. She inspected them without comment, then dropped them into an empty cup at the side of the bed.

"Well," she said, in the voice one would use to close a conversation, "thank you. I guess you'll be going now."

He sat back on his heels, steadying himself with his wings spread against the floor. "Why would you think that?" he said. "I wouldn't abandon you while your friend was still sick."

"And of course I appreciate that," she said dryly. "But I don't think there's much more you can do for us."

"But I want to stay."

"But I don't want you to."

"I wish you'd tell me your name," he said abruptly.

She looked at him coldly. "I see no reason you need to know it."

"So I don't have to think of you as 'that Jacobite girl.' "

"The description suits me."

"I am not your enemy," he said, suddenly intense.

"And I am not your friend," she replied.

He balanced there another moment, watching her, wondering what he could possibly say to win her over, then he rose to his feet. "I'll scare up something for dinner," he said. "Do you have anything or should I go hunting?"

Briefly, she looked ready to protest, and then she shrugged.

"I have dried meat. A few dried apples. Not much else."

"There's a stream nearby. Do you have a fishing rod?"

"There may be one in the storage cabin."

He headed for the door. "I'll see what I can find."

He located no rod or reel among the Jacobites' possessions, but a long-handled net had been packed in with some traveler's clothes. He carried this with him to the stream, and there he caught four trout in half an hour. Afterward he scanned the riverbank for anything that looked promising. There were three varieties of purple flowers rioting along the muddy shorelines. On impulse, he picked a handful.

When he arrived back at Ileah, the girl appeared to be hanging out wash. She had strung a line between one cabin and a pole she had stuck in the earth, and to this she was attaching half a dozen dripping shirts. In the light wind of early evening, the wet clothing made a pleasant snapping sound.

"Do you like fish?" he asked, and she swung around to face him, drying her hands on the front of her blouse.

"It's fine," she said absently. "I built up the fire."

He showed her the flowers. "For you," he said.

He had never seen anyone show such a look of complete bewilderment. She stood absolutely still, hands at her sides, eyes fixed on his face, as if she had forgotten the rudiments of speech and motion. He could not keep himself from smiling. It was ludicrous, actually: an angel offering wildflowers to a Jacobite at an abandoned Edori sanctuary that had recently been overrun by murderous Jansai. He urged the flowers on her again.

"I thought they were pretty," he said. "You've had a tough couple of days. Can we put them in a cup of water?"

Still without speaking, she nodded twice, and gingerly took the blossoms from his hand. In a few minutes she had found a suitable container, filled it with water, and carefully arranged the stems. The whole time she moved as if she were made of glass that had already fractured at some unimagined trauma, which would fly apart into a million pieces if someone laid even a whisper of breath against it.

"Do you want to cook, or shall I?" Jared asked.

"You can," she said in a faint voice. "I'll find another set of dishes."

So they enjoyed a curiously domestic evening around the fire in the sick man's cabin. Jared fried the fish while Tamar laid out a cloth on the floor, setting it with two places and positioning the makeshift vase in the exact center of the fabric. She had already stewed some sort of gruel for the sick man, and while Jared cooked she coaxed a few mouthfuls down his throat.

"Is he any better? Can you tell?" Jared asked.

"His fever seems to have gone down," she said. "But he doesn't seem much more coherent."

As if to belie her words, Peter suddenly spoke a few sharp, lucid phrases. "Jansai," he said. "Killed them all."

She laid him back on the floor. "I know," she said. "Dawn and Daniel and Kate and all of them. But you'll be fine."

"My head hurts," he said.

"Are you hungry? Will you take more food?"

He shook his head fretfully. "Where's Conran?"

"Not here. I don't think he ever showed up."

There was a moment's silence while the girl waited to see if he would say anything else. Jared thought Peter had fallen asleep again, but suddenly he spoke again.

"Tamar."

"Yes?"

"Tamar?"

"I'm here. Peter? Peter?"

But that was all. The hurt man stirred uncomfortably on his bed, sighed heavily, and drifted off. She waited a few more minutes, then moved over to sit before one of the plates she had arranged on the floor.

Jared brought over the pan of steaming fish and served them. She had already cut up some of the dried apples and what looked like shriveled, sorry carrots. The fish smelled better than he would have expected. Maybe he was just hungrier than he'd realized. He lay the pan aside and sat across from her.

"Tamar," he said thoughtfully. "That's a pretty name."

"I'm so pleased that you like it."

"There was a famous Tamar, oh, a couple hundred years ago. You've heard of the Archangel Gabriel, of course? She was his niece."

"I don't think I was named after any angel."

"She was mortal, though both her parents were angels. They say she was very troublesome."

For the first time he saw her smile. He was more pleased than he could have believed possible. "Then perhaps I was named for her after all."

"Would you be willing to tell me," he asked cautiously, "a little of your story? How you came to be a Jacobite, for instance?"

"Born to Jacobites and raised among them."

He felt a surge of alarm. "Your parents weren't among those you found murdered here, were they?"

She shook her head. "They died when I was a baby. Alongside Jacob Fairman. I was raised by their friends."

A stark story there; he could guess at its incredible bleakness and solitude. "I'm sorry to hear it," he said. "No wonder you are such a staunch believer in your rebel doctrine."

"I am a believer because it makes sense," she replied instantly. "Not because I have been misled by fanatics. As you have been."

"I have been taught something that seems to me to be absolute truth. As you have," he said mildly. "I think you have been shamefully lied to, but that doesn't lead me to think you should be executed. It leads me to think you should be educated, perhaps."

"*You're* the one who needs the education," she said.

"All right, then," he said. "Educate me."

She was quiet so long that he was sure he had pushed her too far. When she started speaking, her voice was quiet and precise, a teacher's voice, not a madwoman's. Not a fanatic's.

"We believe the original settlers were brought to Samaria on board an incredibly complex vehicle called a spaceship, designed to travel billions of miles across the landscape of the stars. This spaceship was called the *Jehovah,* and it was a marvel of engineering. Not only could the settlers live on it in comfort during the years it took them to complete its voyage, but it could be programmed to orbit above the planet they chose to inhabit for hundreds or thousands of years.

"So Uriel and Hagar and the rest chose Samaria. And *Jehovah* orbited overhead. In its storage compartments, it held medicines and seeds and chemicals, and it could release these items when people on Samaria had need of them. It was fitted with strange, amazing devices that could focus power on the atmosphere of the planet and make clouds dissolve or draw together. And it was armed with powerful weapons, aimed always at this planet, which could be unleashed whenever certain conditions were met. When an angel sang a prayer asking for a thunderbolt. Or when the people of Samaria failed to gather for the annual Gloria, singing their songs of universal harmony.

"And over time, as the settlers deliberately abandoned their technology, and their sons and daughters grew up ignorant of the most basic tenets of science, they forgot that *Jehovah* was a spaceship. And they began to believe he was a god. And they called the songs they sang prayers. And they worshiped him for the good he could bring them, and forgot that they themselves had created him. That he was their tool, not their creator. That he was their servant, and not their master."

"But why would a spaceship care about the Gloria?" Jared asked, as he had asked Christian. "Why would it care if the people of Samaria live in harmony or kill each other one by one in the most excruciating manner possible?"

She had been contemplating the fire; now she raised her eyes to his face. "Of course none of this matters to a machine," she said. "But the settlers who programmed the ship cared a great deal. They had come from a world so filled with hatred and violence that, so we were told, the planet destroyed itself shortly after the colonists managed to flee. They did not want to see that violence repeated on their new world. They thought if they decreed that everyone came together once a year in peace, they could ensure that they would never descend into the mindless brutality of the world they had left behind.

"And so they fashioned small, electronic devices which would be fitted to every man and woman on the planet," she continued, for a moment fingering the Kiss in her arm. "And impulses from these devices were fed to a computer on the spaceship so it could track how many people lived on Samaria every year. And it could count how many attended the Gloria. And it would calculate by that if there was indeed harmony in the world. And if there were not enough souls gathered together on the Plain of Sharon to meet the computer's requirements, it would send down thunderbolts to threaten destruction."

"And if this story is true?" he asked. "What then? If what controls our lives is a spaceship, and not a god, if we pray for rain or drugs or succor and what responds is a machine, what then? Can we stop our prayers? Can we ignore the Gloria?

Won't we all perish in a rain of lightning if we cease to adhere to Jovah's commands?''

She flung her head back; perhaps she had never considered what would happen if the veil were ever successfully ripped from the god's face. ''Once the truth is known,'' she said, ''we can decide how to act.''

''God or no god,'' Jared said, ''I see no other way to behave.''

''You would worship a machine?'' she said scornfully.

''Well, if it had the power to destroy my world, I would certainly treat it with respect,'' he said.

''But don't you want to *know*?'' she demanded. ''If what you have followed all these years has been a piece of man-made equipment—not a god at all!—wouldn't you want to know the truth?''

Jared spread his hands, and the emeralds in his bracelets glinted coolly in the firelight. ''I'm not so sure,'' he said, giving her an easy grin. ''Wouldn't I feel sort of foolish? I think I'm happy with things as they are.''

''Well, I'm not. *We're* not,'' she said decisively. ''And it's time to discover the truth.''

''And how do you plan to do that?'' he asked softly. ''Or have you and your friends actually located the Alleluia Files?''

''What do you know about them?'' she asked suspiciously.

''That they are the memoirs of the Archangel Alleluia, who is supposed to have actually visited this spaceship. And that she considered the news so incendiary that she hid them somewhere that no one has been able to discover in a hundred years.''

''But she knew we would find them,'' Tamar said confidently, ''when the time was right. And that time is now.''

''Well, then,'' Jared said. ''Where do we begin?''

She frowned at him. ''You have no part of this search. You are not one of our allies.''

''I am not your enemy,'' he said again. ''As you say, it is better to know the truth. I will help you with your search.''

''You said the truth would make you feel stupid. You only want to help us so you can destroy whatever evidence we find.''

''I will destroy nothing. I want to help you.''

''We do not want an angel's help,'' she said positively.

''Are you certain? Think of the places I can get to that you cannot. Inaccessible mountain peaks. The most intimate interiors of angel holds. The homes of the very wealthy and the very devout. What makes you think this Alleluia wouldn't have hidden her files in one of those places? And the Jacobites will never find them if she has. Maybe we should make a list of places to search, and then begin visiting them.''

She was silent a long time, toying with the last remnants of food on her plate. ''Why?'' she said at last. ''Why are you interested? It's not because you want to help us. You'd just as soon all the Jacobites disappeared off the face of Samaria.''

''Or emigrated to Ysral. True,'' he acknowledged. ''But there are political factions besides the Jacobites in Samaria—parties with far more clout than you'll ever have, I'm afraid—and some of them have recently decided it's fashionable to embrace the Jacobite theories. They can create a lot of trouble if they aren't contained or—oh, let's say redirected. My guess is some of them will be searching for these files of yours. And I'd just as soon have my hands on them first.''

''So you can destroy them,'' she said again.

Jared shook his head. He hadn't, in fact, thought the whole thing through this far (he didn't actually think he'd find these Alleluia Files), but as he spoke he knew he told her the truth. ''No, if we find evidence that the Archangel Alleluia discovered a way to walk to the god's chamber and found herself instead in the heart of a huge machine, I think we cannot suppress it. There have been thirty years of speculation on this exact topic, and the rumor is tearing Samaria apart. It's risking our fundamental harmony. We need to know. And we need to know soon.''

She watched him a long time without speaking. She had a gift for silence, he decided; she could fashion it into a weapon or a luxury.

''How can I make you trust me?'' he asked at last.

''I don't know that you can,'' she said. ''I'll think about it.''

He rose to his feet. ''Good enough for now. Will you stay the night in the cabin with him?''

''Yes.''

''Then I'll find somewhere else to sleep.''

She nodded and made no effort to detain him. He hadn't thought she would. He wandered out into Ileah, letting his eyes adjust to the night that had fallen while they were inside. Not much to choose from here, and he was used to his comforts.

But he could make do. He picked one of the smaller huts that appeared to be in passable repair and stepped inside to see what he could make of its interior.

To his surprise, Tamar spoke from the door. She had followed him. "There's an assortment of blankets and bedrolls in the storage cabin. Things that my friends brought with them. You can go through them and take what you need."

He turned to face her, though he could scarcely see her in the dark. "Thank you. And I assume it's all right to build a fire in here?"

"There's wood and kindling behind Peter's cabin. And you can take a light from my fire."

"Thank you again. I will."

So within half an hour he was more or less settled for the night. Once she had helped him start a little blaze in his own hut, she had disappeared, and he didn't expect to see her again till morning. It was full dark but not particularly late, and he did not feel especially tired. But there wasn't much to do in Ileah for entertainment. He sat for a while on the hard ground outside his new home and watched the stars make their slow wheel overhead. Eventually he just gave up, went inside to his hard bed, and coaxed himself to sleep.

Several hours later he woke up from sheer discomfort. His fire had almost died, though a few charred branches still glowed with a malevolent orange light. Jared rose and built up the blaze again, piling on twigs and small limbs and finally two logs. Then he sat back on his heels a moment and watched the leap and twist of the brilliant flames, holding his hands as close as he dared to the source of light and heat.

It was at that moment he noticed the colors of the fire reflected in his Kiss, for the glass seemed to ripple and dance with a pale, undomesticated illumination of its own. He had never seen his Kiss by firelight before—or never paid attention—and he admired its shifting opal patterns.

He wondered what time it was; he was wide-awake. It wouldn't hurt to walk by Peter's hut and see if the injured man, or the whole woman, needed anything he could supply. So, quietly, in case they were both peacefully asleep, he exited from his cabin and crept across the village.

He was not fifty feet from the other hut when he realized that he was not the only one astir. Soft, disembodied music floated to him on the still night air; it had the gentle unreality of starlight, intangible but beautiful. He closed his eyes to listen more attentively. The singer was performing some simple, repetitive melody that must be a lullaby of some kind, but her voice was so clear and so faithful that the music took on an unexpected dignity. Even the childish words became solemn and wise when pronounced by that pure voice; all the secrets to the universe were contained in a single uncomplicated measure of that song.

She sang for another ten minutes or so while Jared stood motionless, clothed in shadow, a shadow himself. When she eventually stopped singing, he heard her speak in a normal tone of voice, a few last soothing words, and then there was silence from the cabin. He waited patiently another fifteen or twenty minutes, in case the sick man should stir again, and the nurse would need to comfort him. But there was no more sound issuing from the cabin; both its inhabitants appeared to be asleep. Regretfully, Jared turned back toward his own bed.

And then caught sight of the Kiss in his arm, still coruscating with sheets of cold fire, crimson and aquamarine and saffron. Automatically, he covered it with its hand, but it held no heat and shot no arrows of pain into his arm. Merely it reveled with a soundless celebration of light, and the debauch looked likely to continue on through till morning.

Peter was worse the next day—or, at least, no better. "I do think the pills are helping, actually," Tamar told the angel, "because every time I give him one, he grows calmer and sleeps. But he should be much better by now, and you see he's not. He's not lucid for more than three minutes at a time."

"I think he needs a doctor's help," Jared said.

He had expected her to protest, but she nodded. "Yes, but the nearest one must be Stockton, and since I have no carts or horses—"

"Do you expect any more of your friends to come here? Or is this the sum total that was supposed to gather in Ileah?"

She shot him a wary glance, so he realized she still did not trust him and might not tell him the truth. "Others might still be coming," she said cautiously. "But they might have been warned away, if someone escaped the Jansai attack. In any case, they are not here now, and soon it will be too late for Peter."

"I'll take him to Stockton," Jared offered.

"You? How?"

He couldn't help smiling. "I'll carry him, of course, and I'll fly there. It won't take me more than an hour."

"You can't carry him all that way! It's forty miles or more!"

"Angels have great strength," he told her. "Didn't anyone ever teach you that? Much greater strength than mere mortals. I could carry a big man across Samaria and only have to rest once or twice."

"But—you're not—he's not—he's my friend and he's my responsibility," she stammered. "Why would you help him?"

"Because I'm a kind man," he said gently. "Because, little though you may believe it, most angels spend their lives helping mortals—answering petitions, solving problems, interceding for them with Jovah. It was why we were put on this world. It is why I prayed for the medicine. I will be happy to take him to Stockton. And," he added, seeing more trouble gather in her face, "*not* mention to anyone that he's a Jacobite."

"I don't have any money," was her next protest.

"The doctor will consider it a favor to Monteverde and be happy to do it. Everyone wants to leave an angel in his debt."

"But—will he be all right? Will he be safe with strangers?"

"Safer than he will be here, dying of infection in Ileah. Come! Surely you trust me this far. I will not turn him over to Jansai."

"I could follow you, I suppose," she murmured. "I could be in Stockton in a day."

"You will wait for me here," he said sternly. "I'll leave this morning and be back this afternoon. And when I return, we'll decide where we want to begin our search for the Alleluia Files."

He could tell by her face that she didn't believe she'd ever agreed to cooperate in this search, but that she didn't want to risk antagonizing him just now. He grinned and, unable to resist, reached out to pat her spiky hair. She jerked her head back but didn't move away.

"When I return, we'll talk about it," he amended. "Get him ready to travel. I'll leave as soon as I've eaten."

Accordingly, less than an hour later, Jared was on his way to the nearest city. Tamar had spent the intervening time preparing Peter for travel, cleaning him thoroughly, feeding him one more time, dressing him in several layers of warm clothing. She had also written a brief note which she tucked into the sick man's pocket, "explaining to him what's been happening," she said when the angel asked. Jared supposed it was composed in some cryptic style that would give no information to any angel or medical official who happened to scan it.

"When he's ready," he said to her gently as she continued fussing around Peter.

She sighed and stepped aside. "He's ready. It's just that I—so many of the others are dead, I want him to be safe—and I do thank you for this, I really do."

"I told you, I'm happy to do it," Jared said, carrying Peter from the cottage and experimenting with the most comfortable grip. The man had probably never had much mass; now, a few days of illness had made him practically weightless. He would be no trouble at all for such a short flight.

"In a couple of hours," Jared reminded Tamar. "I'll be back."

She nodded, and he took off. In deference to his passenger, he flew fairly low to the ground, where the air was warmer, and at a slightly slower speed than he normally would have enjoyed. Once or twice, Peter grunted or stirred in his arms, but for the most part he lay listless and still in the angel's grip.

Stockton was quickly arrived at, and it took only one or two inquiries to find a medical man. As Jared had expected, the doctor was extremely willing to take on an angel's patient and waved off Jared's offer of payment.

"But what happened to him?" the doctor asked as he stripped away the sweaters and shirts to expose the bony chest, still wrapped in Tamar's inexpert bandages. "He looks like he was beaten almost to death."

"That would be my guess," Jared said. "This is how I found him, and he's never been lucid enough to talk."

"Who should I contact when he's well enough to speak?"

Jared spread his hands. "Maybe he'll be able to tell you. I know nothing about him. But you can certainly get in touch with me at Monteverde to let me know how he's doing or if you've found out anything about him."

"I'll do that," the doctor said, shaking the angel's hand.

Twenty minutes later Jared left Stockton and headed back toward Ileah. He had paused to buy a few groceries, because he was tired of fish, boiled jerky, and mashed apples, and he was sure Tamar must be, too. Although they obviously had no reason to stay at Ileah any longer, now that the injured man was gone. Although where she would agree to go with Jared remained an interesting question. He couldn't picture her happily planning to sojourn in Monteverde or the Eyrie, making furtive explorations for the missing files. Well, they would think of something.

Or, he thought as he landed in Ileah and looked around for the Jacobite, perhaps not. For, though the sick man's bed was still set up in one hut and the laundry was still hanging on the line, Tamar was nowhere to be seen. And she did not answer his hail when he called her name three times, with a little less hope each time. No, she had made good her escape, and there was no telling where in Samaria she could have fled to now.

CHAPTER EIGHT

It took a week to sail from Port Clara to Angel Rock, although technically, Lucinda learned, they weren't always sailing. *The Wayward* had two masts and a variety of sails, and when the wind was strong enough, this was the captain's preferred method of locomotion. But *The Wayward* was a powered ship, with a big, clamorous engine locked deep in her lower reaches, and she could travel on any sea, in still weather or riotous, and never be for an hour becalmed.

This and other fascinating facts Lucinda learned from Reuben, first mate of *The Wayward*, or, as he liked to describe himself, "the man who does everything he's told to do and everything else that makes the ship go, and who still gets in trouble if a single thing goes wrong." The captain, a weathered, wiry Edori of about sixty years, had heard this description and grinned. There seemed to be a warm affection between these two men, as well as the three others who crewed the ship, quite different from the stern relationships of the Jansai and Manadavvi seamen she had seen put in to Angel Rock. But then, the Edori were different in just about every way from all the other people of Samaria that Lucinda had encountered.

As on the trip to Lisle, on this journey Aunt Gretchen kept entirely to her cabin, and so Lucinda was free to amuse herself any way she could. Since they were the only two passengers, her single hope of entertainment lay with the Edori crewmen. And of the five of them, Reuben seemed the most happy to oblige.

He was a tall man, but lean, and constant exposure to the elements had deepened the color of his skin to a rich mahogany. He wore his waist-length hair in a loose braid, tied with a strip of leather, and his sleeveless vests or carelessly buttoned shirts showed off his well-muscled arms and chest. Lucinda thought he was quite the most attractive man she'd seen, in Angel Rock or Samaria, and only the most threadbare remnant of guile kept her from saying so. Normally, she said what she thought—to anybody, on any subject. But Reuben was so handsome that she was just a little inhibited, and shyer on some subjects than she would otherwise be. But every time he spoke to her, however briefly, the instant his back was turned she put a hand in exaggerated ecstasy to her heart and allowed her face to register appreciation of his awesome beauty.

The times he talked to her were the highlights of those seven days aboard the ship.

The first couple of conversations were merely civil—though Edori, she had learned, had few of the automatic rituals of reserve most people extended to total strangers. Their welcome was immediate and sincere, and their goodwill was not dependent upon an acquaintanceship of more than a few minutes. It occurred to her to wonder if it would be possible to earn an Edori's enmity, and if so, how, but that was a question she never got around to asking.

That first day, when she spoke with Reuben, it was to ask him simple things: how long the trip would take, how big the ship was, how long he had been a sailor. He showed her around *The Wayward*, told her she could pretty much go where she chose, and introduced all the other crew members to her.

"That's Maurice, he's the captain. He's the oldest of the lot, but not at all hard of hearing, so you can't mock him as you'd like. That's Michael, you'll remember him because he's ugly. Part allali, you know."

Michael had looked up at this description and grinned. He was not as handsome as Reuben, but in any other company he would have been a strong contender.

"He's part what?" Lucinda repeated.

"Ah, now you've offended her," Michael said. "Best go bury your head in shame and let me finish the tour."

"Allali," Reuben said with the most innocent expression imaginable. "It's an Edori word that means anyone not of our race."

"It means," Michael said, "dirty, cheating, lying scum, or

roughly those words, which applies to anyone who's not an Edori."

"Ah," Lucinda said solemnly. "Not a complimentary term, then."

"Well," said Reuben, "not always. Over there are Joe and Ricardo, you'll never speak to them, so you've no reason to tell them apart, but Joe's the tall one and Ricardo's the one with the bad leg."

"He's turned that around," Michael told her. "Rico's the tall one and Joe limps."

She looked from one to the other. They both looked entirely serious. "But who should I believe?" she questioned.

"Me, of course. In addition to being as ugly as a bail of fish bait, Michael's a terrible liar. Never believe a word he says."

"I'll ask them," she decided, and made her way over the coiled ropes and stacks of boxes to where the two men were checking a net and enjoying an amiable conversation.

"If I could just have a minute of your time," she said, and they looked up with that universal Edori grin. "I was sent to ask you—which one of you is named Ricardo?"

"He is," the men said in unison, each pointing at the other. Then they each tapped their own chests. "And I'm Joe," they added.

Lucinda could not keep the laughter from bubbling up. "Oh. Well, that explains everything. It was nice to meet both of you."

So that was how she met the crew members; and then, within a day, she was taking her meals with them, too. That first day, she brought food to Gretchen's small cabin and ate with her aunt, but Gretchen had little conversation to offer except bitter comments on the pitching of the ship and the wretchedness of her stomach. Lucinda saved her own meal for the solitude of her room, and tried not to sigh too loudly over each lonely bite.

The next day, as Reuben called them all down to the galley for lunch, she impulsively asked him if passengers were allowed to eat with the crew. "If not, I do understand," she said, but Reuben instantly waved her to a seat around the small, cramped table.

"Next I suppose you'll be wanting to haul the sails, too," he said. "Well, that can be arranged, mikala! We've always work for idle hands."

"Mikala?" she repeated.

"Young lady. An Edori term."

"And just as polite as the last Edori word you taught me?"

"No, this one is truly respectable. Me you can trust," Michael said, entering behind them. "It would be 'mikele' if you were a young boy. Very nice words. Use them with pride."

"The mikala Lucinda will be joining us for meals from now on," Reuben informed Michael.

"Good! Then perhaps we will raise the level of conversation a notch or two."

Reuben eyed Lucinda with his head tilted to one side. He was grinning. "Do you think so?" he said. "She does not look so much the intellectual to me."

"Well, but it would not take much to impress you, or so I've gathered," she replied, and was rewarded with a burst of laughter from both men.

"I'm thinking she took *your* measure quickly enough," Michael said to his mate.

"At any rate, I'd rather look on her face than your ugly one," Reuben retorted.

The whole conversation had to be recapped for Joe and Ricardo when they entered the galley (Maurice, who never joined the crew for meals, apparently stayed at the helm). Lucinda listened closely, but she still was unable to determine which man was which; the other two referred to them alternately by both names. It was annoying, a little, but it also continued to be amusing.

So the first few days on board ship passed in a lively and pleasant manner, and Lucinda tried not to abuse her privileges by getting in the way. The men were almost always busy, though they invariably had time to spare her a friendly word, and she was grateful just to be given free run of the ship and a frequent smile.

They were a little more than a day outside of Angel Rock before she had her first extended conversation with Reuben. She caught him in a rare moment of laxness, as he leaned over the railing at the bow of the ship, enjoying the cool liquid run of the wind against his cheeks.

"So are you looking forward to getting back to Ysral?" she asked as she came up beside him and put her hands on the rail to steady herself.

"It'll be another week or so before I'm there," he said. "And

I won't be there long before we set sail again. Most of my life is spent at sea, you know."

"I would have thought it would take longer than two weeks to get between Samaria and Ysral," she said.

"Actually, you can do it in less time, if you're willing to run the engine the whole way," he told her. "But that takes fuel, which costs money, and we're so rarely in a hurry that we don't often use it. But many's the time I've been glad to have it in the hold, ready to whisk us across the sea."

"When the wind is calm," she said, nodding sagely.

His face crinkled in a grin. "That, and when the wind is too rough and we want to outrun it if we're able. And if the Jansai are prowling the oceans, looking for easy pickings. Then the engine is our lifesaver."

"The Jansai?" she repeated, startled. "What do you mean?"

He glanced down at her, still grinning, but now it seemed that it was her innocence that amused him. "They're a warlike people, the Jansai, and a covetous people, too. And they've never cared much for the Edori. They aren't above a little theft on the open ocean, if there aren't other ships too close and they think they can get away with it."

"Theft—you mean, they *attack* you? Attack your *boats*? And steal your cargoes?"

He nodded, still faintly amused. She wondered for a moment if he might be teasing her again. "Aye, and sink the boats and all the men aboard them, though that hasn't happened often in the past two or three years. We've got the edge, you see, since our engines are better and our boats are faster, and we keep a keen eye out for any ship sailing the Jansai colors. But there's many an Edori girl weeping because a Jansai warship came close enough to board an Edori cargo boat, and the boat went down with all hands aboard."

"But—surely—can't you tell the Archangel? He would never countenance such actions! You're not Samarian citizens, true, but the Jansai are, and he must be able to keep them in check."

Now the grin faded, to be replaced by a thoughtful, considering look. "Aye, well, in fact the Archangel is none too keen to put a leash on the Jansai, seeing as he's the one who let them out of the kennel," he said. "In public I'm sure he's against the piracy, but he has his reasons for allowing it to go on."

"What reasons? What could he possibly—"

"Well, the Edori have been known to be friendly to the Jacobites," Reuben drawled, "and Archangel Bael would be happy to see all Jacobites quietly removed from the face of the earth."

"Jacobites," she repeated. "I didn't realize any still existed."

He raised his eyebrows. "They wouldn't, if Bael had his way," he said. "But I assure you, there are more than a handful left."

Now she leaned against the railing and stared at the teal sea without really noticing it. "My mother was a Jacobite," she said. "So they tell me. She was a mortal, though born to an angel, and she was raised at Cedar Hills. But somehow she met up with Jacob Fairman and his friends, and she was converted. I thought all the Jacobites were wiped out when Fairman was killed. But then," she added apologetically, "I don't get all the current news about the mainland, and Gretchen doesn't always tell me everything she knows."

"Well, I'd say there are several hundred of them still active, and who knows how many living in secret who would embrace the Jacobite doctrine if it didn't mean their lives," Reuben said. "I was not joking, you know. Bael has made it his mission to exterminate the rebels and their heretical beliefs, and he has licensed the Jansai to do the work for him."

"I believe you," she said, "but I don't see why."

"Because all of Bael's power rests in the notion that Yovah is a god," he said, using the Edori pronunciation of the god's name. "If Yovah is indeed a starship—some machine programmed to respond to certain voice cues—what does that make Bael? The custodian of a piece of equipment. It destroys his position as spiritual leader of the country. It shreds the mystique of the angels. It invalidates his life, basically."

Lucinda gave a small shrug, and felt her wings lift and settle with the motion of her shoulders. She was still gazing sightlessly down at the glittering water. "It still seems to me that he would want to know the truth," she said. "*I* would want to know, if I were Bael."

"Perhaps it's not a truth that we can know," Reuben said. "It's too hard to prove one way or the other. Though we can devote our minds to analyzing the question and coming up with reasonable guesses."

Now she turned to look at him, focusing at last on his face. "And what do you believe?" she asked softly.

"Well, you must understand that the Edori have never worshiped Yovah quite the way you angels and the other Samarians have," he said easily. "So for us it's not quite as big a leap as it would be for some others."

"What exactly do you believe, then?" she said. "And why do you call the god 'Yovah'?"

"Yovah is how the Edori have always said his name, though in the very, very old oral histories we have records of the god being referred to as Yahweh and Jehovah. He seems to be a god whose name has many variants. But centuries ago the Edori chose to call him Yovah, and so we have called him ever since.

"As to what we believe," he said, his voice growing slower and deeper, and losing every teasing edge, "we believe he is one god of many. That he was set above Samaria to watch over this planet, to reward us when we prayed and chastise us when we erred, and to record our names on his eternal scrolls. But we do not believe he is the deity that pervades the entire universe. We do believe there is a god, all-powerful and fantastic, who knows the location of every star and the longing of every soul. This nameless god, we do believe, controls Yovah and controls all the minor gods that look after every other planet in the universe. We do not know his name or his form, but we know he is there, that he hears us, that he watches us, and that he knows us. And that he has given us Yovah because he loves us."

"No wonder Gretchen told me you are all heretics," Lucinda murmured. "This is blasphemy almost as astounding as the Jacobites'."

He smiled. "It is not blasphemy if it is what you believe to be true," he said mildly. "And, as you can see, it is a philosophy that makes it very easy to accept the idea that Yovah is in fact a machine. A starship, if you will. With no other power than that bestowed upon it by men."

"And is that what you believe?" she asked.

He spread his hands in a considering gesture. "I am not entirely convinced," he said. "I think it is a possibility. I think, technologically and mathematically, it could be true. But I am not completely willing to give up the idea of my personal god, standing so close to my homeland that he can cool it with his breath or wet it with his tears. I would be sad to lose Yovah as a god. But I would not be as sad as Bael."

"But you think it is possible? You truly do? That men could

have created something so complex, so wonderful, that for centuries it could imitate the functions of a god?"

"Yes," he said. "I truly do."

"Then I must learn more about these Jacobites," she said.

He laughed, obviously surprised. "So you are not offended? Horrified? Shocked? I thought you would be."

"I have not been raised among the holds," she reminded him. "I do not know what it feels like to be an angel who is revered by the common men. I have learned to pray to Jovah, true, and I have had him respond, but no one but me was much impressed. I have always thought he was my god. And I would be sorry to lose him. But I think I would be more sorry not to know the truth."

"Then," Reuben said, "I have something interesting I should show you."

But he never got a chance. At that moment Michael shouted to him from the stern, and Rico (or Joe) called to him from belowships. "Looks like I'm wanted," he said, and spared a moment to give her a final smile. "We'll talk more later."

She knew she should retire to her cabin and keep out of the way of whatever emergency was occurring, but curiosity sent her following Reuben, a few discreet paces behind. Still shouting, Rico erupted from the galley hatch and raced toward the main mast. He flung himself on it and started to frantically climb the knotted ropes to the top. Lucinda stared in amazement. Just then, she felt a sudden thump and roar beneath her, and the ship lurched forward with such abruptness that she almost lost her balance. Someone had deployed the engine. Rico had made it halfway up the main mast and began calling numbers down to his crewmates. Joe and Michael and Reuben were hauling down sails, coiling ropes, and shouting directions to each other so rapidly that Lucinda could not keep track of who was where or what they said. Maurice apparently was still in the bridge, guiding the boat forward, though it began a disorienting weave from side to side just as it picked up speed. She *hoped* he was in the bridge, and that they hadn't just suddenly run amok.

Someone grabbed her arm from behind, and she almost screamed. "Get belowdecks," Michael ordered. "Now!"

"What's happening?"

"Jansai. Get below!"

"Jansai?" she cried, but he had left her; he was running

across the deck shouting something unintelligible to Reuben. Lucinda stood immobile, uncomprehending, feeling the deck shake beneath her feet as the engine revved to a higher pitch. She could see the bow lift a little against the rocking sea as the ship pushed its way more forcefully through the uncooperative water. Every separate plank and nail seemed to tighten against the strain, to grow sleeker and more sheer, as the ship cut through the water with ever-increasing speed. And yet, Lucinda felt panic rising from the men around her. It was not fast enough.

There was another great boom, louder and more distant, and she whirled to see what had caused it. Something huge dropped into the ocean twenty feet away, sending up a spray of water so broad that she was completely soaked. She wiped her eyes impatiently and stared. So close she could not believe she had not seen it before, a second ship was veering toward them across the waves. Like the Edori vessel, it had dropped its sails, so it must be moving under outside power. It was bigger than *The Wayward* and painted a cobalt black, hard to see against the waves, particularly at night. No flag flew from its highest mast, but it was not difficult to identify its origin: Breven.

A Jansai ship was firing on *The Wayward*.

A second time she heard that buried explosion, only this time she saw the cannon on board the Jansai ship glow with fire a moment before the heavy ball arced across the water. Again, the shot fell short; again, Lucinda and the whole deck of *The Wayward* were drenched with seawater. The Jansai ship kept coming at an alarming pace, angling across the water to intersect with the Edori vessel. Maurice had altered their course, and the whine of the engine continued to increase as *The Wayward* went faster and faster, but it seemed only too obvious that the Edori boat had been caught unaware and could not correct for disaster in time.

Someone grabbed Lucinda violently from behind, and she was whirled around to face Reuben's angry eyes. "I thought you were told to go belowdecks!" he shouted over the roar of the engine. "Do it! Go!"

"I want to help!" she shouted back. "How can I—"

He wasted no more time on words. Heedless of how he handled her wings, he spun her with his hands and hustled her across the deck toward the ramp to the lower levels. She tried to protest and she tried to resist, but he was impatient and furious, and he nearly shoved her through the narrow door. She felt her feathers scrape agonizingly against the tight frame, and she allowed herself to be pushed through rather than suffer further injury. Under her own power, she completed the climb down, then stood for a moment in the hallway, indecisive.

There was another cannon shot, this one sounding more muffled because she was belowdecks; the whole ship rocked with the force of the waves kicked up by the ball as it hit the water. Lucinda heard a helpless shriek coming from the cabin next to hers, and rushed down the hall to see what she could do for Gretchen.

Her aunt was standing at the edge of her bunk, one hand splayed against the wall, and her face completely colorless. "Sweet Jovah save us!" she exclaimed when Lucinda burst into her room. "Is there a storm?"

"There's a Jansai boat coming up—we didn't see it in time," Lucinda said, hurrying to her aunt's side. "We're trying to outrun it. You might be safer sitting down. Or lying down."

"Merciful god!" Gretchen cried. "*Jansai!* Attacking *us*? Whatever for? Will we all be killed?"

"I hope not," Lucinda said. "Please, you must be calm, there is nothing you can do—"

"We must make this boat go faster! We must escape them!"

"Maurice is trying, I believe. Reuben says Edori boats are faster than Jansai ones, and we should be safe, but apparently we didn't see this one coming until it was almost too late—"

"Jovah, Jovah, Jovah, merciful Jovah," Gretchen moaned, obeying the urging of Lucinda's hands and collapsing onto the bed. "I cannot believe this is happening. Jansai attacking. We will all be killed, I know it. We will all be drowned."

"I hope not," Lucinda said again. But the words were barely out of her mouth when another explosion was followed, seconds later, by the crashing noise of a cannonball connecting with wood. There was a terrible sound of rolling thunder overhead as boards were splintered and masts were struck and boxes were knocked askew. Gretchen screamed. Above them, the hoarse shouts of the Edori men tallied the damage and estimated their chances. They sounded afraid, Lucinda thought; and she grew even more frightened.

"But why are they *attacking* us?" Gretchen demanded again. "What have we done?"

"They think there are Jacobites aboard," Lucinda said absently.

"Jacobites," Gretchen repeated numbly. "Why would we— and even if—dear god, if they but knew. Not Jacobites aboard this ship, but an angel. If Bael finds out—ah, dear god, dear god—"

She went on this way for some time, but Lucinda had stopped listening. Yes, indeed, an angel aboard; and Bael would not like it at all if he found out.

"Stay here," she said suddenly to her aunt, and slipped from the room. She ran down the short hallway and up the cramped stairway, hoping no one was close enough to notice her in time to stop her. Up on the deck, the air was acrid and thick with smoke, and the Jansai ship had drawn frighteningly close. The noise—the engine, the shouting, the whining of every timber— was incredible. Lucinda felt her eyes water and impatiently shook her head. She must see clearly. She must think clearly.

She had heard one ball land; she looked around for it. Not hard to follow its erratic trail of destruction—and there it was, fetched up against a toppled stack of crates not ten yards from where she stood. She darted across the deck to retrieve it, knowing that the instant she went into motion, a crew member would notice her. She was right. Someone shouted her name just as there was another *boom,* a singing whine, and a terrifying crash as a cannonball plowed through the wall of the captain's bridge. She heard Maurice cry out, and she saw, from the corner of her eye, Reuben running her way across the deck. She scooped up the spent ball and flung herself aloft.

It was much heavier and much hotter than she had imagined, and she almost dropped it on both accounts as she drove her wings hard against the smoky air. But she adjusted quickly for the weight, and she would not be holding it that long. She attained an extremely low cruising altitude, and circled once above the Edori ship.

Faintly below her, she could hear more shouting—coming from *The Wayward,* coming from the attacker. She could see— or, from this distance, imagined she could see—the Jansai crowded together at the railing of their warship, pointing at her, calling out to their comrades, "Do you see? Do you see? An angel aboard that vessel!'' That should give them reason enough to pause, and so she hovered above the Edori ship, her wings spread as wide and steady as they would go, allowing the afternoon sunlight to turn her feathers golden and halo her yellow hair. If they were really tracking Jacobites, they should abandon their pursuit now, for surely they wouldn't believe that angels and rebels would travel in peace together on the same ship.

But the Jansai boat did not slacken its pace. Maurice, she was glad to see, had not slowed *The Wayward* just because she had left it, and it seemed to her that, imperceptibly, the Edori ship was drawing ahead. The Jansai still followed, and she saw the red glow of their braziers heating up for another round of cannon fire. So she shifted her position and beat her wings against the sullen air, and attained an altitude so high above the warship that she could barely make out its dark colors. And then she opened her hands and let the cannonball fall.

She could hear the mighty crash of its arrival, the thunderous reverberations as it tore through the deck and tunneled through the hull and fell with a great splash into the sea. She had aimed just right; it had smashed through the edge of the stern and ripped away a good chunk of the planking, and even now the cold, excited water must be rushing in on two levels. She balled up her fingers, which felt taut and crackled from the heat they had absorbed, and slowly spiraled down for a better look.

Yes, the Jansai ship had stopped moving and all hands appeared to be furiously attempting to repair the damage. *The Wayward* had pulled another hundred yards away. Lucinda flapped her wings lazily and regained a little of her altitude, slowly pursuing. It felt good to fly, to unfurl her clenched wings and feel the thick, viscous ocean air lay its cushions under her feathers. She would follow from the air for another hour or so, watching out for other Jansai warships and enjoying a little exercise. By the time she landed, surely Reuben would have lost some of the fury she was absolutely certain he was feeling. Aunt Gretchen she could handle; but the Edori's wrath was not something she wanted to face immediately.

As it turned out, Reuben had had other things to worry about than the angel's dangerous maneuvering. The cannonball that had struck the bridge had sent glass and twisted metal spraying through the small chamber, and Maurice had been hit by flying timbers. He was unconscious and bleeding, and there was grave doubt about his chances for survival.

Gretchen, who had always been a competent nurse, had assumed the chore of caring for the captain. Given a compelling task, she had managed to overcome her seasickness and resume some of her usual brisk efficiency, and she already had Joe and Rico running errands and fetching supplies for her. When they were not aiding her, they were helping Michael repair the most extensive damages to the ship. Reuben had climbed into the shattered bridge and taken over the task of piloting the ship.

That left the galley to Lucinda. The space was cramped but orderly; if she did not turn too swiftly from table to grill, she could reposition her wings without knocking anything from the countertops. She was an adequate cook, not an inspired one; she knew how to prepare a meal for three or thirty, but it wasn't a job she sought out. Still, everyone else was obviously occupied, and this was something she could do, and so she went to work willingly.

Michael, Joe, and Rico were surprised and grateful when she called them down for the meal, though they waved off her offers of any further assistance. "Help your aunt with the captain," Michael said. "That's about all you can do."

"Well, and I'll clean up here. And make breakfast in the morning. How long before we make it to Angel Rock?"

Michael looked somber. "If we keep the engine running, we could be there before dawn. But the cannon fire did some damage and I'm not sure how well the engines will hold up. Might be best to drift in under the sails. We're still deciding."

"We don't have much of a harbor at Angel Rock," she said, "but there is a yard where you can do repairs—"

Michael nodded. "We know it. We'll be there a day or two, most likely. But we'll be limping into port, I'm thinking."

He didn't say that they were in any immediate danger of shuddering apart here in the middle of the cold ocean, so she didn't let herself think about the possibility. Much. She of course could fly to safety in a couple of hours, but how could she leave these six behind to drop slowly, inexorably, into the hungry waters? If she knew they were in danger, she could rescue them, one at a time, fly first Gretchen then Maurice then Reuben then the others to Angel Rock or some closer haven, but it would take time, hours and hours, so she would have to know in advance in order to save them all. . . . But they were not in any danger, they just had to be careful. By tomorrow they would be home.

She took a plate of food down to Gretchen, who was nursing the captain in his own spartan cabin. "How is he?" she asked.

"Cold and in pain. I think it's best not to give him anything to eat right now. I think he may have a concussion."

"The food was for you," Lucinda said gently.

Gretchen looked at her blankly for a moment. "Oh. I see. Thank you. Yes, I believe I am hungry."

Lucinda couldn't help smiling. Her aunt was difficult, opinionated and stubborn, but she was so *strong*. Whatever the crisis, she had the skills to rise to it, and forget her own illnesses and fears. A month ago Gretchen never would have admitted that she could be so absorbed in nursing an Edori to health that she would forget her own bodily needs. But Lucinda was not surprised.

"Do you need anything else? I'm going to take dinner to Reuben now."

"No, I believe I've got everything I need. Check with me again in an hour or two."

"I will."

Finally, Lucinda prepared a plate for Reuben and climbed from the galley to the deck to the bridge to deliver it. In the moonless dark, it was something of a trick to clamber over the disordered deck and into the ravaged bridge, careful not to tear her skin or her clothes or her wings on the sharp edges of splintered wood and ripped metal. The bridge, always small, was even more cramped now as planks lay across its tiny floor and jutted into its confined space.

Reuben sat in the captain's chair, hands resting lightly on the rudder, eyes fixed before him on the glinting black surface of the sea. As far as Lucinda could tell, he was guiding the boat by memory alone, for she could make out direction neither by constellation overhead nor instrument panel at his side. There was so little light from the stars that they did not seem to sketch patterns either in the heavens or across the water, and it was impossible to tell where the horizon line lay. *The Wayward* could be anywhere, it could be nowhere; it was suspended in an element as foreign to her as space.

"This must be what it felt like to travel to Samaria on *Jehovah*," she said softly, almost to herself.

Reuben did not start or turn suddenly around, so he must have heard her approach, though he had offered no greeting. "I have often thought that same thing," he said. "But surely the sea is less frightening than the stars."

"You can drown in the sea," she reminded him.

"And you could, I am guessing, drift forever between the stars, lost and disoriented, with no home port to go to. I would choose the ocean any day, I'm thinking."

"I brought you dinner," she said.

Now he turned to look at her, though she doubted he could make out anything of her face in this nonexistent lighting. "And did you cook my dinner as well?" he asked.

"I did. It's not fancy, but it will nourish you well enough."

"Then you have yet another skill I would not have guessed. First you wage war like a Jansai, then you cook like any ordinary woman. There is more to you angels than a man first suspects."

It was disguised as irony, but she clearly read the anger. "I will not allow you to chastise me for doing what I could today," she said, laying his plate before him so she could set her fists on her hips. "It was a simple enough thing, and I was in no danger."

"It was wondrous brave, and you were in grave danger, and I will chastise you if I like," he replied, his voice still under control but a little less so. "As I would reprimand any of my men who flung themselves in harm's way, even to save their fellows. Every minute you were on deck, you were in danger from falling cannonballs."

"I was aloft soon enough."

"And a target even a half-blind Jansai could see! Had they turned their cannons your way while you floated above them in the air, could you have moved quickly enough to evade them? I think not! And one of those shots would have torn through your soft skin much more easily than through the wood and metal and rubber of this ship."

"They would not have aimed at me," she said confidently. "Kill an *angel*? Bael would never allow that. Never."

"How would Bael have learned about it?" Reuben demanded. "If you were dead and every soul aboard *The Wayward*

went down, who would be left to report atrocities to the Archangel? I was close enough to the Jansai ship to see where their
guns were firing. I saw the muzzle slipped free of its support
and aimed toward the heavens. You could have died in seconds,
mikala, great angel wings or no, and not one of us could have
done a damn thing to save you.''

It had not occurred to her—would never have crossed her
mind—that she could have been in any mortal danger, deliberately and maliciously directed at her person. The ball would not
even have had to hit her body; it could have torn through one
of those delicate lace wings and sent her plunging into the icy
water. But it had not happened. She would not think about it.

''I will not apologize,'' she said, lifting her chin, though he
could not see the mutinous gesture in the dark. ''For, say what
you will, I saved all our lives. And I would do it again. Though
you *locked* me in my cabin and forbade me to help.''

''Well, and it was an act of courage and quick thinking such
as I could not have come up with myself, even had I wings such
as yours,'' Reuben said in a softened voice. ''If it were not for
the great fear I had for your life, I would be blessing you and
thanking you now. But my heart stopped in my body when I
saw you swooping away from this ship, and when I thought that
cannon would shred you to pieces overhead, I nearly died myself. I am not used to denying anybody the right to defend himself or his friend. I don't know why it was so hard on me to
see you take a chance I would cheer anyone else for taking.
Maybe I am like every other Samarian, and I think any angel is
a precious thing. But I would not like to live through another
afternoon like this one.''

''No, and neither would I,'' Lucinda said in as offhand a
voice as she could manage after that extraordinary speech. ''Let
us hope none of us is ever at such risk again.''

Moments after that she left the bridge, murmuring some in-
coherent phrase about needing to clean the galley. Well, all
Edori were flirts; she had heard that often enough from
Gretchen, from her friends on Angel Rock. All Edori could
charm the heart from a woman's body with honeyed words
poured into her ear; they were laughing lovers who left nothing
but warm regret behind. And sailors—they were not to be
trusted, they wooed girls in every port from Lisle to Port Clara
to the Ysral harbors, and to not a single one were they true. So

the words of an Edori sailor, sweet though they sounded, were as insubstantial as foam lashed up by a falling wave.

And yet he had sounded sincere, and the anger, she knew, had been genuine; so maybe, the least littlest bit, he cared if she lived or died. And the thought was so amazing, so huge but so intimate, that she could not get a hold of it. It made her shiver, made her sing, made her wrap her wings around herself for comfort and celebration. She stood for maybe half an hour in the tiny galley, cocooned in her own feathers, motionless, thoughtless, buffeted between doubt and fear, and wondered what it would be like to be drowned in an Edori's love.

But her dreams that night were anything but romantic. Lately—since the morning of the Gloria—she had had odd nightmares, filled with fear and violence and desperation. Once or twice, waking at midnight, she would find herself still gripped by a wretched panic, a sensation so strong that she could not believe it was stirred up by nothing more alarming than a dream. It would sometimes be hours before the desolation faded and she could sleep again in relative peace.

But it had been a few days since she had had the nightmares, and she had been so tired this night upon seeking her bed that she had thought she would fall instantly asleep. And so she did—but a few hours later she woke herself by her own crying, soft and hopeless and unfathomable. Her face, her pillow, her hair were all wet with tears; she must have been weeping for some time before her sobs awakened her. She was surprised by the leaden weight on her chest, the sense of loss and helplessness. What could she have been dreaming of, what terrible images or fears had clenched upon her heart in the night? Dimly her mind showed her pictures of broken bodies, bloodied clothing, but she could not reconstruct a narrative. Maybe it was simply that the violent events of the day had gone reeling through her head in a drunken, brutal sprawl, and her mind could not process them rationally. It was not an easy thing to confront the possibility of one's own death, or the deaths of those nearby. She was not used to such sober thoughts; they shocked through her body and transmogrified themselves to nightmares.

She turned to her side and pillowed her head on her hands, but she was a little afraid to go back to sleep. She still felt weary, drained, and sorrowful, for no cause that she could identify (no one *had* died, after all). Even Maurice had seemed stable enough when she last checked on Gretchen before seeking her own bed. Everything would be fine. Reuben or Michael had apparently decided that the engines were whole enough to do their work, for they were still moving through the ocean at top speed and they would be at Angel Rock sometime before morning. They would all be safe there; everything would return to normal. A few more hours and all would be well.

CHAPTER NINE

The tiny harbor at Angel Rock was crowded: in addition to the various small working craft owned by island residents, there were three visitor ships lined up at the dock. Two were Edori and one bore the blue colors of Luminaux, so Lucinda, who had been fearing Jansai, relaxed. No danger lurking here.

Always a sleepy port, Angel Rock at dawn was completely deserted. Lucinda flew in low over the wharf, just in case anyone was astir, but she spotted no one. So she flew on to the Manor, the eight-bedroom inn that she and her aunt Gretchen operated, and landed on the flagstoned walk leading to the front door.

Emmie was standing on the porch, shaking out a rug, which she dropped to the ground when Lucinda touched down. "You're back! We weren't sure when to expect you! Your aunt wrote from someplace a week or so ago and said it might be another fortnight—"

"Is Jackson here?" Lucinda interrupted. "We've got a hurt man on our ship, and we'll need a stretcher to carry him back here."

"He's sleeping, I'm sure." Emmie sniffed. "I'll wake him if you like."

"Yes. Tell him to go to the dock and await *The Wayward*. Then get a good breakfast ready for five or six. I'll go see if I can find Hammet. How many rooms are empty?"

"Four of them."

Lucinda nodded. "We'll put Maurice in one and the others can share. Or—I don't know, they might want to sleep on the ship. At any rate, they should be here within the hour, so please hurry.''

Emmie disappeared back inside, leaving the rug in the dirt. Lucinda hurried on foot down the short road to the Gablefront Inn, run by Hammet and Celia Zephyr. They were a charming, erudite couple who had retired to Angel Rock from Luminaux five years ago; Hammet had been a surgeon of some renown and Celia had been a metalworker. Although Hammet never failed to point out that his specialty had been bone repair, he was the closest thing to a doctor living on the island, and so they all brought him their illnesses, injuries, and aches for healing.

Celia herself answered the door, dressed in an embroidered nightshirt that looked expensive enough to pay for remodeling her hotel. Her salt-and-pepper hair was coiled on top of her head, and her complexion was rosy from sleep. "Why, Lucinda! I had no idea you were back! Is there trouble? Where's your aunt?"

"She's still on the ship that brought us from Samaria," Lucinda said. "There's a hurt man on board. I've sent Jackson to the harbor with a stretcher. Do you think Hammet can meet us at the Manor in an hour or so? I don't know how soon they'll arrive.''

"But of course he can!'' Celia exclaimed. "What's the nature of this man's injury? Hammet will want to know.''

"Concussion and some pretty big chest wounds,'' Lucinda said. "Our ship was fired on by Jansai cannon, and the ball hit where Maurice was sitting.''

"Fired on! Jansai!'' Celia repeated. "I can't believe—''

"I couldn't either. But I was there. No one else was hurt.''

"Sweet god singing,'' the older woman murmured. "Don't you worry. I'll have Hammet over at your place in half an hour.''

Lucinda checked in at the Manor again briefly to make sure both Emmie and Jackson were doing as they were told, and then she glided back to the wharf to waken the harbormaster. Not that there was much he could do, but Foster liked to be apprised of all the events going on in his domain.

"Jansai, yes, they're a terrible nuisance on the high seas,'' he told her as they strolled down to the dock to await *The Wayward*'s arrival. "More than one Edori ship has come dragging into harbor here having run afoul of a Jansai warship.''

"I didn't know anything about this," she said.

Foster shrugged. "I suspect they war on none but the Edori. Who are not the type to complain to the Archangel. He may not even know of the piracy."

"Or he may," Lucinda said, thinking back to her conversation with Reuben.

Foster shrugged again. "Or he may. The ways of the angels are mysterious and sometimes prejudicial to mortals. Which is why I left Samaria twenty years ago."

"Someday you'll have to tell me the whole story," Lucinda said, but absently. She had spotted *The Wayward*'s masts shaping out of the early morning mist. "When we have more time."

There was an excruciating wait (it seemed pointless to fly back to the ship just to get in everyone's way), and then an hour's worth of bustle as the ship docked and Maurice was carried off. The sailors commandeered Jackson's stretcher and bore their captain down the short street to the Manor, following Gretchen's brisk lead. Lucinda trailed behind them, feeling useless and stupid.

Another pair of hours passed in purposeful activity as Hammet examined Maurice, Lucinda fed the sailors, and Gretchen consulted Emmie and Jackson about the status of the hotel while she'd been gone. Everything looked fine to Lucinda: The roof was still on and none of the windows had been bashed in, so she couldn't imagine that anything dreadful had gone wrong. But Gretchen liked to be in control of her environment, and she could not relax for half an hour until she had identified potential problems that had boiled up in her absence.

Reuben slipped away before Lucinda had a chance to talk to him; she guessed he had swallowed his breakfast, then tracked down the doctor in Maurice's room. There was good news, though: Reuben had told Gretchen that he would much appreciate a room at the hotel, though he expected the three others would sleep on the ship. Which meant, for another day or so, she would have the exquisitely wonderful, exquisitely torturous gift of his company.

She busied herself cleaning the kitchen, though Emmie could do it well enough. Gretchen swept through, saying, "Well, nothing's irretrievably broken, and that's a blessing, though a small one," before marching toward the stairway to check on the condition of the upstairs rooms. Lucinda smiled, then she sighed.

It was another half hour before she had any news of Maurice, and that was brought by Reuben himself. Lucinda had drifted into the large parlor and begun automatically to open curtains and neaten the furniture, though Emmie had kept everything in reasonably good shape. She cast a longing glance at her harpsichord, for she found nothing so soothing as music, but she did not want to disturb the hurt man. So she merely dusted the top of it with the cuff of her sleeve, and closed the lid over the keyboard.

"When you've time, you'll have to play a song or two for me," said a voice from the doorway, and she was so startled she almost crushed her fingers under the lid. "At least, I assume you play?"

"I do, and so does my aunt. She taught me. How is Maurice?"

"Your kind doctor says he's well enough and just needs two or three days of quiet rest, undisturbed by gunfire or violence."

"You told him what happened?"

"He did ask."

"Was he shocked?"

Reuben came farther into the room and shook his head. "He didn't seem like a man easily shocked, your doctor. My guess is he's got sharp old eyes that have seen a great deal in this lifetime."

"Luminauzi," Lucinda said with a shrug.

"Well, they are the wisest."

There was a moment's silence while Reuben stared out through the lace curtains and Lucinda tried to think of something to demonstrate her own wisdom. All she could come up with was, "So what will you do now?"

"Wait a few days till the captain's better, then sail on to Ysral," he said, still looking out the window.

"I meant—this minute. Is there anything I can do for you? For Maurice?"

"Where are Michael and the others?"

"They went back to the ship. They said they needed to sleep for a week."

Reuben smiled. "As do I. Perhaps we'll be here longer than a few days."

"There's a room ready for you," Lucinda said tentatively. "If you'd like to go there now."

At last he turned to look at her, smiling faintly, and she felt all her blood rush to her cheeks at the sheer beauty of his face. "What I need more than a bed right now," he said, "is a hot bath. Is such a thing to be found here on Angel Rock?"

"Yes, we have baths in a chamber out back," she said, though it was a struggle to speak normally. Which was ridiculous; she could not imagine why she was behaving so oddly. "I'll have Emmie heat the water. It will be ready in ten minutes."

"And *then* I'll sleep for a week," he said. "When I come down, I'll be so civil and cheerful that you won't know me."

"You may be changed," she managed to retort, "but I don't think a little water and a little dreaming will improve you so much as all that."

"Wait and see," he promised. "Wait and see."

After that, the rest of the day was nothing but dull anticlimax. Reuben and Maurice slept; Gretchen sailed through the house, noting inefficiencies and errors; Emmie trailed behind her, explaining things away and rolling her eyes at Lucinda; Jackson kept to himself in his basement quarters until he was summoned to a chore or an accounting. Most of the neighbors dropped by to welcome them back, but of course Gretchen had no time to visit with any of them. Lucinda listened with far less interest than usual to the recitations of events that had occurred while she was gone (learning from three separate sources that Timothy and Gia had decided to marry, though no one was supposed to know it, and Parker was considering returning to the mainland, though he had not decided if he would live with his son in Breven or his daughter on her farm in Bethel). These were the comforting, familiar threads of her daily life; she was shocked to learn that other faces, other names, could take up so much of her attention that she had little to spare for her oldest friends.

But she was tired and out of sorts. In a day or two, when the Edori sailed away, she would revert to her ordinary self. The Manor would not look so strange, as if the rooms had shrunk down or the furniture had been wrongly arranged; the accents of her neighbors would not sound so provincial and unmelodic. Everything would be the way it should be, as she remembered it, as it had been before she'd left.

• • •

And the next day she did feel much better. She had gone to bed early and slept late, and not stirred once the entire night. She woke to the smell of Emmie's pancakes and bacon, and the aroma was so delicious and so familiar that she instantly felt like she was *home*. And was swept with a great nostalgia for this place that she had known most of her life, and missed more now, at this instant, than she had for the whole time she was away on her journey.

She bounded into the kitchen and had breakfast, chattering with Emmie the whole time. Yes, it was true, Timothy and Gia were marrying but the *real* secret was that Gia was already with child and if Gia's parents ever found out, she would be banned forever from Angel Rock. As for Parker, he had been saying for five years that he would leave the island, but Emmie herself would believe that when she saw his ugly face grinning at them from the railing of an outbound ship.

"But who cares about any of those people?" the housemaid said impatiently, clearing off a place at the table and sitting beside Lucinda. The two were nearly the same age and had both been raised on Angel Rock; neither could remember a day they had not known each other. "Who is that gorgeous man? And how long is he going to stay here?"

"You couldn't possibly be referring to poor sick Maurice, now could you?" Lucinda teased.

"No, I couldn't be. I meant that other one—Reuben, I think your aunt called him. *He*'s enough to make you want to go sailing off to Ysral."

"Don't think it hasn't crossed my mind." Lucinda sighed. "Although—Edori sailors. You're the one who told me never to trust them."

"Well, and I had good reason to tell you that," Emmie said firmly. "That Yacov! Well, and I didn't have much luck with Amos, either, although he was a beautiful man to look at and said sweeter things than I have ever heard coming from a man's mouth. But this Reuben looks like an intelligent, thinking man. So tell me about him. Did you get to know him on this journey? And how is it you come to be traveling on an Edori ship, anyway? I thought your aunt wouldn't consider it."

But the trip home was the very last part of a very long story, and Lucinda was just as glad to turn the talk away from Reuben's manifest charms. There were many other tales to tell Emmie, of the *Gloria* itself, of Bael and Jared and the other angels, of Cedar Hills and Luminaux. And Emmie listened intently to it all, easily remembering names and events and interjecting the occasional shrewd comment on Gretchen's probable reaction to events.

"But the Edori boat," the housemaid said at last, toward the end of the narrative. "What in the world changed her mind about that?"

Lucinda shook her head. "One day I was at Cedar Hills, having lunch with Omar—"

"The Archangel's son."

"Right. And the next day we were scurrying off to Port Clara, bound and determined to take the next ship out. I have no idea what set her off. You know my aunt. It could have been anything."

"No, not quite anything," Emmie said, frowning. "She has strange reasons, sometimes, but once you know them they always make an odd kind of sense. Someone must have said something to her that made her feel like she'd overstayed her welcome. Or made her feel like she was in some kind of danger."

"Danger?" Lucinda repeated incredulously. "In Cedar Hills? It's true someone may have made some comment that she took amiss—"

Emmie leaned forward. "Did you ever ask her," the girl said, "why she left Cedar Hills in the first place? When she brought you here? Did you ever wonder what made a middle-aged spinster bring a small child to the most isolated spot in the whole world? Did she kidnap you? Was she afraid someone would take you away from her? If she just wanted to raise you away from the hold, couldn't she have found a nice little house outside one of the small towns in Jordana? Why Angel Rock? Why did she have to run away?"

"I don't know," Lucinda said blankly. "She never said. It's never come up."

Emmie sat back in her chair. "If I were you, I'd want to find out. And I would think whatever it was, that's the same thing that sent you away from Samaria so fast that you ended up on an Edori boat. With the most handsome man I've seen walking around live in all my days."

After the meal, Lucinda carried a tray up to Maurice's room, where she knew her aunt had spent much of the night. She was surprised to find, instead of a comatose man and a sleepy woman, two wide-awake Edori. Maurice was sitting up in bed, and Reuben was standing over him, grinning.

"You're awake! You're better!" Lucinda exclaimed, laying her tray aside and coming forward. "How do you feel?"

"Like five horses rode over me in the dark, and a sixth one kicked me in the head," the captain replied promptly. "But not so bad, considering. Reuben tells me your doctor has recommended three more days in bed, but says there's no reason I shouldn't heal completely."

"Well, that's good news. Are you hungry? Are you allowed to eat?" She glanced around. "Where's my aunt Gretchen?"

"I sent her off to her bed when I came in this morning," Reuben said. "I don't think she would have gone but she didn't have the strength to protest."

"She must think he's really better, or she wouldn't have left anyway," Lucinda said. She was considering the bacon and pancakes on her tray. "Not for you just yet," she decided. "Reuben may eat this breakfast, if he likes, and I'll bring up some porridge for Maurice."

"But I like bacon," the hurt man wheedled.

"I don't think so," Lucinda said. "But maybe if you do well with porridge, we'll let you have some beef tonight."

She hurried back to the kitchen and returned to the sickroom twenty minutes later, carrying a fresh tray of porridge, tea, and fruit. Maurice ate like a starved man, so she relented and fetched him two slices of bacon. Emmie was still cooking; the other guests had begun to stir and ask for their breakfasts. At the Manor, breakfast was served until every last hungry person had been fed. Dinner, however, was served promptly at six, although anyone who happened to miss this meal could easily cajole one of the women to fix him a cold plate. Gretchen could not abide the thought of anyone going hungry under her roof, though her sense of hospitality warred with her desire for order. Hospitality always won.

"Reuben tells me you've baths out back," Maurice said. "If it wouldn't be too much of an imposition—"

"Jackson can help Reuben take you down there. It's something of a walk and you're still so weak."

So that was quite a procession, the three men limping through the halls and out through the garden, into the sauna—and then, half an hour later, reversing the process. Maurice looked pale and drained after the excursion, and it was no surprise to anyone when he opted for a nap as soon as he'd made it back to his bedroom.

"And you?" Lucinda asked Reuben as they closed Maurice's door and stood for a moment in the hallway. "Has all this activity tired you out as well?"

"Not at all," he said promptly. "In fact, I was just wondering what I might do to entertain myself. You, no doubt, have a list of chores fifteen pages long—"

"I do," she interrupted, "but I've been gone for weeks and the world hasn't ended while they remained undone. I can give you a few hours. Would you like to see the island? Or have you been here before?"

"I've been, but I don't believe I've set foot outside the harbor," he said. "I was hoping you'd have time to show it to me."

"Well, then," she said, "before Aunt Gretchen finds me. Let's go."

They strolled out into the cool spring afternoon and walked at a leisurely pace down the cobblestoned road leading from the Manor to the harbor. "There are really only two roads on Angel Rock," she said. "The hotels and the general store and a couple of the houses are along Harborview, and as you can tell, it's quite short—you can stand at any point and see from end to end. Here," she said as they came to a gravel road intersecting the main one about a quarter mile from the harbor, "is Old Crossing Lane, and most anyone who doesn't live on Harborview has a cottage somewhere along this road. Well, Parker has what you might call a *shack* and it's about a mile off the track, but you get to it by following the road all the way south and then turning left."

"How many people live here? And what do they do?" the Edori asked.

"Twenty-four, including me. Almost everyone works at one of the hotels or in the shipyard or at Coburn's. Coburn's is the general store but you can get everything there—fabric, machinery, grain. Most of us lay in our own supplies, of course, and trade with all the ships that come in, but Coburn picks up things none of us think we'll ever want, and then one day we want it and he has it. He's amazing.''

"When was the island wired for electricity?''

"About ten years ago. It was such a controversy! Because of course some of the residents came here to get away from all that 'newfangled' technology—Foster and Parker and all the old-timers were bitterly opposed to it. Celia and Hammet came from Luminaux, where of course there is *every* luxury, so they were delighted at the idea of installing a generator and powering everything up. But James Sauverne—Timothy's father, you know—he thought electricity was evil and would end in us all being fried in our beds. I'm not sure if he thought the electricity itself would destroy us or if Jovah would be so incensed he'd send thunderbolts rolling down from the heavens, but he was the worst of the whole group. Now, of course, he's got every room in his house wired and he wants to have his own generator installed, except he can't afford it.''

"Where did your aunt Gretchen stand?''

She smiled at him sideways. "On the side of progress, oddly enough. She's so conservative that I thought she'd vote against change, but she's also a businesswoman. And she'd had enough mainland guests complaining about poor heating and insufficient light, and it just galled her to think there were luxuries that she couldn't offer. She wants to consider the Manor as grand a hotel as anything in—oh, Semorrah, I guess—and so she had to argue for change. Actually, I think it was her opinion that swayed the others, because she's a very strong-willed woman, my aunt Gretchen. People find her hard to resist.''

"I like her," he said.

"So do I.''

They had arrived in the center of town. The harbor was before them, the three hotels at their back. Lucinda pointed to the half a dozen buildings, identifying each one—the harbormaster's home, Coburn's store, the house where Gia and her parents lived and where they made candles, curtains, bedding, and all sorts of domestic items. Those were the shipyards, that was the house Emmie shared with her mother and sister, back there was the cottage that was empty now that Dora and Vestry had moved with their three children to a large empty lot at the north edge of Old Crossing Road. . . .

And that was it. No more sights in the harbor. Lucinda paused blankly, not sure what else to point out, and then she gave a slight laugh. "You must feel sorry for us, so few of us living in such a small place—" but he interrupted.

"Not at all. The Edori mostly live in small clans of no more than thirty," he said. "And know each soul as well as they would know a brother's. And count themselves happy and fortunate to have such a close connection to so many. But the Edori also have a great need to come together at least once a year and see *all* their brothers and sisters and cousins and uncles five times removed, and so we have an annual Gathering that everyone attends. And then we are *really* happy," he said, smiling broadly. "For we like nothing so much as living practically on top of one another in one big communal heap."

"I've heard of this Gathering, I think," she said. As she spoke they both unconsciously turned and headed slowly away from the harbor. As they approached Old Crossing Road she headed northward, and he followed her. "I always thought it was like the Gloria. A celebration to Jovah. But it's not?"

"Well, certainly there is much singing, and we direct many of our songs to the god—asking him for livable weather, you know, and good health in the coming year—but I wouldn't say that praising the god is the real motivation for our celebration. Mostly it is a chance to see old friends and family members who have joined with another clan, to tell each other the events of our lives in the past year. Edori have remarkable memories. Most anyone can recite you his clan history for five generations and every event of significance in the life of every living Edori. So the Gathering is as much a time of sharing information as it is a time to worship the god."

"I know that when the Edori lived in Samaria, they were wanderers," Lucinda said. "Are they still? In Ysral?"

"Some are, some aren't. It's very interesting," Reuben replied. They were walking more slowly now, since Old Crossing Road was steeply pitched and not particularly well graded. It would eventually peak on the highest point of the island, then meander down toward sea level again, gradually petering out about a mile beyond Dora and Vestry's place. "There are actually two pretty good-sized towns, not unlike what you've got here, only a bit bigger. Not the size of Luminaux, of course—more like Cedar Hills. And the Edori who live there seem quite happy. They have their businesses and their crafts and their homes and their gardens and their friends and their families. They don't seem to want for a thing. But the more traditional Edori—the ones who are still wanderers—have a certain scorn for these town folk.''

"Allali," Lucinda said with a smile.

He smiled back. "Not quite that bad, but you've got the general idea. The wanderers refer to the city dwellers as the corelli—which means, roughly, someone who loves safety, who is afraid to take chances. And it's true that most of the corelli are Edori who emigrated to Ysral long after the first shiploads came over to explore. The corelli were born in the Edori sanctuaries on Samaria, they were not brought up wandering from Gaza to Breven and back again in a single season. They grew up liking the comforts of the same roof over their heads night after night. They didn't see any reason life should have to be harder than it already was.''

"I can't tell," she said. "If you were corelli or not."

"My mother's people were," he said. "But she fell in love with my father, and chose to follow him as his clan drifted through Ysral. Every summer we would return to Covallah to visit her parents for two months. So I got a taste of both lives.''

"And which did you prefer?"

He smiled again. "Well, you see, I have chosen to wander even farther afield," he said. "But if I were to stay in Ysral? I think I would be corelli. I might journey off from time to time, spend a few weeks with friends in a traveling clan. But I am a man who likes his comforts. And I am lazy enough to not want to work any harder than I have to.''

They had arrived at the highest point of Old Crossing Road, and Lucinda came to a halt. From this vantage, most of the island was laid out before them, a patchwork of cool green and misty gray that came to a sudden shocked halt at the lavender expanse of the sea. The sky overhead was an insistent turquoise, and one billowing white cloud rose voluptuously over the far horizon. There was nothing to see but color.

Reuben took a deep breath, surveying the landscape for a long time in silence. "Well, now, that's a pretty view," he said at last. "The sea changes colors like a child changes moods, but I've rarely seen it just that shade. Is it always like that, or only on sunny days?"

"Mostly that color. Sometimes, on gray days, a little darker. The color it is farther out."

"And at sunset?"

"The sea and the sky are both on fire, and all of Angel Rock seems like a tiny piece of kindling that is about to be dropped into the blaze."

"Well, that is the danger," he said absently. "To be consumed by beauty."

They stood awhile, Reuben turning slowly to take in whatever part of the vista he may have missed, Lucinda noting that a few of the more impatient bushes were beginning to uncurl their spring buds. Soon there would be washes of vermilion and lilac and canary to decorate the pure emerald and stone of the island.

Reuben pointed down to the rocky strip of land that separated the island from the sea. It was low tide; in a few hours, that whole stretch would be underwater. "Can we get down to the shoreline?"

"Not on foot," Lucinda said. "There's no path. I can get there."

He turned his attention to her. "And can you take me there?"

She lifted her chin. "I can. If you trust me."

He spread his arms; an invitation. "Why would I not trust you? Don't angels have the strength of five men? If you say you can carry me, I will feel safe with you."

She felt a rush of—something—excitement, panic, terror; but she nodded with dignity. "Certainly I can carry you. And it is not very far, after all."

"I do not expect to be dropped even over short distances," he retorted.

"No, and you shall not be."

Before she could think about it too long, she stepped behind him and wrapped her arms around his chest. It was like embracing an oak, solid and sturdy and unlikely to break, except that he was warm and muscled and scented more like cedar. . . . She shook her head once, tightened her grip, and drove her wings in short hard sweeps against the air.

Hard to take off from a standing position, carrying a burden nearly twice her own weight, but she was determined to do it gracefully, and she managed. She was aware of the steady, rhythmic beating of her wings, the tensing and relaxing of the sinews across her back, but nonetheless she felt like she was floating through the air. She and the Edori drifted peacefully across the broken terrain, silent and light as milkweed, circled once over the rocky margin of the shore, and settled easily a few yards from the sea. Their feet were on the ground a good twenty seconds before she remembered to drop her arms, and he had not made one movement to free himself or step aside.

But. She released him and instantly bent to retrieve a shell, an opaline fist with spiky knuckles. "Isn't this pretty? You so rarely find them whole down here. The sea comes in too roughly."

"Very pretty," he said, his voice sounding as distant to her ears as her own had, as though he spoke through some formal curtain of restraint. "Do you ever hold one to your ear to listen for the sea?"

"Why would I have to?" she said. "The sea is right here."

"In case you're ever gone from it," he said.

She looked out at the shifting purple water, rising and falling as if it breathed. "I don't think I'd ever be gone from it for long," she said. She looked over at him directly for the first time. "Do you?"

He was bemused. "Do I what?"

"Do you carry mementos of places—and people—that you've left behind forever?"

He answered slowly. "I haven't left that many things behind for what I consider forever," he said. "That's one of the benefits of being a wanderer. You can always wander back to what you miss."

"What if it doesn't miss you anymore?"

"That's a risk," he acknowledged. "And maybe there haven't been that many people—or places—I really expected to miss me."

She began walking along the shoreline, watching her feet because there were so many rocks and hazards. He fell into step beside her. "Mother—family—clan members," she suggested.

She could hear the smile in his voice, though she did not look at him. "They're happy to see me go. Happy to see me return, I'm sure, but not grieving when I set sail again."

"And of course they know you'll be back."

"They know it. I tell them so. I never made a promise like that I did not keep."

"And to how many others have you made that promise?" she asked before she could stop herself.

"Not as many as you might think," he murmured. "The Edori reputation has been somewhat exaggerated."

"Well," she said. "I don't know much about Edori. I don't know much about anything off this island."

He came to a halt and she followed suit. He stood for a moment gazing out at the ocean, as if he had not seen it every day of his life for as long as he had been at sea, and then turned his head so he could survey the short, sharp cliffs that sealed off this tumbled shore. "It's a nice island," he said, as if he had assessed it and found it acceptable. "I'll want to return. Often. Though I would not want to come so often that anyone found me intrusive."

"I can't imagine that would be the case," Lucinda replied. "You know that Aunt Gretchen lives to make every guest welcome."

"And you, Lucinda?" he said softly. "Would you welcome me?"

He had left off examining the beauties of the island and was staring soberly down at her. Her heart had grown so big that there was no room left in her chest for air, and so she was taking short, shallow breaths and finding them insufficient. But she managed to return his look steadily and serenely, and her voice sounded calm, even to herself.

"I would," she said. "Anytime you arrived at our harbor."

He put a hand to her cheek so lightly that it was more a sensation of warmth than an actual touch. His eyes were so dark, night-dark, secret-dark, the dark of forgotten dreams. His skin was the color of old wood, polished by hundreds of loving hands. He was more beautiful than she had imagined a man could be.

"Then I will be back here," he said, "as often as the tide."

"As often as the sea brings you, you mean."

"More often than that. You shall see, mikala. You shall see."

Dinner and the quiet interaction of the evening were much more prosaic but infinitely easier to live through. Maurice had a tray in his room, but Rico, Joe, and Michael joined the rest of the Manor's guests for the six o'clock dinner—for which Lucinda and Reuben had to hurry home in order to be on time. Gretchen knew how to do up a meal in grand style, and for certain pampered guests she offered every elegance, but for ordinary meals, everyone sat down to the table in democratic fashion—guests, innkeeper, even Emmie and Jackson, and all the food was handed round the table. No one had ever complained about this, and the Edori were certainly not going to be the first. The other seven guests were full of questions for their hostess and her niece, wanting to hear all about their trip to the mainland, and so conversation was general and lively. The food, of course, was excellent.

Afterward, some of the guests departed, and the others drifted into the music room, looking for mild entertainment. Lucinda sat in a corner, quietly talking to the young Luminauzi girl who was here with her parents, but she waited patiently for the inevitable request; and it came.

"It's so rare mortals like us get to hear an angel singing," said an older man who appeared to be on a pilgrimage to Ysral with his wife. At a guess, he was a businessman in one of the smaller Bethel towns—well-to-do by his own standards and not embarrassed in any company, but not as sophisticated as a Manadavvi, either. "If Lucinda would be willing to offer a song or two for the glory of Jovah, we would be most delighted."

"Oh, do sing, Lucinda, please do," the young girl begged.

Lucinda rose to her feet, smiling pleasantly. "Of course," she said. "But I don't have to sing the sacred masses if you'd rather hear something else. Although I do know the masses! It's up to you."

A quick murmur running around the room revealed that most people would prefer to hear a contemporary tune, if the angel did not believe that was sacrilege. She nodded and went to the harpsichord. Reuben, she noticed, casually rose and circled the room till he came to rest right across from her, where he might have an excellent view of her face. Well, she had sung for angels at the Gloria; she would not be nervous of a few Edori.

Accordingly, she picked her favorite songs, the ones most perfectly in her range, and let her fingers dance lightly down the narrow keys. She could feel her voice rise, giddy and true, over the remote, tiny music of the harpsichord; she sounded happy, as if she laughed over every note. She could not help smiling. Around her, the audience smiled in response.

Gretchen came over to stand beside her as she finished her

second selection. "That was very nice," she said approvingly, flipping through the pages of a book of music. "I was think-ing—here, I haven't heard you sing this one in a long time."

It could be sung as a solo, but the harmony was sweet. "If you'll sing it with me," she replied, smiling up at her aunt.

"Oh, heavens! I haven't sung in months."

"Just once. Just the first verse."

"Well—" Gretchen glanced at the music again, then nodded briskly. "Well, why not. Scoot over."

So Lucinda made room for her on the edge of the seat, and Gretchen reminded herself of the descant by tapping out her part very softly on the upper registers of the keyboard. They sat side by side, Lucinda playing the accompaniment, and sang the whole song straight through, all four verses, their voices blend-ing in well-rehearsed harmony. They had sung together their whole lives, they knew each other's strong notes and missed phrases, and their voices moved silkily beside each other like images in a mirrored glass. When they finished, Lucinda pound-ing out a few dramatic chords for emphasis, the small audience erupted into spontaneous applause. Gretchen sat there a moment, wreathed in smiles, then leaned over to kiss her niece on the cheek.

"You're a sweet girl," she said, and got up from the bench. Despite the requests of the others in the room, she refused to perform again.

"Too much work!" she said, quite gaily for her, and sailed out of the room toward the kitchen. She was still smiling.

Lucinda sang one more song, a quieter number to induce guests to start thinking about their beds, and then closed the lid. "I think I've had enough performing for the evening," she said with a laugh when the businessman asked for one last number, and came to her feet. They were too polite to protest for long.

Soon after that, everyone dispersed, seeking their various rooms. Lucinda moved mechanically around the parlor, pushing pillows back in place and closing the curtains for the night. She was tired herself, though she should not be. What about the day had been so hard—?

"Your concert tonight reminded me of something I meant to show you when we were aboard *The Wayward*," Reuben said from the doorway, and she whirled around a little too quickly. He should not startle her so; her heart was absolutely racing.

"But then the Jansai came calling, and I didn't have time."

"I can scarcely remember any life before the Jansai arrived, firing at us," she said, summoning a careless smile. "But weren't we discussing treason just about then?"

"We were discussing the Jacobites, yes, and machines that are tuned to music," he said, taking a seat on the plush flowered sofa. "Come. Sit here and let me show you this."

She could not sit on such a piece of furniture; her wings would not allow it. Instead, she pulled up a hassock before him, and let the feathers tumble behind her. His eyes wandered from wing tip to shoulder blade as if he liked the white spill of quill and down, and then he looked at the object in his hand.

"A music box," she said. It was a small silver case with tiny scrolled legs; the top was glass painted with the face of a singing angel. It was held shut with an ornate clasp in the shape of a rosebud.

"Of a sort," Reuben said, holding it out to her. "Can you open it?"

She took it from him with an inquiring glance. "I suppose not," she said, and gently tried to twist the flower. It did not budge. "Maybe it doesn't open?" she guessed.

"Oh, it does, and there's a treasure inside," he said, smiling. "A ring that I bought in Luminaux one day when I had no business squandering my money on trinkets."

"Then you probably shouldn't have bought the box, either," she said. "For it looks quite expensive."

"Well, it was, but at that time I had more money," he excused himself. "Besides, it was made for me by a friend of mine."

"Who sealed it with a lock only you could open."

"Anyone can open it," said Reuben, "who knows the key."

"Holds the key?"

"Knows it," he corrected. "For, listen."

And he sang a sweet, wordless melody in a honey-smooth tenor that made her briefly absentminded to hear. The song was maybe twenty notes long, and when the last note sounded, she heard a sharp metallic click. She looked down at the music box in her hand. The rosebud had flicked to one side.

"Did that—did your song unlock it?" she asked in a wondering voice, holding the box away from her body as if it were an enchanted thing. "I heard a sound—"

Reuben nodded. "Open it. See what's inside."

"How can a song undo a lock?"

"It's an electronic lock. It responds to aural cues."

"I don't understand what that means."

"Well, I couldn't duplicate it myself, but there's a tiny receiver in there that picks up sound. And it responds to the song you just heard. And that song breaks the circuit that wires the lock in place. I'm told that it's a very simple principle, though I admit I found it amazing the first time I saw it."

"I find it a little terrifying."

"Open it," he said again, and when she did not, reached over himself and swung the painted lid upright.

The inside was lined with black velvet and on the velvet lay a silver ring set with an unbroken band of emeralds. The stones alternated in cut, a square gem beside an oval one, all the way around the band.

"Oh, how pretty!" Lucinda exclaimed, instantly forgetting her unease over the lock. "May I try it on?"

"Certainly."

It did not fit the first finger she tried, but slid smoothly over the ring finger of her right hand. In the muted light of the drawing room, the emeralds looked sleepy and content, rich with thoughts and dreams of their own. She turned her hand this way and that to see what secrets the light could uncover.

"I can understand why you did not try to resist buying this," she said, "though I do have to wonder if you had a lady in mind when you made your purchase."

"Well, I did," he said, smiling, "but I changed my mind before I saw her again. When I realized I would rather never see her again than part with my emeralds, it seemed like a good time to make my farewells."

"Are you *sure* those Edori tales have been exaggerated?" she murmured.

He laughed. "Well, some of them."

Regretfully, she took the ring off and laid it back in its case. "Where did you get it?"

"Luminaux, of course. The most beautiful things in the world are to be found there, though we try to make them elsewhere as well. But nothing I've found in the mainland or Ysral compares with the treasures I have come across in the Blue City."

"Thank you for showing it to me."

He picked up the box once more and held it at his eye level. "Now, how do you suppose I lock it up again?"

"I would think you sing another song?"

He nodded. "Good guess. But not quite right. I sing the same song—backward."

"The same notes in reverse order?"

He nodded again. "Listen." And he sang again in that delicious, offhand tenor, the same few notes that he had sung before but arranged in the opposite direction. The silver rosebud slipped into place as his last note sounded. Reuben looked over at her and grinned.

"Isn't that clever? Who would have thought of such a thing?"

"Let me try," she said, and took the box from his hand. "Do I have to be on exactly the same pitch as you? Or do I just have to have the intervals of the notes correct?"

"I assume the pitch doesn't matter. I don't pay much attention when I unlock it, I just start singing."

She nodded, then sang. She was a quick study, and the melody was very simple, and she had been paying attention. She got it right, first try, for the lock snapped open under her fingers. She laughed softly.

"I'm impressed," he said.

"I want to try something," she said. "If I sing it deliberately wrong, what will happen?" So, a little more haltingly, she offered the song in reverse, but changed the last note. The rosebud did not move.

"A true key in a real lock, with only one correct fit," she said. "I am still amazed."

"I will have to commission him to make a box for you," he said. "And have it programmed with some impossibly complex song that will take you days to master. Not to mention how hard it will be to learn the song in reverse."

She had stopped listening; she was gazing down at the painted angel on the lid and remembering something. "You know, this is so strange," she said slowly, still looking down. "I'd almost forgotten. A few months ago we had a spell of dry weather on the island. It's so cloudy here, especially in winter, that we all love sunny days. But at this particular time we were running low on fresh water, so we all agreed that a few hours of rain would be welcome. So I went aloft and prayed for storm.

"There are many prayers for weather," she went on more slowly, "and the prayers that call for snow and those that call for thunderstorms are very different, but in each there is a passage that is identical. Just a couple dozen measures—maybe a page of written music. What comes before and after varies radically from song to song. But there must be some combination of notes that tells Jovah we want precipitation, and the *kind* of precipitation is determined by the rest of the music.

"So the rains came, and we all filled our cisterns and barrels and cook pots. And after a few hours we agreed that we had had enough, and I went aloft again. And I sang the prayer for sunshine, for the dispersal of clouds. And in the middle of that song I realized there were about twenty-five measures that were identical to the ones in the song for rain. Except they were in reverse order. I had never sung the two prayers so closely together before, and so I had never realized it."

"Even so, I'm surprised you noticed. A song sung backward sounds nothing like the composition as it was intended."

She smiled faintly, finally looking up at him. "I am good with music," she said. "I remember notes and phrases. If an artist saw one image on a canvas and in a mirror, wouldn't he instantly recognize it as the same piece? That is how it is with me."

"So Yovah perhaps operates on the same principle as this little box," Reuben said. "The prayer for sunshine reverses the prayer for rain. What other prayers might be mirror images of each other?"

She spread her hands. "There aren't many other prayers you would want to reverse. If you asked the god for medicines, you would not then ask him to scoop them back up again. The same for grains and seedlings. I suppose, if you had begged for a thunderbolt and then no longer wanted it to fall, you could sing that song backward—" She paused a moment, then laughed. "Although, to be frank, I don't believe that is one I could do in reverse without a lot of practice. It's a *very* complicated piece."

"And how often have you prayed for thunderbolts?" he asked, smiling.

"Never," she said, smiling back. "In fact, that is the danger of learning such a song. You have to practice it in pieces, and sing something else in between, so the god does not really smite you when you are just learning your lessons.''

''Ah,'' he said, nodding wisely. ''I always wondered how that was done.''

She was about to describe to him the days she had spent learning her prayers, Gretchen tirelessly and exactly going over every note, every song, teaching the young angel prayers she herself would never offer to Jovah. Gretchen believed that no one but an angel could call directly upon the god; but she knew the songs, every one. She never had to look at the music to correct a missed note.

But Gretchen herself entered the room before Lucinda could say another word. ''Goodness, Lucinda, are you still up? Don't you realize how late it is? I'm sure you've taken up quite enough of Reuben's time today, now let him go to bed, and you be on your way, too. Go, now. No argument. I'll see you in the morning.''

And in fact, she *was* tired, so tired that thoughts and disconnected bits of song were floating through her mind in no particular order. So tired that she could barely marshal a good night for her aunt or a smile for Reuben, who rose to his feet but did not follow her through the door. As she left the room she heard him ask after Maurice. In three minutes she was in her own chamber, undressed and lying under the covers. In four minutes she was sound asleep.

Three days later *The Wayward* sailed from Angel Rock. In those three days Lucinda had almost no opportunity to speak alone with Reuben. Gretchen kept her busy, cleaning out the recently vacated rooms, going over the storage bins with Jackson, dragging out the spring linen with Emmie's help, and generally running errands. Soon enough she began to suspect that Gretchen's desire for her assistance really masked her determination to keep her niece from spending too much time with the attractive Edori sailor. Not that she blamed Gretchen. If she'd been the aunt, she would have found much more time-consuming tasks for her niece to perform.

And she was not sure it was a bad thing to find herself separated from a man who would be sailing away any day now, to return who knew how often, if ever? But she sighed as she buried her face in the clean, cedar-scented folds of the spring sheets, and her steps were slow every time she left the inn.

But the morning Reuben and Maurice packed up their scarce belongings and carried them to the ship, Lucinda abandoned all pretense of scrubbing the kitchen pantry, and accompanied them down to the harbor. Jackson had come with them so Maurice could lean on his arm if need be, but the captain seemed perfectly able to navigate the street on his own. He was paler than an Edori should be, but quite cheerful, and he seemed delighted to be returning to his ship.

Lucinda skipped along beside them, carrying two baskets. "This is bread, Emmie and Aunt Gretchen baked it this morning, so it's quite fresh. And this is roasted salmon, but it will spoil soon, so you have to eat it tonight, Aunt Gretchen says. But there's dried beef in here, too, that will last a few days. And there are oranges and limes, although they aren't very good this time of year, but better than nothing. Is there anything else you need? I could run back to the inn and fly to the ship in no time."

"This is plenty. This is generous. You'll have to thank your aunt for us," Reuben said gently. "She has been most kind."

She was chattering, and she knew it; but he was leaving, and how would she say good-bye? and so she couldn't stop. "And she says anytime you're near Angel Rock, you're to come stay with us, even if you all want to sleep on the ship, you're to come have meals with us. And she says if you *want* to stay at the inn, there will always be room—"

"Ship's good enough for a whole man," Maurice said with a smile, "but next time I've been shot by Jansai, be sure I'll take her up on her hospitality."

And that was it, they were at the harbor, Joe and Rico had come ashore to help the captain carry his things on board. In a few minutes they would be gone; she might never see any of them again. Reuben had promised to return, but what did an Edori's promises mean? This might be the last time she ever laid eyes on his beautiful face, saw the sun send white streaks down the sleek black braid—

And she was, somehow, alone on the cobblestoned street with Reuben. Jackson had disappeared with the Edori, and none of the usual onlookers seemed to be present on the dock this morning. Reuben was looking at her intently, his expression more sober than normal, as if he was finding this farewell no easier than she was.

"It's a week or two to Ysral, depending on the weather—and the Jansai," he said, with a small grin. "And a week or two there. And a week or two back. So you may see me again in as little as three weeks, and certainly before two months are out."

She kept her eyes on his, afraid to look at him too closely, afraid to look away. "Maurice might not want to come back so soon," she said. "And he's captain."

"Ah, Maurice had visits from half the people of Angel Rock while he lay there pretending to be sick. Your doctor was asking about some new medical machine that he thought they were building at the Augustine school, and your harbormaster wanted some tool he'd heard about that only the Edori craftsmen make. Maurice has a dozen commissions on the island. He'll want to come back."

"I look forward to seeing you again," she said, because if she didn't say it straight out she would never say it, and maybe he didn't know? "I'll miss you while you're gone."

"Well, I'll think of you while we're away, and that way I won't miss you quite so much," he said, smiling a little. "And here—you take this, and it will help you remember me."

He had caught hold of her hand and now pressed a rounded metal object into her palm. She knew without looking that it was the music box.

"I can't take this," she protested. "It's so special—it was made for you by a friend—"

"It's so special," he said, smiling broadly now, "that I promised myself I would only give it to the girl who could learn the key."

"The key—to the box?" she said, stammering a little.

He shook his head slowly, smiling still, and laid a fist against his heart, but he made no other answer. She felt herself blushing. From the ship, someone called his name in a loud, impatient voice.

"You must go," she said. "I'll look for you. In two months."

"More likely less," he said. And without another word, he bent down and kissed her quickly on the mouth. Then he sprinted for the ship, leaped up the gangplank, and called something to whichever sailor was already hauling on the ropes. In a matter of moments *The Wayward* began to move, idling out toward open sea like a girl coyly slipping away from her guardian's notice. Reuben and, she thought, Michael stood at the railing and waved to her so vigorously that she finally lifted her free hand and waved back. But she did not want to. Her heart was leaden, her whole body was cold; even her lips, where she could still feel the pressure of his kiss, seemed icy and bloodless in the playful spring air. He was leaving, he was leaving, he was gone.

She watched for another thirty minutes as the sails of the ship grew smaller, indistinct, and finally invisible against the hazy blue of the eastern horizon. She should return to the inn; Aunt Gretchen would be wondering where she was. (Aunt Gretchen knew very well where she was.) She had a dozen chores to do, and the activity could not but do her good, wake some of her shocked, abandoned blood, prod her heart into motion again. She was a fool to be standing here, forlorn and bereft, watching the waves swallow the shadow of a vanished Edori boat.

She gave one long sigh, shook her head, and made herself turn back toward the inn. She had not taken three steps when she felt a faint shift and roll inside the silver box. So she stopped in the middle of the street and softly crooned the short melody that would turn aside the silver rose. The lock slid back, and she lifted the painted glass lid.

Inside was the emerald ring.

He would return as he had promised.

CHAPTER TEN

Tamar had two strokes of luck as she fled from Ileah. One came almost immediately, twenty minutes after she snatched up a few bundles and the rest of the dried beef and hurried west down the road. She had gone less than two miles along her way when she heard a dull rumble behind her and, looking back, saw a big farm transport vehicle bearing down. She scrambled out of the way (in her experience, the drivers of the big trucks weren't always careful about keeping faithfully on the road) and slowed her pace to watch the truck pass.

She was surprised when it came to a growling idle beside her. A man riding high on the elevated driver's seat waved down at her; she saw heads pop up in the windows of the mammoth cabin behind him, children's faces, children's eager, indiscriminate waves.

"We're on our way to Semorrah! Looking for a ride?" the man called down to her.

It was almost outside of her experience that anyone could extend such kindness to a complete stranger, but then, she had heard many tales of the friendly midland farmers who picked up wayfarers just for the company. The presence of children on the truck was reassuring; even a man who offered assistance so he could eventually turn to assault seemed unlikely to do so in the presence of little witnesses. Even so, had she not been desperate, she probably would have refused.

"I don't think I can pay you," she called back up to him.

He waved a hand in a dismissive gesture. "No, no, I don't want your coins. Just wanted to save you a few hot, weary miles."

The angel would be back in half a day; on foot, she was unlikely to get far enough to elude him. It was a gamble, but she was running out of safe choices.

"Then, yes, thank you very much," she said. "How do I climb in?"

Three giggling boys swarmed out of the back of the truck and demonstrated for her the footholds and handholds built into its thick metal sides. She hauled herself aboard and tumbled into the cavernous cabin, a huge, rattling, odoriferous compartment that seemed stocked with all manner of mysterious cargo. She could smell leather goods and what might be grain; in addition, there were boxes that could contain anything. The truck roared into its traveling mode again, and Tamar felt the vibrations enter her bones from every part of her body in contact with the metal—her feet, the palms of her hands, her hip against the interior wall. The droning ricocheted through her head and set up a steady quiver in her back teeth. It was instantly too noisy to hear anything except the roar of the motor. She could not imagine how she would endure this for more than five minutes.

But it was a hundred and sixty miles to Semorrah. They might be traveling at a rate of thirty miles an hour or so (she had no aptitude for judging the speed of a motor vehicle). She had a day of this to endure.

Two of the boys made their way to her side, nonchalantly navigating the piles of merchandise and bracing themselves against the unsteady sway of the truck. One of them carried a sheepskin rug in his hands, the other what looked like an over-sized feather pillow. They offered these to her silently. When she stared at them blankly, they went into a pantomime routine: the one laid the rug on the jouncing floor, the other placed the pillow on top of it then sat himself squarely in the middle, crossing his legs under him. He grinned up at her as if to say, "See how comfortable?" and she could not help smiling in return. He jumped to his feet, almost fell over when the truck took a rapid turn, then held his hand out to indicate that she should now sit down.

So she did, and was relieved to find that the padding sub-stantially cut down the awful vibrating sensation. In fact, if she was careful, she could lie on one side, half curled up but com-fortable enough, and still remain within the shelter of the pillow. She gave the boys a big smile of thanks and they laughed back

at her. She was glad it was too noisy to talk. Otherwise, she
was sure, they would want to sit and visit with her, and she had
no conversation to offer young farm boys whose lives were so
serene that they could so joyously welcome grim strangers into
their midst.

So she rearranged her body, piling all her bundles under her
head to further cut the vibration, and lay completely supine. The
boys watched her till she closed her eyes. She did not hear them
rise and leave her (she couldn't hear a thing), but when she
peeped out through half-closed lids, they were gone.

She sighed and turned to her other side, punching the pile of
clothes under her head to make it more comfortable. She had
Evan's jacket, one of Dawn's sweaters—she had run to the
storeroom cabin and just grabbed anything that looked useful,
anything that she could fit into one fairly tight bundle. She had
left Peter's pallet unmade, the breakfast dishes scattered on the
floor, the well uncovered, the laundry on the line. . . .

Well, of course, it was not laundry at all. The red shirt was
a warning signal, a message of danger, a sign that said TROUBLE
LURKS HERE; PASS BY. All Jacobites carried a bit of red clothing
with them and never wore it—unless they had been taken prisoner, unless they were in the company of enemies and did not
want their friends to unwarily approach. The angel had asked
her if she expected any more Jacobites to arrive at Ileah. She
did, but she expected them to take one look and run back the
other way.

He would think, if he knew, that she was warning them of Jansai predators. But she considered the angel a danger just as great.
All this talk of helping her to look for the Alleluia Files—! As if
she would trust an *angel* with such a task! With *anything*. Everyone knew that angels had nothing to gain, everything to lose, if
the spaceship *Jehovah* was exposed for the combination of machinery and fraud that it was. She had no idea what his plan was,
how he expected her to help him betray her friends, but she was
smart enough to know no good could come of colluding with an
angel.

She punched her makeshift pillow again and turned over, trying to find a position that was comfortable for even five minutes.
He had not seemed as indiscriminately evil as she would have
expected. He looked neither debauched nor cruel, and he had
certainly been kind enough to her and Peter. *He had reasons to*

be kind, she reminded herself, for naturally he wanted to win her over. Thus the courteous manner, the helpful acts, the gift of flowers which she could not, to this hour, fathom.

It would be easier to hate a man—an angel—who was coarse or abusive. This angel, this Jared, had seemed sincere enough and, actually, good-hearted; but of course it was all a facade. A shame that a man with such a pleasant face should use it as a mask for malevolence, but there it was. An angel was only good to propagate lies; how many times had she heard Conran say that? "The only favor an angel will grant is the favor of a quick death." It was not like one pair of sympathetic eyes could overcome all her bitter training.

She rolled to her back and stared at the shaking ceiling overhead. There were half a dozen small windows near the top edge of the truck's walls, and these let in a little light and even less wind. Not that she needed to see, and she was getting resigned to breathing only tainted air. But it was a way to judge the hours of daylight left.

How far were they from Semorrah? How fast were they traveling? Would they drive straight through to the merchants' city or stop for the night somewhere along the road? There might be any number of small villages along the way, offering cheap inns and poor food, but Tamar doubted she had enough money in her pockets to pay for even the least expensive room. She would prefer driving straight through, or even camping out for the night.

Although, as usual, her desires were not to be consulted. When the driver did halt, about two hours after he'd picked her up, they took a quick break for an afternoon meal. Tamar found herself feeling oddly shaky and disoriented as she carefully climbed down. The driver stood with his back to her, shouting directions to the children. Beside him was a woman, most likely his wife, whom Tamar had not noticed before.

The woman smiled at her sympathetically. "I know just how you feel," she said. "It's so noisy in the back of the trucks, and say what they will, I'm convinced there's something in the fuel that swirls around in your head and makes you feel sick. If I've been on the road all day, riding in back like that, there are times I sit up and retch all night. Truly. But you'll feel better if you walk around a few minutes now."

"I'm fine," Tamar said faintly. "Why are we stopping?"

"Well, the boys get terribly wound up if we don't let them out every few hours," the woman said with a laugh. "And I had some personal needs to tend to. And I thought we might as well all have a snack. Are you hungry or is your stomach too queasy from the ride?"

Tamar thought about it a moment and was surprised to discover she had an appetite. "I could eat a bite," she said cautiously. "I have a little food with me—"

The woman waved her hand. "Oh, heavens, no, I've brought enough to feed half the merchants in Semorrah! It's a good sign that you're hungry. I don't think you'll suffer too much."

"And I don't want you to think I'm complaining," Tamar said earnestly. "It was so good of you to offer me a ride."

The woman smiled again. "Arthur loves to help people out. He was so poor growing up, you know, and as he tells it, so many people were doing him favors, giving him odd jobs so he could earn a little extra money, helping his father on the farm when his dad got sick—well, he says he could never pay back to others all the things people did for him. I always thought that was such a positive way to look at life, don't you think? Because most people are always complaining about how others have done them wrong. It's one of the things I like most about him."

I don't care about this. I don't know you people, Tamar wanted to say, but despite herself, she was a little intrigued by the story. To have met with so much kindness in your life that you felt you could never repay it; there was a new thought. Of course, she had had some experience in that area, for she had been taken in and cared for by people upon whom she had no claim at all. But their affection had bound her only to them; it had not opened her heart to the world at large.

Perhaps the fault was in her, and not in her mentors. She was too suspicious and unforgiving by nature to expect good from everyone around her. Or perhaps she was right and this Arthur was wrong, and someday he would offer succor to the wrong fellow and be murdered for his pains. Now there was a dour thought to nurse on a sunny day. She shook her head to clear out the melancholy.

"I'm Tamar," she said, just to have something to say. She rarely offered anyone her name first.

"Gena," the woman replied. "The boys are—well, I'll tell you their names, but I won't expect you to remember them!"

And indeed, Tamar forgot them as soon as Gena reeled them off, but she smiled politely and made sure to glance at each cheerful young face.

Then she helped Gena spread out a blanket on the grass and cover it with plates and cups and baskets of food. The boys came yelping up and plopped themselves on the checkered cloth; their father followed a bit more sedately. For a while everyone ate in virtual silence.

"So, Tamar, what's taking you to Semorrah?" Arthur asked after he learned his passenger's name.

"My cousin may have a job for me there," she said.

"And you came from where?"

"Stockton."

"All that way on foot!" Gena exclaimed. "You must be exhausted!"

"I had a ride partway. I don't mind walking."

"What kind of job?" Arthur wanted to know.

Tamar smiled. "Well, my cousin works at a hotel, and I said I'd take anything. I can cook, I can clean, I can even tend horses—and I understand they have a lot of horses in Semorrah, since they don't allow motor vehicles inside the city."

"It's good to know horses," Gena said approvingly. "Arthur thinks machines are the answer to everything, but my father always relied on horses and they served him well."

"Mark my words, another fifty years, you won't see a workhorse in the country," Arthur said. "Some people may still ride them for pleasure, but I say, it's not that much pleasure to ride a horse."

"Well, it's not exactly a pleasure to ride in your smelly old truck, either," Gena replied with a sniff.

He laughed. "No, but it's twice as fast! And ten times as strong and can carry a hundred times more. The days of the horse and the ox are over, I'm afraid."

"What hotel does your cousin work at?" Gena asked. "One of the big ones? They have such lovely hotels there—so fancy! For myself, I see no reason to waste good money just to stay in a pretty room twenty-five stories over the city, though I will say I like the view from some of those big public towers. But if all I'm going to do is lay my head down on a pillow and sleep, well, I'd rather save my money and settle in someplace a little less expensive. As long as it's *clean*. I will not abide a dirty room.''

"I don't exactly remember the name of the hotel," Tamar admitted. Actually, she was hoping for a little guidance from her hosts. "She said it was a nice place, not too fancy but the kind of place a woman would feel safe in if she was traveling alone or a man would feel free to make a business deal in. Only about fifty rooms, she said, but big enough to have its own taproom and stable. I think it was called the—"

"The Berman House?" Arthur interjected. "I've often thought about staying there, but I've always had such good luck with the Greystone that I've never bothered to change."

"The Berman House?" Tamar repeated. "That sounds— where is it located?"

"Oh, it's a few streets over from the River Walk. Still in the fashionable part of town, but not quite as pricey," Gena said. "It's Cathedral and Market streets, isn't it, Arthur?"

"Yes, exactly," he agreed.

"That's it!" Tamar exclaimed. "Cathedral and Market! I kept thinking she said Market and Church street, but then I thought, no, there isn't a *Church* Street in Semorrah."

"Not that I ever came across. Must be the Berman House, then. Good for you," Arthur said, beaming. "Not a bad place to work."

"So when will we get to Semorrah?" Tamar asked. "I'm not sure how far away we still are."

"Oh, not till tomorrow morning," Gena said. "We could drive lickety-split all day and make it there by tonight, but it would be dark, and of course we can't bring the truck into the city, so we'd have to find the warehouse on the east side and then still try to cross the bridge tonight and find our rooms, and frankly, it's just too much work. Better to arrive fresh in the morning and deal with all the details then."

Arthur was nodding. Tamar felt her heart sink; Gena did not seem like the kind of woman interested in camping out for the night. "And do you plan to stay somewhere along the road, or just sleep in the truck overnight?"

"Oh! My! The truck! No, no, there's a town not twenty miles from Semorrah. The cutest little inn you ever saw. We stay there every time we go to town. They always have room. I'm sure you won't have any trouble getting accommodations."

"No, I hope not," Tamar said, but of course she could not afford to pay for luxuries like a room for the night. Well, she'd talk to the proprietor, quietly, when she arrived. He might be willing to trade a few hours' labor in the kitchen for a pallet in the stables. That had worked for her in the past. She would see what arrangement she could make.

But then she had her second stroke of luck.

They had climbed back into the truck and taken off at what seemed a faster pace with increased volume. Or maybe the strain of the past few weeks was finally catching up with her. Tamar squirmed on her pallet, punching the jacket one more time to improve its possibilities as a pillow—and her hand encountered a crumpled wad somewhere inside the coat. Frowning, she sat up and dragged it across her lap, turning it inside out and looking for a way inside the lining. If it had been ripped open, it had been neatly sewn shut again; but that just made it more likely that something had been deliberately hidden inside. Documents, maybe; incriminating papers. Evan had been notorious for keeping maps and personal letters that most Jacobites had trained themselves to destroy. She found a weak hem and tugged. The threads gave way with a quick, silent spiral.

She stuck her hand inside the ragged tear and pulled out the balled-up papers. Not letters and maps, oh no. The indiscreet Evan had amassed a sizable sum of money, all new dollars of various denominations, currency good across the three provinces. She stared for a moment, hardly believing her eyes, and then quickly counted the bills. Not a fortune, not by any measure, but enough to see her to Semorrah and keep her from sleeping in any barns along the way.

Like Arthur, she was benefiting from the kindness of good friends and chance acquaintances. Maybe she could learn from this a lesson of generosity in return.

They made the inn before nightfall and were all assigned rooms. Tamar agreed to join her benefactors for dinner, although she would have preferred an hour of solitude; but they had been so nice to her that she hated to appear aloof. She ate quickly, pleaded a headache, and went straight up to her room. Even the muted clink and buzz from the taproom below her sounded like blissful silence after the ordeal all day in the truck. She washed up, climbed into bed, and was asleep in five minutes.

The next day, the ride did not seem quite so torturous, but that might have been because she knew it would be brief. And sure enough, before they had been on the road an hour, she felt their speed slow enough for her to make herself heard over the noise.

"Are we there already?" she asked one of the boys. "In Semorrah?"

"In Eastgate," he replied. "But there'll be a wait. There's always a lot of trucks lined up trying to get to the warehouses. This is the boring part."

And indeed, it took nearly another hour, moving at a crawling pace, to navigate the crowded roads into the industrial city that serviced Semorrah on this side of the Galilee River. Tamar thought she would go mad with the inactivity, though it was certainly a relief to have the noise and vibration cut down so dramatically. She was even reduced to playing cards with the boys, who taught her a simple gambling game. She promptly lost every hand. Feeling magnanimous and giddy, she gave them the copper coins she'd gotten in change from the innkeeper when she had paid for her room last night.

At last, the truck came to a wheezing halt—somewhere indoors, because the level of light had filtered down to almost nothing. The boys were instantly climbing down the outside of the truck, and Tamar was only seconds behind them. Arthur was in earnest conversation with someone who looked like a dock official, and they appeared to be discussing the quality and quantity of cargo in the truck. Tamar looked around to locate Gena.

"I think I'll be heading on now," she said as politely as she could. "All I have to do is find my way to the bridge and I'm in Semorrah, right? So I don't think I'll wait."

"Oh, I was hoping you—but I know you're in a hurry to see your cousin," Gena said. "Remember, we'll be at the Greystone for three days if you want us for anything."

"I think my cousin can get me everything I need," Tamar said.

"And maybe next time we come to town, we'll stay at the Berman House, and we can visit you," Gena said a little more happily. "That might not be for a few more months, but look for us, all right?"

Tamar could not imagine how, in less than twenty-four hours, this woman could have formed enough of an attachment to her to care if she ever saw Tamar again. "Certainly," she said. "Enjoy your visit to the city!"

And she finally escaped, quickly walking out of the warehouse and not once looking back. It was sunny outside, and this close to the river, everything had a haloed, misty appearance. Although even that asset did little to make Eastgate attractive. The district reminded Tamar of the grimiest parts of Breven, all blocky buildings, oily cobblestones, and noxiously fumed air. Trucks lurched down every street or rumbled at idle before every warehouse door. Men dashed from doorway to doorway or shouted orders down from unwashed windows. Everything was a productive, graceless bustle.

Tamar wove her way down the sidewalks and streets, aiming for the river edge of town. It was impossible to mistake her direction. From every point of Eastgate, she could see the two bridges that spanned the Galilee River—the broad, serviceable, unadorned bridge that carried the majority of traffic, and the slim, elegant bridge that was the city's most famous link to the Jordana coastline. It was to this second structure that Tamar made her way through the cluttered streets of Eastgate. White, lacy, and spider-thin, it was the first thing of true beauty that the traveler to Semorrah encountered, and it was impressive indeed.

She remembered this bridge. She had been here once with Conran and two others, maybe ten years ago. She couldn't remember why; she thought Conran had had some contact in the city he had wanted to meet with, and he had brought the others as camouflage. Yes, Elinor and Dawn had traveled with him, posing as his wife and sister; Tamar had been his daughter, and they were a farming family in town for a holiday. Conran had never said much about the actual meeting with his friend, but in their free time, they had done a lot of sightseeing. It had been fun.

But instructive, of course. Conran had made several points about the idleness of the rich and the contrast between the wealthy and the poor, and he had shown them the abandoned slave markets where, centuries before, Jansai had sold their captured Edori. She had always suspected that Conran was part Edori, for he knew every detail of the tribe's history and often made references to Edori values or lifestyles. She had never had the nerve to ask outright.

So she had a collection of visual memories in her head, of
the fabulous bridge, of the delicate, marvelous, impossible architecture that made the whole city one extended fairy-tale castle. And now, as she crossed into Semorrah, the memories came
clearer, snapped into sharper focus. She paused as she reached
the center point of the bridge so she could gaze down at the
water foaming below her, and then look up at the milk-white
spires and dainty towers of the city itself. She knew it was an
evil place, everyone said so; but certainly it was magnificent.

She spent her first hour in Semorrah merely wandering
around. She paused at a street vendor's to buy a meat pie and
ate it as she walked. Not only the city, but the people in it
seemed steeped in a gorgeous opulence; their clothes, their
scents, their conversation seemed rich with useless but beautiful
adornments. She had been feeling fairly unkempt before; now
she felt positively filthy.

Although she had cleaned herself thoroughly back at the little
inn, she found the public baths and paid the fee to spend an
hour in a private room. If she was going to get a job at a fairly
high-class establishment, she needed to look a little less like an
urchin. Once she had washed herself vigorously, she checked
herself in the mirror. The brown coloring was fading from her
spiky hair, leaving it streaked with gold, but she decided that
wasn't particularly bad. She could dye it again before she left
Semorrah. Her face looked weary and pinched, and her clothes
were definitely motley. Those details she would have to attend
to.

So she shopped the street bazaars till she found a stall of
cheap but fashionable clothes, and she bought an embroidered
emerald dress that made her eyes look painted on by a wide
brush. She also bought a handful of inexpensive cosmetics and
applied them as she stood before the mirror in the vendor's
booth. She didn't know how it was she had acquired this skill,
but she had always been good at making herself up, enhancing
the features she wanted to emphasize, downplaying the others.

"Well, now, you don't look half so much the starved rat you
did as you walked in," the vendor said approvingly when Tamar
turned away from his mirror. She supposed that was a compli-
ment. "My wife can do the same thing. Look like death one
moment, take a little rouge and mascara, and look like an angel

of mercy the next minute. I admire a woman who knows her assets, that I do."

Tamar practiced a smile on him. "Would you hire me?" she asked.

"If I had need for a worker, I would," he said promptly.

She nodded. "Good. Thanks for the mirror." And she left.

She'd already walked past the Berman House once, just to make sure it was the kind of place she had described to Arthur and his wife. But from the outside, it looked perfect: respectable, a little old-fashioned, in good repair. Not the kind of place to attract wild young men out for a good time, or the haughtiest of clientele always looking for fault with the hotel staff. Or Jansai. Or angels.

Now she returned to the Berman House and made her way to the back. The man who answered her knock was older, stately, uniformed, and authoritative; she knew at once he was the steward who oversaw the whole staff.

"I'm looking for work," she said. "Are you hiring?"

He examined her for a moment in silence, and she endured the scrutiny without flinching. She had worked at enough big establishments, encountered enough housekeepers and butlers like this man to know they prized their talent at judging human nature above almost everything else. A fidgety woman looked untrustworthy. A slouching woman looked slovenly. A young girl looked flirtatious. An old woman looked weary. It was best to be neutral, indeterminate, and serene.

"We have a few positions available," he said at last. "What are your skills?"

He didn't look like he would favor a jack-of-all-trades, so she skipped all mention of horses and detailed her experience in the kitchen and bedchambers. She mentioned a few of the places in Luminaux where she had held jobs, giving the names of the people she had worked under; he nodded twice, which was a good sign.

"Can you serve?" he asked when she was done. "Wait tables?"

"I haven't done it often," she said promptly. "Only at taverns, where there was not much need for formality. But I didn't spill anything and I didn't mix up my orders."

It was the right answer; it showed a willingness to work but didn't claim skills above her ability. He nodded again.

"We have housing available to the employees who wish it," he said next. "It is not required that you stay there, but it is preferred, so that you can be instantly called upon if there is a need. Would this suit you, or would you be looking for other lodgings?"

It would, in fact, be perfect. She had only worked one other place that offered this arrangement, and she hadn't dared hope the Berman House would provide the same amenities. "I'd like to see the room," she said, so she didn't sound too eager.

That pleased him, too; she had a little discrimination. "Certainly," he said. "When would you be willing to start?"

"Tonight, if you need me," she said. "Later in the week if that is more convenient for you."

"Tomorrow morning," he said. "You may move in tonight, if you wish. Let me show you the room."

And as easily as that, she found employment in Semorrah.

The next month was as close to contentment as Tamar had come in a long time. Until this year she had enjoyed her life in Luminaux, but the last few months had been so marked with terror and grief that she had forgotten what those easier days were like. The trip to Breven and back—the horror in Ileah—all had been brutal, bloody, awful episodes. She felt like she had been running, hiding, and fending off fear for so long that she might never remember how to unclench her stomach and relax again.

But life in Semorrah, life at the Berman House, was easy, easy, easy. Oh, certainly, she worked hard every day, and the hours were long, and the physical demands were severe. Jasper, the steward, saw to it that she was trained in every aspect of cooking and serving, so every day she was lifting heavy pots, stirring thick stews, carrying laden trays into the dining area. He also came to quickly trust her to go to market, so he sent her every other day to purchase potatoes, vegetables, spices, fruit, bread, and other staples. (He himself oversaw the selection of wines, while only the head cook was permitted to buy meat.) She loved the responsibility, loved the diversity of duty; she had never minded menial work, and she liked to stay busy. She knew that he liked her, and it pleased her more than she had thought possible. She had not realized that anyone's good opinion mattered to her, especially the good opinion of someone she doubted she would know more than a few months.

Then again, perhaps she would stay in Semorrah forever. She could not return to Ileah, she was afraid to return to Luminaux, and she had no idea where to look for the rest of the scattered Jacobites. They must be somewhere, and someday she *would* seek them out again. But for now, Semorrah would take her in, give her shelter, peace, and purpose. For now, Semorrah was a haven.

On her free afternoons, she strolled through the city. It offered any number of diversions. She most often went to the concert halls and live theater productions (there were cheap seats in the back, good enough for her) and watched and listened in amazement. There were three art museums in the city and one historical museum, and she wandered through each of these slowly, gazing intently at every painting and sculpture, reading every word of each descriptive card. She went once to the science museum, but it confused her, all the electrical wires and generators and demonstrations of light, sound, and motion. She preferred the gentler contributions of humankind.

She also found the book fairs and the student exchanges where books on almost any topic could be purchased for pennies. She could have borrowed books for free at any of the city's four libraries, but she did not want to put down her name and address on any application and so leave behind a record of her existence. But she did make herself go back to the main branch, at least one day a week, and ask for admittance to the old manuscripts room. Here, in carefully controlled cases, were a few of the documents left behind by the original settlers, composed in the old language that had died out six centuries ago. No one could read it anymore, except the oracles, a few learned angels, some of the engineers who studied the ancient texts—and the odd, natural linguist like Tamar.

One of her schoolteachers in Luminaux had discovered Tamar's aptitude for language and mentioned it to Conran, who had thereafter insisted she spend an hour a day learning the settlers' difficult, archaic phrases. She had hated it, aptitude or no, but she had learned it to please Conran. It had been five years or more since she had had a chance to look at any of those old texts, and every now and then she had wondered if she had forgotten the language. But here in Semorrah, as she puzzled over the words of the first Samarian visitors, she was reassured. She remembered enough of the language to understand their references to weather, plague, and planting; and so all Conran's insistence had not been in vain.

Though she still could not understand what value such a skill could have.

Although she went to the Semorran library every week, she much preferred the hours she spent reading other material— mostly badly written novels about unlikely lovers. Tamar had never had much time for reading in the past, though Conran was a great book lover and sometimes would entertain them all for hours by reading out loud from his favorite authors. Now she found entertainment and company in the historical romances he would have despised.

She herself was a little horrified to learn that her taste was so low; she could not stop herself from reading an entire series of love stories built around mortal women who had won the affections of angels. There was something so fantastical, so unreal, about the events depicted in these novels, that they took her completely away from her own dull, circumscribed life. And there was so much detail about daily life in the angel holds, an existence which heretofore she had not wasted a minute trying to imagine. After she had read the first six or so, she was sure she could behave with the correct etiquette at a dinner party at the Eyrie or sing the angelica's part at the next Gloria.

One day, as she sat reading in the small garden behind the Berman House during her break, she was accosted by a young girl named Jenny who worked beside her in the kitchen. She didn't think to close the book and hide the cover in time, and Jenny exclaimed aloud at the title.

"Oh, that's my favorite! *Susannah the Stolen*. It's so romantic! And it's based on a true story, you know, which most of them aren't. But I have to say, I never thought *you* were the type to read books like this."

Tamar liked Jenny. She was a farmer's daughter who had come to the city to escape the advances of a neighbor boy and "learn more about the world at large." She was buxom, brunette, worldly, but unspoiled, and Jasper was training her to become assistant to the housekeeper. At times Tamar thought Jasper had a secret desire for the lively Jenny, though she doubted he would ever indulge it since she was at least thirty years his junior and he seemed far too proper. Still, it had crossed her mind that the match might be good for both of them.

Clearly, she was reading too many romances. In the past, such a thought would never have popped into her head.

"I never knew I was the type to read them, either," Tamar said a little ruefully. "But I really, really like them."

"Have you read *Edori Angelica*? That's about Gabriel and Rachel, and it's so good. Maybe that's my favorite. That or *Susannah the Stolen*."

"*Edori Angelica*? No, I'll have to look for it."

"I've got a copy, I'll lend it to you. But I know once you read it, you'll want a copy for yourself."

They talked books awhile longer, then regretfully came to their feet; time to return to work. At the door, Tamar impulsively turned to Jenny and said, "I have the day off tomorrow. If you're not scheduled, maybe we can go into town together and shop. Or go to a concert. Or something."

"Oh, that would be great! I need a new blouse, I spilled gravy all over my good pink one, and I just *can't* get it clean. I have to work the evening shift, though, so we'd have to be back early."

"Fine with me," Tamar said, smiling. "Let's do it."

And it was amazing how such small things—a conversation in the garden, a plan for entertainment the following day, an assignation with a friend—could make the pleasant world that much more enjoyable. Tamar felt herself smiling all evening as she worked, caught herself humming that night as she went to bed. Anticipatory elation. For such a small joy . . .

But the next day, she and Jenny laughed their way through the bazaar, bought more clothes than either one had intended, ate more rich foods than was good for them, and generally had a splendid day. When Jenny returned to the Berman House, Tamar accompanied her, too tired to stay out the rest of the evening on her own. Instead, she lay for hours in her bedroom, reading *Edori Angelica* and dreaming over the stern, sculpted beauty of the Archangel Gabriel.

Over the next couple of weeks the friendship between the two young women prospered. As it turned out, there were many things Jenny knew that Tamar did not: how to flirt with strange men in public cafés, how to identify rich men over poor ones, who the most prominent merchants of the city were, and the names of their wives and children. When they stood on the more well-traveled street corners of Semorrah, Jenny would point them out to her and name them off; she even knew the names of visiting Manadavvi and a few of the Luminaux celebrities who came to town. It did not occur to her that she would ever meet and mingle with these people. She was merely fascinated by their wealth and their air of royalty.

"Though I *will* go to the Gloria someday," she told Tamar one evening as they worked in the kitchen preparing to serve the evening meal. "Anybody can go, you know, and *everybody* who matters is there. Bael and Mariah, Omar, Jared, Mercy—all the great angels, and then of course Christian Avalone and Ben Harth and all the Manadavvi—"

It had given Tamar a start to hear Jared's name drop so casually from Jenny's lips; it made him seem real, substantial, alive, and that made him seem dangerous. But she could not bring herself to ask about him, could not admit she had met him. How could she ever explain those circumstances in Ileah? Best to forget the meeting ever happened.

And yet, not ten minutes later, he was to seem even more alive and more dangerous than ever.

Jasper had come into the kitchen, a rare event, and gravely watched them a moment to make sure they were hard at work. "We have angelic guests tonight," he said finally. "They must be served with particular dispatch and courtesy. Which of you wishes to wait on them?"

"Oh, me, me, please, me," Jenny said instantly, then quickly gave Tamar a guilty look. "I'm sorry, of course if you want to, you can take the tray out. It's just—"

Tamar smiled and shook her head. "Please. You. The thought of serving angels terrifies me."

Jasper nodded. "You must take great care to step around their wings, as their feathers will trail on the floor by their chairs," he said. "On no account brush up against their wings, for they hate their feathers to be touched. Other than that, treat them with the same degree of civility you would give any guest."

Jenny was almost dancing in place. "I will—I know—I won't touch anybody," she promised. "Oh, this is so exciting! Tamar, is my hair in place? Are my eyes smudged?"

"And try to behave with dignity and calm," Jasper added.

Jenny nodded, her attention on Tamar. Tamar reached out to pat some of the brown curls in place, but really, there was no fault to be found in Jenny's bright eyes or eager smile. "You look perfect," she said.

They loaded up the tray and Tamar helped her through the door, then turned back toward the kitchen. But curiosity made her pivot again and slip into the hallway that led to the dining room. If she was careful, if they were sitting at just the right table, she could get a glimpse of these majestic visitors and still remain in shadow herself.

Yes, there they were, at the best table at the far end of the room, closest to the fire. The first person she recognized was Christian Avalone, who sat facing her, though he was looking at one of his companions. The angels sat in profile to her, a man and a woman; Jenny was bending over the man, so she did not immediately see his face, but the woman looked kindly and amused. Not the expression Tamar would have expected on any angel's face. Her wings were small enough to imply that she was short, and they were flecked with spots of amber, beige, and copper. She looked, Tamar thought, well-worn and comfortable, and at the moment she was smiling broadly.

And then Jenny stepped back and Tamar was staring at the angel Jared. Who appeared engrossed in conversation with his host and not interested in inspecting the shadows for lurking Jacobites. Nonetheless, her heart had immediately exploded inside her rib cage; her throat closed down in astonishment. She backed quietly into the hallway till she was invisible from the dining room, and then ran into the kitchen. And there she stood, gulping for air and trying to think, till Jenny burst into the room.

"It's Jared! Did you see?" Jenny exclaimed, practically throwing her tray to the counter and waltzing around the stone floor. The cooks working over the steaming stove looked over in astonishment at her antics. "He's the most handsome of all the angels, and so polite! He thanked me every time I laid a piece of silverware on the table. His eyes are as gray as storm clouds. He's wearing his emerald bracelets, the ones he always has on in formal pictures. I can't wait to take out the second course."

He had not seen her, of course; he had not come here looking for her. There was no need to panic, no need to run. "Who is with him?" Tamar managed to ask, amazed that her voice sounded so steady.

"Well, Christian Avalone, of course. And the angel Mercy,

who leads the host at Cedar Hills. She's really the nicest angel of them all, so everyone says, and she comes to Semorrah all the time. She and Christian Avalone are great friends.''

"I'm glad you're enjoying this so much," Tamar said, now producing a smile. Her heart was slowing; she was feeling a little calmer. He had not seen her.

"Well, but I feel guilty. Do you want to take out the salads?"

"Oh, no! Angels make me nervous. I'd be sure to step on their feathers or drop the spoons in their laps. You do it, and then tell me everything they say."

They seemed to stay at the inn forever, Christian and his divine guests, debating the god knew what policy or trade agreement. It was exquisite torture to Tamar to have the angel so close, to feel so at risk, for such an extended period of time. Yet she knew she was safe. He was unaware of her existence. He would be gone in a few hours, and then all would be well again.

The angels left the inn without encountering the Jacobite, but the incident left Tamar deeply shaken. It had been stupid to think she was safe in Semorrah. It was one of the great cities of Samaria; at any point it could be filled with visiting angels or touring Jansai. Perhaps there was no reason to think they would recognize her—even if Zeke had been captured and forced to betray his friends, how would they know her face? But if she was filled with this much fear every time she saw a pair of arching wings, she would be in for a miserable existence in the river city.

Accordingly, and with great reluctance, she made plans to leave. She found herself unwilling to walk off in the middle of the night, leaving Jasper and Jenny to wonder at her whereabouts, so she wrote herself a letter and mailed it one afternoon when she was running errands. Jasper himself brought it to her when it arrived at the Berman House the following day. He looked, even for Jasper, unwontedly serious.

"I hope it is not bad news," he said.

Of course it was. She opened it and read it in the kitchen, right in front of them, and felt her face grow pale. "My sister has taken ill," she said. "They don't know if she—and she has three babies, and there's no one to take care of them—"

"Oh, Tamar, do you have to go?" Jenny wailed, but Jasper silenced her with a look.

"I must. As soon as I can, I think," Tamar said. She put her hands to the bow at her back that held her apron in place, as if she would strip it off now and flee from the house. Then she dropped her arms, took a quick, indecisive pace around the kitchen, and came to an abrupt halt. "I must check the bus schedules. Maybe I can leave in the morning." She gave Jasper a pleading glance. "That is—if it's all right that I leave so soon. I know this isn't much notice—"

"Do what you must," he said, in such a kindly voice that she felt even more wretched for leaving. But she had to. She had no choice.

That night, as she packed her sparse belongings, Jenny came to the door and asked mournfully what she could do to help. Tamar was edgy and weary and just wanted to sleep, but she was touched by Jenny's obvious sadness and did not have the heart to send her from the room. They stayed up most of the night talking.

Therefore, when Tamar left the Berman House early the next day, she was exhausted and a little depressed. She took a ferry to Westgate on the Bethel side of the river, because she had decided to explore that province; she wanted to be as far from Breven as possible. Westgate, almost a mirror image of its sister city, offered few amenities but Tamar wanted only one: a bus station. She found it quickly enough, and spent a few minutes studying the roster of schedules.

Not that it helped her; she knew very little about Bethel, and none of the destinations sounded familiar. She wanted a town that was small and sleepy, a place where angels were unlikely to drop by and news of the world was infrequently reported. The town of Shepherd's Pass sounded promising, and when she checked its location on a nearby map, it seemed perfectly suited to her needs. It was situated in the heart of the province's rich farmland and appeared to be miles from any major crossroads. She would buy a ticket to Shepherd's Pass.

During the two-day bus trip, she mostly slept, although she did read one of the books Jenny had insisted she take. It did not hold her interest as much as she had hoped; perhaps she had outlived the brief phase of her life when she could read for mindless pleasure. When she could neither sleep nor read, she stared out the window at the gentle green countryside and tried not to brood too blackly.

Shepherd's Pass was everything she'd hoped for, half a dozen intersecting streets lined with the requisite grocers, bankers, and general stores. There appeared to be two hotels, and she chose the least prosperous-looking one. She had saved most of the money she'd earned, but she was by no means rich; a few weeks of idleness would see her bankrupt. She must spend wisely, and find work again immediately.

Therefore, the next morning she made the rounds of the shops, looking for employment. To her dismay, she found that there wasn't much need for labor in Shepherd's Pass, not even at the stables where she could almost always count on a job.

"But they're hiring at Isabella Cartera's spread, so I heard," a groom told her.

"Hiring for what? Who's Isabella Cartera?"

"She owns the biggest farm holding in Bethel. Inherited it from her husband, but she's done a fine job of running it. Must be a hundred people working there, house and fields, but they're always looking for more hands."

"I've never farmed," she said. "Do they use machines?"

He nodded. "To plant and harvest. Big and scary. Give me a horse any day. But she's got stables, if you truly want to work with horses, and the house is huge. They must need cooks and chambermaids. I'd go out to Cartabella and give it a try."

He rented her a horse and gave her directions, and she rode out to Cartabella that afternoon. He was right; the place was monstrous. The house itself was palatial and gracious, but most of the other buildings looked industrial, efficient, and impersonal. She counted two dozen barns, stables, milking sheds, warehouses, and other unidentified structures before she gave up.

And one woman owned all this. Wealth, indeed.

She rode straight to the section of property where the livestock appeared to be quartered, then dismounted and tied her horse to a convenient fence. She had decided that, this time around, she would avoid the kitchens and the living areas where there would be the greatest concentration of people. If there was work in the stables, that was what she would take. Animals were less likely to recognize or betray her; and she would not feel any rush of sadness if she suddenly had to leave them behind.

The first person she saw was a young man, a boy, really, who said sure he could direct her to the head ostler and that wasn't much of a horse she was riding, was it? No, she agreed, it had been rented, but it had gotten her here in one piece and that was all she asked of it. He had his own horse, he confided, a two-year-old gray mare, though he didn't have much time to ride. Still, he was allowed to stable her here for free, so he could visit her every day and bring her an apple from the dinner table.

Tamar cared very little about his joys and grievances.

"The head ostler?" she reminded him gently, and he led her into the maze of corrals and stables that had to cover a full square mile of property. The head groom was deep in conversation with another man, but ended that conversation soon enough and came over to inquire civilly about Tamar's business. He looked only slightly taken aback when she said she was looking for work (some men, she had found, were reluctant to hire women for the stables) but admitted that he could always use another pair of hands.

"You'll have to give me a demonstration," he said. "Saddle and unsaddle, hitch and unhitch, show me you can ride, pour a measure of grain, show me how you'd wrap a sprain. Don't mean to doubt you, but there's plenty say they know horses that don't know horses."

She wasn't offended in the least. She was always glad to have a chance to prove herself, because she knew she was good enough to win over anyone but a confirmed misogynist. And, despite her intentions of maintaining her distance from her next employer, she could not help liking him. He was a bluff, weathered, middle-aged man who seemed both powerful and at ease. Then again, she had liked most the people she had met who worked with horses.

"Tell me what you want done," she said.

He put her through her paces with three separate horses, one a skittish filly who seemed to resent any handling at all, and nodded wordlessly each time she finished a task. She knew she was doing well; she felt confident and in control. So she was not surprised, though pleased and grateful, when he shepherded her out of the stables and offered her his hand.

"I'm Gene," he said. "I'll be your boss. Can you start today or will you need a few days to get settled?"

"I've got to return my horse to Shepherd's Pass," she said. "I can be back in the morning."

"Good enough."

"I take it there's a bunk here for me?"

"Dorm," he said. "Small room, but all to yourself. Food's good. Not much entertainment."

She smiled. "I don't require much."

"People in trouble rarely do."

Her smile faded and she gave him a swift, arrested look. He shrugged. "Not my concern," he said. "You do your work, that's all I want. I'll go tell Isabella you're on the payroll."

She nodded and turned away without another word. But during the whole ride back to the city, and during much of the night while she lay awake in her hotel room, she wondered. Was that why Jasper had been so kind to her—and Arthur and Gena, and even Jenny? Had it been so obvious, so stark on her face, that she was running from terror or persecution? She had thought she was solitary and self-sufficient, hiding her troubles and relying on no one but herself, and all along, people had been extending their helping hands. She was not sure she would be willing to take in a fugitive, offer her a job, and ask no questions. Why had these people been so ready to give her a chance?

The speculation, which should have comforted her, made her shiver instead. She did not want to rely on the goodness of strangers; that would lessen her own strength, dull her wits, lull her to security. She was not safe here, would be safe nowhere that she could imagine, even once she was with the Jacobites again. It would not do to let down her guard. She would take this job, because she needed it, but she would not stay for long.

CHAPTER ELEVEN

Spring in Bethel was lovelier than spring in Gaza, because it came sooner and more rapturously. In Gaza, the landscape altered overnight, it seemed, from winter brown to summer green, without the exotic riot of flowers that changed the Bethel terrain to a pastel candyland during this most playful of seasons.

Still, Jared would have preferred being anywhere in Bethel but the Eyrie. And even the Eyrie wouldn't have been so bad if he hadn't had to spend his time there with Bael and Mariah.

It was entirely his fault, of course, since he had come here of his own free will, but he had not expected to be stuck for three days or more. Mariah had practically greeted him with the news that they were planning a dinner party that he simply *must* stay for, and while he was here he could renew his friendship with Annalee Stephalo, surely he remembered her? He almost felt as if Mariah had been lying in wait for him anytime these past three months, plotting how she could enmesh him in her social schemes and force him to make an extended visit. He had not thought quickly enough to manufacture an important engagement back home, so he agreed to stay till the party, and then cursed himself roundly every hour for the next seventy-two.

It was not that the Eyrie was a bad place. On the contrary, it was quite the most beautiful of the angel holds, and the one gorged with the most history. Built atop the steep Velo range, it was carved from the glowing rosy stone of the Velo Mountains and therefore possessed a warm, eerie incandescence even in the deepest tunnel. It was a labyrinth of levels and corridors that only the residents were required to navigate; the main public area was a broad plateau that anyone could reach by climbing a massive, serried stairway cut from the mountain itself. This stairway was lined with shops and vendors' booths and was always crowded with noisy, excited visitors, and Jared found it a little tedious anytime he had to use it. Mostly, of course, he just used the public landing spot at the top of the compound and made his way inside from there.

The most distinctive feature of the Eyrie was its constant music. At all hours of the night and day, rotating shifts of singers gathered in a small chamber in the uppermost reaches of the hold and offered harmonious prayers to the god. The singing could be heard from any point in the Eyrie, and it could, Jared knew from experience, calm a man in a rage or cheer an angel in despair.

Although, on this trip, not even music was enough to improve his spirits.

Truth to tell, he had been in a fairly black mood when he arrived here, though such a humor was alien to one usually so sunny-tempered. He could not believe he had lost the Jacobite woman. He had not been entirely surprised to find her missing from Ileah when he returned from Stockton, but he couldn't imagine how she had escaped him so completely. She could not have gotten far on foot, and he had scoured the area nearby, looking for likely hiding places: cliffs hanging over the river, dense stands of trees. But he could not locate her. It seemed likely someone had picked her up as she hurried along the road, but he could hardly stop all the trucks and transports traveling the routes fanning out from Ileah. And he had no idea in which direction she might have run.

So he had left Ileah in a pretty foul temper indeed—although he wasn't sure why he should be so angry. It was not as if she had been at all cooperative. It was not as if she had supplied him with any good ideas for continuing his search. Still, she was a Jacobite and he had thought he could make use of her, and now she had disappeared. And he wasn't entirely certain where he should next turn his efforts at finding the Alleluia Files.

So he had come to the Eyrie, not because he really expected to find the files there, but because he had promised himself he would search all the possible hiding places. He had expected to stay half a day, maybe overnight if courtesy demanded it; he had not expected to be roped into Mariah's entertainment plans.

"Once a year, we plan a dinner for the, shall we say, upper

echelon of Bethel society," she told him. "As the highest tax-payers in the province, it's only fair that they get some recognition for the wealth they have poured into the Eyrie's coffers. And of course there is no higher honor than being invited to sit at a table among angels as among equals."

Jared thought perhaps some mortals would be less impressed by that equation than others, but he preserved his silence. Despite the fact that she had been married to Bael for nearly thirty years and lived at the Eyrie most of her adult life, Mariah still seemed to possess the sort of blind hero worship for angels that Jared expected to find only in the very young and the very unsophisticated. In his experience, angels had at least the same number of flaws and vices as the average mean-spirited mortal, and Bael could probably multiply that figure by a factor of one hundred. But still, Mariah seemed besotted; and that was probably just as well for her. Better to adore your husband than to despise him.

Bael had greeted the news of Jared's extended visit with hearty approval. "Always glad to see you here, my boy, always a pleasure to talk with you!" he declared in his booming voice. "And how were things in Monteverde when you left? All well, I trust?"

It seemed like years since he had left Monteverde. "All well," Jared replied pleasantly. "It is colder there than it is here, of course."

"Ah, but spring will not lag long, even in northern Gaza," Bael said. As always, the very tenor of his voice made everything seem like a divine pronouncement; Jared half expected his command to make the flowers open a month sooner and the ground to amaze itself with greenery. "But you are welcome to enjoy our spring while you are here. We must find other ways to entertain you as well."

"I thought I'd take a look around your archives, if you didn't mind," Jared said boldly. He'd had a moment to give this some thought; he believed he could pull it off without arousing suspicion. "One of Ben Harth's daughters was at Monteverde a few weeks back, doing research for some school paper. Some history class. She was asking about the Archangel Delilah, about whom I found myself surprisingly ignorant. I know that she ruled from the Eyrie, and that there was some short interruption of her tenure, but I couldn't tell her the whole story. I thought you might have some biographies of her here?''

"Yes, we do, I'm sure we must," Bael said. "The archives would be the place to look. Make yourself free of them. Myself, I've never been able to locate a single thing I wanted there. The place has not been organized as well as it could have been. But look all you want."

So that was dangerous ground lightly skated over; he had not even mentioned Alleluia's name. He spent some time that afternoon poking through the bookshelves and boxes of the archives, but it wasn't like his hopes were high. As Bael had said, the place was so badly organized that it scarcely had any logic at all. He would be lucky to find a couple of volumes about the flamboyant and much-beloved Delilah, let alone any information about the reclusive Alleluia of the brief period of glory.

In fact, he did find two histories on Delilah, both of which devoted entire chapters to the temporary Archangel, but did not heap her with praise.

"During Alleluia's reign," said one, "the storms and the tempests grew in frequency and fury. While it was true that Alleluia herself was able to fly to any site and calm the storm, no matter how violent, she was not able to successfully mobilize the other angels, which was perceived as a distinct failing on her part. Not until Delilah regained her ability to fly and was once again on the seat of power did the storms abate and the god again choose to listen to the voices of all the angels."

Well, that didn't make it sound as if Alleluia had transported herself to the deck of the spaceship *Jehovah* and conversed with the machine who controlled the weather and the fate of Samaria.

Jared laid the biographies aside and continued to search through the mayhem, but since he had no idea what he was looking for, his search was hardly systematic. Merely, he picked up books, glanced through them, put them down, opened cartons, poked inside, shut them again. He was looking for anything that looked like it might hold sound. In his experience, recordings were always put on small silver disks or larger black disks that could be inserted in specialized machines; but in Alleluia's day, perhaps, other mediums had existed. Still, a random search through the cabinets and cupboards of the archives yielded nothing promising. And he had not thought it would.

Sighing with frustration, Jared swept his wings behind him and sat on the dusty stone floor. If he had been the Archangel

Alleluia, possessed of a dangerous but important secret, where would he have hidden evidence? If he had been married to an engineer of some genius, he thought he might have recorded his memoir on some highly customized equipment and kept it close to his side. After her brief stint as Archangel, Alleluia had been the oracle at Mount Sinai for nearly forty years (according to this unsympathetic chapter on her life, which also noted that such a quiet, regulated existence had seemed more suited to her temperament and her talents than a great role in the public eye). True, the oracles, like the angels, received a steady stream of visitors looking to offer petitions to the god; but the oracles' retreats were much more inaccessible and sternly guarded than the angel holds. And the Augustine school had been built at the very foot of Mount Sinai, so Caleb Augustus's equipment would have been easily available to her. And she would have felt safe there; the oracles' retreats were famous for creating auras of shelter and haven. All in all, it seemed like a good bet for a hiding place. Sometime in the next few weeks he must go to Mount Sinai.

He had barely reached this conclusion when he heard delicate footsteps cross the stone floor and a sweet, hesitant voice call out his name. "Jared? Are you in here? Jared?"

He came to his feet just as Annalee Stephalo drifted into his line of vision. She was a small, frail blond girl, who dressed always in diaphanous pinks and melons and wore her hair in a wild cloud of curls. She had the tiniest hands and the biggest eyes Jared had ever seen. Her father owned a mining concern in southwestern Bethel, and she had been living at the Eyrie for more than a year.

Jared couldn't stand her.

"Oh! There you are!" she said in her breathy voice as she rounded the corner and saw him waiting there. "My! In these shadows you look so tall."

"Are you looking for me, Annalee?" he said coolly. A stupid question since she obviously was.

"Yes, it's nearly time for dinner and Mariah thought you might need to be reminded," she said. She was looking around the room with a small frown on her dainty face, as if trying to comprehend where she was. "There are certainly a lot of books here, aren't there?" she said at last.

"Indeed, there are. History books, mostly. Accounts of the

hold. Tales of past angels and Archangels. Are you interested in history?'' he added maliciously.

"Oh, no! Reading gives me a headache.'' She paused for a moment, her eyes trained on the floor, then lifted her face to give him a single, soulful look. It was a trick she repeated often, and it was generally effective; her eyes were so enormous and so blue that every time you saw them again, full force, you were shocked at their depth and brilliance. Even if you didn't like her. "I'm sure you're a great reader, Jared. You're so clever.''

"Well, not clever enough to make heads nor tails out of half the stuff in here,'' he said briskly. He bent over to retrieve the two books on Delilah (even though no one at Monteverde really wanted to read them, he may as well pretend so, and take them back).

"You didn't find what you were looking for?''

"Not exactly. How soon is dinner? Do I have time to clean myself up beforehand? I'm a little dirty.''

Unexpectedly, for she was generally a demure girl, she came a few steps closer. "I don't think so. Here, let me dust you off a little.''

And she proceeded to brush her hands lightly across the front of his shirt, down the smooth hips of his leather pants, and across the very tips of his wings. Despite himself, as her soft fingers touched his feathers, he felt himself shiver and almost flinch away. He was astonished. Angels hated to be fondled, could not abide any except the most intimate touch on their sensitive wings. More than one mortal had discovered this to his rue as an angel had reacted violently to some invasive contact. Annalee had grown up among angels—she knew this—and yet here she was, intently stroking the edge feathers of his wings with a slower and more deliberate motion. Each fingertip left a trail of fire; his whole body leaped with unwilling response. She touched a finger to her tongue and reached for him again as if to smooth down a wayward quill.

Jared took a deep breath and stepped backward, out of reach. "I think not,'' he said.

Again, she gave him that upswept look, a world of heavy meaning in her eyes. "I think I've improved you as best I can.''

Jared tilted his head back, eyeing her haughtily, but she gave him no time to reply. "We must hurry,'' she said in her breathless voice, and turned for the door. "I believe Mariah is waiting."

And so he followed her from the room into the tunnels of the Eyrie, and wondered if he had misread the whole incident. Had she meant something by it or not? She seemed too childlike to be attempting to seduce him (and she had certainly chosen a bad time for it if they were expected at dinner in five minutes), but no mortal familiar with angels *ever* initiated such casual contact.

Unless she meant something by it. And there was no reason to think Annalee Stephalo wasn't on the lookout for a liaison with a well-known and potentially powerful angel. Her father had planted her here in the Eyrie, after all, a place where ambitious parents often sent their daughters for extended visits. Even if these girls did not succeed in marrying an angel, it was no disgrace to take an angel for a lover, especially if the union produced an angel child. Such good fortune could settle a young girl for life, for she and her child then became the responsibility of the hold; and the honor of being an angel's mother was one that profited her entire family.

Still, Richard Stephalo had position and wealth enough of his own; he didn't need angel grandchildren to secure his status in life.

And perhaps she had only been trying to be helpful, making him look presentable for Mariah's little dinner. He was too suspicious, he disliked too many people; and he was too irritable at being stuck here in the Eyrie. He should not be attributing manipulative motives to a simple act of kindness. He sighed again, silently, and caught up with Annalee as she preceded him down the hall.

Dinner was formal but not as much of an ordeal as Jared had anticipated (*that* would come in two nights, when all the landowners of Bethel were gathered for their annual banquet). As ranking guest of honor, he was seated by Mariah, but she spent most of her time talking to the young man on her left. Jared was too far from Bael to be forced to converse with the Archangel, but of course it was impossible to miss any word uttered in those silver, gorgeous tones. Jared tried not to listen, but he took in some impression of the conversation—something about wheat tariffs and land taxes. He'd had the same discussions himself over dinner at Monteverde. He sighed again, and signaled the servant for another glass of wine.

Two more tedious days to go. He did not see how he could possibly bear it.

He escaped into Velora the next morning before anyone could find him. Velora was the small town situated at the bottom of the Velo Mountain; it had served the Eyrie since the hold was founded. The grand stairway, that conduit of commerce, connected the hold with this bustling, merry little city, but Velora was much to be preferred as a place to do business or enjoy an afternoon's shopping. Jared spent most of the day sitting at outdoor tables of sidewalk cafés, thumbing through his histories of Delilah, and wishing he had better reading material. He did walk through the bazaars, just for something to do, and bought a handful of shirts and gloves simply to have something to show for his day.

In the afternoon he returned to the Eyrie and found himself in an unexpected tête-à-tête with the Archangel.

He had decided it would do him no actual harm to see if the Alleluia Files could be found on one of the disks left in plain sight in the Eyrie's music rooms, and so he was on the lower level of the compound, looking for an empty chamber. Bael opened the door to leave the very last one just as Jared had lifted his hand to knock.

"Oh! Sorry. Thought it might be empty," Jared said, stepping back a pace. Although Bael was considerably shorter than he was, the Archangel's pure physical presence was so forceful that he exuded an air of power even in the most casual situation.

"Nonsense! Don't apologize. I'm quite through," Bael said, beaming up at him. "In fact, wait. I'm not. I'm glad you're here. I've a new piece of music I'd like you to listen to, if you've got a moment. Perhaps you're in a hurry?"

"No, no hurry," Jared said, and the two men stepped inside. Bael shut the door. The room was small, acoustically perfect, and barely furnished; the singer, or the listener, was supposed to concentrate all his attention on the music, not the decor. Still, there were two stools, and Bael gestured for Jared to take one. Jared sat while Bael fiddled with the controls on the cabinet in the wall.

"There! Isn't that nice, now?" the Archangel said, coming

over to sit by Jared. The music issuing from the hidden speakers was a duet, male voice over flute, and Jared listened critically a moment. Dark music, melancholy and brooding. Not quite Jared's style. "He does have a talent, does he not?"

"Omar's new piece?" Jared guessed. Bael nodded.

"He brought it to me this morning. I told him I would critique it with my usual harshness, but I find it hard to judge my own son. I think he's a maestro."

"He's very good," Jared said. "I take it he's come in for your dinner party a day early? That must make you happy."

"Yes, it's always a treat to see my son. As you will know, when you yourself marry and produce children."

"The day seems far away," Jared said, amused.

"You're not so young that you can afford to be putting off the inevitable for long," Bael said with a quick frown. "It is good for any angel to breed, but for one in your position, it is essential. I tell you this not only as your friend, but as your Archangel. It is well past time for you to marry. May I suggest a proper girl such as Annalee Stephalo, who is even now visiting at the Eyrie? She has attractive manners and a desirable background. You could do worse than turn your eyes her way."

So that answered that question. Not the girl's father, but her Archangel, had encouraged her to dally with the visitor from Monteverde. "I do not find my affections leaning in her direction," Jared said softly.

Bael nodded. "Fine. Then some other girl. There must be plenty of eligible young women among the Manadavvi who would not look upon your suit with disgust."

"Thank you," Jared said faintly. "I will bear your advice in mind. I assume you give the same to your son—who is my age and older, and unmarried himself?"

"He is not angelic, so his responsibility to reproduce is not as high as yours—but yes, we have had this discussion," Bael said seriously. "It is the duty of every righteous, intelligent, and devout man to marry, and marry wisely. I have a special interest in Omar, of course, and am keenly desirous of seeing him settled well. And I have ideas on that score, and he is not loath to entertain them. But his case is entirely different from yours."

Jared was conscious of a sudden overpowering desire to fly to Cedar Hills and repeat every word of this conversation to Mercy. He could hardly wait to hear her caustic comments on

Bael's attempts to pair off the world to his own specifications. But. He was by now ruffled enough to let some of his own ire show. "Marry him off to an angel," he said flippantly. "Then she can be named Archangel, and he'll still have the power, if not the position."

He was shocked when Bael turned those wild prophet's eyes on him with a fanatic intentness. "Such a plan might please Jovah," the Archangel agreed. "And my son is such a man as could be expected to appeal to any woman, even an angel girl who has her pick of suitors."

I was not serious, Jared wanted to say, but Bael clearly was. It was a wholly new thought to Jared, but he realized instantly it had been a scheme long gestating in the Archangel's mind. And why not? From Bael's perspective, it made a great deal of sense. It put his son in power; it kept him deeply connected to the rule of Samaria. It allowed him to continue whatever political and religious policies he had instituted over the past nineteen years. . . .

"Tell me," Jared said slowly, "does Omar feel as you do on most topics that concern the realm?"

"We discuss most of my important decisions before I make them," Bael said. "I have found my son to be a clear-eyed adviser. At times we disagree, but he has most often conceded later that I have been correct. At other times I have allowed his opinion to sway me and have not been sorry. He has gifts for statesmanship that are very great, and which many do not appreciate because he stands in my shadow."

Not an entirely straightforward reply, though clearly the Archangel had answered Jared's question in the affirmative. "On the Jacobite issue, for instance," Jared said, very quietly, "he concurs with you?"

"Anyone who holds dear the safety of Samaria and its continued existence must concur with me on the Jacobite issue," Bael said sharply. "The Jacobites are extremely dangerous. They are seditious both politically and theologically, and those who believe in them court destruction by the hand of Jovah."

"I have heard," Jared said, still softly, "that you have been at some pains lately to—drive the Jacobites from the shores of Samaria. I confess I had not realized you were so passionately against them. But perhaps I have heard wrong, and you do not direct violence against the rebels?"

He was not sure Bael would answer, for it was an accusatory question, but the Archangel nodded his silver head. "I wish them gone from Samaria, yes," he said. "Think about it, Jared! Do you not see the risk they pose? To be telling people that the god does not exist—! The god who nurtures us, watches over us, saves us from flood, delivers us from famine—the god who, with a single thunderbolt, can destroy our entire world! Is it not dangerous—is it not terrifying—to anger such a god? Do you not realize that no one in Samaria is safe if a single Jacobite remains to preach of heresy?"

Sweet Jovah singing, then everything Christian had told him had been true. This was a zealot speaking, a man who felt his goal was so just that he could not envision setting any limits to attain it. And yet, and yet . . . "I agree, the hazard is great," Jared said cautiously. "But I do wonder how you plan to usher them from Samaria. I suppose you could shepherd them all to Edori boats and ship them off to Ysral—"

"Jovah hears every whisper uttered in Ysral as clearly as he hears every word spoken here," Bael said sternly. "We are no safer if they emigrate. They must be eliminated—or converted."

"Eliminated?" Jared repeated. Surely Bael would not admit . . .

The Archangel turned his mad eyes to his visitor. His face burned with a righteous fever; he lifted his hands as if to invoke the will of the god. From the speakers around them, Omar's voice suddenly burst free of the flute in a dark and portentous solo lament. "They must be executed," Bael proclaimed. "They must be cleansed from the face of Samaria. Their blood must be spilled so that the blood of innocents is not shed. They have betrayed their god, and they must die."

Jared stared at him, too stunned to say another word. Bael stared back, his face alight with passion, and stabbed his finger suddenly in Jared's direction.

"And all who do not agree with me must be questioned. And all who do not see the truth must be enlightened," the Archangel continued. "Who knows how far the heresy has spread? Who knows how many the poison has tainted? Look to your devotions, Jared. Jovah sees all, and judges all, and avenges all. And no one is safe until we are all back in Jovah's arms."

• • •

After that, the visit to the Eyrie ceased to be merely tedious and
began to seem almost dangerous instead. Jared was miles from
embracing the Jacobite theories—though he did concede they
had a certain logic to them—but by Bael's criteria, he was most
certainly a heretic. Which made him suspect. Which put him at
risk.

Seeing Omar that night over dinner did nothing to improve
his sense of security. The Archangel's son approached him in
the few minutes before the meal when they all milled about in
the drawing room.

"My father told me you had honored the Eyrie with a visit,"
Omar said with his usual suave smile. "How long are you
here?"

"I've been persuaded to stay through the party tomorrow
night," Jared replied. "But then I must get back to Monteverde.
I've been gone too long."

"Oh? Where else have your travels taken you?"

To Ileah, where I consorted with Jacobites, Jared thought
about saying. He cursed himself for his unwary tongue. "I was
in Cedar Hills a while back, and then in Semorrah with Christian
Avalone," he said easily.

"Business? Pleasure?"

"Wanderlust. I never stay still for long."

"I like Christian, but I wonder at some of the company he
keeps," Omar said idly. He was studying his glass of brandy as
if it was a scrying crystal, filled with visions. "Solomon Davilet,
for instance. Christian knows how opposed my father is to rapid
technological advances, and yet he insists on encouraging the
very men who are investing all their resources in such development." He looked up quickly to catch Jared's frown. "I don't
know if he's aware how much this has displeased my father."

So; another warning, or so it looked to Jared. "Christian's a
businessman," Jared said lightly. "He's looking for the profit.
I don't think you have to ascribe to him any more ambition than
that."

"Well, Christian is a smart businessman," Omar said. "He
sees that my father has only one year left of his tenure, and he
thinks the next Archangel may view his projects with more le-
niency."

"But he has no idea who the next Archangel may be."

"No," Omar said. "That is why it would behoove him to move slowly with his developments."

The supper bell rang just then, which Jared was grateful for, till he went into the dining room to find himself directed to sit by Annalee Stephalo. She gave him that dramatic look, suddenly raising her eyes to his face, as he took his seat next to her.

"Good evening, Jared," she said in her soft voice. "I haven't seen you all day. Have you been keeping busy?"

Worse and worse and worse. He knew it would be best to keep his head clear, but at this moment he couldn't bear the thought of getting through dinner entirely sober. He signaled the servant for a glass of wine, and drank half of it with his first swallow.

But the morrow brought a welcome respite. Jared had just emerged onto the central plateau, preparatory to flying down to Velora for the day, when he happened to investigate the commotion of a new arrival coming up the grand stairway. It was a cadre of liveried servants carrying boxes, luggage, and cartons; beside them, holding up her skirts with one hand and looking very cross, toiled Isabella Cartera. Jared broke into a grin and paused, waiting for her to arrive at the top of the stairwell.

"Isabella! Invited to the Eyrie to partake in the grand banquet, I see!" he greeted her, clasping her hand and helping her up the last few steps. "I'm glad to know you are still considered part of the upper echelon of Bethel society."

"Why is it," she fumed, "that two of the most-visited places in all of Samaria require you to arrive on foot? You can travel by private bus all the way to Breven, and through it, if you choose. You can ride up and down the streets of Cedar Hills or Monteverde in your truck, and Luminaux can be navigated by any means possible. But to get to Semorrah you have to leave all your vehicles behind you on the banks of a river and ride a horse into the city—and to get to the Eyrie, you actually have to *walk*! You have to *climb*! This is not the life to which I have been accustomed, I assure you. If it were not for the honor of the invitation, which has been growing paler as the day progresses, I would not be standing before you now, hot, windblown, and in a temper."

"Next time you must arrange to have an angel meet you in Velora so you can be flown into the hold in style," Jared said, amused. "Had I known you were coming, I would have been your escort myself."

She put back the lace confection that had shaded her head from the warm spring sun. "Yes, and had I known you were here, I would have sent for you," she said, gazing up at him. "Which reminds me to ask, why are you here? Surely not for Mariah's little dinner party?"

He grimaced. "I made the mistake of dropping by two days ago and have been coerced into staying. I leave with the dawn tomorrow, I promise you."

"Well, I am very glad to see you," she said decidedly. "For I cannot bear any of the others who will be present. You must sit by me in the drawing room and flirt with me all night. It will make Mariah so angry. She does not approve of my morals at all."

Jared grinned; Isabella was fast recovering her customary good humor. "If you wish, I will take you down to Velora with me now, and we can commence the flirting right away," he suggested.

She laughed up at him. "I have just *come* from Velora," she protested.

"This trip will be much easier. I will carry you."

"Very tempting. I should—but all right. Give me twenty minutes to find my room, change my clothes, and rejoin you out here."

"You must greet Mariah, too, of course. I should give you half an hour. Maybe an hour."

She grinned. "I will not trouble Mariah just yet. Twenty minutes. It is good to see you, Jared."

Therefore, his second afternoon in Velora passed much more pleasantly than his first. Isabella could not resist dragging him back to the bazaars he had frequented the day before ("Say what you will about Velora being the most provincial of the angel towns, it still has a market that far exceeds the merchandise at Shepherd's Pass"), but he didn't mind that. He didn't mind carrying her purchases for her, either, or allowing her to hold up a sweater to his chest to determine if it might fit her son ("For you're about the same size, though you're a little more muscular"). Isabella was like a chorus of harmony after a month of dissonance, and he was glad to be in her company.

   Later, they sat at one of the outdoor cafés and sipped iced drinks laced with alcohol. "So tell me the grim roster," she said. "Who besides me is expected at this dismal dinner?"

   He laughed. "I'm not sure of the entire guest list. But I did hear Mariah mention a few names." He reeled them off; Isabella alternated between nodding agreeably and grimacing sharply. "And of course, we have the usual assortment of Bael's court— Omar is here, and Annalee Stephalo, who has been my particular bane this visit."

   "Has she really?" Isabella asked with her throaty laugh. "Throwing herself at you, is she? You've been a friend of mine for fifteen years, Jared, but if you marry her, I'll never speak to you again."

   "Glad to hear it. Now at least I have a reason to give Bael when next he proposes her as my bride. Sorry, can't do it, Isabella Cartera will drop me from her list of friends."

   "Although Bael is right. It is time you married. Or at least took a lover or two."

   "I have had my share of lovers, though I thank you for this interest in my life," he replied, amused but a little discomfited. "As for marriage—"

   "I know, it is a wretched business, and I was much happier after my husband had the good sense to die," she replied. "But you do have a position to uphold. And there are people who might think you a little less—flighty—if you were settled with some sober girl, raising your family and staying home of nights."

   "From you of all people! Bael, yes, or even Mercy, but you—!"

   "I have always been respectable, Jared, whatever my other failings. It is good advice. Though I do not blame you for rejecting Annalee Stephalo or any other bride of Bael's providing. But surely, among your own people—the Manadavvi must have produced some charming young women who are only too eager to share your bed and your fortune."

   "Dangerous to dally among the Manadavvi," he told her. "They're too near Monteverde. Too much ill will is created if nothing comes of it. You must see that."

   "Yes, unless there was some great and overwhelming attraction . . . But I know! You must come to me at Cartabella. I am having my own party in two months—one which I trust will be much more pleasant than the one we are suffering through now. I am hosting a wedding for my niece, and there will be all sorts of young women present. Girls from good families, too—bright, educated girls who have been schooled at Luminaux and Semorrah. You might find one there who is a little to your liking. How does that sound?''

At present, one more social engagement—even at Isabella Cartera's—sounded dreadful, but the offer was a kind one and he knew he should not refuse. "It sounds most delightful," he said. "Tell me exactly when it is, and I shall be there."

She laughed at him. "You must try to feign more enthusiasm when you arrive," she said. "Don't worry, I shall entertain you royally. And who knows? Perhaps you will find yourself a romance."

They stayed in Velora until the last possible moment, then flew back to the Eyrie in time to change for dinner. Isabella told Jared that she could only bear these events by dressing in the most outrageous manner possible, and true to her word, she appeared in the drawing room attired in a flimsy white gown that was almost transparent. She had also bedecked herself with ropes of diamonds around her throat and her wrists, and in the braided coronet of her hair, so that she glittered wickedly when she made the smallest movement. Mariah stared at her wrathfully and almost could not bring herself to cross the room to greet her, but Omar, Bael, Richard Stephalo, and most of the other male dinner guests were by her side in moments. She laughed delicately, extended her hand to each man in turn, and sipped from her wine while keeping her eyes on the face of whoever happened to be talking. Jared, watching from a distance, couldn't help smiling. To such heights of sophistication Annalee Stephalo could only aspire.

He had been resigned to having Annalee as his dinner mate, and he was right, but when he arrived at the table, he was pleasantly surprised to find the oracle Jecoliah seated on his other side. She was peering about in her usual shortsighted way, but smiled at him cheerfully when he sat beside her.

"Jared! I thought I heard your voice across the room, but since I could think of no reason you would be here—"

"Ill luck," he responded, which made her laugh, though she

tried to strangle the sound. "How are you, Jecoliah? I have not seen you since the Gloria."

"Well, and happy to have spring here again," she said. "Quickly, before the others are seated. Who is sitting near us and on my other side? I see very poorly these days and I am too embarrassed to ask for the names of people I should know."

So he obligingly sketched in the composition of their table and pointed out the luminaries at the other tables. Then, while the meal was served, he took advantage of this rare chance to have an extended conversation with the oracle.

"You might be able to answer a question for me," he said, leaning back in his chair and sipping his wine (Manadavvi vintage, unless he greatly missed his guess, and very good). "Someone questioned me about the oracle Alleluia the other day, and I found I knew little about her—except that she was Archangel briefly, and oracle forever—"

"And the Jacobites have taken her up as their patron," Jecoliah added calmly.

Jared started violently, then glanced around quickly to make sure no one was paying attention. "Well, yes," he said, in a lower voice, "but here that's a word that it isn't even wise to whisper."

Jecoliah rolled her milky eyes but obligingly left off discussing Jacobites. "She was truly a great oracle," she said. "Any question she put to the god was answered immediately. Anyone who came to her for advice left knowing exactly what to do. She trained hundreds of acolytes and priests, and she had a great reverence for the power of Jovah."

"You sound as if you knew her."

She smiled. "No, she died before I came to Mount Sinai. But her successor was the oracle Deborah, who had known Alleluia her whole life, and Deborah trained me. And so I heard all her reminiscences about Alleluia's greatness. And of course, had it not been for Alleluia, neither Deborah nor I would have been acolytes, let alone oracles."

"How so?"

"In those days, as today, acolytes were most often chosen from the wealthy families—it has always been considered an honor to have your son or daughter serve the god for a year or two. But Alleluia felt acolytes should be culled from the poor as well as the wealthy—and from those who were disadvantaged in other ways. Deborah was almost completely deaf, you see, as I am almost completely blind. In fact, we both came from the village of Chahiela, where people with disadvantages such as ours can live in comparative freedom.''

"Chahiela," Jared repeated. "It is in southern Bethel, is it not? Almost on the ocean."

"Exactly," Jecoliah confirmed. "It is quite a prosperous little place now, though when it was founded, it was very small. And it still boasts a large community of the deaf and the blind, in what is the older part of town. As I say, Alleluia brought Deborah in from Chahiela, and when I was a girl, Deborah brought me to Mount Sinai. I myself have made it a practice to bring in acolytes from the school in Chahiela—and had a great deal of success, I might add. I find that a child who is deaf can somehow concentrate more intently on the words of the god, and someone like me who can scarcely see a man's face can with ease read the words the god prints on the interface. I do not know why this would be so. But I am thankful for it."

"Very interesting," Jared said, and he meant it, though he didn't see how any of this benefited him in his search. "Though I can't imagine how you or anyone can read the words of the god. I have been to the oracles' retreats and seen the holy language written on your screens, and I have not understood a thing."

She smiled. "That is because it is written in the divine language, which common men have forgotten," she said primly. "You must study a long time to learn it! Although most of those who are to be oracles simply one day look at the words and understand. It is one of the ways we know we have been chosen by Jovah."

"And you have been oracle—how long now?"

"For nearly thirty years."

"You must have been fairly young when you assumed your duties."

She nodded. "No one expected Deborah to die as she did, so quickly. She was nearly eighty, of course, but she had always been in good health. But then—she had a partial failure of her heart. One day she was fine, the next day she could not speak or walk, though it was clear that she could still understand—and think. Her last few days were terrible to witness. It was obvious that there were things on her mind—things she wanted to tell—and over and over again she asked for me to come to her room. And I would come, and I would send everyone else out, and she would take me by the hand and draw me down to the bed. And no words would come from her mouth, though she tried and tried to speak. She moved her hands in that strange language of the deaf—which I did not know—but when I brought her pen and paper, she could not write a word. I stayed with her as much as I could, hoping she would regain the power of speech. But three weeks later her heart stopped entirely, and she died in the night. It made me very sad." She paused, shook her head, and smiled away the ghosts. "But it also made me very busy! For I had overnight become the new oracle, and there was much to do."

"I wonder what it is she wanted to tell you," Jared said.

"So do I, sometimes. But no great mysteries have arisen that I could not solve—no locked cabinets that I could not find the key for, no dreadful events that she could have forewarned me about. I think she was afraid, and looking straight into the face of death, and wanted the assurance of the god's love. And that I gave her. So I don't worry about it anymore."

"Do you think—" Jared began, but was stopped by a small, speculative touch on his arm. He turned instantly to find Annalee smiling up at him with a wistful, plaintive expression.

"Oh! I'm sorry!" she said in her soft, exclamatory whisper. "I didn't realize you were still talking."

"What is it, Annalee?" he asked with an edged calm.

"It's just that, after dinner, I know Mariah is going to ask for entertainment. And I thought—if you had no objection—you would be willing to sing a duet with me? Something simple, of course, I know my voice is no match for yours, but Mariah made me promise that I *would* get up and sing, and I am shy to be singing by myself in front of all these strangers. But if you were beside me, well—"

He let her go on for a few more tangled sentences, mentally consigning Mariah to eternal damnation, before nodding sharply three times. "Of course. I am happy to serve as Mariah's amusement," he said. "Did you have a song in mind?"

Well, she had several, all silly love songs with preposterous lyrics, and all equally distasteful to him. "Choose what you will," he told her. "I am familiar with each of them."

As soon as he could, he turned back to finish his conversation with Jecoliah, but she had become engrossed in a discussion with the miner on her other side and showed no indication of ending it soon. In frustration, he addressed himself determinedly to his food, not looking up till he had cleaned his plate and finished his third glass of wine.

As he had expected, the soiree following the meal was even worse than the dinner itself, highlighted by his own performance with the wispy Annalee. He did his best not to make eye contact with Bael, Mariah, or Richard Stephalo while the painful duet was in progress, for he could not bear to see the satisfaction on their faces; likewise, he could not look at Isabella, because he knew she would be laughing. The applause that followed the song was extravagant, but not enough to make him agree to an encore, and he swept the assembled company a bow before stalking away from the pianoforte. He went straight to the servant holding a tray of wineglasses.

"You'll be too ill to leave in the morning, if you keep drinking all night," Isabella murmured in his ear, and he turned to give her an idiot's grin.

"Nothing will make me too ill to leave in the morning," he informed her. She took the glass from his hand, deliberately sipped from it, and handed it back. He added, "I'm considering making my exit now, in fact."

"But you've been so gracious all evening! You can manage another hour or two."

"I wouldn't be so sure."

"I hope you plan to be in a better mood when you arrive at Cartabella in a few weeks."

"I hope you plan to provide me better diversions."

She stretched to her tiptoes to kiss him on the cheek. "Oh, yes!" she murmured in his ear. "And if you don't like the youthful ones, I'll amuse you myself, in any way you care to name." She drew back and favored him with a brilliant smile. "Now how's that for a rash and breathless promise?"

He wished suddenly that his head was clearer; but surely she was just flirting. "I think I'll find myself tolerably well amused, thank you very much. I'm looking forward to the visit, in fact."

The smile still lurked in her eyes. She could probably read every thought in his head. "You're not," she said. "But I assure you it will be better than this."

"I've no doubt of it. In two months, then."

"In two months."

He stayed till the first of the guests began filtering out, and then he made his farewells to Mariah and Bael. He slipped up to his room, fell instantly into bed, and slept the sleep of the reprieved man. In the morning, he was up with the dawn, packed in five minutes, and hurrying through the corridors before anyone else was awake. At the public landing space on the Eyrie's highest level, he flung himself from the mountaintop as if he was fleeing from doom, his wings working mightily, his face straining toward the skies. He could not get high enough fast enough; he flew at top speed, straight north from the Eyrie, for as long as his wings could bear the exercise.

He would never go back to the Eyrie as long as he lived.

CHAPTER TWELVE

"Well, Jared, it doesn't sound so awful to me," Mercy said mildly three weeks later. "You had two boring dinners and half a dozen conversations with people you didn't like. No worse than your average Gloria."

Christian was laughing. The three of them had come together, unexpectedly, in Semorrah, and the merchant had insisted on taking the two angels out to dinner. So now they were seated in the well-appointed dining room of a quiet little inn called the Berman House, sharing one of the best meals it had been Jared's privilege to eat in a long time. And the company was better than he had had since he left the Eyrie, too.

Jared had only been back in Monteverde for a couple of weeks before he had felt compelled to leave again. He had wanted to apprise Christian of the results of his quest so far. And Monteverde had been so peaceful that he did not feel he needed to stay—and so chilly that he did not want to. Mercy's presence in Semorrah had been a delightful, unplanned bonus.

"Well, I commiserate with him on the Annalee Stephalo question," Christian said. "I don't know what it is about her that is so off-putting, for she's a pretty enough girl, and her manners are for the most part acceptable."

"She's stupid, but she's harmless," Mercy said briskly. "And I wouldn't want to see Jared entangled with her, but he's a grown man, after all! He ought to be able to have a civil conversation with someone he doesn't much care for, and not let it ruin his life. I hate to say it, Jared, but it's time you grew up and acted like an adult."

"And this is the reason I was so happy to see you when I arrived in Semorrah," Jared said, smiling at her lazily. "Because you always make me feel so good about myself.''

''Nothing like Mercy's tender love,'' Christian agreed. ''She spent the morning telling me I was a wicked father, and that if I didn't intend to raise my own sons, I should marry a woman who'd do it for me.''

''Matrimony seems to be the theme on everyone's mind,'' Jared murmured. ''I know the nicest Bethel girl. She's currently staying at the Eyrie as the guest of the Archangel—''

''I didn't say you were wicked,'' Mercy informed Christian. ''But you are neglectful. And your boys are adorable creatures whom you should enjoy spending time with.''

''I do enjoy them,'' Christian said mildly. ''But by all means come to Semorrah as often as you like and we can parent them together. They like you. They'd be overjoyed to have you around more.''

''It's not *me* they need more time with, Christian, but you.''

''I give them as much time as I have. And I think I'd prefer to discuss Jared's failings, if you please.''

''I'd prefer to discuss Bael's,'' Jared said. He nodded over at the merchant. ''I don't know how much Christian has told you of what he discussed with me last time I was here,'' he said to Mercy. ''But from him I learned that Bael has undertaken a systematic plan to eliminate the Jacobites from Samaria. Frankly, I didn't believe him—but Bael all but confirmed it for me while I was there. It was very chilling. All this time I have merely believed him to be obstructive and narrow-minded. But now I think he might be—'' He paused, searched for a word, and reluctantly found it. ''Evil.''

''Oh, come now, Jared!'' Mercy exclaimed. ''Misguided I'll allow, but nothing stronger than that.''

''I agree with Jared,'' Christian said coolly. ''I think Bael has misused power, and done it deliberately, and knows that his motives would not bear close examination.''

''His motives! The safety of the realm!'' Mercy replied. ''I am not one of these radical thinkers who believes that every lunatic with some view to propose deserves to have his hearing in the public market! Like Bael, I believe the Jacobites present some risk to us and to our society—''

''But would you have them murdered out of hand?'' Christian demanded.

She stared back at him. ''Well, no. I would perhaps try to

reeducate them—and I would not willingly allow them a forum for their views, but I . . . Well, the Librera tells us that every life is sacred. I would not take one without the direct mandate of the god.''

"I believe Jovah has given Bael no such mandate,'' Christian said.

There was a moment's silence while Mercy glanced uncertainly between the two men. Christian and Jared had agreed before they set out for the Berman House that they would not discuss the validity of the Jacobite claim with Mercy—she was too devout to entertain even a philosophical doubt about her god—but they had felt reasonably secure in discussing the fate of the rebels themselves. They were sure Mercy would not consign anyone to a brutal death.

"What is your proof?'' she asked suddenly. "What is it you have seen or heard that makes you think he is actually committing executions?''

Christian nodded at the other angel. "I believe Jared has the most recent firsthand knowledge.''

So Jared told them about his adventure in Ileah and his conversation with Bael at the Eyrie, and saw Mercy's face grow lined with worry and Christian's mouth grow taut with anger. "I cannot believe it,'' Mercy said, more than once, but it was clear she was beginning to. And then Christian filled her in on rumors he had heard about the Jansai, in Breven and in Luminaux, sweeping through on the Archangel's orders to flush out Jacobites and bring them to justice.

"Some of this I had heard, but not the details—I thought they were just being harassed, relocated—'' she murmured.

"Relocated where?'' Christian demanded. "If he wants to eject them from Samaria and will not allow them to emigrate to Ysral—''

"And yet—they *are* a danger. They *do* put Samaria at risk,'' she said faintly.

Christian threw his hands in the air. "Then we are done with this conversation! You clearly side with Bael—''

"I do not! I believe his principles are right but his methods are completely wrong!'' she fired back. "If he is truly doing these terrible things, he must be stopped! And we must pray to Jovah that whoever succeeds him as Archangel can solve this riddle in a more humane fashion.''

The men exchanged glances. "But who will replace him as Archangel?" Christian said softly. "The god has not spoken. And Bael has his own ideas."

"What can you possibly mean?" she asked sharply.

"It's no secret he'd like to hold on to power," Jared said. "How better than through his son? Find a compliant angel to wed with Omar, convince the god that this angel would be a suitable candidate, and—" Jared snapped his fingers. "That quickly she takes over his post. That quickly Omar steps into his father's shoes. And believe me, the son adheres to his father's teachings."

Mercy stared at him. "But that's absurd. There are no compliant angels. All have minds of their own."

"Do they?" Jared said a little grimly. "I can think of half a dozen young angels who might be the suitable age to marry Omar. And all of them are half in love with him already. He's an attractive man, is Omar. More attractive if he can offer someone that kind of power."

"But he can't! Jovah has never named an Archangel at the behest of the angels before."

"How do you know? How do you know how he picks his candidates? The god exists to offer counsel to men, but how do we know he doesn't appreciate a little advice from mortals now and then?"

"Jared. That's blasphemy."

"All I'm saying is, Bael seems to think he can convince Jovah that his son should wed the next Archangel. And I wonder why Bael thinks that if he hasn't done a little research and discovered some compacts that were worked out in the past between the Archangel and the god."

Mercy rubbed her temples with her fingers. "But if that's so . . . Then what are we to do? How can we stop him? From killing the Jacobites, from putting Omar in his place? What can we possibly do?"

"Well, first, I think we must spread the information around a little," said Christian briskly. "You and Jared must let your angels know what Bael is doing, and that you don't like it. You must talk with the Manadavvi and your privileged land holders—and even, if you're up to it, Mercy, to the Jansai—and let them know that Bael's actions do not meet with your approval."

She was frowning at him. She looked anxious and a little

afraid. "It will cause no end of dissonance," she said hesitantly. "When there is disagreement among angels—"

"I know. But is there not dissonance created even now by Bael, as he murders helpless men and women? Does not the Librera instruct all of us to live in harmony? All of us—Edori, Jansai, Manadavvi, angel, mortal—Jacobite? And is not that harmony even now being destroyed?"

"Yes, yes, you're right, it's just that—it will be hard. But it will be done."

"We need to make sure we stay closely in touch," Jared added. "The three of us. We need to let each other know anything we find out."

"Ah! I'm glad you brought that up," Christian said. He leaned over to retrieve a leather bag he had brought with him, and he resettled it on his lap. "I have lately invested in a small mechanical marvel which I think you might find useful. Here. I procured one for each of you."

And he reached in his bag and pulled out two thick black cylinders, maybe five inches long, studded with mysterious buttons and switches. He handed one to each angel. Mercy took hers gingerly, but Jared examined his with interest. It weighed about half a pound, featured a small grill on one blunt end, and smelled like chemicals.

"I cannot even imagine what this might be," Jared said.

"Long-distance communications device," Christian said. "Its transmission travels along a sound path that very few other machines can intercept, so it's virtually a dedicated line. It can be programmed to contact up to ten different receivers, but I couldn't think of who else you would want to contact except each other—and me. So that's all I programmed them for."

"What are you *talking* about?" Mercy demanded. "Sound waves and communication devices—"

"Unless I miss my guess, I can be sitting in Monteverde and use this little contraption to talk to you while you're sitting in Cedar Hills," Jared said. "Am I right?"

Christian nodded. Mercy set her communicator on the table with a snap. "That's not possible! And if it *was* possible, it would be—it would be wicked! Yes, it would, Christian, don't you laugh at me!"

"Why wicked? How can something this innocent be considered harmful? A device that makes it possible for friends to converse even if they're not in the same room?''

"Because technology in and of itself is harmful! Because it leads to war and destruction!''

"The whole Gloria was broadcast across Samaria, and we haven't slipped into war and destruction yet,'' Christian reminded her. "Technology is not always to be feared. It can have repercussions, yes, but these little communicators offer no hidden terrors. They are just a way for you to keep in touch with Jared and me.''

"I don't like them,'' she said flatly.

"I understand that,'' Christian said gently. "And I do respect your feelings. And you don't have to use them. But will you allow me to show you how they work in case an emergency arises and you find you need to get in touch with one of us right away?''

She eyed him mutinously for a moment, clearly unsettled, but unable to marshal any convincing arguments. This had been a difficult evening for her. All the things she believed in were being challenged, all the things she abhorred were being forced upon her; and yet she was too honest to deny that times were growing desperate and dire measures were called for.

"May I show you?'' Christian asked again. She looked over at Jared, who gave her a sympathetic smile.

"I don't like them,'' she said again, but she picked up her cylinder.

Christian took Jared's. "It's very simple,'' he said. "This yellow button turns it on. These ten buttons are the ones you push when you want to contact someone. I am number one. You, Jared, are number two, and Mercy is number three. I'm Jared and I want to call Mercy. So I flick on the yellow switch, and then I punch the third button.''

Instantly, the cylinder in Mercy's hand emitted a soft peeping sound. She gasped and dropped it, but Christian caught it before it rolled off the table.

"Now I'm Mercy and I want to see who is contacting me. I push in the red button.'' The beeping stopped. "I put the grill end to my mouth and I say, 'Jared, is that you?' Then I push the green button, and put the grill end to my ear.''

Jared took his own communicator back from Christian. "What do I do now?'' he asked.

"You push the green button again. It toggles you between

transmit and receive. You speak into the grill now.''

Jared put his lips to the end of the cylinder. "Hello? Mercy? Are you listening?" He turned the grill to his ear.

"No, you must push the button again. All right." Christian spoke next in a high, squeaky falsetto. "Why, Jared! You gave me such a fright! Don't you know it's past midnight?"

Mercy grabbed it from him. "Give that to me. Hello, Jared? How can you tell if this stupid thing works?"

"Push the button. Put it to your ear."

Jared spoke back into the microphone. "You can hear it coming out of the speaker. It's a little creepy."

Her eyebrows flicked up. "I can hear your voice! Right in this little tube!"

"And you'll be able to hear it over a distance of a thousand miles," Christian said. "There might be some static from time to time, especially if the weather's bad. And sometimes if you're deep in a mountain range, the transmission isn't too clear. But essentially you should be able to talk as easily as you are right now."

Jared gave Christian a big grin. "I like it!" he said. "What other fun stuff have you merchants been hiding from the angels?"

"Everything else Bael has put a moratorium on," the other man replied promptly. "You'd be surprised at some of the prototypes that exist. And next year—if Omar is not Archangel— you will begin to see some amazing machinery make its way onto the open market."

"Christian—!"

He smiled over at Mercy. "Well, you will. None of it anything to alarm you, dear heart. But machines and technologies that will"—he spread his hands to indicate a canvas of rich, incredible beauty—"color every inch of your world."

"My world is quite bright enough as it is, thank you."

"And let us not be sidetracked from the issue at hand," Jared interposed. "We are not concerned with the influx of new technologies sometime in the uncertain future. We are concerned with keeping in touch with each other, now, during this crisis. Mercy, do you understand how the cylinders work?"

She gave him a frosty look. "They seem simple enough."

"Fine. I take it we should keep these by us at all times, in case someone is trying to contact us?"

"If you can," Christian said. "I'm sure there will be times that won't be convenient."

"And perhaps we should plan to meet again in—a month?— to see what any of us has learned or done."

"That sounds agreeable," Christian said.

Mercy smiled with what appeared to be an effort. "You do not have to wait a month to come see me, or talk to me only on this little machine," she said. "Either of you."

"Very well, then," Christian said, smiling back at her much more warmly. "Then I won't."

Jared was so surprised by the tone in the merchant's voice (and minutes after he'd called her "dear heart," too!) that he yawned and stretched his arms above him, just to distract himself with motion. Come to think of it, they had been sitting here for hours. He was starting to feel a little cramped in the back of his legs, in the upper muscles of his arms, his right arm particularly—

Mercy was looking over at him with a frown. "Jared. That's odd. Look at the colors in your Kiss."

He lowered his arm quickly to see the glass heart of his Kiss dancing with small impatient flames. "Huh," he grunted. "Did the same thing a few weeks ago when I was sitting by firelight. Must be a reflection. Never noticed it before."

"Nonsense, I'm sitting right here and my Kiss is as pale as a chip of ice," Mercy said. "Do you feel any pressure? Any pain?"

Well, he did, but he was not about to admit it to Mercy. "No," he said. "I think it's just the firelight. Every Kiss is unique, you know. Each one probably responds to a different set of stimuli—light, color, motion, heat."

"The presence of your true lover," Christian added. "Isn't that what the legends say?"

"The legends that only the young girls believe," Mercy said with a sniff. "Jared, I think maybe you should go see a priest, or even one of the oracles."

"Mercy, I'm fine! Thank you for your concern. Anyway, I think it's the firelight. Look, Christian's Kiss is filled with just as much color as mine is."

And Mercy glanced over at the merchant, whose glowing amber Kiss could be glimpsed through the fine white lawn of his shirt. And then she looked sharply into his face, where a faint smile and a fainter blush made him appear both self-conscious and a little amused. And then she herself colored deeply, and caught her breath, and looked away; and nobody could think of a word to say for at least two minutes.

"Well, I think I'll tell our host that we're ready to pay our bill," Christian said at last, in the most calm and pleasant voice imaginable. "It looks like we're all through here."

So that was a strange ending to an otherwise fairly productive day, but Jared made no comment to Christian as they retired to the merchant's home. Mercy, who had come to Semorrah on other business, was staying elsewhere, and planned to leave early in the morning. They made brief enough farewells, then separated for the night.

Jared lay awake a long time in the elegantly appointed room that Christian always reserved for him, and stared up at the ceiling watching the white lights of Semorrah flicker across the tile. Well. Christian had always been fond of Mercy—everyone was—but Jared could not believe that the suave, sophisticated businessman could actually have fallen in love with the matronly angel. And, since the last of her children had been born nearly fifteen years ago, Mercy had shown surprisingly little inclination to take on lovers, something most angels did as a matter of course. She had seemed content, fulfilled, and energetic, running Cedar Hills, raising her three daughters, and overseeing the lives of all her friends. She had not seemed to want for anything.

Jared turned to his side, spreading his left wing over his body like a quilt. But it had been startling indeed to see the amber lights sparking in Christian's Kiss, moments after the merchant had spoken of true love. Mercy was right; most people believed that the stories of sympathetic kinship between Kisses were romantic fairy tales designed to appeal only to the young and foolish, and yet . . . There were enough stories about predestined lovers brought together by their flaming Kisses that you almost had to give them some credence. Susannah and her Archangel lover—that was the most famous tale. Come to think of it, didn't the legends say that Rachel's Kiss would light every time she heard Gabriel sing, and that his took fire every time she was hurt or in danger?

Jared shifted irritably. He could not get comfortable, though Christian's expensive furniture was not at fault. His own Kiss had glowed with secretive, insistent colors tonight, and he had felt its dull ache deep in his arm before it had occurred to him to check for the source. He had seen the colors, but not felt the pain, one time before, and then in the ransacked camp of Ileah when he heard the Jacobite girl singing. . . . According to myth, of course, the Kiss would light only for your true love, your soul mate; it should not respond at random to the presence of dozens of possible candidates. Surely Jovah did not think the young rebel girl was Jared's one true love. And even if the god had so decided, it seemed ludicrous to think that the fugitive Jacobite was staying at the Berman House, ordering room service and haughtily directing the staff to wait upon her. Surely it was nothing more than a reflection of the firelight and a chance pressure on his arm. No matter what Christian said.

But he did wonder where Tamar had gotten to.

He wondered even more late the next day, when Christian freed himself of his other duties and met Jared for a late meal on the rooftop patio.

"Good afternoon, angelo, I trust you are enjoying yourself," Christian greeted him before directing three servants where to place various trays of refreshments. "I know how easily you get bored, so I'm pleased you've curbed your impatience long enough to join me for lunch."

"I know that the food here will only be tolerable if I eat it in your company," Jared retorted.

Christian seated himself and waved the servants away. "True," he said, unfolding a napkin and spreading it over his silken trousers. They looked very expensive. "It's a little trick I have for encouraging my guests not to linger. You should try it at Monteverde."

"None of my guests ever linger. In fact, I rarely have guests, because I am never home. My mother and my sister complained of this delicately last time I was there. So my plan is to return immediately and not stir outside my doors until I leave for Isabella Cartera's."

"Give la Cartera my love."

What you have to spare, Jared was tempted to say, but did not. "So! You said you might come back from your meeting with news."

"Yes, and so I did, though I don't know how valuable it is.

I told you I have—a contact—who feeds me information on Bael's activities."

"Yes, and I wish you would tell me—"

"I cannot. If I have no discretion, I have nothing. But I trust this source."

"Very well. And you learned?"

"Up till now, Bael has been operating pretty much at random—going to the known Jacobite hideouts and hoping to roust a few dissidents. He's also given the Jansai license to raid Edori ships on the open sea."

"That's new," Jared commented.

"He says not. I think the scale of the attacks has been stepped up a little. But, anyway, till now they have just been looking for potential Jacobites, not anyone in particular."

"And now they have names and faces?"

"A few," Christian confirmed. "They've always known the name of the de facto leader, a man named Conran Atwell. He's pretty much run the group since Fairman died. But apparently now they've put together a list of eight or ten of the Jacobites they consider the most dangerous or the most persuasive, and they've found somebody who's willing to supply descriptions as well."

"Which I assume you have copies of."

Christian nodded. "Even better. Apparently some artist in Bael's pay sketched up portraits based on these descriptions, and so we have pictures. Would you like to see them?"

"Of course. Just so I'll know them when I come face to face with any escaped Jacobites."

Christian laid aside his fork and took up a small leather portfolio that he had brought with him. "This is the key one. Conran. Looks like any old man you might meet on the street."

Jared took the paper and studied it a moment. True enough, but even in this badly rendered sketch, the man possessed a certain force of personality. He had been limned with high cheekbones, dark eyes, and a full mouth; the thinning hair, lightly shaded to indicate gray, must once have been black. "Is he Edori?" Jared asked.

"I don't know. Does he look Edori?"

"A little. He has that—undomesticated expression."

"All the Jacobites do. At least in these pictures."

Jared glanced at the next three and heard Christian pronounce their names, but none of these portraits conveyed the same sense of intensity as the first one. Two of them were men; the third was a woman. Jared forgot their features immediately.

"I confess I'm not sure I'd recognize any of them if I passed them on the street," Christian said. "So I don't know how the Jansai will. But I suppose—"

"Jansai?" Jared repeated.

"Oh, yes. Copies of these have been circulated to all the interested Jansai. There's a reward for their capture, too. Not much for your run-of-the-mill Jacobites, mind you, though for Conran Atwell I believe the sum is fairly substantial. As it is for this woman, for some reason. She doesn't look like she'd be particularly ferocious, now, does she?"

And Christian handed him a portrait of Tamar.

And Jared felt the Kiss in his arm explode in a painful burst of fire.

"I know this woman," he said carefully.

"Really?" Christian sounded amazed. "During what unlikely social function did you make her acquaintance?"

"In Ileah. I told you. There was a Jacobite there. This is her." The shape of the face was not quite perfect, and the expression of the mouth was too serene, but it was Tamar; there was no question. "I can't imagine that she could be on anybody's list of criminals most dangerous to the realm. She scarcely had enough strength to keep body and soul together."

Christian took the picture back to study it more closely. "Perhaps she has unsuspected depths. She looks here like she's fairly determined."

"Indomitable," Jared agreed. "But—powerless. I have never seen anyone who looked so alone and friendless."

"Well, she'll certainly be friendless if Bael's Jansai catch up with her," Christian said. "Where do you suppose she disappeared to?"

"I wish I knew," Jared said. He took the portrait back. "Could I get a copy of this? Of all of them, when it comes to that?"

"Certainly. I'll have copies made immediately. So you plan to look for her again?"

"For any of them. Although, based on my luck with Tamar, I don't know that I'll be able to convince them that I am not the enemy."

"Well, they must come to trust us, and you're as likable as any angel," Christian said. "Though that's not saying much. Where do you plan to look?"

"You're the one with the mysterious connection to information. Where do you suggest?"

"Ysral," Christian said promptly. "That's where many of them are thought to have sought refuge. And the Edori, of course, have welcomed all of Samaria's castoffs for the past hundred years."

"All right, then. That's where I'll try. Right after Isabella's party."

"I'd love to join you for the fete," Christian said with a grin. "Unfortunately, I have other plans that weekend. I was invited, you know."

"Well, Isabella promises to introduce me to any number of respectable and charming young women. I have to admit I'm dreading it."

"For a man with your gifts and attractions, you seem remarkably eager to escape romantic coils."

"With respectable young women," Jared said with a grin. "I do not mind entanglements with the reprehensible kind."

"Mercy was right," Christian said. "It's time you grew up."

Jared considered his friend for a long moment. "Since you brought up her name," he began, but Christian forestalled him with a laugh.

"Spare me the fatherly advice. From you it would be ludicrous."

"She'll never leave Cedar Hills," Jared went on unheeding, his voice slow and serious. "And she's not likely to jeopardize a friendship that means as much to her as yours does. And— you know—"

"And I don't believe I expressed an interest in your opinion, anyway," Christian interrupted.

"We've spent the past two days discussing *my* love life."

"Which is of some interest to the realm. Mine is not. Besides, I have already produced two fine heirs. I appreciate your concern. But I've no wish to discuss it."

Jared hesitated, shrugged, and finished his meal. "How quickly can you get me the copies?" he said at last. "I'd like to leave today if possible."

"Within the hour. You will let me know as soon as you discover anything—or anyone?"

Jared patted his hip and grinned. Christian had devised a waist sling for carrying the communications device, and Jared had made a point of wearing his around the merchant's house all morning. "I'll contact you immediately. Good enough?"

"Good enough. Good luck."

In the afternoon, Jared left for Monteverde, though it was impossible to reach the hold before dark. Still, he was impatient to get back, and he actually enjoyed flying at night. He liked the way the ground slowly disintegrated beneath him and the blackness of the night intensified around him; he especially liked the sensation of being suspended in a net of starlight, cold and brilliant. Some angels complained that they grew dizzy or lost their way when they attempted to fly after sundown, but Jared always felt his mind hone down to a diamond-hard clarity; his bones were suffused with exhilaration. It was like breathing the god's air, clean and intoxicating. Jared loved it.

It was past midnight when he arrived at Monteverde, so it was late the next day before he was up and making the rounds. His mother greeted him with her usual affectionate sarcasm— "Is that my son? Have you remembered my existence?"—and Catherine more helpfully filled him in on events that had transpired in his absence. But Monteverde had been quiet. No Jansai, no Jacobites, no predatory women. He could use a spell of quiet reflection.

Except all his meditations led him back to Tamar.

Where *could* she be? Was she in danger? How could he find her?

Why had his Kiss lit once in her presence, and once when she was nowhere nearby?

Or had she been nearby? Had she been in the Berman House? Not that she could have been a guest there, but perhaps she had come to the door while he sat there, selling something or asking for information. Or perhaps—stupid man not to have thought of this before!—she had sought employment there. She had seemed like a woman who would not be afraid of hard work, and she was certainly presentable enough to be hired at a place like the Berman House. He should have investigated. He should not have so cavalierly dismissed the significance of the agitated Kiss.

If she was still at the Berman House, he could have Christian seek her out immediately. His hand went to the cylinder at his waist, and then he paused. But she didn't know Christian and would be suspicious of any wealthy merchant who came asking after her. Of course, she knew Jared and was suspicious of him, anyway, but somehow he felt this was a task that was supposed to fall to him. He could not redirect it to his friend.

Therefore, two days after his return, he sought out his sister. "I have to go to Semorrah for a day or two," he told Catherine, who rolled her eyes in resignation.

"Didn't you tell me yesterday that you would be here until Isabella Cartera's grand dinner party?"

"I did, but I lied. But I'll be back in a day or two. Promise. And this time I'll stay. Well, a few weeks. Until the wedding."

"I don't believe you. But go. Go. Have fun disporting with Christian Avalone and the Semorrah girls. We do just fine without you."

He felt like he should justify himself, but when he opened his mouth to explain, he found that it was too complicated. Therefore, he smiled, shrugged, and let her think what she would.

He left that morning for Semorrah and arrived in the city by early evening. Without even stopping at Christian's, he made his way to the Berman House and, after a few inquiries, found his way to the steward who oversaw the entire staff.

"I was wondering if you could tell me if you had ever employed this young woman—or seen her anytime this past month," Jared asked. He unfolded the portrait of Tamar that Christian had given him. Mysteriously, the merchant had been able to produce a copy in minutes but would not explain how that had been possible. "She's fair, with short, light brown hair and green eyes, and she's called Tamar."

The steward had taken the portrait just as Jared pronounced the name, and he started visibly, shaken either by the word or the picture. He studied it for just a few moments before handing it back.

"I know her," he said quietly. "Is she in trouble?"

Jared considered. "She could be in danger," he said. "But not from me. Please believe I mean her no harm. I could have

Christian Avalone vouch for me if that would reassure you."

The older man made a brief, quickly repressed gesture of negation. *No, no, I need no character references.* "I could not betray her to you even if I would," he said. "She left two days ago, somewhat abruptly."

"Did she tell you where she was going?"

"To her sister, who had fallen ill. She did not leave an address or anything personal behind. My own opinion was that something had frightened her and she felt the need to run away. I was sorry she did not trust me enough to confide in me."

Jared refolded the paper and slipped it back in his vest pocket. He was cursing himself for failing to heed the pressure of his Kiss that night he had dined here with Christian and Mercy. She had been here, not fifty feet away, and he had sensed it somehow. . . . "Do you think she might come back someday?"

"I hope so. But I doubt it."

"Would you get word to me if she does?"

The steward considered. Jared had to like him for it, though his was the soul being weighed; but he was glad to see Tamar had won at least one friend during her sojourn in Semorrah. "I would be willing to tell her you want to speak to her," the old man temporized.

"Fair enough. Tell her that I think she is in danger, and that Christian Avalone will give her sanctuary. She won't believe you, but tell her anyway. I appreciate your willingness to help."

The steward inclined his head. He had a certain majestic dignity; he probably led a much more productive, demanding existence than Jared had even contemplated. The thought was somewhat lowering. "It is a privilege to serve the angels."

"And you don't have a clue where she might have gone? You don't know this sister's name or what province she lives in?"

"I believe the sister was fabricated. Had she given a direction, I suspect it would have been false."

All too likely. "Thank you again for your assistance," Jared said. He added impulsively, "And for your kindness to her. I will look for her elsewhere."

But as he left the Berman House, feeling completely dejected, the question remained: where? It seemed unlikely she could have made it from Semorrah back through Jordana to Breven and thence to safety in Ysral, particularly if Jansai were looking for her and knew her face. So she was probably in Bethel some-where, taking odd jobs and trying to avoid drawing attention to herself. There were any number of places to hide in Bethel—small towns or farming communities, for instance, and there were literally hundreds of those—and he did not know how he would begin to comb through them all.

Well; it was back to Monteverde now, because he had prom-ised. But he would leave early for Isabella Cartera's and make a few unscheduled stops on the way. Maybe he would get lucky. Maybe he would find the Jacobite where he least expected her.

CHAPTER THIRTEEN

Lucinda had never known time to pass so slowly. During the first three weeks after *The Wayward*'s departure, every day seemed a thousand hours long; the sun seemed to crawl toward its unreachable zenith of noon, then descend hesitantly, reluctantly, toward the indifferent bed of the sea. Night was interminable, rubbery, each minute stretched to accommodate ten. No dreams could speed the passage of the hours, and sleep, of course, was unattainable. When—impossible to delay any longer—the next dawn made its unwilling debut, there was no need to look forward to any hope of relief. There was no diversion, no employment, engrossing enough to nudge a single hour into a faster pace.

Well. If this was how it felt to be in love, Lucinda could not imagine why the poets praised the state so exultantly. She found it a wretched business all in all.

She did not speak a word of her unhappiness to Gretchen, who most assuredly would not approve of romances conducted with Edori sailors. Nonetheless, the older woman sensed that something was wrong, and eyed her niece often with a measuring glance. Several times during those three dreary weeks, her aunt would surprise her with a quick, pouncing question: "Do you have a headache?" "Are you suffering your monthly distress?" "Is your stomach bothering you? I have a potion you could try." To all inquiries Lucinda answered firmly, "I'm fine." She was fine. She was just heartsick. And lonely. And terrified of never seeing Reuben again.

And more terrified of having him sail back into the harbor at Angel Rock.

Every night before she went to bed, she softly sang the notes

that unlocked the silver box, and she took out the emerald ring
Reuben had given her. She wore it while she slept (on the rare
occasions she actually slept), and it gave her a peculiar, bitter
comfort to wake in the middle of the night and feel its weight
around her finger. Each morning, she replaced it in its case and
sang the measures in reverse, and then she hid the box under a
pile of clothes in the bottom drawer of her dresser.

But still she wondered if she would ever see him again, and
what she would say to him, and if he would remember what he
had said to her.

But it was stupid to brood over an absent Edori lover. There
was much to do here, and she threw herself into work with a
desperate frenzy. Fortunately, this was the beginning of their
busiest season, and all the innkeepers were preparing for the
influx of summer visitors. Every room had to be cleaned from
top to bottom, curtains washed and repaired, bed quilts changed
from winter wools to summer cottons, every window washed,
every floor waxed. The garden needed to be planted, the cellar
needed to be cleaned of last year's dried potatoes and jars of
old fruit preserves. There was enough work that no one's hands
needed to be idle, and no one's brain needed to be set in the
same miserable, unproductive whirr.

During the middle of that third week, the inn began to fill up,
and Lucinda became the most attentive hostess imaginable. She
could not do enough to feed the guests, prepare them special
meals, show them around the island, entertain them in the evening. She was perfectly willing to play cards, learn board games,
sing, engage in charades or any other activity someone might
dream up. And when the guests retired for the evening, she
instantly returned to the kitchen to help Emmie finish the night's
dishes and organize for the morrow's breakfast.

And still the days dragged by.

She tried to avoid gazing out toward the harbor more than
twenty times a day, looking for familiar sails. Every day, driven
by a restless energy, at some point she flung herself aloft and
flew as far as she dared from the safety of the island. But inevitably, as she circled back, she made one pass over the open
sea that stretched between Angel Rock and Yrsal, counting the
ships she could see plowing through the dense lavender waves.
There were more this time of year than any other time, and some

of the ships were Edori-built, but none of them was *The Wayward*.

While she flew she sang, for she was practicing new music and did not particularly want Gretchen to hear it. She had spent a good portion of her free time scoring the prayer for thunderbolts from the god—note for note, in reverse of the proper order. She had selected it because it was the most complex of the prayers and she had figured it would be the most challenging, swallow up the biggest chunk of her time. She was surprised to find that, performed backward, it was an eerie, haunting piece, with its own distinct melody that lingered in her mind. She scored the reverse harmony for it as well, though she had no one to perform it with, and learned the descant once she had memorized the notes to the prayer itself.

But even singing could not take up whole days, even flying could not. She could take every prayer in the angels' hymnal and write it backward, forward, medley and fugue, and still the days would idle by like lovers on their way home from a dance. There was no joy in the world anymore. And every day was a hundred years long.

But at the end of that third week she got a letter from Reuben. He sent it with an Edori sailor, who approached her one afternoon with a broad smile on his face.

"I'm an observant man, I am, and it looks to me like you're the only angel living on this little island," he greeted her, and the familiar, lilting Edori accent made her welcome him with a smile. "So it occurs to me your name must be Lucinda."

"It is," she said. "Can I help you?"

"I've all I need, thank you kindly," was the prompt response. "But I've brought something for you that I'm hoping you'll be glad to see. It was sent with many instructions to guard it carefully and make sure it was delivered safely, and I cannot help but think the sender was most anxious that it come to your hand as soon as might be possible."

"Oh! Is it—did Reuben send it?" she stammered, feeling her face wash over with heat. "I mean—is it from another Edori?"

"Aye, Reuben sia Havita himself. He'll be sorry to hear that you were not more pleased to be receiving news of him."

"No, I *am*! Don't you say that!" she exclaimed, before she realized he was teasing her. She felt her blush intensify. Tentatively, she smiled at him. "Please, may I have the letter?"

So he handed it over, still laughing, and she hurried down to the edge of the harbor, where Aunt Gretchen was least likely to see her. Then she carefully snapped the seal, unfolded the single page, and devoured its contents.

It was relatively short, for, as he noted, he had learned just five minutes ago that *Horizon* was heading for Angel Rock and so he had little time to put pen to paper. "In the future I'll be smarter! I'll start my next letter the instant I hand this over to Marcus, and by the time I find a ship to take it to you, it will be a thousand pages long. At least that is how I feel—that if I wrote a few words every time you crossed my mind, I would fill about a hundred pages a day.

"I know I told you it could be as little as three weeks before I saw you again, but now I think it will be three weeks more than that, for we have set sail directly for Breven without a pause at Angel Rock. Yet we will not tarry on the mainland, and Maurice has already promised me that we will pause a day or so on your island, and so you see I will be able to keep my word to you. Maurice is nicely recovered, by the way, though he has made dreadful demands on our sympathy and hopes to receive more coddling from your kind aunt when we make our way back to the island. I tell him that he must reinjure himself if he hopes to get any special attention, for I was there four days and never got more than a reproving glance. . . .

"I miss you more than I can put into words. Strange, is it not? For if you count the hours we spent together, they were not so many. But I remember each one. And I tell myself that I did not delude myself and that you remember them as well, each hour, each minute. Well, I shall find out soon enough. Look for us before another three weeks are out. Reuben."

She read the letter five times before she even looked up. Then she closed her eyes, touched the letter to her heart, opened her eyes again, and read it a sixth time. Three weeks. She would see him again in three weeks. Such a short period of time, after all! The days would fly by!

As it happened, the days were filled with enough incident that they did hurry by—but they left Lucinda feeling uneasy and a little bewildered. And they left Aunt Gretchen in a most peculiar state of anxiety.

For they had a distinguished guest come to the island: Omar, the Archangel's son.

He arrived a week after Reuben's letter, and he made his way immediately to the Manor. Lucinda was on the front stoop sweeping away debris when he walked up, his baggage in his hand.

"Lucinda?" he called when he was still a few yards away, and she looked up inquiringly. When she recognized him, she dropped the broom and hurried forward, her hands outstretched. "Omar! What brings you to Angel Rock?"

He set his suitcase hastily on the road so he could take both her hands in his, and he smiled down at her intently. "Part vacation, part investigation," he said lightly. "It has been a hectic few weeks since you left, and since I have heard such restful things about your island, I thought I would give myself a little respite and check it out. And when my father heard where I was going, he told me that he has considered coming here for a week or two of relaxation, but he would await my report before making any plans. So you see I come as emissary for the Archangel, and you had best treat me well if you want the chance to entertain so august a personage."

It was wonderful to see someone from Samaria, even someone she scarcely knew, and the light, teasing note in his voice chased away her ever-present melancholy. Lucinda felt herself grow giddy with pleasure. "Well, I like to think we would treat you kindly for your own sake, and not your father's," she said gaily. "But now you put us on our mettle."

"I did not write ahead for a room," he said. "And the sea captain told me these are busy days on the island. Is there room for me here? Or must I look elsewhere?"

"You're in luck, because we have only one room open—and it's my favorite," she replied. "How long do you plan to stay? Do you know?"

"Not more than a week, I think," he said, picking up his suitcase again. "But I am on no particular schedule."

"So how is everyone in Samaria?" Lucinda asked over her shoulder as she led him into the inn. "Your father? Mariah? Mercy?"

"I haven't been to Cedar Hills, but when I stopped at the Eyrie everyone there was well and expressly told me to give you their good wishes."

They were inside now, and Lucinda began pointing to doors and stairways. "That's the parlor. Many of the guests gather here in the evenings, and we sing or play games. There's the dining room. We serve meals promptly at eight, noon, and six, but you can generally convince Emmie to feed you at any time of the day. That door leads to the back where the water rooms are. Up here," she continued, starting up the stairwell, "are the guest rooms. Yours—should you find it satisfactory, sir—is the one at the very end of the hall. We have guests in all the other rooms, so I do hope you like this one!"

She flung open the door as soon as they reached it, and they both stepped inside the room. It was fairly small but nicely appointed, with a lovely view of the harbor through thick lace curtains. The four-poster bed was plush with a satin quilt; the desk, the armoire, and the chest of drawers were all constructed of a warm honey wood that glowed in the white morning light. On the walls were two paintings of Angel Rock done by some visitor more than a decade ago.

"But how charming!" Omar said, pivoting slowly to take in the furnishings, walking across the room to gaze out at the harbor. "I wonder that you don't keep such a pretty room for yourself!"

Lucinda laughed. "My room is smaller, crammed with *things*, and has no view to speak of, but since I'm rarely in it, I don't really mind. So you like it, then? You'd like to take it for the week?"

He turned back to smile at her. "At least a week."

"There's not much to divert you in Angel Rock," she warned him. "A week is about as much as most people can stand."

"And what are the entertainments?" he asked. "So I can work up my enthusiasm in advance."

"Well, many of our male guests like to fish," she said. "A few of the residents maintain fishing boats, and they'll take you out very early in the morning and stay out with you as long as you want. Have you ever fished?"

"Not in the ocean. In lakes and rivers. I like it. Do you?"

Lucinda laughed and shook her head. "Not at all! I don't mind eating fish, or even boning it and cooking it, but the idea of actually taking a live thing and sticking a hook through its mouth or its gill—awful. I can't do it. Besides—" She flicked her wings delicately. "I'm not much good on a small fishing craft. I don't exactly fit."

"You could trail your feathers in the water as bait," he suggested.

She laughed again. "Yes, and have eel nibbling at my wings! I don't think so! So I mostly stay away from the fishing expeditions."

"What else is there?" he asked.

"Well, in the summer months, some people go swimming off the north beach, but it's really too cold for that now," she replied. "There are a few pretty walks around the island—but it's not a very *big* island, and the walks don't take very long."

"And for entertainment in the evenings?"

She felt the laughter bubbling up again. Strange, she didn't usually find it this amusing to describe the charms of the island—but she knew where Omar came from, she knew how sophisticated his pleasures usually were, and Angel Rock could in no way match them.

"Well, lately the Jomarsons—who have been with us for six days—and Mrs. Temple, who has been here for three weeks—have been writing a play which they hope to perform in a few days for whoever can fit in our parlor one night," she said. "I'm sure they'd be delighted to have you contribute your wit to the composition of the play, or your acting skills to the performance. I've also learned how to play some pretty complex board games, which I could teach you if you don't already know them. And sometimes Hammet and Celia invite us over to the Gablefront Inn for an evening with their guests. Generally then people take turns singing, or reciting poetry, or telling funny stories. Usually it's quite enjoyable."

"Yes, it all sounds delightful. Why are you laughing at me, you silly child? Do you think I'm too jaded to enjoy simple pleasures?"

"Well—yes! After the Eyrie, and Luminaux, and Semorrah—"

"The Eyrie and Luminaux and Semorrah are the very reasons I have come to Angel Rock," he said firmly. "I find their pace too taxing. I must have quiet! Or I shall go mad!"

This last was said very dramatically, in obvious jest, and Lucinda laughed again. "Well, you shall have it here," she observed. "Come along downstairs. We'll tell Aunt Gretchen you've come to stay awhile."

They returned to the ground floor to look for Gretchen, whom they finally discovered in the orchard that grew some distance behind the house. She was frowning up at the riotously blossoming apple trees.

"Aunt Gretchen! Goodness, why are you looking so fierce?" Lucinda exclaimed. "I think the trees look gorgeous."

"Dory said she saw insects boring into her peach trees this morning, and I was just wondering if I would need to spray," Gretchen replied. "I don't see any evidence of trouble—but then, better too much prevention than a season ruined. What a bother! Well, I'd best go tell Jackson the glad news. You know how he hates spraying for bugs."

"Aunt Gretchen, we have a new visitor from the mainland," Lucinda said, since it seemed possible that Gretchen could stalk right by them, intent on ruining Jackson's day. "Do you remember Omar? Bael's son? You met him at the Gloria."

Gretchen did a strange, abrupt halt, spin, and stare, so that she seemed to be jerked from one plane of existence to a wholly different and less pleasant one. She dragged her eyes once from Omar's face to glance at her niece, and then she returned her attention to the Archangel's son.

"Yes. Of course I remember you," she said in a completely uninflected voice. "I just did not expect—what brings you to Angel Rock?"

Mystified by Gretchen's odd response, and hoping Omar didn't notice it, Lucinda spoke in a quick, bright tone. "He's come to rusticate for a few days and escape the grueling pace of the mainland. He says Bael may come to Angel Rock sometime in the future when *he* needs a vacation. Won't that be nice? Has he ever been here?"

"Not that I know of," Gretchen said, still in that strained voice. "I don't recall that any of the Archangels have ever come to the island."

"Lucinda has been telling me of all the pleasures in store for me," Omar said. "She laughed, but I confess, I did not expect so much! If I go out fishing and I'm successful, what do I do with my catch? Bring it back to the Manor for cooking?"

"Oh, yes! Emmie loves to make fresh fish. But you have to

catch enough to feed all the guests, because we wouldn't want anyone to feel slighted," Lucinda said.

"So if I only catch two, I should throw them back before we head for land."

"Unless they're two *very big* fish," she said solemnly, and then the two of them laughed. Gretchen gave them the smallest, unhappiest smile.

"Yes. How enjoyable for you," Gretchen said, seeming to speak almost at random. "Excuse me, Omar. I must go find Jackson. Lucinda, I'm sure you'll do what you can to make our new guest comfortable." And she hurried off.

Omar looked after her with a small frown. "Well! She seems very upset about her destructive bugs."

Or something, Lucinda thought. "Aunt Gretchen gets very focused on something, and that's all she can think about," she said lightly. "But she's a wonderful hostess. Let's go back to the house so you can unpack. Lunch will be ready in another two hours. Are you hungry?"

"Starved."

So Omar was settled in and introduced to the rest of the guests at the noon meal, where he managed to charm even the prim Mrs. Temple. Lucinda didn't see him again until dinner, because she got swept up in the orchard frenzy, and spent the entire rest of the day under the apple trees with Jackson and her aunt. They sprayed all afternoon, covering themselves with a noxious, choking chemical residue, and she never saw a single bug.

But she had cleaned herself up by dinner, which she looked forward to for the first time in nearly a month, and a very pleasant meal it was, too. Omar enthralled every guest with tales of the Eyrie and descriptions of the Gloria, painting vivid pictures of the great events and popular angels, and fielding all the questions the others put to him.

Except one. "And who's to be the next Archangel?" Mrs. Temple asked as dessert was being served. "Has that been decided?"

Omar looked grave. "The god has not yet spoken on that issue, which concerns my father greatly. All the oracles have been consulted, but Jovah has chosen not to answer this particular question."

"And what happens if no Archangel is named before the next

Gloria? It is next year that the new Archangel should sing for the first time, am I not right?''

"Indeed you are. My father, of course, is willing to carry on his duties as long as is necessary—but he has served nineteen years, and grows weary. He is as eager as anyone to see the next man—or woman—chosen."

"Do you think it might be a woman?" Ed Jomarson asked.

"Historically, the Archangel has been female roughly a third of the time," Omar said. "We have had several male Archangels in a row, so—yes, I think the chances are good that the god will select a woman."

"Mercy?" Lucinda asked.

Omar spread his hands in a diplomatic gesture of denial. "Mercy is not an old woman, but she would be by the time she had been Archangel for twenty years," Omar said. "Most often, the Archangel is in the prime of life—thirty or thirty-five, often young enough to still bear children. Delilah, of course, was barely twenty-five when she took over the role. But I do not remember any Archangel who was older than forty when he or she was named to the office."

"Then who?" Lucinda asked. "Are there many female angels between the ages of twenty-five and thirty-five living in Samaria?"

"Oh, there are several—quite lively, intelligent women, too. We'll just have to see what Jovah decides. It may be months before he lets us know. And it may be tomorrow."

"This is quite intriguing," Mrs. Temple said, quivering a little in her seat. "It makes it seem so much more exciting when you hear about it all firsthand. Now I cannot wait to see who is chosen."

That conversation ended the meal, and they all moved by common consent to the parlor. The Jomarsons and Mrs. Temple instantly went to work on their play, arguing in low voices over the wording of a line of dialogue. Three of the other guests got out a board game, and four others dealt out a hand of cards.

"That appears to leave you to entertain me," Omar said to the angel. "I spy a harpsichord in the corner. Is it too much to hope that you are allowed to play music at night, or will we disturb the others?"

"No, no disturbance!" Ed called out. "In fact, we consider

our evening quite ruined if Lucinda doesn't play for us at least an hour."

"Will you?" Omar asked her again.

"Gladly. Unless you would rather play? We have music, if you neglected to bring any."

"I'm not good on a keyboard," he said, following her over to the instrument. "A flute I have mastered with some gracefulness, I like to think, and I've been practicing on a lyre, but I don't have either with me."

"Well, you could sing," she said, seating herself on the bench. "For I know you have the skill for that."

He had picked up a book of music and was flipping through it. "Let's see. I know this piece, and this one, and—here. One of my favorites. Do you know it?"

He set the open book before her. "But this one is so sad!" she exclaimed.

"No, no, sweet and wistful. You don't want to play it?"

She ran her fingers over the opening chords, minor and dark. "I'll play it. You take the melody."

She let him sing the first verse solo, playing the accompaniment very softly, and she had to admit the piece was more moving than she remembered. Or perhaps she was swayed by the power of his voice, gorgeously grieving over the words of heartache and loss. In any case, she felt like crying before the chorus was reached. She added her voice in ghostly treble counterpoint, and the room instantly seemed haunted by echoes of sadness. She continued singing harmony through the second verse, and the third, and when they finally wrapped up the final chorus, the mood in the whole room was one of profound dejection.

Lucinda herself sat a moment with her hands on the keyboard, recovering her good temper and quite unable to speak. Omar sat beside her, seemingly lost in a reverie of his own. It took a voice from across the room to break the silence.

"But, Lucinda, can't you play something happier?" Mrs. Jomarson asked plaintively. "You're making my heart break!"

Murmured assents from the others caused Lucinda to toss her hair back and summon up a smile. "You see?" she said to Omar, and without consulting him, offered up the chords for a completely different song. This one was lively and fun, full of looping melody lines and a tricky harmony. He laughed, but joined in, and allowed her to pick the next few selections as well.

"I see we have completely different styles," he said several songs later when she paused. "I have been accused before of having a sober turn of mind, but you're the first one who's forbidden me to choose *any* of the music."

"And it seems so unlike you," she said, allowing her fingers to wander at random over the keyboard. "For you seem to be such an amusing, entertaining man. But your music—! I remember now. At the Gloria you did a very solemn piece as well."

"They say a man's true nature is revealed in his poetry and his song," he said lightly. "Whatever else he conceals about himself is inevitably revealed in verse."

"And is that true of you?" she said, looking at him sideways. "Are you a sad man in your secret, concealed heart?"

"Sad?" he repeated. "I would not say that. Serious, yes. These are serious days. A man needs to be earnest and sober."

She thought of the voyage to Angel Rock on *The Wayward,* the attack by the Jansai, Reuben's contention that the Archangel encouraged such piracy. She thought of the Jacobites, hounded from Samaria at Bael's instigation. She wondered what the son thought of the father's policies. Serious days, indeed.

But she smiled at him. "But you must meet grave challenges with a serene heart," she said. "You must seek happiness where you can. A joyful song floods my whole body with delight. That makes me stronger."

He gave her a deep, deferential nod, almost a bow. "You seem formed for joy," he said. "That makes you delightful to be near."

She surveyed him a little more speculatively, but her smile lingered. "And you have a very graceful way of flattering," she observed. "By week's end, I shall be so under your spell, I shall begin to believe you when you say things like that."

"Why wait that long?" he murmured. "Believe me now."

She laughed aloud, pleased despite herself. Before she could make an answer, some stray movement at the corner of her eye turned her attention to the door. Aunt Gretchen stood there, seemingly rooted in place, staring across the room at the couple by the harpsichord. Her angular face seemed bony with worry; her dark eyes were sharp with concern. Her hands twisted in her apron, furling and unfurling it with completely uncharacteristic disregard for an item of clothing. But she was not looking at Lucinda. Her gaze was fixed on Omar.

Lucinda glanced again at the Archangel's son. And what could Aunt Gretchen possibly know about Omar that would make her stare at him as if he was bad news direct from Jovah? Omar had opened a book of music and was idly flipping through its pages. He did not seem to notice the intense, despairing gaze that was trained on him from across the room. He found a selection that pleased him and offered it to Lucinda with a smile. She played it, but this time her heart was not in it. She could not imagine what, but something was greatly amiss.

Yet Gretchen said nothing to her the next morning, by which time most of Lucinda's odd uneasiness had evaporated. Omar had elected to spend the morning on one of the boats (promising to bring back a basketful of fish), so he could not disturb them with his presence. By the time he returned, sunburned and happy, Lucinda had managed to forget her aunt's strange reaction of the night before. She welcomed him into the kitchen, she incorporated his fish onto the night's menu, and she shooed him out of the house so she and Emmie could finish preparing the evening meal.

Which was delicious, and everyone said so. Afterward, the Jomarsons and Mrs. Temple cornered Omar to see if he'd be willing to take a part in their play, to which he agreed. He spent the rest of the evening huddled with them, discussing his part and the rehearsal schedule. Lucinda was surprised to find that she was a little disappointed—she had enjoyed his company the day before—but she amused herself playing card games with the other guests.

And two whole days were gotten through in this manner; and she had only thought of Reuben three or four hundred times in those two days; and she would see him again in as little as twelve days, perhaps. So she was not unhappy.

The next day, all the cast members commandeered the newly sprayed orchard and practiced their lines and argued over stage directions. No one was allowed close enough to overhear a word of dialogue, so Emmie and Lucinda took lunch out to them, left it a hundred yards away, and scampered back to the house, laughing.

That evening after dinner, Omar did manage to break free of

the playwrights and join Lucinda at the harpsichord again. "They're charming people, but do give me an hour's mercy!" he whispered in her ear. "I really cannot abide one more discussion about Jack's proper pronunciation—my character is named Jack, you see—or why he simply wouldn't say such a thing, though I think he would. Had I known how grueling this would be, I would never have agreed to take part."

"Nonsense, I'm sure you'd be completely bored if you weren't doing the play."

"I wouldn't be bored, I would be exploring the island with you," he said promptly. "Do you realize I have scarcely said a word to you for a whole day? I didn't realize that was the bargain I would be required to make."

"When do you perform?"

"Tomorrow night. Here in the parlor, I believe. I suppose we can seat twenty or so in the audience, though it will be a tight fit."

"Yes, we're supposed to invite everyone from the Gablefront to come for dinner and the theater. I think it will be fun."

"And the day after tomorrow? Can I have your complete, undivided attention?" he asked.

"Well, I don't know about that," she demurred. "But I can show you around the island."

"Good. It's a promise. Save the whole day for me."

They sang two songs together, a compromise of styles, for they chose some of the familiar folk songs that everyone loved despite their sad themes. Not wishing to alarm Gretchen again, Lucinda closed the instrument after the second song and suggested they join the others in a card game. And so the evening passed with a pleasant conviviality, and Gretchen, when she looked in, appeared to be content.

The next day the actors spent completely in seclusion while the staff of the hotel prepared for the evening's entertainment. Jackson, under Gretchen's direction, rearranged all the furniture in the parlor to create a makeshift stage and three rows of seats. Emmie and Lucinda cooked, baked, marinated, and grilled for what seemed like hours. Celia sent over two trays of desserts with a note promising ten people for the evening's festivities. Lucinda caught herself wondering what she should wear. Such excitement over a silly amateur play!

But the evening was fun. Celia, Hammet, and their eight visitors arrived promptly at six, and the expanded dinner table was quickly alive with conversation and laughter. Everyone lavishly praised the meal, and the wine flowed freely. The actors perhaps imbibed a little more than the others, for a few of them declaimed their lines over dessert, causing Ed Jomarson to leap up and clap his hand over his leading lady's mouth.

"I think it's time to raise the curtain!" Hammet called out, so the whole lot of them rose to their feet and jostled into the parlor. Ed had spent some time that afternoon rigging up dramatic lighting, and this elicited cries of "Very nice!" and "Isn't this impressive!" as the members of the audience found their seats.

The play itself was thoroughly bad, a comedy of manners involving a wealthy Bethel burgher who unknowingly insulted his neighbor's wife, and none of the actors could speak a convincing line. But no one in the audience was minded to be critical, and all the more outrageous insults were applauded wildly—including, Lucinda suspected, a few that were improvised on the spot. Omar and the Jomarsons' daughter had a love scene that had probably been more sedate when rehearsed in the orchard; but here, egged on by catcalls from the audience, the two actors indulged themselves with a prolonged embrace and many meaningful glances. Lucinda could not help noting that Omar's attentions to the Jomarson girl—his expressions, his tone of voice—seemed very similar to those he had used with her. Perhaps the man was both a flirt and an actor by nature.

The final scene had been written as broad satire and was played as grand farce, and everyone in the parlor was laughing helplessly as it drew to its ridiculous conclusion. On Ed's signal, Jackson cut all the lights. In the sudden darkness, Hammet could be heard calling out, "More! More! Author!" The houselights came back on to a standing ovation. Even Gretchen, lurking watchfully in the back of the room, was on her feet and smiling.

"Oh, the good god love us," Celia said, fanning herself with her hand. "That's one to go down in the history books. I can't remember the last time I've laughed so hard."

"Anybody interested in a little more dessert?" Gretchen said loudly, speaking up above the chattering crowd. Everyone answering in the affirmative, they all trooped back to the dining room. The day ended on a note of high hilarity and sweet confections, and everyone went up to their rooms that night full and happy.

And everyone slept in the next morning except Lucinda and Omar. They met early in the kitchen, packed a day's worth of food, and took off on foot before anyone else had crept down for breakfast.

"It wasn't nearly as awful as you'd led me to believe," the angel chided the reluctant actor. "Or—well, it *was,* but it was more fun than I'd thought it would be."

"Thanks to plenty of wine and an audience hungry for diversion," he said. "But I thank the great god watching over all of us that no one I know was here to witness my humiliation. And you cannot tell a soul what you once saw me lower myself to do."

"But you were very convincing," Lucinda said. "Particularly in the love scenes. I thought surely you had developed a passion for Ed Jomarson's lovely daughter."

Omar groaned and then he laughed. "If I thought you really believed that, I would go out in the next fishing boat and fling myself into the sea. But enough about that wretched play! Tell me about the island. Where are you taking me?"

So she showed him the main roads and took him on the long, winding path that circled the island. But she did not lead him to the beach she had shared with Reuben; she did not offer to take wing and fly him to any of the remoter peaks of Angel Rock, although she had done this for many guests in the past. But not this guest. She was not sure why.

They ate their lunch sitting on a short cliff that teased the ocean to furious spray twenty yards below them. The sun was warm enough to make them drowsy but not hot enough to make them cross. The wind was playful and surprising, stealing one of Lucinda's linen napkins before she could catch it, and brushing the brisk, damp sea air through their hair.

"Isn't this a beautiful day!" Lucinda exclaimed after a long moment of contented silence. "Do you see why people come to Angel Rock? Do you see why I love it here?"

"I do see," Omar said after a pause, and replying in a more serious voice than Lucinda expected. "And I'm glad to think that you've been so happy here. But I think it's time you considered coming back to Samaria. Permanently. This is no home for an angel."

Lucinda stared at him, taken completely by surprise. "What? But this has always been my home. Why should I think of leaving?"

Omar spread his hands. "It's a rock in the middle of the ocean. There is nothing here—nobody here. You see a few odd Edori every other week. Maybe a Manadavvi boatload now and then. Where is your companionship? Where is your society? You're an angel, Lucinda! You're one of Jovah's elect! You were put on the earth to help carry out the god's commandments and to bring him the petitions of the voiceless mortals. How can you serve humankind if you are so far from them they do not even know your name? How can you serve the god if he never hears your voice raised in prayer?"

"I raise my voice in prayer," she said, though at the moment her voice was strangled with disbelief. "I've asked for sunshine and for rain—I've prayed for medicine and received it. There are people here who need me, and I've served them—"

"But, Lucinda! There are—what, twenty people living on this island? On Samaria, you could serve thousands. You could live the true life of an angel, with all the reverence and adoration that commands. You could be part of the life of a hold, which is exciting and fulfilling and demanding. You could join other angels to sing masses to the god. You could lead the Gloria!"

"I thought only the Archangel led the Gloria," she said sharply.

"And how do you know the next Archangel will not be you?"

She simply stared at him.

"We wonder why the god has not named the next Archangel," Omar went on, more slowly. "Could it be because he is not familiar with her name? Because he is not familiar with her voice?"

"He knows my voice," Lucinda whispered. "He knows my name."

"He has not seen you function in Samarian society. He has not seen if you can command the respect of angels and the adoration of mortals. He has not been able to judge you. But if you return with me to Samaria—"

Lucinda laughed in amazement. "You think to promise me the role of Archangel, which no one but the god can bestow, if

I will only return to the mainland with you? I think you go a little too far.''

''I make no promise. But I tell you the truth. The god has chosen no one and we do not know why. But it only makes sense that he is observing us all, looking for clues, looking for weaknesses. How can he choose you if he cannot observe you? Do you not want to be considered for the greatest honor any angel can achieve?''

''Well, frankly, I've never given it any thought,'' Lucinda replied. She was still shocked and more than a little bewildered, but alert now and not ready to be outmaneuvered by Omar. ''But offhand I would say I would be the last angel Jovah would name to the post.''

''And why?''

''Because—'' She stopped, at a loss for words. Omar leaned closer.

''Because you live remote and isolated, unused to the ways of angel society.''

''Well—perhaps.''

''But if you came with me to Samaria—''

''But I don't want to go with you to Samaria! I'm happy here!''

''For how long? For the rest of your life? To live and die solitary, unknown and unsung? Come to us for one year—for six months. Discover if you like the life, or if you hate it. Then decide if you want to return to Angel Rock forever. If at all.''

She wanted to refuse outright, to tell him she had no interest in the gaudy, frenetic life of the mainland, but the words would not come. She remembered her weeks in Samaria after the Gloria, the color and pageantry of the cities and the holds. Well, she had enjoyed herself then. She had felt more alive and excited than she ever had. And she had wanted to go back—for a visit, nothing more!—though not right away. As a special treat. Once every few years. For a month or less.

But to live there? To make that her permanent home?

To be considered for Archangel—?

She scrambled to her feet, hastily brushing crumbs and seeds from her lap. ''I don't want to talk about this anymore,'' she said rapidly. ''Angel Rock is my home. These are my people. The god—or you or anyone else who looks for me—can find me right here.''

And she flung herself forward off the edge of the cliff, diving straight toward the ocean before pulling herself up in a close, sharp curve, driving her wings hard against the heavy sea air. She flew high, higher, straight toward the clouded outline of the sun, so high that Angel Rock shrank to a black stone in the ocean below her, and she could not see Omar at all.

She avoided her guest for the next two days, and he wisely made no move to approach her. To her extreme irritation, she could not stop thinking about what he had said. Oh, not the business about being the Archangel—that was a lure he had no right casting. But about Samaria. Living there. At least for a while. A few months. To determine if it would be the right place for her after all.

Aunt Gretchen would rage against such plans, she knew. Would resist them with all her considerable strength of will. But if she decided to leave, simply take wing one day and fly toward the mainland, there was no way Aunt Gretchen could stop her. Though she would not want to part that way, secretly or in anger. She would want her aunt's blessing. Which she would never get.

Although she could *ask*.

If she wanted to go.

Which she didn't. Not really. Although, for a month, or maybe two, could it really be such a bad idea?

She tried to think of other things, but could not. Even counting the days till Reuben's arrival (seven now, or so she thought) did little to distract her. She wondered what Reuben would think of her moving to Samaria. She thought he would not like it, especially if *The Wayward* did not go often to the mainland. But if it did . . . Well, he might have an opinion to offer her; she would listen to his advice.

And then she would make up her mind.

All the soul-searching left her abstracted and a little fretful, though she tried to hide her preoccupation behind her usual light cordiality. Nonetheless, she caught Gretchen's eyes on her more than once, sharp and considering, and Emmie asked her a couple of times if she was brooding over something.

"If it's that Edori sailor, though, I don't want to hear about it," Emmie added. "Because I warned you! Don't be thinking about him."

At dinner that second day Lucinda made a point of sitting by Omar and engaging him in idle talk. He slanted her a quick, sideways look but easily joined in the conversation, relating a funny story about an adventure at Coburn's general store that had everyone at the table laughing. Afterward, in the parlor that she had shunned for two days, Lucinda sat at the harpsichord and softly played a few sweet melodies. Omar joined her within five minutes.

"Am I to take it that I have been forgiven for suggesting the unthinkable?" he said, seating himself beside her.

"If you promise not to say another word about it, yes," she said. "Are you in the mood to perform tonight? What would you like to sing?"

"Songs of farewell," he said. "I leave in the morning."

She was conscious of an unexpected jolt of some unidentifiable emotion—regret? relief?—but her hands did not falter on the keys. "Your week is up, then. It seemed to go quickly."

"Too quickly. But I'll come back in a few months, if I may."

"We'd be glad to have you."

She selected a few ballads, a little mournful but completely to Omar's taste, and they sang duets while the other guests murmured in the corners. Between selections, they talked quietly of inconsequential things, and the hours passed without any unpleasant interchanges.

But late that evening, as Omar rose to go to his room, he paused to look at her intently. "Think of what I said," he said soberly. "Any hold would welcome you. For any length of time. And the Eyrie would be honored to have you."

She did not reply, but she nodded once, her eyes still on her music. He lingered another moment, but when she did not look up, he made her a brief bow and left the room. In the morning, when she emerged for a late breakfast, he was gone.

That afternoon, as Lucinda lay napping in her room (she had gotten very little sleep the past two nights, for there was so much on her mind), Gretchen burst in without knocking. "Open the drapes, we need a little light," her aunt said without preamble, stalking to the closet. Lucinda sat up in bed, marveling. Gretchen threw open the closet doors. "What will you want? Summer clothes, I suppose, but you'd best take a few warm things. You never know about weather."

"What—? Aunt Gretchen, what in the world—"

Gretchen was pulling out shirts and vests, tossing them on the bed when they suited her, and jamming them back in the closet when they did not. "You won't really need your nice clothes—maybe one dress, and the rest can be those sturdy trousers you like so much. Here, do you want to bring this? It's rather pretty."

Lucinda came to her feet, sure she must still be dreaming. As instructed, she drew open the curtains and let the room flood with afternoon sunlight. But even by this illumination, nothing seemed clearer. Gretchen was still rooting through her hangers, looking for acceptable items.

"You may as well take this blouse. I've never liked it, but I know it's one of your favorites. And shoes! Well, I suppose you should bring your boots and then those sandals you like so much."

Lucinda crossed the room, took her aunt by the arm, and pulled her forcibly away from the closet. "Aunt Gretchen, what are you doing? Why do you think I'm taking a trip? Where do you think I'm going?" *Samaria?* she wanted to ask, but she couldn't think that was possible. But then, where?

Gretchen faced her, her expression stony and set, her eyes wild with anger or conviction. "Ysral," she said. "By the next boat out."

Lucinda dropped her hand. "*Ysral!* But—this is ridiculous. Stop a minute. Tell me what's going on."

"I think you need to get away from Angel Rock for a while. A few months perhaps. I have friends in Ysral. You can visit them."

"You do not have friends in Ysral! You've never mentioned them if you do. And why do I need to go away from Angel Rock? For Jovah's sweet sake, sit down and tell me what is going on here."

A moment longer Gretchen stood ramrod stiff, and then all the energy seemed to leak suddenly from her thin body. She sagged forward, drained and exhausted.

"I don't think you're safe here anymore," Gretchen said in a low voice. "I never should have taken you to the Gloria."

Which made no sense either. Lucinda shook her head once as if to clear it, then took Gretchen's arm again, and led her to the bed. She pushed her aunt down to the mattress and took her own seat in a nearby chair.

"Start at the beginning," she said. "What's wrong? What are you afraid of? What does it have to do with me?"

Gretchen sat shapelessly where Lucinda had set her, staring before her at sights distant from this room and this time. "Bael," she said at last. "He has remembered you exist. And he has taken an interest in you again. And I want you as far from him as possible."

"And why?"

"Because he killed your mother and your sister. And he is an evil, evil man."

Delirium, delusion, madness; and yet she spoke so calmly. Lucinda felt a cold, chilly hand spiderwalk down her spine. "My mother died on the side of the road, my sister in her arms," Lucinda said gently. "Bael had nothing to do with their deaths."

Gretchen nodded, her eyes still fixed on some point in the wretched past. "Before Bael was named Archangel, he spent much of his time at Cedar Hills. He had been Michael's foster son, you know, and they were very close. He was almost as outraged as Michael was when Rinalda—your mother—joined the Jacobites, and he concurred with Michael's decision to keep her imprisoned at Cedar Hills. Although, in fact, he recommended harsher punishment for her. But Michael was not in the habit of condemning young women to death."

Lucinda caught her breath sharply, but said nothing. After a moment Gretchen went on. "When you and your sister were born, no one was more horrified than Bael. He made no secret of the fact that he considered it an abomination that an angel should have been twinned in the womb with a mortal. He even claimed that Jovah had warned him that the arrival of such twins signaled the end of Samarian society as we knew it. Now, how would Jovah have told him such a thing? I asked the oracle Deborah if she had received that message from the god, and she said Jovah had commented on the arrival of the twins but she had not interpreted his remarks in just that way. It was Bael's own great hatred that led him to concoct such a lie."

Gretchen paused a moment, but Lucinda absolutely could not think of a word to say. Gretchen's voice dropped a few notes lower, and her next words came more slowly. "It was a miserable winter that year. Colder than I have ever seen it, anywhere, at any time. You know the story—a few weeks after you were born, Rinalda escaped from her locked room into the icy winter night, carrying your sister in her arms. And was found two days later, frozen to death. And everyone at Cedar Hills thought it was sad, but probably for the best.''

Gretchen raised her eyes suddenly, and they were fierce with an old torment. "But I know Bael helped her escape, because I saw him lead her down the corridor. I saw that baby in her arms. And I know, as surely as I am sitting here today, that he chose that night, that winter night, to set her free—with no coat, with no boots, with no haven anywhere for miles. Because he wanted her to die on the side of the road, and he wanted that baby to die with her. And I have known from that day on that Bael is a murderer, no matter that he is the most revered angel in Samaria.''

"But—did you tell anyone? Michael? My father? Anyone?''

Gretchen shook her head. She had dropped her eyes again, and when she spoke, she addressed the floor. "There was no one to tell. There was nothing to say. Rinalda was dead, and a day later, so was your father. But three years later the god announced that Bael would become Archangel when Michael's tenure was ended. I knew then that you were no longer safe in Samaria. And I brought you to Angel Rock, and raised you as best I could, and kept you from Bael as long as I was able. And I was a fool to allow you to return to Samaria, for he has remembered you, and sent his son to court you, and you are no longer safe if he knows where you are.''

Melodrama; nonsense; and yet . . . She could not deny that Omar had been courting her, in a peculiar, unsettling way, and he had been very attentive to her at the Gloria. Lucinda remembered suddenly that Omar had come to visit her at Cedar Hills, and that the very next day, Gretchen had abruptly insisted they return to Angel Rock. Gretchen had been so eager to leave Samaria that she had agreed to travel on an Edori ship. Had she feared Omar even then? Feared Bael?

Lucinda leaned forward and put her hand on the older woman's arm. "Aunt Gretchen, I do not want to run away, from Angel Rock and from you,'' she said softly. "I am not afraid of Bael—''

"Well, you should be!'' Gretchen exclaimed, suddenly frenzied. "For he has killed Jacobites other than your poor mother, and he is willing to stop at nothing to erase them all! He is dangerous, he is ruthless, and his son is power mad. And if you do not realize that, you are in even more danger than I thought. You must be gone from here as soon as possible."

"But I don't want to go to Ysral! I don't know anyone there, I don't—"

"I have a friend there. He'll take care of you. He can be trusted."

"Who is this friend you have never mentioned?"

"His name is Conran. He knew your mother."

"He knew my *mother*! I didn't realize the two of you had any friends in common."

"A few, but Conran the best of them. I have not seen him in nearly thirty years."

This was more and more like an unsettling dream, full of disconnected words and images. Lucinda ran a hand through the snarls in her hair, wishing she could untangle her thoughts as easily. "Then—how do you know where he is? How do you know he can still be trusted? How do you know anything?"

"I hear from him now and then. For Rinalda's sake, he has always had a great deal of interest in you. So I have sent him letters from time to time. He'll be happy to see you."

"And he's in Ysral? Is he Edori?"

"No," Gretchen said sharply, for of course she did not like Edori. "He's a Jacobite."

And Lucinda stared at her aunt, and her whole world disintegrated around her, foundation, form, and essence. For if her aunt was a secret Jacobite, and had been for twenty-five years, then nothing Lucinda had believed in was solid or could be relied on. And nothing made sense or conformed to any rules. And there was no safety in Ysral, or anywhere.

Five days later *The Wayward* pulled into Angel Rock, bound for Ysral. And Lucinda boarded, half her belongings in her hands, and sailed away from the island toward the cautious, unpredictable welcome of strangers.

CHAPTER FOURTEEN

Life at Cartabella was not nearly as enjoyable as life in Semorrah, but it wasn't bad, either. Gene was a strict boss when it came to treating the horses properly and keeping the stables clean, but other than that he left his workers to their own devices and had little commentary to offer on their lives or personal habits. The other grooms were an odd assortment of misfits, mostly taciturn older men who dealt with animals much better than with people and were just as happy to be left in solitude. Gregor, the young boy who had first greeted Tamar upon her arrival, was the most tiresome of the lot, always looking for entertainment, conversation, or distraction; but most of the other grooms ignored him, so Tamar found it safe to do so, too.

She ate in the common mess hall, where all the ostlers, gardeners, and field-workers took their meals, and there was a constant stream of visitors into the stables, but it was possible to pass an entire day without having more than a brief exchange of words with anyone. At night, Tamar retired to her tiny room, spent five minutes reveling in the blessed privacy, then read for an hour before falling into a deep, exhausted sleep. Working in the stables was hard, demanding labor, but she welcomed the physical challenge. The more strength required of her body, the less energy she had left to funnel to her mind. She was glad to have a couple weeks of simply not thinking.

Although she would have to think again, someday. She could not spend the rest of her life in seclusion on Isabella Cartera's well-run farm. She would go mad, that was one consideration; but it was a waste of her life, that was another. She must find her friends again, take up the search again, once more have the courage to tell Samaria the truth about Jovah and the Alleluia Files.

The more she thought about it, the more she thought Conran and the others must have gone to Ysral. It seemed the only safe choice for the long term. So she must join them there, but it was insanity to try to leave from Breven, Kiss or no Kiss. Perhaps there would be ships departing for Ysral from Port Clara or one of the other harbor cities. She would work here a month or two, save all her wages, then travel in careful stages to one of the other ports and see if she could book a passage out.

That much she eventually decided, over a fortnight's attempts to avoid thinking at all; she could come up with no other solutions for her life. So for now she would just exist.

The only really disturbing part of her life these days was the music in her head. It was the oddest thing. She still had bouts of the strange vertigo that had troubled her since she had had the Kiss installed, but for whatever reason, these had ceased to worry her. Actually, at times, when the day was particularly dull, she welcomed those dizzy sensations of whirling above the earth in giddy, looping patterns. If she closed her eyes (and wrapped her hands around the railing of a corral or some other convenient hold), she truly felt as if she was flying, climbing straight into the cloudless blue sky, plummeting downward in a terrifying free fall, then spinning back upward in a whirling climb of cartwheels. She wondered where these fantasies came from (some head injury she had suffered in the past, perhaps, though she could not remember any this serious), but somehow the sessions did not seem as alarming as they had at first. She enjoyed them; she actually looked forward to them.

But the singing, at least at the beginning, did unnerve her. It had begun while she was in Semorrah, but in that bustling city, it was easy to believe the faint, indistinct music was coming from an outside source—someone in the next house practicing a melody, a street vendor trying out a song. But after she had spent a few days in the quiet confines of Cartabella, the music became clearer—and more internal—as if it originated inside her head, somewhere at the back of her skull, and vibrated in the space between her ears.

She could not shake away the sweet, liquid notes; she could not clap her hands over her ears and shut out the music. More than once she stared wrathfully down at the Kiss in her arm, convinced that it was some kind of receptor picking up the music on a frequency tuned only to her brain, and narrowly broadcasting on a band only she could hear. For she had never had this experience before she had been Kissed by the god. Surely that was not a coincidence.

Yet mistrusting the Kiss did not stop the music—nothing did—and she had no choice but to listen to it. Eventually it was so clear that she could distinguish every note, every nuance, every catch of the singer's breath. After a while she could sing along.

For her personal muse sang one piece over and over again, an eerie, complex melody that seemed neither sad nor exultant, though it had a peculiar power that made it a hard song to ignore. And then, for several days in a row, the singer performed what seemed like a different number, though within a few measures Tamar was convinced it was merely the harmony line to the first song. She experimented, humming the melody she knew beneath the descant in her head; yes, they fit exactly.

Thereafter, whatever part the singer took, Tamar took the other, whistling or humming along with the disembodied voice; and in this way, over time, she lost her distrust of the music as she had lost her fear of the vertigo. She knew she should hold on more tightly to her outrage and suspicion, but she could not. She did not have the strength. And for some reason, she was not afraid.

It was like having a secret companion, here on this friendless farm, a voice to listen to in the dark. She thought she might actually be sorry if the singer ever abandoned her abruptly and she was left once again in silence.

But it was not to be expected that her period of calm would last forever, and inside of three weeks it began to fray. Isabella Cartera was hosting a wedding, a grand event, and dozens of guests began to arrive at the compound.

"These are the rules," Gene told his staff the morning after the carriages began pulling up at the house. "There's always at least one ostler waiting at the front door. Most of Isabella's guests will come in some kind of motorized car, but a few of them will arrive by carriage, and some will arrive on horseback. We must be ready to take the horses instantly and stable them.

"Some of the guests will want to ride in the mornings. More will want to ride in the afternoons. Any guest who wants to borrow a horse may do so. If any guest is riding alone, offer to accompany him. If he declines, note when he leaves and make sure he returns. If he has not returned by the time your shift ends, notify me. If he returns, but the horse looks abused or mistreated, notify me. Every time one of our horses is returned to the stable, check it thoroughly for burrs, soreness, lameness—any problem a novice rider might overlook.

"We will not let Isabella's horses out before dawn or after dusk, unless it is a special ride authorized by Isabella. However, guests may take out their own horses at any time, and some of them may wish to ride at odd hours. One of you must sleep in the stables at all times so someone is available to serve the guests at a moment's notice. You will take turns sleeping here—we'll make up a schedule.

"Isabella's guests are to be treated with unfailing politeness. Call them lord, lady, sir, madam, angelo, or angela as the case requires. Some of them may be a little arrogant, but I expect you to overlook that. If someone is actually rude to you, or unkind to the horses, I expect you to report that to me immediately."

He continued talking for a few more minutes, but Tamar's mind had disengaged. *Angelo? Angela?* Were angels coming to Isabella Cartera's? That had not previously occurred to her, although she should not be surprised; Isabella's wealth was such that she undoubtedly moved in the highest circles of Samarian society. Which was composed mostly of angels.

Well, but angels never rode horses. They were notoriously inept in the saddle, their great wings creating all sorts of problems for themselves and their beasts. None of them would have any reason to come to the stables. She was safe.

Nonetheless, the days leading up to the wedding at Cartabella were filled with other disagreeable incidents. For instance, the visiting nobility were not always as noble as their lineage might suggest. And some of them found it quite curious—and intriguing—that a woman would be employed in the stables.

Tamar had her first taste of this only two days after the guests began arriving. Three young bloods—from southern Jordana, she guessed by their accents—found her alone in the stables and began pressing for her personal history.

"Say! Last time I went to fetch a horse, the groom was old, ugly, smelled of tobacco, and fondled himself with his free hand while he held my bridle in the other," said the tallest one, dressed in clothes that were perfumed like money. "I much prefer a pretty girl like you."

She schooled her features into neutral stiffness. "Which are your horses, sirs? I will bring them from the stalls for you."

"And will you ride with us if we ask you nicely?" said one of the others, a small blond with a handsome face but close-set, narrow eyes. "We're unfamiliar with the land around Isabella's farm. We might get lost."

"I have been instructed only to ride with the ladies," she said woodenly. It was not true, of course, but she suspected Gene would back her up.

"Ah! And were you imported just to service the ladies?" the tall one said, unmistakably stressing the word "service." "For I do not recall you being here the last time I visited Isabella."

"No," she said baldly.

"And how long have you been a groom?" he asked. He seemed to be the leader of the group; in any case, he was the one who kept edging closer to her no matter how she attempted to sidestep him.

"Long enough. Which are your horses, sirs? I will bring them out for you."

"I'm afraid my mare may have pulled her right foreleg," her tormentor continued in a soft, silky voice. "Will you put her through her paces for me so I can see how she handles? I'm sure you've got a gentle touch that she'll respond to, though normally she only allows me to ride her."

"Perhaps one of your friends can oblige you," Tamar replied. "I have work of my own to attend to."

He was beginning to get testy. "I assure you, I am asking what I would ask of any groom," he said coldly. His other companion, the one who had not yet spoken, touched him gently on the arm.

"Oh, let it be, Devon," he said in a calm voice. "Let the girl go to her work, and let's get on with the ride."

Devon jerked his arm away and stalked across the stable to where a restive, high-strung palomino pranced nervously in her stall. "Fine," he snapped. "I'll take care of my mare myself."

Tamar nodded gravely and turned to the other two noblemen, who appeared slightly embarrassed by their friend's fit of temper. "Sirs?" she repeated.

"The black is mine," said the third man, pointing. "And Alan's is the bay with the white nose. We'll await you outside."

That was the most chilling of the incidents, but more than one of the other visitors expressed a great deal of interest in her presence, her appearance, and her ability to perform her job. She treated them all with a noncommittal courtesy, rarely made eye contact, and never allowed herself to come close enough to be touched.

She mentioned none of this to Gene until the skirmish with Devon, and then she felt it best to speak up before one of the noble lords complained to the head groom. "If I behaved wrong, tell me," she finished. "I'll do what you say."

But she had gambled correctly. He frowned, and nodded thoughtfully. "Hadn't thought about it before," he said. "You hear stories about how lads like that treat the maids and the upper servants, but as I haven't had too many women working for me in the stables, it didn't occur to me. . . ." His voice trailed off. He studied the pattern of halters hanging on nails in the far wall. "Well, we'll take you off the night shift. There's one worry done away with. Could make you point person at the front door all day—you might get a few comments still, but there'd be too many people about for anyone to corner you and try a mischief."

Yes, but at the front door she'd be highly visible to anyone who happened to drop by Cartabella—angels, noblemen, anyone. "You could put me in charge of exercising the estate horses," she said. "That way, I'd mostly be out of the stables but I'd still be working."

He nodded slowly. "That's fine with me. Still might run into a few hotheads now and then who think any woman is fair prey."

She gave him a quick, demure smile. "But if I'm exercising the horses," she murmured, "I can just ride away."

He grinned back. "Fine. Your call. Something else comes up, let me know, and we'll work it out. But don't be afraid to tell me about it. I know the gentlefolk. Not so gentle."

So that comforted her, though she wondered if her coworkers

might resent her for getting preferential treatment. If they did, they did not say so. Gregor did comment on her new duties ("Better you than me. I'd rather feed them than take them out for exercise"), but didn't seem to feel she'd received any privileges. All in all, she felt she was surviving Isabella Cartera's influx of visitors relatively well.

Although, the next day, she was not so sanguine.

She had risen early to give special attention to Lunacy, a two-year-old filly that Gene had recently acquired. The horse had picked up some bad habits from her previous trainer and didn't like to be handled by women, though she was small-boned and delicate and clearly destined to be a lady's mount. Tamar wanted to accustom the filly to a woman's voice and touch before she attempted to take her on a long ride—or turned her over to Isabella Cartera.

Lunacy backed from Tamar's hand before she had even opened the stall door, and whickered plaintively as if to call for help. "You have no idea how this hurts my feelings," Tamar told her in a low, steady voice. She always talked incessant nonsense to the nervous horses; it usually calmed them. "To have you reject me in this way. I'll have you know I've never abused a horse. Never will. You're completely safe in my hands."

The dainty ears flicked forward, and the big, intelligent eyes watched her warily. Tamar could not help smiling. Lunacy was irritating, no question, but Tamar felt a certain kinship with her. Just so she pictured her own reaction—to anyone, male or female—if she was suddenly transmogrified into a horse.

"Now, I know you've been fed already. Come out with me to the corral. We're going to see how you take the saddle and bridle this time. Don't you want to learn how to behave prettily enough to have Isabella choose you as her favorite mount? She's quite the most important person on the farm, you know. Everyone will admire you if she's your rider."

Eventually, Lunacy allowed herself to be bridled and led from the stall. Once outside in the golden spring morning, she pranced a little—nerves, maybe, but Tamar thought it might be a small celebration of her delight in the lovely day. She smiled.

"All right. Let's walk once around the corral. I'll just hold the bridle, like this, and you can walk beside me, and you can see how easy it is, just walking, just having a nice little chat."

They circled the corral twice, Tamar talking all the while, and Lunacy's initial skittishness quickly evaporated. Tamar considered trying to mount for a brief ride, but thought she'd wait a day or two, till the horse was used to her voice and her presence. Then she'd see how Lunacy reacted to a saddle and a rider.

"See. Wasn't that easy?" she said, coming to a halt and patting the filly's nose. "Would you like a little sugar? Would that make you like me better?"

"Doesn't take sugar to make *me* like you better," said a smooth voice behind her, and she whirled so suddenly that the horse whinnied and tried to jerk the lead rope from her hand. It was Devon and his blond companion Alan, and they were both smiling at her in a menacing fashion.

"She's a beauty, now, isn't she," Devon said, coming closer to run his manicured hand down the horse's nose. Tamar tried to step away, but she didn't want to let go of the bridle. She kept thinking there must be some way to spin around, leap onto the horse's back, and gallop away. "Not too well trained, though. Is that your task—to break her in?"

"My favorite kind of work," the towhead drawled. "Breaking in a new filly."

Both men laughed. Devon was already as close to Tamar as he could get; now the blond stepped forward, crowding her against the horse. Lunacy neighed and backed away, but Devon's hand was on the halter, and his iron grip forced her to a standstill.

"I like them spirited," the tall man observed, "but not so stubborn they can't be taught."

No way to get on the horse and ride off. Tamar stood frozen in place for five seconds, then lunged forward and ducked under Devon's arm. There was a flurry of motion as the horse reared backward, both men yelled, and someone dove after Tamar. She felt hands close on her arm and jerk her back; she whirled around with the motion and lashed out with her free hand, making solid contact with someone's chest. Alan's. She heard his small grunt of surprise, and his clutch on her arm loosened. But before she could do more than think of running away, Devon's arms snaked around her from behind, and he crushed her to his chest. She could feel his heart pounding, hear his sudden ragged breathing, smell his mixed scent of cologne, leather, and finely starched linen.

"I think we deserve a little more courtesy than that," he murmured in her ear, drawing her even closer. She felt her ribs protesting the strain, and there was a terrific pain building up in her right arm. Perhaps Alan had bruised her when he grabbed her. "Alan, show the young lady how we prefer to be treated."

She could not back up but she whipped her head from side to side as the blond leaned closer, clearly intent on kissing her. "Feisty," he said with a laugh, and placed his hands on either side of her face, holding her still. She kicked out furiously, missing his groin but connecting with her knee, causing him to howl and hop backward. Devon was laughing; she could feel his chest shake. As soon as Alan regained his balance, he rushed forward and slapped her viciously across the cheek.

"Stupid bitch!" he exclaimed. "Would you like to see what we could really do to you if we wanted?"

She pursed her mouth to spit at him. But before she could act, before either man could speak again, the air around them suddenly changed. It grew both shadowed and iridescent, as if the sun were filtered suddenly through a vibrant, translucent awning. The air ruffled around them; a rapid, muffled rhythm seemed to offer up the heartbeat of the wind itself. All three of them gaped upward. All three of them grew loose and stupid in a moment's quick shock.

It was an angel hovering barely ten feet above them, looking like Jovah's wrath personified. He blocked the light with his outstretched wings; his arm was extended in an accusatory gesture. The bracelets on his wrists glittered with baleful emerald light, and just below his shoulder, the Kiss in his arm blazed like a miniature sun.

"And this is what noblemen consider a fitting pastime for their idle hours! Devon Malpasson and Alan Parlair—I recognize both of you. Who are you troubling now with your ugly faces and your ill-bred desires?"

Not until the angel spoke their names did Tamar's attackers actually release her. "Let's get back to the house," she heard Alan mutter. Devon snarled, "What mix is it of his?" but she could feel him slinking past her with much less of his usual arrogance. For herself, she could not move a muscle, not to retrieve the drifted horse, not to run to the stables, not to cover her face in mortification. For the angel could just as well have called out her name—he knew it. She knew his. The angel Jared, leader of the host at Monteverde.

He waited till the other two had stalked away, then canted his wings and came down for a noiseless landing. He looked not at his feet or the terrain beneath him, but straight at her; and while he watched her she could not turn her eyes away.

She had remembered the tangled brown hair, the shape of his face, even the timbre of his voice. She had forgotten the color of his eyes, gray and stern as a father's reproach. She had to force herself not to open the conversation with an apology. He came a step closer, still staring at her, and she stiffened her backbone and stared right back.

"So. You made it safely from Ileah, I see," he said, the sarcastic edge very faint in his voice.

"I did," she said. "How was Peter when you left him?"

"In good hands. I did not linger to watch his recovery. I wanted to hurry back. In case I was needed."

She winced a little; but she would not be cowed. "You did not rush back because you feared for my safety," she retorted. "You wanted information—secrets about my friends. I left before you could try to force that information from me."

"Wrong on all counts," he said, and now his voice showed a certain grimness. "I wanted—I still want—to help you, and possibly help your friends. And even if I was after information, I never would have resorted to the tactics those two fellows tried. You were safer with me than you have been at any time since."

Tamar did not exactly sniff, but the sound she produced was fairly close. "I have been in no danger."

"Well, you will be," he said soberly, and reached inside a pocket on his leather vest. It had not escaped Tamar's notice that he was very casually dressed, in tight leather leggings and a sleeveless vest; and he was, by any standard, more appealing than the last two men she had just viewed. Not that it mattered, not that she cared. "The Archangel—who, as you know, is not fond of Jacobites—has managed somehow to come up with a portrait that resembles you. And this he has passed along to all the Jansai and any other mercenary souls who might be willing to make an easy dollar by bringing you to the Eyrie. Not a great likeness, but a passable one, don't you think?"

He handed over a piece of paper. She looked down at her

features, ill-drawn but unmistakable, and felt a chill hand wrap bony fingers around her heart. "You drew this," she whispered. "To frighten me."

"It is not a skill I have," Jared replied coldly.

She looked up at him, blindly now, seeing not his face but her own, chalky and blurred on the much-folded paper. "But—I don't—why?" she stammered. "There is no reason—I am not someone Bael should care about one way or another."

"Oh, he has other portraits, which I've got copies of. A man called Conran—I can see by your face you've heard of him— a couple of others. But you and Conran seemed to be the two he was most interested in. Don't ask me why. I wouldn't have pegged you as the dangerous type, myself. Stupid, maybe, but not dangerous."

The epithet cleared her mind and restored her vision instantly. "Just because I don't trust you is no reason to call me stupid," she said fiercely. "At least I'm alive, which is more than I can say for many of my friends. And who knows if trusting angels isn't what killed them?"

A strange, reluctant smile crossed his face. "I have to give you credit for spirit, if nothing else," he said, almost as if he spoke to himself. "What can I do to make you believe me? For you have to believe me. We need to leave Isabella's the day the wedding is over. I must take you to Ysral. I don't think you'll be safe anywhere else."

"Ysral? Why should I go to Ysral?" she demanded, though she had decided just a few days ago that was her ultimate destination. But she would not travel anywhere with this man, not a mile, not an inch.

"Because it's not Samaria, for one thing. And because I believe the rest of the Jacobites are there, for another."

"How would you know anything about the Jacobites' plans?" she said suspiciously. "How do you know about these—these portraits? Where do you get all your information?"

"I have a friend. Christian Avalone, do you know of him?" She nodded. "He's a merchant who has no love for Bael. And because Bael has no love for the Jacobites, Christian has decided to help the Jacobites where he can. Also, I suspect that in his heart Christian likes the idea of a mechanical god instead of a real one. Christian has only a very small heart, you know—most businessmen do—and that would simplify his life considerably."

"You talk in riddles," she said. "And nothing I have heard about Christian Avalone makes me trust him any more than I trust you."

"Then it appears we are at a standstill," he said lightly.

She waited, but he said nothing more, which was very annoying. She had quite enough anger left to counter everything he said with a good, hard insult, but she felt ridiculous just standing there looking at him when he did nothing but stand there in return.

"Did you come here searching for me?" she asked, just for something to say.

"No, I had another reason for coming to Isabella's. I am as astonished to see you as you are to see me. Though not surprised to find you in trouble."

She scowled at that, but even through her narrowed eyelids she could see the residual opal glow on his arm. "And why in the world is your Kiss all lit up like that?" she said irritably.

He glanced at it, as if he hadn't noticed, and then gave her the most peculiar smile. "And why is yours?" he asked in return.

Quickly she checked, but it was true. The pain she had taken for Alan's mishandling was the result of a pulsing, swirling fire in the depths of her Kiss. She felt both bewildered and very, very wary. She looked back at the angel. "Why does it do that?" she asked. She remembered the stories she had heard—but Ezra had told her they were fairy tales—surely the angel was not about to tell her—

He was still smiling. "Legends say your Kiss will light when you meet another person with whom you have some—bond," he replied. She had the sense that he was editing. "There appears to be some sort of link between us. For instance, I know you were working at the Berman House in Semorrah." She could tell that her face showed her astonishment; he nodded. "The night I had dinner there, my Kiss flared just like this. I didn't figure it out till later, then I returned to Semorrah looking for you. Jasper told me you had gone to visit your sick sister."

He had the story right; he must be telling the truth. "And now?" she breathed.

"Minutes after I arrived on the farm, I felt a kind of pressure in my arm. I couldn't believe it—after all the time I've spent looking for you, could you possibly be here? And then, a few hours later, the pressure became intense. Painful, actually. They say that the angel Gabriel felt fire in his Kiss when his angelica Rachel was in danger. All I know is that the pain in my arm sent me out of the house in a hurry, looking for you.''

She stared bleakly down at the Kiss again. Yet another reason to hate it! First dizziness, then music, and now an uncontrollable, undesirable link to the angel Jared. ''I should never have had this installed,'' she muttered darkly. ''It has caused me no end of grief.''

''And will not serve its intended purpose of hiding you from the Jansai,'' he added. ''For they will not be looking at your arm, but your face.''

''There are no Jansai at Cartabella.''

''Do you plan to stay here your whole life?''

She did not answer.

''And anyway, I know for a fact that Isabella trades with the Jansai,'' he went on. ''Just because you haven't seen any doesn't mean they won't show up. And then how will you defend yourself? Isabella is not the type to ruin a good relationship with a Breven merchant just to save a nameless servant.''

''I don't think you need to concern yourself,'' Tamar said evenly. ''I have taken care of myself so far without your help.''

''But things are much more risky for you now,'' he said urgently. ''Your life has taken a very hazardous turn.''

''And what do you know about the hazards of my life till now?'' was her furious reply. ''What do you know about the deaths I have witnessed or the indignities I have suffered? What do you know about my terrors or my dreams? What do you know about me at all?''

He was silent a long moment, watching her, this time not responding to her anger with a flare-up of his own. ''Very little,'' he said at last. ''But I would like to know it all.''

Which was not the reply she had expected. She flung her head back, taken by surprise, but there was really no answer to that. Not saying another word to him, she stomped across the corral to retrieve Lunacy, and led the horse none too steadily to the stable. The angel let her pass in silence.

Once inside the aromatic dimness of the stable, she paused to catch her breath and marvel over the events of the past half hour. Menace on all sides; hard to know what to fear most. Oddly enough, she felt as much exhilaration as fear, at least in regard to the angel. She didn't trust him, of course, but somehow she did not hate him as she should. Something to do with that damned Kiss, no doubt.

Only after she had stood there a moment or two and her eyes had adjusted to the relative darkness did she realize that Gene was standing there, watching her. The soberness of his expression made her realize that he had witnessed at least some part of her adventures.

"None of my business," he said diffidently, "but if that angel was one of the ones bothering you, I'm not afraid to go to Isabella even so. Some of the angel folk are no better than the gentry."

"No," she said quickly. "He had some advice for me that I didn't want to take, but I'm not afraid of him. I didn't mean to worry you."

He nodded slowly, thinking it over. "You know him, then? The angel Jared?"

"I've met him before. Very briefly."

"They say he's the best of the lot. But I just wanted to let you know that if there was something to complain about, you shouldn't let the fact that he's an angel stop you."

"No. No complaints," she said. "But thank you anyway."

And she had stabled Lunacy and led out one of the other estate horses before she realized she had barely exercised the filly at all. So she was not succeeding particularly well even at the specialized job she had been assigned; but somehow she did not think it was entirely her fault.

Jared came out to the corral the next morning to watch her work. She was leading Lunacy around on a halter, talking nonsense words, when out of the corner of her eye she spied the angel approaching. Tamar made no attempt to acknowledge him, but it was a little hard to overlook him when he swung himself up to the top railing of the fence, swept his wings behind him, and hooked his feet over the bottom rung. The day was hot, and Tamar felt her hair beginning to stick to her forehead as the sweat built up along her scalp. She was covered with bits of straw and no end of horsehair, so all she needed to look really attractive was to have perspiration redden her face and flatten her short hair.

Not that she cared how the angel viewed her.

Jared watched her in silence for perhaps half an hour while Tamar did her best to ignore him. But finally his presence goaded her to such supreme irritation that she wrapped the reins around her hand and hauled the horse over to his perch.

"What?" she exclaimed.

Jared merely raised an eyebrow. "What what? I'm just sitting here enjoying the fine day."

"You are not. You're trying to distract me."

"I didn't say a word."

"Well, you're *staring* at me."

"I will endeavor to turn my eyes elsewhere," he said. And suiting action to words, he let his gaze wander past her, to the maze of buildings that housed the granaries, the dairies, and the machinery.

Tamar almost stamped her foot. "Have you come to frighten off Devon or any of his friends? Is that it?"

"No, I told you, I'm just enjoying the sunny day."

She pushed her hair back with her free hand. "Perhaps you'd like to ride? Not Lunacy, of course, because she'd throw you, but one of the other horses?"

"I don't ride, thank you. But I appreciate your thoughtful offer."

This time she did stamp her foot. Without another word, she stalked off, practically dragging the horse behind her. Once inside the stables, she settled Lunacy in her stall and chose as her next subject a great, spirited bay stallion that Isabella loved to ride. He hadn't been exercised in a day or two, though, so he needed a good hard gallop. Quickly, Tamar saddled him and led him out into the daylight. She mounted and headed off toward the acres of open parkland that constituted one of the main attractions of Isabella Cartera's land. There were a number of riding trails here, some more challenging than others, with a few low jumps thrown in for good measure. She would ride as far and as fast as the horse would go.

They had been out only twenty minutes or so, taking the empty trails at a good clip and clearing the ornamental hedges with room to spare, when once again Tamar realized she had company. The angel was following them overhead, making lazy loops back and forth over the pathways she had chosen, wings outstretched in an easy, untroubled glide. It did not take much cogitation to realize that no matter where she took this horse—or any other horse—the angel planned to follow.

Either he was stubbornly desirous of rousing her to fury, or he really did believe she was in danger.

That night after dinner, Tamar went to Gene. "I heard you telling Gregor that Isabella's new saddle arrived in Shepherd's Pass," she said. "I could ride to town and fetch it, if you'd like. I know Gregor hates to leave the farm when there's this much excitement going on."

Gene looked at her long and consideringly. Tamar kept her face empty of any expression except neutral helpfulness. "That would be fine," he said slowly. "Take Harmony, though. Isabella's planning a hunting party tomorrow and she won't want any of the good horses to be missing."

Harmony was a swaybacked old mare with a sweet disposition but very little energy. The least valuable horse in the stables. So Gene had read her right despite her innocent face. "I'll leave in the morning."

"Should be able to make it there and back in a day, but if something holds you up, you should stable the horse at Gwierson's," the head groom went on. "Saddle's been paid for, but I could give you a little cash in case there's a problem."

"I wouldn't think there'd be a problem," Tamar said. Her throat hurt her to speak. He was being so kind.

He shrugged. "Suit yourself. Leave as soon as you're ready."

So that night she packed up as many of her meager belongings as would fit in an inconspicuous bag that might seem appropriate for a day trip into the nearest town. She'd already gotten three weeks' worth of wages, and she counted out the money. Enough to take her to Port Clara easily; enough, she hoped, to buy passage to Ysral.

She slept badly and woke with a headache before dawn had really opened its lush eyes. No reason to lie here any longer, fretting, so she rose and dressed and hooked her duffel bag over her shoulder. When she arrived in the stable that was Harmony's home, she was surprised to find Gene there before her.

"Just wanted to look her over quickly before you set out," was his explanation. "And I remembered last night. Still a down payment on the saddle. So here's enough money to cover it."

Impossible to refuse when phrased that way, so helplessly she accepted the roll of bills he offered her. The outer denomination was almost as much as the small stash she'd managed to accumulate.

"I can't—what if I lose it?" she stammered.

He shrugged. "It's not much. Don't worry about it. Ride carefully. Remember—Gwierson's is the place."

She nodded. "Thanks." She shrugged, because she wanted to say more and could not think how.

He gave her one of his rare grins. "And if any of those boys asks me where you went, I won't tell," he said.

She smiled back. "I'm sure they'll miss me."

"Won't we all."

She nodded, murmured her thanks again, and freed the horse from the stall. Too much weighted conversation like this and she would be in tears before she could get out the door. Gene followed her outside but had no other comment to make. Once on horseback, she waved good-bye and he returned the gesture. Then she was off into the sweet, fresh coolness of morning.

On her own again. Running again. Would she ever come to rest?

Shepherd's Pass was even sleepier than usual, as Tamar discovered after dropping off Harmony at Gwierson's. The clerk at the bigger of the two hotels, which also doubled as the bus terminal, was not sure when the next transport was due in or where it might be headed.

"Will it come in sometime today?" Tamar asked impatiently. Oh, yes, there was always at least one bus a day. He just couldn't remember which one it would be. "Can anybody tell me? Is there a schedule anywhere I can look at?"

Now, he might have a schedule for her. Hold on just a minute. She waited in gathering irritation while he rummaged through some old papers and an assortment of maps.

"Except I don't think this is still the right timetable," he told her as he finally handed over a creased and faded slip of paper. "I'm pretty sure the schedule changed a year or so ago."

So that was fairly helpful. Tamar glanced at the days and numbers on the chart he'd given her, but it was pointless to try to plot a route based on obsolete information. "I'll just hang around for a while, then,'' she said, ''and see what comes in.''

While she waited she bought a little road food and filled her canteen with fresh water. She was resigned to spending the whole day lurking outside the hotel, but she cheered up immensely when, two hours after her arrival, a big, odoriferous bus rumbled through the town's quiet streets. She waited till the single passenger disembarked, then crowded up to the doorway to address the driver.

''Where are you headed?'' she asked.

''Azolay,'' he replied. It was a river city south of Castelana, not nearly as important as either that city or Semorrah, but a sizable place nonetheless. From there she should be able to find a bus anywhere.

''How much for a seat?''

''Twenty.''

''When do you leave?''

''Five minutes.''

''Let me get my bag.''

She slept most of the way to Azolay, a trip that took the rest of the day. Whenever the bus stopped for more than ten minutes, she disembarked to walk off the kinks in her legs or refill her canteen. Practically no one, it turned out, wanted to ride from Shepherd's Pass to Azolay, so the bus was almost empty and she had a whole row of seats to herself. She didn't feel like reading, she was not in the mood to talk to strangers, and she refused to let herself think, so sleep was the only option.

They arrived in Azolay a little before sunset. Like Semorrah, Azolay derived all its income from commerce. In the past fifty years it had expanded rapidly, serving as a market for much of southern Bethel. It was not nearly as pretty as Semorrah, however. For one thing, it had none of Semorrah's graceful, harmonious architecture, but instead was built of a hodgepodge of brick, stone, marble, and granite in a completely unplanned manner. For another, it still had a raw, new edge to it, because its wealth and prominence had been so recently achieved. But all its energy and its random structure gave it a certain constant charm. You were never quite sure what you would encounter anytime you turned a corner: a new theater, an old mansion, a freshly paved street leading down to the docks.

Jansai driving through town in one of their big transports, whistling at the girls and throwing fruit rinds into the alleys.

Tamar drew back sharply when the first truck passed, melting into the shadow of the nearest building. *Damn*. That had been so careless. Because she had seen so few Jansai in Semorrah—and none at all near Shepherd's Pass—she had forgotten how far the gypsies loved to roam. Of course they would be in Azolay, or even Castelana and the other river cities. All that kept them out of Semorrah were those narrow streets that would not accommodate their massive trucks.

She had best remain invisible tonight and be on her way first thing in the morning.

She already had her ticket for Port Clara. She had picked it up before leaving the bus terminal where she had been dropped off, and it had cost her far more than twenty dollars, too. She would be grateful yet for Gene's gift, which she still hadn't had the nerve to count. Would she really have enough money left to pay for passage to Ysral?

With that in mind, she chose the cheapest hotel she could find that still looked like it had passable standards of cleanliness. Another restless night; seemed like these days she could only fall asleep on a bus. She tossed and turned until the sky had lightened enough to make it reasonable to get up and dress.

She had a quick breakfast at an outdoor café right on the river's edge, then strolled along the pier for a while, watching the barges go by. She had asked Jasper once if you could sail from Semorrah all the way to Ysral and he had laughed at her. Then he had explained the differences between riverboats and oceangoing vessels, although frankly the distinctions weren't all that clear to Tamar. Too bad, though. It would save her some time and grief if she could board a ship now and close her eyes till she arrived at her destination.

She had just brushed the crumbs from her lips when she heard running footsteps behind her, and sudden alarm made her whirl around. Too late; hands closed on her arms and harsh shouts called reinforcements over from two streets away. She was surrounded by three men, though it seemed like thirty. She lashed out with her feet, with her fists, and the Jansai struck back with what seemed like hundreds of gloves and boots. Someone clouted her on the head, knocking her momentarily blind, and she heard a voice shout out, "Stupid! He wants her alive!" Another attacker was trying to bind her wrists, but she snaked her hands away from him and ducked low, butting her head into his stomach. There were cries and grunts all around her, and voices coming closer. Panic made her insane. She clawed her way down someone's bare forearm and, for a moment, felt the deathgrip on her arms lessen. She broke free.

She ran flat out down the cobblestoned street, sobbing breath into her lungs, feeling her legs nearly wrench out of their sockets with each huge, desperate stride. Behind her, angry shouting; before her, a few early-morning risers, staring and pointing at this amazing sight, a wretched woman fleeing from a horde of Jansai attackers. If she could reach a shop door, a clump of friendly onlookers, anything that could pass for safety—

Eager footsteps pounded up beside her. She felt a hand clutch a fold of her blouse and heard the material rip as she lunged away. Her lungs were on fire; her legs were lead. Her head was about to burst with pain. Again the hand reached out from behind, this time closing on her arm with a sharp, merciless grip. She cried out and almost tumbled over backward as she was dragged to a halt. The Jansai slapped her once, hard, and received calls of approval from his companions, racing up a few yards away. Tamar summoned every last ounce of strength and punched him in the chest as hard as she could. He struck her again with a blow so vicious it sent her reeling, falling, somersaulting into the river or into the air or into that well of vertigo that was so deep now she did not think she would ever climb out. . . .

But there were arms still wrapped around her from behind, hands gripping her crossed wrists, she could not be falling, she could not be flying, she must only be dreaming the battered, brainsick dreams of the dead. Oddly enough, she felt no fear, now that she was comatose or possibly even killed; she felt relieved, serene, but very, very dizzy. It was pointless to try to open her eyes, so she did not, but she almost started to relax, to enjoy herself, to give up the constant, impossible fight. She probably was dead, then; she could not imagine that mere loss of consciousness would be enough to make her surrender to the Jansai. To anyone.

"Are you all right?" asked a worried voice in her ear. "He hit you so hard. Have you passed out?"

It was Jared's voice. Astonishment made her open her eyes after all—very widely as she took in the diminutive landscape below her, shrunken river, miniature boats, tiny trees. The vertigo rushed back, and her hands twisted in his hold to clench on his wrists.

"We're *flying*," she whispered.

"What did you think we were doing? Are you all right?"

All sorts of words rose to her lips, but none of them were answers to his questions. She still could not fathom how he had come to be here, how he had scooped her up and carried her aloft while her senses were too shattered to process the information. He had saved her—again—he had found her every single place she had run to. She did not even need to ask where they were going, but her mouth shaped the words anyway.

"Where are you taking me?"

"Ysral."

CHAPTER FIFTEEN

It had been with a certain amount of dread that Jared winged his way to Cartabella for Isabella's grand event. If he had not promised, he would not have gone. The lure of possible bedmates—lifemates? whatever—had not been strong enough to make him anticipate the trip. But it served one good purpose: It had been his deadline. After the wedding, he had decided, he would go to Ysral. For that reason alone did he greet the wedding with any anticipation.

And then, to arrive at the estate and feel that peculiar, urgent pressure in his arm. Jovah rejoicing, was it possible that Tamar was anywhere in the vicinity? If so, it was a stroke of luck so unexpected as to be stupefying.

But it was true; and he had found her; and she still had no use for him. But he had her measure now. He was not surprised that she refused to believe him, was still less surprised when she disappeared from the farm two days after he made his appearance. And pleased, rather than disappointed, when the head groom refused to divulge her whereabouts. She had the knack of winning unlikely supporters, this proud, lonely ragamuffin. If the man would not tell an angel Tamar's whereabouts, he would not betray her to less savory individuals.

But this time Jared refused to let her slip through his fingers. Armed with the portrait and the sure knowledge of her danger, he felt justified in tracking her down—it was for her own good, after all, and not merely a selfish, almost incomprehensible desire on his part to see her again.

It was not hard to pick up her trail. She would have had little choice but to head for Shepherd's Pass, and a few inquiries there elicited the information that she had escaped via bus. The hotel clerk was not particularly clear on *which* bus, but the driver of the next vehicle that pulled through was able to give the angel a much better rundown of the schedules. Azolay seemed the likeliest choice.

Jared reached the river city late that night and rose early the next morning to see if he could discover his tiresome, elusive Jacobite. The minute he had arrived in Azolay, he had seen the Kiss in his arm flicker with an unsteady light and felt a faint, even tremor against the bone. She was here, then. He had guessed correctly. The realization filled him with a sense of elation out of all proportion to the significance of the triumph.

He had trouble sleeping, so when, at dawn, he decided it was futile to stay abed any longer, he rose and dressed. The streets were barely light, so it seemed pointless to go out hunting Jacobites. Instead, he pulled out his cylindrical communicator and punched in Christian's number.

"Do you know what time it is?" were the first words out of Christian's mouth. Not quite the cheery greeting he had used the only other two times Jared had contacted him. "This better be awfully damn important."

"Not really. I just couldn't sleep."

"Where are you, anyway? You sound very close."

"Azolay."

"Why did the god bring you *there*?"

"Chasing an escaped Jacobite, and I think I've found her. That's what I wanted to tell you."

"Good. Thanks for keeping in touch."

"No, don't switch off! I also wanted to let you know that I'll be in Ysral for a few days. In case you were looking for me."

"I thought you would have gone there sooner."

"I was at Isabella's. Actually, I should still be at Isabella's and she'll be furious when she realizes I'm gone. If she complains to you, tell her it was important."

"I'll tell her I hate you myself for waking me up at this hour. Just so you know, from now on I'm turning off my communicator while I'm sleeping. You won't be able to wake me up again."

"I already apologized for that."

"No, I don't believe you did."

"Well, I'm sorry, then. I'll talk to you some other time."

"When you have news. Good-bye, Jared."

"Good-bye, Christian." But the merchant had already disconnected.

Time to leave, anyway. Jared headed down to the hotel restaurant and ate a quick breakfast. He had planned to go to the bus terminal and wait there most of the day, since it seemed logical that Tamar would head out on one of the big, anonymous transports. But over his meal, he started getting restless and edgy. What if she found a farmer with a big truck or a family in a horse-drawn gig who seemed friendly and harmless and offered her a ride? What if she rented her own horse, paid for passage down the river on a barge, or found some other conveyance out of Azolay? What if she slipped out of the city limits before he had located her, while he was foolishly hanging around the bus station, hoping she would arrive? There were too many variables. He could easily lose her again.

So he paid for his meal, stepped outside, and instantly flung himself aloft. He could patrol the whole city in something under ten minutes, flying in low circles over the colorful assortment of houses, office buildings, schools, shipyards, bakeries, theaters, and parks. He was too high up to get a good look at people's faces, but close enough, he thought, to trip the sensor in his Kiss that would alert him to Tamar's presence.

He was right about that, as he discovered on his second pass over the city.

He was flying over the edge of the river, swinging back toward Azolay proper, when a sudden sharp stab in his arm made his whole body flex with adrenaline. Sweet Jovah singing, how could she have fallen into danger again so quickly? He banked and descended, looking around madly for any disturbance on the ground below him. Within a few seconds he had spotted the battling Jansai and the struggling woman, and he angled as fast as he could in their direction. He nearly cheered in relief when Tamar broke free, but he had to alter his course to intercept her as she ran, and he lost a minute readjusting. He felt terror pump through his heart when the Jansai pursuer caught up with her and struck her that blinding blow. He accelerated his pace, dove low over the grappling figures, and plucked the woman from the arms of her Jansai attacker. A few more deft wingbeats and they were above the river, across the river, arrowing into Jordana, and headed for the eastern coast of the continent.

•　•　•

Except for that one brief exchange when she asked where he was taking her, neither the angel nor the Jacobite volunteered much conversation for the next few hours of the flight. Once or twice Jared shifted his grip on his passenger so that she rode a little more comfortably; she did not resist, but lay passively against his chest. At first he thought she might be sleeping, for she was as motionless as a child dreaming in her father's arms, but then it occurred to him that she might have suffered a concussion from that final blow. Which worried him deeply enough that he brought them in for a landing an hour or two before weariness would have dictated that he take a rest.

He touched his feet to the ground and sank to his knees all in a single motion, so that he could lay Tamar on the grass without requiring her to stand. Until all movement ceased completely—until she was half sitting, half lying on the ground, supported by his arm—she did not open her eyes. When she did, he was struck again by their pure, undiluted green innocence.

"Why are we stopping? Are we in Ysral?" she asked.

Which alarmed him further. "No," he said sharply. "It will take us two days to fly across the ocean, and we aren't even at the coast yet. I thought you might want something to eat or drink."

"I don't have any food," she said. "And I lost my canteen."

He had never seen Tamar helpless or even at a loss, and it filled him with an almost uncontainable anxiety to see her so dazed and disoriented. "How's your head?" he asked abruptly. "You're acting so strangely. I think that Jansai must have injured you when he struck you."

She put a hand to her temple as if checking to make sure that her skull was still intact. "Maybe," she said uncertainly. "I don't think I'm bleeding."

"You don't have to be bleeding to be hurt."

"I think I'll be fine."

"Are you hungry?"

"No. Thirsty, a little."

He helped her swallow from his own flask and then wondered if he should have. If she really had a concussion, shouldn't he keep her from food and water? And if she had been seriously injured, shouldn't he get her to a doctor? But they were in Jordana now, not four hours' flight from Breven, and there could

be Jansai at every small town and oasis they came to from here
to the coast. It was hard to know how far her picture had been
circulated. He hated to take unnecessary risks.

"Does your head hurt?"

"A little. The flying makes me dizzy. Just like it did before."

Now she was talking nonsense. Worse and worse. "Before?"
he said cautiously. "But you've never flown with an angel before, have you?"

She shook her head once, then stopped abruptly as if the
motion pained her. "Not real flying. I told you. Sometimes I
get dizzy. Ever since I had the Kiss put in, I would feel like I
was floating in the air. And that's just how it felt while you and
I were flying. And then sometimes I hear music."

"Just now you heard music? When we were flying?"

"No," she said impatiently. "Before. In my head. Like someone was singing. I was afraid at first, but after a while I liked
it."

None of this made any sense; clearly she was delirious.
Whether or not he liked it, he was going to have to get her to
shelter and a doctor's care, the sooner the better.

"Listen, Tamar," he said, speaking slowly and distinctly.
"We're going to rest here for a few minutes. Then, when you
feel well enough, we'll fly on a couple more hours. There's a
little town about fifty miles south of Breven. I think we'll be
safe enough there for the night. Then tomorrow morning we'll
head for Ysral."

"Over the ocean," she said drowsily. "Flying and flying for
two whole days."

"Well, no. We'll fly for a day, then find a trading ship headed
for Ysral and take shelter on it for the night. Then we'll fly on
to Ysral the next morning. It usually wouldn't matter what kind
of ship we chose—Jansai, Manadavvi, Edori—but you being
who you are, I think we'd be safest with the Edori."

"I think so," she murmured.

He could not keep his worry to himself anymore. "Tamar,
are you all right?" he said sharply. "You seem so—lost. I'm
afraid you were seriously injured back there. I've never seen
you so—so—"

"I can't fight anymore," she said. "I can't. My head hurts.
I can't think straight. Do what you want. I can't fight you."

Without another word he slipped his flask back in his pocket, scooped her up in his arms, and carefully levered them both back into the wind. She nestled her cheek against the soft leather of his vest and curled her hands against her chest like a child. She was asleep before they had even reached flying altitude.

The town of Marquet boasted only one doctor, who looked to be about a hundred years old and not likely to go running off to Jansai with tales of suspect new arrivals. Tamar was awake while he examined her, though barely, but she was able to answer all his questions in coherent sentences. She admitted to a headache, said it was not severe, and told him without a moment's hesitation that she had slipped and fallen that morning, cracking her head against a wooden bench.

"Don't feel a bump," the old man muttered, poking under her hair with the tips of his fingers. "Couldn't have hit it too hard. But the brain's a tricky thing. You can shake a baby hard enough to kill it just by scrambling up its brains. Fact. Doesn't take much of a blow to make an adult woozy for a few days."

"So is she all right?" Jared asked for the tenth time.

The doctor was repacking his kit. "Hard to say. It's a good sign that she can walk and talk and remember her name and what she had for dinner yesterday. All her reflexes are good. It's a bad sign that she wants to sleep so much. It would be a very bad sign if she started vomiting. If that happens, let me know."

And then you'll do what for her? Jared wanted to ask, but did not. Brain injuries were notoriously difficult to treat; he had heard that a long time ago. "Can she eat? Drink?"

"Moderate food intake. No alcohol. If she goes twenty-four hours without vomiting, she can eat pretty much what she wants."

"And all this sleeping? That's bad?"

"Try to keep her awake for a few more hours. Till nighttime, at least. Then wake her up every couple hours all night. If you can't rouse her, get in touch with me."

"We're leaving in the morning. Unless you think that's unwise."

The doctor shrugged. "You're flying?" Jared nodded. "High altitude might increase her headache. Try to stay as low as possible. If she gets worse, land as soon as you can."

"All right. Thanks for your help." The doctor left.

By this time it was early evening and the sun was dipping flirtatiously below the horizon. They had taken a single room in the small hotel, because Jared wanted to be near Tamar if she needed attention during the night. He stood now at the small window, looking out toward the vast darkness of the sea. Common sense told him he should stay in Samaria another day, making sure Tamar was healthy; fear told him they could not linger a minute longer than they had to, not this close to Breven, not with Tamar apparently such a magnet for trouble. Either way, she was at risk. And he felt safer in the air. They would leave tomorrow morning, and see how well she did.

He turned to face her, smiling with an effort. "Are you hungry?" he asked. "You haven't eaten since breakfast."

"I could eat a little," she said cautiously. "I think."

They went down to the hotel's dining room and ordered a simple meal. Tamar had nothing more than soup and half a roll, but the food seemed to revive her a little. Jared could not help watching every bite she took. "How's your stomach?" he asked when she pushed away her dishes. "You don't feel like you're going to throw up, do you?"

"Why? Am I supposed to?" she asked.

He smiled. "No. Very bad sign if you do, the doctor said."

"Well, then I'll try very hard not to."

He hurried them back up to their room, not eager to have strangers walk into the restaurant and catch sight of them. But it was still relatively early and the doctor had told him to keep Tamar awake as long as possible, so now he was faced with the task of entertaining her.

"We could play cards," he suggested. "Board games. I'm sure the innkeeper could lend us something."

She wrinkled her nose. "I don't know many games. And I don't think I could concentrate on learning."

"You could tell me the story of your life."

"Too much effort," she said with a yawn. "You could tell me yours."

"Too dull," he said with a quick smile. "You'd fall asleep for sure."

"You could sing to me," she said. "I'd like that."

He almost couldn't believe she'd said it. It would never have occurred to him that Tamar would consider his singing mesmerizing enough to hold her complete attention. But, "Certainly," he said. "Let me know when I hit on something you particularly like."

So—keeping his voice soft enough to avoid disturbing any sleepers in the nearby rooms—he offered her a selection of brisk, upbeat marches, a few comic ballads at a breathless pace, and the tenor part to one of the sacred masses that had been written in the heroic strain. She seemed to like the music more than he would have predicted. At any rate, she listened fairly closely and did not fall asleep.

"I know a song," she said suddenly when one of his selections came to a rousing close. "I just learned it. Maybe you'd like to learn it, too?"

She was going to sing for him? Heat danced across his Kiss just in anticipation. "Of course. Is it very long?"

She seemed a little puzzled. "No—well, parts of it repeat. I'll just teach you the main part. See how you like it."

So in a soft, sweet soprano, she crooned a wordless melody for him, hands clasped before her, serene and unselfconscious as a young girl singing for her family. He felt the fire in his Kiss intensify; he felt a skittering uneasiness run along the base of his hairline and all the way down his spine.

"I know that song," he said slowly when she had finished. "Or at least—I don't know it. I've never heard it before. But it sounds so familiar. . . . Where did you say you learned it?"

"It's the song in my head. I told you," she said. "The one I hear when I feel like I'm flying."

Now the prickle spread to his elbows, underarms, and knees. He felt spooked and uneasy, in the presence of some eerie phenomenon that he could not identify or understand. "You learned that music—from a voice in your head?" he repeated. "That doesn't make any sense."

She nodded emphatically, her eyebrows raised in agreement. "Tell *me*," she said. "I didn't like it much when I first heard it, either. But I've gotten used to it. And the song is pretty. Would you like to hear it again?"

And he stared at her and felt the chill creep through his whole body. She was mad or delirious or touched by a strange, uncomfortable gift, and the latter possibility seemed the least likely. Yet he was filled with a desire to shield her, restore her— even believe her—so fierce it made him a little insane in return. He did not move a muscle; if he approached her, he thought, nothing would keep him from taking her protectively in his arms.

At any rate, nothing would prevent him from guarding this frail woman with his life, not until she was recovered, not until she was Tamar again, whole and spirited and unafraid.

"Sing it again," he said softly. "I'll listen closely, then next time I can sing it with you. I'll learn it before the night is through."

In the morning, she was better, though still not the feisty, suspicious Tamar Jared was accustomed to. He had slept badly, waking up every few hours to make sure she was still breathing, but she seemed to have made it through the night untroubled even by a nightmare.

"How do you feel? How's your head?" he asked her over breakfast, where she put away more food than he had ever seen a woman eat.

She gave him a look of exasperation. "What did I tell you the first time you asked me that? And the second and third and fourth time?"

He smiled reluctantly. "You said you were fine."

"Well, the answer hasn't changed. So stop asking me. Now eat your breakfast and let's go."

They had lingered in Marquet long enough to buy her a change of clothes, a simple tunic and pair of leggings that would be comfortable enough to travel in, and then they took off. Within an hour they were over the ocean, vast, mysterious, and multicolored, and Tamar stared down at it with an unwavering fascination. The air over the sea was cooler, heavier, laced with scents and vapors found nowhere else in the world. Heeding the doctor's instructions, Jared flew as low as he could, though it would have been easier to cruise through the thin air higher above the water. So they had not made it as far as he would have liked by the time he started to grow weary, and he began watching the waters below them for a likely ship to take them in for the evening.

He had seen plenty of Jansai traders as they made their way above the ocean, and a few Manadavvi ships—even one bearing the Semorran flag, though he hadn't realized the river merchants ran their own cargo across the ocean. Edori vessels were scarcer, and it only belatedly occurred to him that those ships were following a different route, specifically to keep clear of the Jansai traders patrolling the waters between Breven and Ysral.

Yet, before sunset, he spotted something even better than an Edori ship: a Luminauzi pleasure boat, stately, luxurious, six decks high. It plowed through the ocean at a deliberate pace, in no hurry to arrive anywhere; its passengers were the jaded, bored elite of a wealthy society, and for them, the journey was the entertainment.

"Jovah watches over us," he murmured, spiraling down toward the massive ship. Its sixteen blue flags whipped smartly in the ocean breeze, flying from every protuberance and railing. "We'll get a royal treatment here."

Tamar, watching the great ship grow larger and larger, seemed less sanguine. "Are you sure? What if they have no room for us?"

"They'll find room." For a moment he took his eyes off his target and glanced down at her. "Angels are welcome everywhere, didn't you know? Just because *you* hate us, you do not realize that everyone else in Samaria considers us precious and lucky."

She rolled her eyes in disbelief but made no comment.

But he was right, of course; the whole population of the ship, or so it seemed, turned out to greet them as they landed. Tamar (who would have thought she was shy?) fell a little behind him, taking shelter in the shadow of his wings. Jared, on the other hand, gaily greeted the captain, the crew, the passengers who crowded up to ask where he'd come from and where he was headed, and could he stay the night? Could he sing for them? They had a little theater built right on the ship, they had been taking turns presenting their own skits and melodies, but to have an angel aboard, well, that would really be something special!

That easily was everything arranged. The captain led them to a grand stateroom, larger by half than the hotel room they'd been in the night before, and fitted with more amenities. Tamar wandered around it for a full ten minutes, touching the silk of the bed hangings, the porcelain of the sink, the highly polished wood of the furniture.

"Even in Luminaux, I never stayed in a place so fine," she said wonderingly. "Is this how ordinary people live?"

"Well, not ordinary ones," Jared replied. "But more than a few of the wealthy, yes. And this is nothing compared to the

luxury the Manadavvi can muster up. It's a little wasteful, I have
to admit, but it does feel wonderful."

She nodded wordlessly.

He was disappointed, but not surprised, to learn that she did
not want to accompany him when he joined the rest of the passengers for dinner and the evening's entertainment. "Are you
all right? How's your head?" he asked, because he couldn't help
himself. But she seemed to have forgotten she had laid a pro-
hibition on those questions.

"My head hurts a little. I'm tired," she said. "If I could get
something to eat, I think I'd just like to go to sleep."

"I'll have food sent down to you." He hesitated, standing
halfway between her chair and the door. "Would you rather I
stayed here with you? I'd be happy to do so."

She smiled somewhat maliciously. "Your public awaits
you," she said. "You can't disappoint them or they'll throw
you off the boat."

"I don't want to leave if you want me to stay."

She laughed at him. "Oh, Jared, oh please, I'm so afraid
when you're not by me," she exclaimed, her hand pressed to
her heart. He had to grin.

"All right," he said. "I'll see you in a few hours."

If not for the nagging (and surely unnecessary) worry about
Tamar, Jared would have enjoyed himself pretty thoroughly for
the rest of the evening. The meal, served to him at the captain's
table, was the best he'd had in weeks, and the dinner conversation was quick, witty, and light. Afterward, nearly three hundred people adjourned to the theater built into the very heart of
the ship—a professional stage, velvet-covered seats, acoustics
as good as anything he'd heard in a Luminaux music hall. The
angel sang for nearly an hour, a mix of sacred and secular songs
that seemed to please his audience equally.

"Well, this has been the best part of the trip so far," a young
woman named Mira told Jared afterward. She and a much older
escort had been seated at the captain's table with him; she was
slim, chic, bored, and beautiful. She had smiled at him covertly
all during dinner whenever her friend had become engrossed in
conversation with someone else. Jared suspected she was not an
angel-seeker in the classic sense, but a woman who had no
qualms about trading her youth and beauty for status and ac-

quisitions. "The rest of the entertainment has been quite dull by comparison."

"Thank you," Jared replied gravely. "I am so rarely able to outperform wealthy amateurs and the retired Luminaux musicians who sign on with cruise ships such as this."

Mira narrowed her eyes at him, trying to decide if he was jesting or chastising her, but the captain interrupted them before she could reply. "Everyone has been raving about your singing," the man said. "And those who couldn't cram themselves into the theater are complaining loudly about what they've missed. Would you be willing to stay on board another day and sing again tomorrow night?"

Jared thought quickly. The ship cruised at a rate much slower than he could fly, yet it did go forward toward their destination. And the rest could not hurt Tamar, even if she insisted on staying cooped up in their cabin for the next whole day. And they were in absolutely no danger from Jansai, here on a pleasure boat in the middle of the ocean. "I hate to impose," he said, just to make sure the offer was sincere.

"No imposition! An honor! A favor to me and my guests."

"Then we'll be glad to stay another day."

After that, it was impossible to leave without tarrying for a drink or two, so all in all it was much later than Jared had planned before he returned to his stateroom. He crept in quietly, thinking Tamar must be asleep already, and she was. She had considerately left a small sidewall light on for him.

He trod silently to the bed and gazed down at her still form. Now he could study her with an intentness he was not rude enough to attempt while she was awake. Asleep, she was relaxed and unguarded, her face open and serene; there was none of that fierce suspicion that colored her every waking expression. She looked so young.

She looked so familiar.

The first time he had seen her, back in Ileah, he had thought hers was a face he should know, though he had put the thought down to a wayward fancy. Now he frowned, studying her more closely, running his eyes over the angle of her cheekbones and the shape of her closed eyes. She looked like someone he should remember, but he could not place the features. He watched her till she turned restlessly in her sleep, almost as if embarrassed by the continued scrutiny, and then he shrugged and moved away.

There was a plush curved-back chaise lounge and a couple of armchairs in the attached sitting room, but neither of these would accommodate a sleeping angel. With a sigh of resignation, Jared plundered the pillows from the chairs and arranged himself as best he could on the carpeted floor, gathering his wings close about him for a blanket. He did not expect to sleep well but, drugged by exhaustion, he did; and it was full morning before he even stirred.

To find Tamar standing over him, arms akimbo, fully dressed. "That can't be very comfortable," she said. "Why didn't you wake me up last night and tell me to sleep on this little curvy couch thing?"

"I didn't want to wake you," he murmured, rubbing his eyes and stifling a yawn. "You looked so peaceful."

"Well, I bet you have a horrible ache in your neck from sleeping like that all night."

Jared sat up. Shoulders and arms a little stiff but the hard floor had done him no harm. "No, I'm all right. How are you? How's your headache?"

"I feel fine, thank you for asking," she said very precisely, as if, by pronouncing the words very clearly, she could impress the answer on his brain and prevent him from asking again. "How was your little concert last night?"

"Everyone loved me," he said, hauling himself to his feet. He felt unkempt; he needed a quick shave and shower. "So much so that they invited me—us—to stay over another day."

She gave him a darkling look. "And you said?"

"We'd stay. No reason not to."

Tamar grimaced and shook her head. "Great. So we're stuck here another whole day?"

"Are you in any particular hurry to get to Ysral?"

"No, but—"

"Then stop complaining. Try stepping outside of the cabin for a couple hours. You might enjoy yourself."

She glanced down at her tunic and leggings, now wrinkled from a day of travel. "I don't feel like I really fit in."

Jared grinned. This was the first time he had seen her show an interest in her appearance. "I've no doubt," he said solemnly, "that there is a boutique on board that will be able to satisfy your every fashion requirement."

She scowled. "Well, I don't have enough money to spend on such silly things and I refuse to let you spend any more of yours."

"Trust me," he said. "It will be free, and given with delight. A small price for the shipowners to pay for the privilege of having an angel aboard as a special guest. Give me twenty minutes to make myself presentable and I will prove it to you."

Tamar made a small sound of contempt but said nothing as Jared slipped inside the luxurious bathing room. Breakfast first, the angel decided as he shaved, and then they would see how the Luminaux merchants would outfit this vagabond girl.

The day that followed was one of the most pleasant Jared could remember spending in the recent months of his life. While Tamar commented in a constant, sarcastic undervoice on the superficial wasteful life of the Luminauzi elite, she could not help but enjoy some of the pleasures wealth could bring. She thought the food was marvelous, for instance, and ate heartily; Jared suspected that at many times in her life she had not had enough to eat, which explained both her slender figure and her appetite now. She was vociferously disdainful when they found not one but three boutiques on the lower levels of the cruise ship (although one catered exclusively to men). That didn't stop her from going in and trying on fifty different outfits, by Jared's count. The clerk at the second store tried to convince her to buy two complete ensembles—one for day wear, one for evening—but she resisted mightily until the woman came over for a whispered conference with Jared.

"Is she afraid of the cost?" the salesclerk asked the angel. "For the captain has assured me this is his gift to you in recompense for your wonderful concert last night."

"They're free, Tamar," Jared called out to her. The word felt peculiar and delicious on his tongue. Tamar. He had only addressed her by name once or twice before. "The captain's gift to you. You'll offend him if you do not accept at least two outfits."

"I am not so greedy," she shot back at him, but as she spoke she stood in front of a tall mirror, admiring herself in a gown of dark green. She had already chosen an embroidered silver tunic and trousers (for casual wear, of course), but she seemed to be having difficulty parting with this number.

"We'll take them both," Jared told the salesclerk. "She'll wear the silver now, and you can have the gown sent to our cabin." He gave her the stateroom number while the saleswoman beamed with pride.

"We're taking advantage of these kind people," Tamar told him a few minutes later as they strolled around the upper deck and watched the ocean unroll beneath them.

"The only payment they want is a little graciousness from you," Jared replied. "Do you think you can manage that?"

"Well, I'm not sure," she growled. "I don't think it's in my repertoire."

"Shall we practice before dinner? I'll be the captain and you can be—well, you can be yourself. Can you give me a big smile and say thank you?"

She instead gave him a black scowl but was unable to hold the frown in place. Instead, an infectious laugh broke through. "Why, Captain! I do so much adore the beautiful new clothes! How can I ever thank you enough? Shall I come to your cabin in the middle of the night and show you the depths of my appreciation?"

"I don't think you need to go quite that far."

"No? Good thing we're rehearsing this in advance or I would have committed a terrible social error."

They were interrupted frequently by passengers coming up to thank the angel again for his concert and ask for an introduction to his lovely friend. Tamar never did more than smile and murmur a quick thank you, but that was good enough since the visitors really wanted to talk to the angel. She could not contain her edged remarks as soon as they'd drifted out of earshot, however, and her acid observations had Jared laughing helplessly more than once.

When Mira and her companion paused to say a few words, Tamar dutifully engaged the older man in conversation while Mira delicately flirted with the angel. As soon as the two had moved off, hand in hand, Tamar gave Jared a wicked sideways glance.

"I just had the best idea," she said. "If you're too uncomfortable sleeping on the floor tonight, I can think of a bed on this ship that would give you a very warm welcome."

"I think there's already two in that bed," he said.

"How much would you like to bet," she said softly, "that if you wanted a place on her pillow, she'd be the only one in that bed?"

"You'd lose," Jared replied. "He paid for the cabin."

"She'd still find a way. I'll wager if you will."

"You don't have a dollar to bet with. Besides, the only way to find out is for me to try to seduce her, and I don't want to."

"Don't let me hold you back," she said, a trace of malice in her voice. "I'd rather sleep in the room alone, anyway."

"I can't think of circumstances," he said in clearly enunciated words, "under which she would be my type."

"But I know so little about you," she purred, and she had gotten Mira's inflection exactly. "What exactly *is* your type?"

Lost souls with the courage of heroines, he wanted to say, but did not. "Why, Tamar, I didn't know you were so interested," he said softly instead, as much for the pleasure of using her name as for the chance of provoking her. "You've never seemed too fond of angels, so I'd abandoned hope long ago, but if you think you'd like to please me—"

"It would please me to see you dumped into the ocean," she snapped, but then she burst out laughing about two seconds after he did. The laughter changed her face utterly, made her glow with an unsuspected radiance. This was Tamar as she was meant to be, he thought; how many times in her life had she had the chance?

After they strolled around the deck, Jared took her below to show her the theater, and then they investigated the game rooms nearby. These were half-full with passengers pursuing every imaginable entertainment. There were card games, board games, and athletic contests, and two harpsichords had been set up in a corner for those who wished to practice their music. There was a library for the readers, a buffet for the eaters, and a guided tour for the curious.

"What's your pleasure?" Jared asked.

"I've never played any of these," she said, eyeing the board games and their array of chips, marbles, and counters. "Are they hard to learn?"

"Oh, for dull, silly girls like you, they might be," Jared said offhandedly.

"Fine! Then I won't ask to learn!"

"No, no, only joking. Here, Devil's Hand is one of my favorites. You start with ten colored marbles lined up on each end
of the board—"

It was a game simple to learn, though nuanced with complex
strategies, and Tamar delighted him by learning it rapidly. He
had thought she might take to a game like this, for it required
quick wits, a lively sense of self-preservation, and a streak of
pure though theoretical ruthlessness which he'd had no doubt
she'd be able to muster. On the fourth game, she almost defeated
him; on the fifth one, she did.

"Oh, I like this," she exclaimed. "Let's play again."

"Let's make it more interesting," he said. "Let's play dou-
bles."

There were two older, unalarming men sitting nearby, playing
their own round of Devil's Hand. Invited to join the angel and
his friend, they assented with alacrity, though they refused to
play on the same team.

"I'll take the young lady, though, if she'll have me," said
one, smiling over at Tamar in a friendly way. Jared was relieved
to see her smile back. "I've been watching you. You learn
fast."

"Well, I've never said no to an angel before," said his friend.
"I think we're all set."

So they played four more matches, splitting the victories
evenly. Tamar was jubilant when they finally left the room,
though Jared cautioned her not to be an unbearable winner.

"I will be if I want to be," was her instant response. "Let's
go back and play tomorrow."

"Tomorrow we'll be on our way to Ysral."

"Even better."

Dinner was a little more of a strain. Mira and Tamar had a
hard time covering their dislike of each other, though Mira made
no ill-natured remarks and Tamar said almost nothing at all. But
it fell to the men to make most of the conversation, a task they
were not used to with pretty women at the table, so talk was
disjointed and frequently clumsy. Everyone was just as glad
when the meal was over and it was time for the angel's performance.

The concert went well again this night. With Tamar in the
audience, Jared didn't mind singing a little longer, so he took
the time to perform all the requests that listeners called out to

him. He enjoyed singing, and he felt a strange, liquid elation at the knowledge that Tamar was listening to every note, every word. It did not escape his notice that while he sang his Kiss hazed over with a muted golden light. He would have given a lot to be close enough to see if Tamar's Kiss also reacted to the stimulus of his singing.

But, "You have quite an impressive range" was all she said as they finally headed back to their cabin.

"You liked the concert?" he couldn't help asking.

She unlocked the door and preceded him inside. "I imagine everyone did," she said.

This night, she insisted he take the bed while she slept on the chaise lounge, where, as she pointed out, her body was more likely to fit. He agreed only when she told him she would sleep there whether or not he lay on the floor, and he knew she was stubborn enough to do so. So he got a good night's sleep, and she claimed that she did, and the next morning they resumed their interrupted trip to Ysral.

It was somehow more awkward and more intimate, this flight over the eastern half of the ocean. Jared had carried this particular bundle from Azolay to the Samarian coast, and from Marquet to the middle of the ocean without feeling quite this degree of self-consciousness. Maybe because, during those first legs of the journey, Tamar had been half-sick and fainting, almost oblivious to her surroundings—and now she was alert, interested, and very animated. It was hard to overlook or ignore her.

Not that he wanted to. But they were suspended over the ocean, by the god's great grace, and she was completely helpless to free herself from him. It did not seem like the courteous time to begin a campaign of flirtation.

So he took her in his arms, cradled her against his chest, asked civilly if she was comfortable, and did not give in to the impulse to hold her tighter than necessary. And flew across the great, variegated sea with as much speed as he could generate.

She wanted to see everything; she wanted everything explained. "Where's that boat from? Why is the water different colors? Why is it so much colder up here? How fast can you fly? How many miles can you cover in a day? How fast do the boats go? Is that an island? Could we land there if we had to? When will we be in Ysral?"

She did not seem to be nearly as self-conscious as he was, so by and by his initial awkwardness wore off. And yet, despite the brisk ocean breeze, despite the mingled odors of salt and fish and seaweed that laced the heavy air, he never lost the fresh-washed smell of her hair or the sweet, unidentifiable scent that he thought must be the natural perfume of Tamar's skin.

After an hour or two she fell mostly silent, speaking only at rare intervals, and eventually she began dozing with her head propped against his chest. Jared flew on more rapidly now that he could concentrate on the task, and he watched the miles melt away below them. The ship captain had told him they were only three hundred miles from Ysral; it would be an effort, but they could probably make it that far by early nightfall.

And then they must seek out the Jacobites and then . . . well, Jared had not thought beyond that. Getting Tamar to safety had become his only concern.

They were possibly another hundred miles from the coast (two or three hours' flying time) when Jared became aware of Tamar growing limp and heavy in his arms. It was like she had crossed from sleep into coma, and her bones increased their weight and her muscles lapsed into elasticity. It reminded him of how she had felt on the first part of the flight, between Bethel and Marquet, and he was instantly alarmed.

"Tamar," he called to her over the noise of the wind and his own wingbeats. "Tamar? Are you awake? Is your headache back?"

She did not answer, did not stir. Her mouth had fallen open and bruises seemed to have appeared, magically, under her eyes. Quickly, Jared dropped down, losing altitude, hoping the thicker air closer to the water would revive her, but she did not shift position. He tightened his grip, shaking her a little, but nothing made her respond.

Now in a virtual panic, he cruised as close to the water as he dared. He continued speaking her name in low urgent tones, hoping the sound of his voice would penetrate her guarded dreaming. He wished there was someplace he could land—the smallest rock, a mere foothold—so he could throw cold ocean water across her face and shock her awake. But there was nothing.

He must find a ship, and quickly. Jovah guide them, now as

never before, for this must be a safe ship, a place he could land with the sleeping Jacobite.

He altered position again, gaining a few hundred feet of altitude so he could command a better view of the sea. The sudden shift in pressure seemed to register on Tamar's consciousness, for she tossed her head and drew her hands against her chest.

"Tamar!" Jared exclaimed in great excitement. "Tamar, can you hear me?"

"What?" she asked groggily. "My head hurts. Where are we?"

"Over the ocean. I'm looking for a ship."

"My head hurts," she repeated. "I just want to go to sleep."

"No, talk to me. Stay awake. Talk to me."

"I don't feel like talking," she said pettishly. "Why won't you let me lie down? Why are you hurting me?"

"Hurting you? What's hurting you?"

"My head," she said, and then she began to cry. Sweet Jovah singing, she broke his heart. He could not even pause to comfort her; he could not squeeze her hand or brush away her tears.

"Don't cry," he whispered, pushing his wings harder, trying to go faster, feeling the strain from the joint at his back to the very feather edge of the tip. "Tell me what you were dreaming."

"I wasn't dreaming," she said, but then she began to recount for him a series of disconnected, fragmented tales and images. Jared did not bother listening closely. Was that a shadow on the horizon, a patch of cobalt blue against the ultramarine of the sea around it, or was it the outline of a ship a dozen miles away? He veered in that direction, silently praying.

It was a ship. And merciful Jovah, it flew the white falcon flag of the Edori. It was headed away from Ysral, not toward it, but that didn't matter now. Jared's arms tightened convulsively on the girl.

"And then the room changed colors, and somebody else was in the room with me and it was an angel but it wasn't you—"

They were above the ship now and Jared circled once to make sure any lookout would have time to spot them. Yes, there were two men—no, three—on the deck, shading their eyes and gazing upward. One of them was waving his hand in a gesture of welcome, while another one headed toward the narrow doorway that led to the lower reaches of the ship, presumably to tell the news. Angel overhead; company for dinner.

Jared landed on the pitching ship as gently as he could, coming to his knees. Almost without his volition, Tamar slipped from his hold to lie half on the deck, half in his arms. Her eyes were open but she gazed around unseeingly, and she seemed both bewildered and afraid.

"Where are we?" she whispered to Jared. "This isn't Ysral."

Most of the crew hung back from the new arrivals, but one, a dark good-looking young Edori, came over and gazed down at them gravely. "Your friend looks ill. What can we do to aid her?" he asked.

Jared was immensely grateful for the instant offer of help. "I think all she needs is a place to lie down. She suffered a head injury four days ago, but yesterday she seemed perfectly fine. I'm sorry to trouble you—"

"No trouble," the Edori said. "I take it you were on your way to Ysral?"

"Yes, but I realize you were sailing west. Please don't alter your route for us. All I want is a bed for the night."

The Edori gave a brief, private smile and tossed his waist-length braid back over his shoulder. "I was not so eager to leave Ysral. I would not mind a quick return," he said. "But we will see what the captain says. Where in Ysral are you headed?"

Jared laughed weakly. "I'm not sure where. I would like to return this one to her friends." He hesitated, but the Edori were notorious sympathizers. He added, "Who are Jacobites."

The Edori lifted his eyebrows, glanced at the angel's wings which so obviously proclaimed him anything but a friend to the Jacobites, and nodded neutrally. "Many Jacobites have settled in Ysral," was all he said. "I'm sure you would not find it hard to locate them."

"I swear you can trust me," Jared said. He had never been around so many people who regarded him with suspicion; as a rule, an angel had the entrée anywhere. "She will tell you so herself."

"When she can speak," the Edori said, sinking to his knees in one graceful motion. Tamar had turned on her side, facing toward Jared, and she seemed to be crying softly. "I have a little skill in healing," the Edori said. "What is her name?"

"Tamar."

"Tamar," the Edori said in a firm, insistent voice impossible to ignore. "Tamar. I am Reuben. I will help you. Tamar. Turn and look at me, and say my name."

To Jared's surprise, Tamar straightened a little, seemed to pull all her bones and muscles back into their accustomed places, and shifted position to face her questioner. "Reuben," she said obediently.

But now he was staring down at her as if an apparition had unrolled itself here on this ship in the middle of the ocean. "Yes, I can see you belong with the Jacobites," he said softly. "And there is someone with them that you will very much want to meet."

CHAPTER SIXTEEN

Life in Ysral was not, Lucinda had found, much different from life on Angel Rock. For one thing, the accommodations in both cases were comfortable but hardly grand; in the small town of Sahala, she lived in a modest six-room, two-story house that she shared with five other people. For another, the communities were both small and self-contained. Sahala was bigger, of course—about a thousand souls to Angel Rock's twenty-four—but it had no greater level of activity or commerce. A few traders arrived every day, a few left, but the town's core community of Edori and Jacobites remained basically unchanged.

Lucinda's arrival had created an uproar.

The resident Edori had been the first to greet her with that unselfconscious warmth and directness that, in anyone else, would have seemed rude or overwhelming. "Look, Martha, it's an angel!" "Well, look at you, child. Have you come to live in Sahala with us? I've never spoken to an angel before. I've never been this close to one." "Jonathon, have you said hello to the angel? What's your name, young lady, I didn't catch it."

So that had been odd enough, though Lucinda had answered as pleasantly and openly as she could, but then there had been the cold, strange greeting of the Jacobites. They had not come immediately out from their stone houses, but gazed at her from behind shuttered windows and half-opened doors. She could not blame them for feeling a profound hostility toward an unknown angel visitor, but still it made her feel awkward, humble, and lonely as she stood in the center of the small town, stared at by everyone.

But Reuben was still at her side. He motioned to one of the

young Edori boys who had crept close enough to touch Lucinda's wing. She flicked it nervously from his curious fingers. "Go tell Conran I'm here," he said. "Tell him I've brought a friend who needs shelter. Tell him she is to be trusted."

The boy nodded and darted off. Lucinda managed to slant a smile at her escort. "I didn't know you were well enough acquainted with the Jacobites to call them by name and have them trust you," she said.

He grinned back. He seemed completely at ease, not worried in the slightest that he and his companion might be repulsed. "Didn't you say your aunt wanted you to seek out Conran?" he answered.

"Yes, but you spoke just now as if you know him."

"Everyone knows Conran. He's that kind of man."

"I'm afraid," she said suddenly.

Reuben reached out and took her hand in a warm, unbelievably comforting clasp. "If they won't take you in, we'll put you with the Edori," he said. "My family's tribe is traveling just now, but they'd gladly take you in. Neither Bael nor Omar would be able to find you if you were with them."

In a few minutes the little boy returned, scampering in front of a small delegation. *These must be the Jacobites,* Lucinda thought, for they certainly were not Edori. They did not have the Edori's unvaried dark coloring and smiling faces; this group, three men and two women, were mostly fair and uniformly suspicious. The leader appeared to be a stocky older man with grizzled hair and a look of lively intelligence. At any rate, the others let him precede them, and the Edori fell back to admit him through their ranks. Lucinda could not help herself. She edged behind Reuben and peered out at the Jacobites from behind his shoulder.

"Well, Reuben, this had better be good," the leader said, coming to a halt a few paces from the new arrivals. His voice was clear and ringing, but he did not sound angry. Astonished, maybe, but not at all unprepared. He seemed like the sort of man who was never caught unprepared. "Bringing an angel to Sahala is much like setting a hawk among the rabbits."

"Ah, Conran, you were never a frightened rabbit running for your life," Reuben drawled in his usual lilting tones, and Conran's face relaxed slightly into a grin. "Besides, I have a message from a lady who advised me to bring this angel to your very doorstep. And I've never yet known you to scoff at any news that came from a woman's mouth.''

"A lady?'' Conran repeated, but his whole face had sharpened into anticipation. He tried to peer at Lucinda's face, but she drew farther back behind her human shield. "And where have you just sailed from, my friend?''

"You've heard of the place, I'm sure,'' the Edori said.

"Angel Rock,'' Conran said. "And this particular package came from a lady named Gretchen.''

"You've guessed it,'' Reuben said. "So now will you be willing to take her in? For that's the request I'll be making.''

Conran reached out a hand to draw Reuben to one side. Reuben was tall and well muscled, but the Jacobite had considerable strength, for his push dislodged the Edori. "And you must be Lucinda,'' Conran said as the angel came into view. "I have wanted to meet you for a long time. Twenty-eight years, to be exact.''

He was strange and intimidating, but he exuded a powerful charisma for all that. Still nervous, but much more hopeful, Lucinda extended her hand. The Jacobite took it in a crushing grip. He studied her face with an unnerving intentness that slowly gave way to a sort of incredulous wonder.

"Yes,'' he said at last. "You look very like her. There would be no mistaking you.''

Lucinda remembered suddenly that this man had known Rinalda in her age of wild passion. "My mother?'' she said shyly. "I look like my mother?''

For a split second she thought he looked surprised. Well, who else could he have thought she resembled? "Yes, that you do,'' he said.

"Did you know her well?''

"I did. A long time ago. I had heard that she bore two daughters, and I am pleased to meet this one at last.''

Lucinda sighed, inexplicably saddened. "Yes, two daughters, but my twin sister died.''

"She did?'' Conran asked sharply. "I did not know that.''

"Oh, yes. As an infant. The story is very tragic.''

"Ah.'' Conran looked briefly hopeful, then his face clouded over again. "Yes, I suppose she is dead, at that. A tragedy, indeed. But to have saved one of Rinalda's girls—that is a triumph in any case. Have you come to join the Jacobites, young lady? Or why are you here?''

"She is here because her aunt fears for her safety," Reuben interposed. "Gretchen is afraid that Lucinda has drawn the attention of Bael and his son Omar. She wanted Lucinda away from Angel Rock."

"Well, she can stay here as long as she likes," Conran said. "We are not likely to deny refuge to anyone hunted by the Archangel."

"And I want you to tell me everything," Lucinda said. "Everything you know about my mother. Everything you know about the Alleluia Files. I want to understand it all."

"I will tell you," he said. "And if you become a believer, like your mother, I will count myself a fortunate man."

He turned away to shout to four others who had followed him, waving them forward to meet the angel. Reuben added in a voice only Lucinda could hear, "He is fortunate anyway, merely to have you near him. That much I could tell him for myself."

But once she had settled in to Sahala—and once Reuben was gone—her life did not materially change. There was no mysterious initiation into the Jacobite fraternity. She felt no sudden access of belief, no zealous devotion to the cause. Conran explained what she did not already know about the Jacobites, and the information intrigued her, but did not wholly win her over.

The most interesting piece of news was what Conran considered verification. Jacob Fairman, according to Conran, had long believed *Jehovah* to be a spaceship, not a god, and he claimed that the oracle Deborah had once assured him he was correct.

Lucinda frowned at this revelation. "An *oracle* also knew that the god was really a spaceship? That seems very unlikely."

"Jacob said that Deborah had been charged by Alleluia to guard this secret with her very life and not to impart it until she, too, was on her deathbed. Because it was imperative that someone know the truth about *Jehovah,* but that the knowledge was too inflammatory for the whole world to learn. So Alleluia told Deborah, and one presumes that Deborah told Jecoliah—although, if that were so, I would have expected Jecoliah to have spoken up before now. Although perhaps she does not see the slaughter of a few hundred Jacobites as significant enough to break a silence of a hundred years."

"Why was it imperative that someone know the truth? If Alleluia found the truth so shocking, why not let it die with her?"

"*Jehovah* is a man-made piece of equipment. I don't know how much experience you have with technology, but it always breaks down. I will grant that *Jehovah* must be more sophisticated than the trucks and radio transmitters our engineers have cobbled together, but no doubt it, too, needs periodic maintenance. So someone needs to know what it is so that someone can make sure the machine gets fixed."

Lucinda was still frowning. "If I was an oracle who had guarded such a secret for most of my life, I don't know that I would be sharing that information with any wild-eyed radical who showed up at my door. And then watch him stir the whole country into bloody controversy and not say a word to anyone else."

"As to why she would have told him—well, Jacob Fairman was a very persuasive man. If anyone could have charmed confidences from an old spinster, it would have been Jacob. If you were to meet him today, I venture to guess you would be telling him your most cherished secrets within ten minutes. It was the effect he had. As to why she told no one else—she died shortly after this conversation took place. She was not in a position to tell anyone anything."

"What made him think to ask her in the first place? Why did he even begin to wonder about the god?"

"There had been speculation in the scientific community for years about the true nature of *Jehovah*. Thirty years before Jacob Fairman began proselytizing, there were two young graduates of the Augustine school who postulated the idea that 'Jovah' was really a machine, based on their largely unproven theories of flight mechanics and weapons systems. Their ideas created quite a stir among the scientists and intellectuals of the time and were violently opposed by the angels. Nothing really came of their speculations, but from time to time, students would come across their papers and start the debate all over again. Jacob Fairman had been a student at the Augustine school, of course, so he'd heard all the theories. He just came to believe in them more devoutly than most."

"And how did you come to believe?" Lucinda asked.

"I went to the Augustine school. I heard the whispers. And I had not been a particularly faithful man to begin with. Engineers, as a rule, are not. They look for the logical explanation behind the mystical event. For instance, we have spent some energy trying to determine why angels can fly."

"We have wings," Lucinda said with dignity.

"Ah, but in so many other ways you are completely human. In fact, current biological thinking says you're mutants, but not naturally occurring ones. Someone tampered with your physical makeup some seven hundred and fifty years ago, and you've bred true ever since."

"No one tampered with us," Lucinda said coldly. "Jovah selected a few trusted men and women, and fitted them with wings. Back when the colonists first settled Samaria."

"That's what the Librera says," Conran agreed. "But there are very old texts, written in the ancient language, that say otherwise. That talk about how the original angels were created by the scientists and biologists among the settlers. That even describe how clumsy the first angels were as they learned to fly."

"How could you read such texts, even if they exist?" Lucinda demanded. "Only oracles know the old language."

Conran grinned again. He radiated energy and confidence, and did not seem at all annoyed by her questions. Rather, he enjoyed knocking aside her skepticism with feasible answers of his own. "Ah, but one of the courses taught at the Augustine school is linguistics," he said. "Some of the ancient engineering manuals that can be found even today in the archives of the angel holds are written in that tongue. And old Caleb Augustus, he got his hands on these books, and it just killed him that he couldn't read them. So he had his wife the oracle teach him the words. And he set up a class to teach them to others."

"That doesn't seem right," Lucinda said. "That's holy knowledge."

"All knowledge is holy," Conran replied. "And all knowledge should be shared, or it becomes profane."

Lucinda rubbed her temples. She was not entirely convinced, of course. As an angel, she had some responsibility to her god and to her people; she could not rashly abandon them for a few facile theorems. And yet Conran was even more plausible than Reuben, although he had not, she realized, given her any more concrete evidence. He just had such a compelling voice that everything he said sounded true. It was hard not to leap to her feet and cry out, "Yes, I believe!"

"It's all interesting," she said at last. "And some of it makes a great deal of sense. But I would need more proof than this before I became a convert."

"Fair enough," he said amiably. "But it is good of you to ask—and to listen."

She had not asked her questions of the other Jacobites. She was rather shy of them, for they were a strange, passionate, suspicious, and ill-kept lot. They looked like they had lived hard, lean lives, managing to survive by the scarcest combination of wits and luck. Despite Conran's welcome, they all mistrusted her; and they had a peculiar habit of staring at her face as if they could not believe the precise arrangement of her features.

There were, in addition to Conran, about fifty Jacobites living in Sahala—the only survivors, he told her, of a band that used to be about four times as strong. She was shocked to learn of Bael's campaign of extermination, though she found this easier to believe than tales of orbiting spaceships. Gretchen had hated Bael, though she had managed to conceal that violent emotion for most of Lucinda's life, and Reuben also had ascribed terrible crimes to the Archangel. Lucinda did not doubt that Bael had ferociously hunted down the Jacobites; he would have considered it his duty.

It was not surprising that those fifty survivors looked at her askance, and so Lucinda made little effort to get to know them. Oh, once or twice at Conran's invitation, she joined them when the whole group assembled in the evenings, but she was fairly uncomfortable at these events. They spoke ardently about their beliefs, contemptuously of the complacent Samarians who were too thickheaded to listen to reason, idealistically of how they would bring the truth to every last soul on the mainland. Lucinda left these meetings even less in sympathy with their cause than she had been before. They were zealots, or possibly madmen; she trusted them very little more than they trusted her.

On the whole, she felt more at ease with the Edori. The house she lived in was an Edori house, owned by people who were in some remote manner relatives of Reuben. Then again, from what she could tell, all Edori considered themselves kin, so perhaps they did not in fact have blood ties. She had not completely figured out how the inmates of the house were related. There were two older women who appeared to be in their sixties; a young woman about Lucinda's age, who had a baby boy; and a young man who did not seem to be brother, son, or lover to any of the others. They treated each other with great affection mixed with hilarity. They loved nothing so much as a joke at another's expense, though none of the tricks were ever cruel.

None of them were ever in the house if they could help it. They spent most of their time in the garden, in the town commons visiting their friends, or off on pursuits Lucinda had not yet identified. Though constructed solidly enough, the house had an impermanent feel, as if at any point its residents might dismantle its stones, cart its components along with them on some impromptu journey, and rebuild the whole thing somewhere else on a more satisfactory site. The furnishings were exotic, colorful, and completely unplanned, so that a red print sofa warred with the blues and grays of a handwoven rug. No one ever gave a thought to mealtime until someone in the house admitted to hunger, and then two or three of them would throw together a dinner from whatever ingredients happened to be in the cupboard.

But none of this discomposed them or made them add a little foresight to their days. On the contrary, Lucinda had never met such happy, carefree, spontaneous people. They made her laugh. They made her feel welcome.

They reminded her of Reuben.

He would be gone at least two weeks, he had told her the evening before the day he had to depart again. *The Wayward* had stayed in port a week while Maurice gathered his next cargo, but that time had gone by wickedly fast. He hated to leave her among strangers, especially since she had been whisked so abruptly away from home, but he knew she would be cared for here. He would not worry while she was among his people. And he did not say, but she heard the unspoken words, the warning behind his farewell: *I am a sailor. I am Edori. I will always return to you, but I will always sail away again.* If she were to love him, she would have to expect to be left behind over and over again.

And it seemed obvious that she loved him.

Nights, when the manic fervor of the Jacobites had left her cold and the cheerful charm of the Edori had failed to warm

her, she lay in her bed and dreamed again of the hours she had
spent with Reuben. They had been a week on *The Wayward,*
traveling between Angel Rock and Ysral, and during that week
Lucinda had learned what it meant to take an Edori lover. She
had not often lain with a man, for it had not been possible to
take casual bedmates from the small population of Angel Rock,
but she had a little experience gained from likable strangers who
had visited the port. But those encounters were nothing like
making love to an Edori.

There had not been room enough for both of them on the
narrow bunk in the ship's cramped cabin. So Reuben had spread
layer after layer of blankets on the hard floor, creating a mattress
of quilt and cotton. And he had pulled her down beside him and
covered himself with her white wings and buried his face in the
blond fall of her hair. She had thought she would be shy or
nervous, but she was neither. She ran her fingers through the
black silk of his hair and laughed when he murmured incomprehensible endearments in the Edori language. Then caught her
breath as he began to run his hands slowly, intently over the
curves and hollows of her body.

No, nothing in her past had prepared her for the utter annihilation and rebirth of making love to an Edori. Or perhaps,
more truly, nothing had prepared her for the ecstasy of being in
love.

And the complete desolation of seeing the loved one walk
away.

When she could think about anything besides how much she
missed Reuben and how little she understood the Jacobites, she
turned her mind to speculation about what she should do with
the rest of her life. Much as she liked the Edori, she did not
envision living in this little house forever. And she had a hard
time picturing herself gradually succumbing to the illicit allure
of the Jacobite enterprise. Could she return to Angel Rock? And
when? And if she did, what then? Would she spend the rest of
her life mooning over Reuben, violently happy on the few days
a year that *The Wayward* was in port, dreamily depressed every
other hour of her life? How would she occupy her time? Running the Manor, cooking and cleaning for mainland guests? Perhaps Reuben and Maurice and the others would allow her to
travel with them from city to city, continent to continent—but
how would that be any more fulfilling?

It seemed unlikely that she could return to Samaria, at least as long as Bael and Omar were in power. And what would she do in Samaria, anyway?

What would she do anywhere? What was her purpose in life?

It was when her thoughts reached this tangled conclusion that she could stand it no longer. She flung herself into the cerulean sky and flew until she was dizzy. She thought she could outrun her thoughts, but they inevitably kept pace beside her, until she had exhausted herself so much that she could no longer think.

But one thing she did have to say for Ysral: It was simply beautiful.

Of course, legend had long described the small continent as rich, warm, and exquisite, and in this case, legend had not lied. It was situated on a slightly more southern plane than Samaria, and so, summer and winter, it was wrapped in idle, sultry breezes. Its soil was fertile and imaginative, and everything seemed to grow there, from the standard crops that could be found on Samaria to flowers and grains of the most amazing hue and variety. The Edori, of course, were lazy farmers, most of them preferring to live off the largesse of the undomesticated land, but even their haphazard attempts at raising corn and wheat and soybeans were met with fabulous success. The rivers ran with water so sweet that even the children preferred it, and nowhere was there hunger or need or want.

But there were the marks of man's presence, a thing which, Reuben had told her, had caused bitter dissension among the Edori. For centuries, the credo of the Edori had been to live in harmony with the earth, in harmony with man, and for that reason they had failed to build permanent structures and turned their backs on farming. But in Ysral, the corelli had built cities—small ones, to be sure, but immobile nonetheless—and altered the landscape to suit them. And the renegade scientists had moved the Augustine school to Ysral, and evidences of scientific advancement were everywhere.

For instance, Edori in Sahala could communicate via a mysterious transmitter with their families not only in nearby Covallah but traveling throughout the remote sections of the continent. They could drive mobile vehicles that were quieter, smaller, and faster than anything Lucinda had seen on the mainland. They had developed remarkable recording equipment that caught her voice one night in an impromptu concert and played it back for her the very next minute.

"All of this takes energy and creates waste," Boyce told her gloomily one evening when she asked about a swift little car she'd seen racing away from the city. Boyce was the young man who lived in the house with her. He seemed both attracted to and repelled by the new technology, though he had been able to explain to her every single thing she'd asked about. "We have always prided ourselves on offering no hurt to the people around us—or the land. But to power our vehicles, we use fuel that we dig from the earth, doing who knows what harm to the soil beneath? And everything we manufacture has left behind some residue—some gas, or toxin, or pile of burned waste. There is not much now, but if we continue at this rate, what then? What kind of evil will we have created?"

Lucinda nodded soberly, though she was not really clear on the problem. She had asked him to take her to the Augustine school and he had said he would, but not for another week or two. It was, she learned, almost a daylong ride away (and that if they borrowed one of the fast little cars), and Boyce had other projects under way at the moment. But soon, he promised. Lucinda had sighed. She had learned very quickly that the Edori had no concept of haste. She supposed she would be older than her aunt Gretchen before Boyce finally escorted her to the university.

A small voice at the back of her head gave her a brief, chiding lecture: *You have scarcely been here two weeks, and already you're bored and looking for entertainment,* it said. *You will have to learn how to amuse yourself better than this.*

But then, the very next day, diversion arrived in a form she would never have dreamed possible.

She had been with Boyce and two young Jacobites who were friends of his, helping them go through some old history books Conran had found. Conran had wanted to know if the books had any value, if they should be shipped to the Augustine school, kept here, or thrown away, and he had suggested Lucinda be invited to help catalog them. She couldn't imagine why, except she supposed her view of history was very different from the Jacobites'. Obediently, she had spent most of the day with the other three, leafing idly through page after page of rather dry historical renderings, and listening to the other three talk about electronics. It had not been the most exciting afternoon of her life.

And then suddenly a young Jacobite woman burst into the room, flushed with excitement and important news. "Did you *hear*? They've found Tamar! They've just brought her to Conran's house."

"Who's Tamar?" Boyce asked a second before Lucinda could voice the words, but the Jacobites were on their feet.

"Where did they find her? How did she get here?" one of them demanded.

"Tamar! Conran thought she was dead!" the other said.

"No, she's here, she's fine. Although she hurt her head a few days ago, Reuben says, and she—"

"Reuben!" Lucinda and Boyce exclaimed in unison. Now they, too, were on their feet, and all four of them had impatiently pushed aside their books.

"Is Reuben back?" Lucinda asked breathlessly, while Boyce said, "How did she end up on *The Wayward*?"

"I don't know the details, I just came up to tell you," the girl said, turning for the door. The others came hurrying after her.

There was a small, agitated crowd outside of Conran's house, growing larger by the minute. Whoever this Tamar was, she was certainly popular, Lucinda thought. Not that she cared about missing Jacobite women returned from the grave. But if Reuben was back a whole week early, that was miraculous news indeed.

He was there; she could pick out his tall, well-balanced body even from a distance, even in a pack of Edori. She was so focused on him that for a moment she did not take in an even more astonishing sight: an angel, standing a little to one side of the main knot of people, explaining something to one of Conran's friends.

What strange coincidence would bring two angels to the Jacobite stronghold of Sahala within two weeks of each other?

As she drew closer she was able to identify the angel, although she did not know him well: Jared, the leader of the host at Monteverde. She could think of no reason he would be here. She increased her pace to a run (it was too short a distance to reasonably fly) and made it to the edge of the crowd before Boyce or the others.

Reuben saw her. He looked straight at her and held her eyes
with a gaze that might have been speculation and might have
been warning. In any case, it was not the expression of joyful
welcome she expected, and it stopped her cold. But then his
face softened and he motioned her forward, and she gently
pushed her way through the crowd to his side.

But when she arrived, he was not looking at her. Like everyone else, he was watching a painfully thin young woman who
was improbably dressed in an exotic silver outfit and speaking
in a low voice to Conran. She had her back to the angel and so
Lucinda could not see her face, and she looked inquiringly back
at Reuben.

"Tamar," the Edori said, and the mortal turned his way.

And Lucinda stared at a young woman with her own eyes
and her own face, who stared back at her as if she had been
knifed in the heart.

CHAPTER SEVENTEEN

If Conran had not taken her arm, Tamar knew, she would have fallen backward onto the hard stone of the walkway. Vertigo again; but this time caused by the shock of an unbelievable vision. That was her face, that angel's face. That was the outline of her cheek and the color of her eyes. That was her very expression, stupefied and incredulous. The angel put a hand to her mouth in a mirror image of Tamar's own gesture.

No one spoke for what seemed like hours. Of all the people who could have stepped forward to offer explanations, it was the angel who first gathered her wits into a coherent sentence. "So you did not die when our mother did," the angel said slowly. "I wonder who it is, then, that they found in her arms that night."

More madness; the words made utterly no sense. Perhaps she was dreaming again. She had had such dark, fantastical dreams ever since that Jansai had struck her on the head at Azolay. They would come over her, waking or sleeping, and sometimes she had a hard time distinguishing nightmare from reality. That must be what was happening now.

But Conran was speaking. "She knows nothing about that," he said sharply. "She was never told who her mother was or that someone like you existed."

The angel spoke again in that same slow, marveling tone; she had a voice like liquid copper, molten and glinting. "Well, I was told that she was dead. And all this time . . ." The angel stepped forward, hands outstretched; Tamar would have flinched backward, but Conran's body held her in place. "Tamar?" she asked. "That's your name?"

Tamar nodded. It was impossible to speak. She had heard this
voice before, over and over, singing in her head. The more the
angel said, the more certain she was. "I'm Lucinda. I'm your
twin."

Everyone had wanted to speak to Tamar at once, but she was
so exhausted she could do no more than pass from figure to
figure, submitting to brief, fierce hugs, and whispers of gladness.
Tired as she was, she could not keep herself from doing a mental
tally, noting who was present and who was not, and guessing
from that who had fallen at the Jansai's hands. But maybe not.
They must have thought she was dead, and here she was, weary
but alive, coming face-to-face with her double in the most bizarre encounter imaginable.

Within minutes, Conran shooed everyone away. "Tomorrow,
when she's rested," he said in that voice that was never coun-
termanded. "She'll talk to you all then. For now, let her regain
her footing and have a moment or two of privacy."

Except it was not privacy, of course. Conran allowed three
others to follow them into his house: the Edori Reuben and both
angels. Tamar was so disoriented and dumbstruck that she still
felt dizzy, and she was comforted when Jared took her hand as
they walked through the narrow hallway.

In a few minutes they were all seated on dilapidated furniture
set up in a small living room. Lucinda, Tamar could not help
noting, had gravitated toward the Edori. He had ensconced himself in a wide, battered armchair and she squeezed herself beside
him, wrapping her wings around her shoulders so the edges
trailed on the floor before her. It did not look at all comfortable,
but the angel did not seem to mind.

Tamar seated herself at random on the edge of a plaid sofa.
Jared at once pulled over a stool and settled beside her, shaking
his wings out behind him. He immediately took her hand again.
Conran straddled a straight-backed chair and laid his arms along
its top.

"First, I'd like to hear the story of what happened to you,"
he said, addressing Tamar. "I went to Ileah. I knew you had
gone there. When there was no sign of you or the others—"

"I arrived a few days after the others, I suppose," she said.
She was trying to keep her voice even, but to her own ears it
sounded dreary and strained. "The Jansai had arrived a day or

so before me. There were twelve dead and one gravely injured. I buried the dead and nursed the living."

"Who?"

"Peter. He's still alive, I believe." She looked over at Jared, who had his eyes trained on the floor. "This angel took him to Stockton to seek medical attention."

Conran, too, glanced at Jared but instantly returned his attention to Tamar. "And then?"

"I moved on to Semorrah. And from there to a wealthy farm outside of Shepherd's Pass. Where I found Jared again." Again she looked at the angel. This time he met her eyes, a faint smile on his lips. Well, at this exact moment she was not ready to go into all her dealings with him, all her fears and suspicions. "He told me that Jansai were looking for us—you, me, Duncan, a few others—they had portraits that someone had drawn of us."

"Where did they get these portraits?" Conran asked sharply.

She shrugged. "From a Jacobite traitor, I suppose. I've been thinking about that. Zeke seems the most likely."

"Zeke! What makes you think he's fallen into the Jansai's hands—or the angels'?"

"He went with me to Breven," she said baldly. "I watched him try to board an Edori ship. I watched him get taken by Jansai. If he wasn't killed outright, he probably found a way to buy his life. Zeke did not have much stomach for torture, you remember. And he was always a passable artist. He could have rendered our likenesses well enough."

"So Zeke—or someone—gave our pictures to the Archangel," Conran said evenly. "And we all suddenly became much more at risk than we believed."

Tamar nodded tiredly. "Jared told me I was one of the ones they were particularly looking for. I could not imagine why." She glanced at Lucinda. "Till I saw her. Bael must have realized who I was, although even I did not know."

The angel leaned forward. She had not, since they seated themselves, once taken her eyes from Tamar's face. "What did they tell you, then," she asked, "about your mother and your birth?"

Tamar rubbed a hand across her forehead. "That she and my father had been Jacobites, devoted to the cause. That they had both died in the raid that killed Jacob Fairman. I never learned many details, but somehow I had come to believe that one of them at least was a Manadavvi. I take it that wasn't true. I take it none of the stories were true."

"She was the daughter of an angel, and she lived in Cedar Hills," Lucinda said. "She left the hold to join the Jacobites, but she was captured a few months before the raid that killed Fairman. My father—our father—was an angel at the hold, and he had always adored her. So I was told. While she was kept prisoner there they became lovers. And you and I were born."

"Twins. Angel and mortal," Jared said, speaking for the first time. "It had never happened before. And has not happened since."

"They took me away from her instantly," Lucinda continued. "One night, a few weeks after we were born, she managed to escape with you in her arms. But the night was bitterly cold, and she found no shelter. Two days later they found her dead at the side of the road, a dead baby in her arms." Lucinda took a deep breath. "Apparently, however, the baby was not you."

All eyes in the room turned expectantly toward Conran. He looked astonished. "What makes you think that I—"

"Tell us," Tamar said shortly. "You have lied to me for twenty-eight years. I think I deserve to hear the true story of my life."

"I told you what your mother wanted you to know," Conran replied.

"My mother is dead. Now tell me what I want to know."

He nodded and spent a moment looking down at the floor, as if he was organizing his thoughts or remembering an old tragedy he had long since managed to forget. "It was the coldest winter anyone could remember," he began, in the low, emphatic voice of the born storyteller. Everyone fell silent to listen. "Even in southern Jordana, where the seasons are usually not so harsh, it was colder than a man could stand to be outside for longer than an hour. The Jacobites were still stricken from the loss of Jacob Fairman, and no one was sure what to do next. Most of us had scattered to the homes of friends and family members who were tolerant of our incendiary politics. Elinor and I were staying in Luminaux in the house of her brother's son.

"News came about Galena, one of the Jacobites, who was spending the winter at her sister's house near Cedar Hills. Her sister was some sort of domestic who was employed by the angels, and she had only begrudgingly taken Galena in because

Galena was about to have a baby. Galena had written to Elinor asking if she could come when the baby was due, and now, during the worst winter of the century, it was her time.

"So Elinor and I traveled to Cedar Hills. But by the time we arrived on Galena's doorstep, tragedy had already come to visit. The baby had been born amid much bleeding, strangling on its own cord, and unable to draw more than a single breath. And this baby had nearly killed Galena in the process. When we walked in the door, the sister began screaming, blaming us and our heresies for the baby's death and her sister's desperate condition. She ran from the sickroom and locked herself in her own bedchamber, and would not emerge to watch her sister die.

"Elinor and I turned to tending Galena, but we knew we had come too late. Within an hour Galena died in Elinor's arms. I was still ripping the mortuary cloths to use for wrapping the body when there was a furious clamor outside. Someone pounding at the door, someone crying to be let in. I ran to the door and threw it open, and on a frigid blast of air, in tumbled Rinalda."

He paused a moment, rubbing his hands together; he seemed, even in this close, warm house, to be suffering again from that freezing air and a chilling discovery. "Elinor and I dragged her to the fire and began stripping her body of wet clothes. She did not have the strength to weep or speak, though we pelted her with questions. We were stupefied to find, as we pulled back the sweater nearest her skin, an infant girl swaddled in rags and strapped to Rinalda's chest.

"The baby was rosy and warm, kept safe from the bitter air by the heat of the mother's body. We had heard, through Galena and her sister, that Rinalda had given birth to twin girls, one angel, one mortal. Elinor held the child in her arms and exclaimed, 'Rinalda, is this your baby girl?' And Rinalda gathered up every last bit of strength she had and whispered back, 'Keep her safe. Guard her from all the angels. Never tell her who her father was or who I was. Never let her seek out those who have betrayed me—and will betray her. Never! Promise me this!' Elinor protested, but I promised for both of us. Only a few hours after this Rinalda died."

Again, Conran paused; again he seemed to shiver from a remembered cold. "We had other friends in Cedar Hills," he said slowly. "While Elinor watched that baby, I ran out into the awful night to the house of a friend who had use of a horse and cart. He and I took Rinalda and Galena's baby and threw their bodies into the back of that cart, and we drove as far from the lights of Cedar Hills as we could stand. And then we dumped those corpses on the side of the road, brutally unprotected from the malice of winter, and left them there for anyone to discover. And may I say that I have not, since I was a boy, believed in the existence of the god, but that night for the whole drive back to Cedar Hills, I prayed for those two wretched, abandoned souls.

"When I returned to Galena's sister's house, Elinor was gone. She had taken the baby to another friend and left Galena for me to prepare for burial. This I did. It was while I was sorting through Rinalda's clothes one last time that I found a roll of fifty gold coins sewn into a pocket. I put them aside to give to her baby girl at a time that would seem appropriate.

"The next morning, when Galena's weeping sister finally emerged from her room, I told her that we had wrapped the dead baby in the dead woman's arms. I remember that she nodded and seemed pleased. 'Good. Galena will keep her warm,' she said to me. I thought of that frozen body out on the Jordana highways, and said nothing.

"Elinor and I stayed for the funeral and left for Luminaux as soon as we could, the purloined baby in our arms. It was two days before we thought to give the child a name. I wanted to choose something rebellious and wild, for Rinalda would never have given her daughter a traditional name culled from the Librera. But Elinor was adamant. 'We will call her Tamar,' she said. 'For the Tamar of legend was also a seditious mortal born to angels. It is a name that will serve her well.' And Tamar she thereafter became."

He fell silent again, now reviewing a more recent history, and then he sighed. "We did what we could for that baby," he said. He still had not raised his eyes to look at Tamar, or any of them. "We gave her whatever love we had. We taught her the things we knew. We raised her on what we still believe is the truth. But it has been a hard life for her, as it has been for us, and I have wondered more than once what would have happened to her had Rinalda not stolen her away from her prison in Cedar Hills."

He sighed deeply and finally looked at his audience, glancing from face to face as if gauging how deeply each listener had been struck by the story. Tamar herself was numb. Her head was pounding, her eyes felt oiled in acid; she could not move, she could scarcely think. She did not want to hear one more word of this terrible story.

"And I wonder," Conran said with a little more passion, "why she picked that night of all nights to flee from Cedar Hills. Surely there had been other opportunities to run—or would be again. Why the night so cold that no one could survive it?"

A small voice spoke from the other side of the room. Or at least the voice seemed small. Perhaps Tamar's ears had merely shrunk down. "Because that was the night Bael chose to help her."

"*What?*" That word was much closer, much louder, leaping from Jared's lips. "Who told you that?"

"My aunt Gretchen. She says she saw Bael sneak into my mother's chamber that night and usher her from the hold. She says Bael wanted her to die in the winter night. She says that's why she took me away from Cedar Hills."

Conran nodded soberly. "It is about what I would expect of him, to murder a helpless girl in a cruel and clever way. And it makes me glad to think that we have fooled him all these years by keeping Tamar alive and whole. Would that we could have saved a hundred more just like her."

Tamar shut her eyes. She could not keep the room in focus; Conran spoke awhile longer but none of his words registered. She heard various voices call out her name but she did not have the strength to respond. Her head expanded and contracted with a slow, painful rhythm, and all she wanted to do was sleep.

"There's a room upstairs," Conran said, and suddenly she was swept up in someone's arms—Jared's, she knew, for she had become quite familiar with the feel of his arms around her. He climbed a short stairway and within minutes had laid her on a narrow bed. She had a confused impression of shapes and shadows around her, and she caught fragments of whispered consultations. "Let me stay with her," a woman said, and a man protested. Tamar did not care if all of them camped out on the floor or abandoned this room, this house, this village utterly. She turned to her side, and she slept.

•   •   •

Dreaming again. Or perhaps not. It was hard to tell sleep from reality, nightmare from memory. Light and dark fenced and feinted, gleaming thrust and parry; figures bulged into menace, then melted into sweet brilliance. More than once, someone held fiery liquid to her mouth, and she drank, spilling droplets down her cheek and into her collar. When she cried out in her sleep, someone was instantly at her side, cool hand on her forehead, low voice chasing away terror. She never saw this person's face, but she was not sure; it could have been a parade of people, dozens of hands, or it could have been the disembodied spirits of her imagination.

Once in a while she was sure she woke, fevered but lucid, and then she opened her eyes. Somewhere in the room there was a low, electric light that threw all the shapes into unwavering relief: the tall dresser, the cracked cheval mirror, the straight-backed chair placed a few feet from her bed. Every time she woke, she felt a moment's surge of panic, a desperate sense of desolation, till she looked over at that chair and saw the familiar sight: angel wings draped across a sleeping body, white feathers drifting across the floor. Only then did the fear subside, only then could she sleep again.

And has it come to this? she thought crossly during one of those brief clearheaded periods. *That I cannot sleep without an angel by my side?* But these past few days she had grown so dependent on Jared's strength that now she could not sleep unless he was there to guard her. She woke; she craned her neck till she could catch a glimpse of those sleek wings; and then she slept again.

It was morning before she woke again to the instant sensation of health. Her body felt light, hollowed out but clean, no longer harboring pain or the mysterious clouds of the brain. She shifted position under the bunched sheets, testing the resilience of her muscles, and the bed creaked beneath her weight. She heard the angel in the nearby chair rustle to his feet. She pushed herself to a seated position and turned to smile at him ruefully.

But it was not Jared who stood there watching her, half hopeful and half afraid; it was not Jared whose presence had calmed her in the night and watched over her fretful dreaming. Tamar stared unsmilingly at Lucinda, and her sister stared back.

•　•　•

The mortal woman was the first to speak. "Was it you here all night?" she asked in a neutral voice.

Lucinda did not come a step nearer; she appeared to be waiting for an invitation. She twisted an emerald ring on her finger as if she could not check the nervous gesture. "All night," she said, "though the others came by often to check on you. Jared came to the door almost every hour. He was extremely worried."

Jared. And there was a problem she would have to consider very soon, for how had it happened that he had become so essential to her peace of mind, so necessary to her happiness, that his was the first face she looked for when she woke? "I think I feel better," she said cautiously. "Someone gave me some medicine."

"Conran. He thought it would help you. Jared says you were hit on the head."

"Well, I've been hit on the head before and it never knocked me senseless for five days," Tamar said irritably. Lucinda smiled, then tried to hide it.

Tamar studied the face so like her own, truer than a mirror image. Of course the hair was not a ghastly shade of half-dyed brown, as hers was, and the eyes were not shadowed with a week of delirium, but it was her nose, her chin, her own hesitant, questioning expression. "I don't like angels, you know," she offered. "None of us do. I have been taught that they are the source of all the wretchedness in the world."

Lucinda allowed her smile to grow, and she came two steps closer to the bed. "Well, I wish I could say that I've heard only dreadful things about the Jacobites, but to tell you the truth, I never heard much about them on Angel Rock. So I have no long-standing prejudice against you."

"I still cannot quite believe it," Tamar said. "No one ever told me I had a sister."

"They told me you were dead," Lucinda said earnestly. She had gathered the courage to push her chair closer to the bed, and now she sat beside the invalid. "I used to ask my aunt Gretchen to tell me the story over and over again, till finally she refused to repeat it one more time. I think I was always hoping it would have a different ending. Not until last night did my hopes come true."

"I can hear you, you know," Tamar said abruptly. "Singing.

And I can feel you flying. At first it frightened me, it made me dizzy, and I didn't know what was happening. But after a while I grew to like it even when I didn't know what it was. Then Jared took me into his arms and flew across the river, and I recognized the sensation. Flying. I must have felt it every time you took wing."

"I think I have been having your dreams," Lucinda said in a quiet voice. "Dark and violent, full of despair and bloodshed. I would wake sad and wondering in the middle of the night."

"Some of them were not dreams," Tamar said.

Lucinda nodded. "That's what I was afraid of. That makes it even worse. But how could this be? I never dreamed of you before."

"Not until the Gloria," Tamar said. "That's when I had the Kiss installed in my arm. I hoped it would make me invisible to the Jansai, which it did not. All it did was make me dizzy with your flying and put your singing inside my head."

"My singing? Surely you could not hear my voice."

"Oh yes, I could," Tamar said. "Things without words. One song over and over again." And she hummed the first few bars of the music she had been hearing for the past two months. Lucinda grew very still.

"That's impossible," the angel whispered. "No one knows that melody but me."

"And the descant," Tamar added, and hummed a few notes of that for good measure. Lucinda appeared almost stricken.

"I believe you," she said, still in that low, amazed voice. "But I do not see how it can be so."

"The first time I heard you was the morning of the Gloria," Tamar said. "I was standing on the streets of Breven and your voice came from some transmitter, broadcast all the way from the Plain of Sharon. I couldn't move. I couldn't think. My Kiss actually ached in my arm. I thought it was because I had only had it installed the night before. But it must have been responding to the sound of your voice."

Lucinda was shaking her head as if shaking away the doubt, and when she spoke, there was the barest teasing edge to her voice. "And does that make you more likely to believe in the existence of Jovah, that he could make your Kiss respond to the sound of your sister's singing?"

"It makes me more convinced of the existence of the computer *Jehovah*,'' Tamar retorted, ''for only a machine could track the lives of separated siblings.''

Lucinda laughed aloud, a sound both rare and familiar to Tamar; so, too, did she laugh, on the infrequent occasions when she had cause. ''You Jacobites have an answer for everything, as I have been learning,'' she said gaily. ''But it will take more than a little plausible scientific theory to make me discard my god.''

Tamar smiled back. ''I am willing to try to convert you,'' she said. ''I am willing to tell you all about the life of a Jacobite—and then I suppose I must ask you to tell me all about the life of an angel.''

Lucinda's smile faded, and she grew instantly sober. She gazed at her sister with a serious, intent expression. ''I am afraid of you, a little,'' she said in a quiet voice. ''Because your life has been so hard, and my life has been so easy. Because you have no reason to trust me or Jared or any of us. And because I want you to like us—to like *me*. I have only known you for one day and already I am afraid to lose you. You have no reason not to walk away from us, from me, and I don't know how to make you stay. I don't know how to tell you how much it means to me to have found you—after all this tragedy, after all this time.''

Tamar was not in the habit of adopting strangers; she was not used to making room for newcomers in her heart. But this woman, this stranger . . . All Tamar's habitual wariness deserted her. All her defenses undid themselves of their own accord. ''I don't know that I could leave you behind even if I wanted to,'' she replied slowly. ''Even if I crushed this Kiss in my arm, I think I would still hear your voice. I have become attuned to you. *Jehovah* woke the bond, but I think it is a bond past breaking. I am afraid, too, but not of losing you. I am afraid of what it means to have found you.''

Lucinda flowed to her feet and threw her arms around her sister. Neither was Tamar used to indiscriminate hugs from chance-met acquaintances, but she did not draw back. This felt familiar, this felt right. Even when those delicate wings came curving around her shoulders, wrapping her in a texture that was half lace and half sinew, she did not pull away. It was as if she was embraced by her own soul, insubstantial but indestructible.

She felt her bones give up their accustomed fight and her blood go dancing backward in her veins.

The sisters talked without pause for the next two hours. It was not until a voice outside the door offered the enticement of food that they were willing to allow a third party to disturb their long reminiscing. They had been right to keep the door closed so long, Tamar thought with disfavor as the room was suddenly filled with an army of well-wishers: not only Conran and Jared, but Reuben and what must be half the Jacobites living in Sahala. Two of them swept her off the bed into energetic embraces, then began to interrogate her about the details of her last three months. Tamar sighed, smiled, and submitted.

She caught Jared's eyes on her from across the room, but could do no more than nod when he raised his eyebrows at her in a questioning look. Yes; much better. To prove it, she ate more food than she had managed in the past forty-eight hours, and for the first time in twice as long did not feel nauseated when she had finished her meal. Some wonder drug in Conran's potion, but that was hardly a surprise. If there were such a medicine available, Conran would know about it and have some at his disposal. Conran knew everything.

Except the location of the Alleluia Files. None of them knew that.

It was another hour before Tamar was able to convince them all to leave the room so she could bathe and dress herself. Of course, no one left until Conran ordered a general exodus, and even then two or three of the Jacobite women were indignant to learn that he had included them in the general retreat. The two angels also left the room, both with regretful backward glances, and Tamar luxuriated in the first solitude she had known for what seemed like months.

But she was back among her people, ready to take up the fight again. She cleaned herself and put on fresh clothes and rejoined them, feeling lighthearted and happy as she had not felt since she left Luminaux for Ileah.

The instant she descended the steps she was caught up in their fervor again. "Tamar, Duncan says the Edori engineers have found a way to communicate over long distances with a simple transmitter device. It works over a thousand miles, can you imagine?" "Tamar, Horace says there is a merchant in Semorrah who is sympathetic to the cause. Christian Avalone, have you heard of him? They say he is a very powerful ally." "Tamar, how many were killed at Ileah? Jani wants to record the names."

This was the community she remembered, urgent and speculative and knocked about by dreams. Whatever kindness she had been shown by well-meaning strangers in Jordana, in Semorrah, in Bethel, these were the only friends she could remember. She answered their rapid-fire questions when she knew the answers and shot back questions of her own when she did not; she laughed when the remarks were outrageous and grew sad when the news was grim. She knew the cadence of every voice and the history of every last soul, and she rejoiced to be among them again.

But as she talked with one eager group and waved to another, her attention was caught by a still, waiting figure in the back corner of Conran's living room. It was Jared. He watched her without intruding, without reaching out a hand to separate her from her comrades, without questioning their doctrine or railing against their heresy. And she thought, almost at the same time, *He has returned me, against his deepest principles, to the circle of my friends* and *I would leave them all for him.* And the thought made her shudder and turn away from him, because she could no longer withstand his grave and searching look, and she did not want to go to him before all her friends and take his hand in hers.

Not until late that evening did Tamar have a chance to speak to Jared privately. As she had expected, Conran had turned her homecoming into an occasion for a celebration, and so the whole Jacobite population of the village turned out that evening for a bonfire. Horace had gone hunting with some of the Edori and brought back two deer and the carcass of an unidentified beast whose cooked flesh tasted much like rabbit. These were roasted over the fire ("specifically," Tamar overhead someone say, "so that half will be burned and half will be raw and the whole will be inedible"). The meat was supplemented with a marvelous array of fruits, potatoes, breads, and sweets, and Tamar ate to the point of pain. Some of the food was wholly unfamiliar to her—raised, she supposed, in this strange and fertile terrain. It all tasted wonderful.

As darkness fell and spirits rose Tamar was able to slip away from the close attention of her Jacobite friends. Over on one end of the campground, Conran was telling stories by the magical yellow light of the fire; a few yards away, others were standing in a group, gossiping. It was not hard to spot the angels, their wings making distinctive silhouettes and menacing shadows against the uneven illumination of the fire.

"So odd," Jared was saying to Lucinda as Tamar strolled over. "At any other gathering I've ever been to, this would be the point at which someone would come up to me and ask for the favor of a song."

"Yes! I was just thinking that!" Lucinda exclaimed. "Even on Angel Rock, everyone considered it such a treat to hear an angel sing."

Jared laughed softly. "Well," he said, "I think we must concede that we are out of favor here."

"Not entirely true," Tamar said, and they both turned to welcome her. "They are pleased to have me back among them, and they thank you for that. But no one really knows what you want with the Jacobites or how long you plan on staying."

"That's a question I've pondered myself," Lucinda said with a sigh. "Not that everyone hasn't been extremely kind to me, but I cannot hide in Sahala the rest of my life. And I doubt that the Jacobites would want me."

"They probably don't want me, either, but I'm staying," Jared said. "I came here to learn about the Alleluia Files, and I'm not leaving until I learn where they are and what they say."

Tamar laughed. "Nobody knows that," she said.

"Then I suppose I'll be staying for a very long time."

Tamar laughed again, but Lucinda's attention had wandered. "There's Reuben," she said. "I'll catch up with you two later."

"*Edori angelico,*" Tamar murmured, for they had had time, in that long afternoon discussion, to cover such topics of interest as handsome angels and Edori lovers. Lucinda appeared flustered, then she laughed, and then she slipped away.

"Well, she seems happy," Jared said.

Tamar looked at him curiously by the shifting light. "How well do you know her?" she asked.

He shrugged. "I'd only met her a couple of times till this week. She lived a very sequestered life, as she may have told you—"

"Yes, on Angel Rock."

"In fact, until she came to the Gloria, I'd never met her or heard her story. Why?"

"I just wondered. If you'd known Lucinda, it seems you should have recognized me immediately. Reuben did."

"Reuben appears to have known Lucinda much better than I did," Jared replied dryly. "And Bael must have memorized her features as well, for he seems to have instantly connected the two of you once he saw your portrait."

"That still makes no sense to me," she said, shaking her head. "Even the fact that I am Rinalda's daughter—Lucinda's twin—makes me no more dangerous to Bael than any other Jacobite. I cannot imagine why he would want to hunt me down."

"I'm sure he has his reasons," Jared said with a smile. "I'll ask him next time I see him."

Tamar smiled, but quickly grew serious again. She said, with some difficulty, for she was not trained in gratitude, "I never got a chance to thank you."

"For what?" Jared said flippantly. "For hounding you all over Samaria and stealing you from your home?"

"For saving me from death at the hands of Jansai," she said soberly. "Or the hands of Bael."

"It was self-interest, of course," he said. "I thought the Jacobites would be more pleased to see me if I had you in my arms."

She was irrationally disappointed; she felt all that splendid food turn to spiky granite in her stomach. "Well," she said shortly. "You did save my life. And I appreciate it."

She turned away, back to the fire, back to her friends, but Jared stopped her with a hand on her arm. "I was only joking," he said quietly. "Had I arrived a minute later—too late to save you—I don't know what I would have done to those Jansai. Called down lightning bolts, I think, that would have burned all of Azolay to ashes. I don't remember the last time I've been so frightened. I suppose I've never before seen someone I cared about in danger."

But that was worse; now the stone in her stomach had erupted into flames. She felt heat rise in the unlikeliest places, up her elbows, across her brow. "Well," she said, and she could hear that her voice was grooved with panic. "Well, I don't suppose—

I guess the Jansai don't usually go around attacking your friends. You wouldn't have those kinds of friends, I mean."

Now he was smiling, and even by this light she could see the mischief in his face. *"Jacobite angelica,"* he murmured. "You *do* know that, in some quarters, I am considered the odds-on favorite to be the next Archangel?"

"I can think of no one more ill-suited," she snapped, and he laughed out loud.

"No, neither can I," he agreed. "But the field of candidates is woefully thin."

The dangerous moment seemed to have passed. Tamar was both relieved and sorry. "Won't your friends miss you if you stay too long in Ysral?" she asked. "Won't they wonder where you've gone?"

"Some of them know. Most of them wouldn't worry. I have a reputation for being a little irresponsible, you know. A little undependable."

"Oh, yes, an excellent Archangel," she murmured.

"So, anyway, no one guards my whereabouts too closely, and people are quite resigned to doing without my valuable presence. Even at Monteverde, where I am supposed to be in charge of everything, my mother and my sister have accustomed themselves to taking over my tasks. I don't think anyone will miss me."

She tilted her head to one side and regarded him. "So what *do* you care about?" she asked. "You blithely abandon your duties at your own hold, and it's obvious you don't want to be Archangel, and apparently nothing can keep your attention for more than a day or two. Don't you have any passions? Any convictions? Anything you would risk your life for?"

"You said that to me once," he said suddenly. "In Ileah."

"Did I? I don't remember."

"I'm not sure I know too many people who would risk their lives—for anything," he said.

She gestured broadly with both hands. "Everyone at this campfire tonight," she said. "For their ideals. For the chance to express their beliefs. For their friends. All of us would hazard our lives—all of us have already done so. I don't think you can truly say you've lived until you know what you'd die for."

"You're too young to talk about dying a martyr."

"And you're too old not to have found a cause."

He smiled a little bitterly. "Why is it that every time I talk to you, I end up feeling like a wastrel and a rogue? Most people like me, you know. I wish you did."

"I do," she said quickly, too quickly. She liked him too much, and that was a tendre that would come to no good. Jacobite angelica, indeed. "And I did not come here to censure you. I came to thank you for saving my life."

He nodded majestically. "It was an honor," he said, his voice grave. "I would say that I would gladly do so again, except that I would not gladly see you in danger again. But you worry me. You do not seem like the kind of woman who sees much value in keeping herself safe."

"I am cautious enough most of the time," she said. "You don't need to be anxious on my account."

He smiled again but looked wholly unconvinced. "Something tells me," he said, "that I shall live to see you made a liar."

She laughed. "Then I hope you will be with me," she said, "so you can rescue me from my folly."

"So do I," he said, not laughing at all. She could not hear the words he added under his breath, but she thought they were, "And I plan to be."

Even if she had had an answer to that (which she did not), she had no chance to make it. A group of Jacobites suddenly swirled around her, enveloping both Tamar and Jared in an enthusiastic eddy. "Back to Conran's—he's got some Edori wine!" someone called out as the crowd swept by, and Tamar allowed herself to be caught up in the general merriment.

There were too many of them to fit comfortably into Conran's small parlor, but they managed it anyway, women perching on men's laps, children sitting cross-legged on the floor, a few restless souls lurking in the doorway or pacing back and forth between the kitchen and the living room. Tamar found herself wedged into an oversized armchair next to Jani, with Horace balancing himself on the padded arm. He had one hand braced against the wall, one arm wrapped around her shoulders.

"So when do we go back to Samaria?" someone asked, and everyone in the room raised their glasses to toast that venture.

"Can't stay here the rest of our lives like whining dogs run out of the house," someone else called out. "Our place is in Samaria. That's where our mission is."

"Yes, but if we all die trying to accomplish this mission,

who's left to tell the truth about *Jehovah*?'' Conran asked reasonably. ''Everyone in this room has had a narrow escape from death in the past three months. Shouldn't we wait till the furor dies down?''

There was a general outcry at that, most of it vehemently opposed. ''I say, let's go right back at them!'' Duncan said very loudly, and half a dozen of the other young hotheads cheered. ''Head straight to Breven and take out a few Jansai to pay them back for the Jacobites they've murdered.''

''I'm on the first boat back!'' Horace cried, jumping to his feet. On the instant ten more followed suit.

Conran stood patient and inflexible at the front of the room, and waited for the uproar to calm down. ''Go to Breven, and most certainly it will not be the Jansai who end up dead,'' he said when the noise had faded enough for him to be heard. ''I say again, why not wait? I am not talking forever, you understand, but a few months, less than a year—''

''Why wait?'' a woman called out, and a few others echoed her. ''Wait for what?'' someone else asked.

''Wait till the next Gloria, perhaps,'' Conran said. ''When the new Archangel is chosen.''

''The *Archangel*—'' Twenty voices spoke in stupefied unison. ''Why do we care who the *Archangel* is?'' Jani wanted to know.

''Because we don't know who the Archangel will be,'' Conran said calmly. ''And it may be someone who is—not favorable toward us, perhaps, but more tolerant. More open-minded. Someone who might rein in the Jansai and allow us to live in peace. Is not that a possibility that merits the wait of a few unimportant months, mikele? Is it not?''

As always, his use of an Edori word (this one meaning ''children'' or ''young boys'') brought a rippling laugh from his fellow Jacobites. ''But what shall we do in Ysral for nine months or more?'' someone demanded. ''Farm? Raise cattle? I don't think so!''

''And why not?'' Conran said. ''Are you too good to work with your hands, doing honest labor?''

''I would rather carry the truth to the unbelievers than dig holes in the ground for corn to grow, yes!''

''Well, whether you are preaching or whether you are merely biding your time, you have to eat, so you will work and I will work and everyone in this room will work, and I don't want to hear a single word of complaint from any of you."

That would shut them up for a minute, Tamar thought with a private smile, but of course it didn't. Duncan flung out a new question almost before the words were out of Conran's mouth. Tamar let her attention stray as she looked around the room. Again, against her will, she was counting heads and tallying up the losses. She could not entirely sympathize with the fanatics who were so eager to rush back to Samaria and engage in a hand-to-hand struggle with death. She would not mind a few weeks, or a few months, to recover from her own encounters with that dark and powerful warrior.

Her eyes wandered to Jared, who was leaning against one wall with his wings held as compactly to his body as possible. She wondered what he thought of all this, if he secretly despised the passionate but aimless Jacobites, if he envied them for their conviction—or if, as she had thought long ago, he was really here as a spy and a traitor, and was even now gathering evidence against them.

But she did not believe that. It could not be true. Even if her own heart could not be trusted, Conran was not a man easily deceived, and Conran seemed to have no quarrel with the angel. It was a small comfort, but she would take whatever portion she was served.

Talk had turned now, as it always did, to the elusive object of their obsessive quest. "But what of the Alleluia Files?" a woman asked, and again the crowd was unanimous in its murmuring response. "Yes, we must keep looking." "Dawn had no luck breaching Mount Sinai, did she? I thought not." "But if they are really at the angel holds, as we all believe, how shall we find them? I don't think there is a disguise good enough to get one of us into the Eyrie."

"The Alleluia Files are not in the Eyrie," Jared said, speaking for the first time and drawing every eye. Most of the Jacobites viewed him with mistrust, Tamar saw, and a few watched him with actual dislike.

"And may I ask how you come by this information?" Duncan asked with sarcastic politeness.

Jared shrugged so slightly that his wings barely shifted. "I looked for them," he said. "In the music rooms and the archives of the hold. I also searched for them at Monteverde. It's possible

that I overlooked them somewhere, but the holds seem like unlikely hiding places, anyway.''

''And where would *you* have stored them, if they had been
yours to hide?'' Horace asked.

Jared regarded him coolly across the room. He might be accustomed only to open-armed welcomes, as he had told Tamar
earlier, but he was not in the least cowed by snarling hostility.

''If I was the oracle, I would most likely have secreted them
in Mount Sinai,'' the angel replied. ''I take it you've looked
there and been unsuccessful?''

''We've never gotten past the outer rooms,'' Conran said
briefly. ''Dawn tried to gain admittance to the inner chambers
a few months back but was not able to manage it.''

''We need a young girl we can offer as an acolyte,'' Jani
said. ''Or a young boy. One who can be sent to the oracles to
be trained at Mount Sinai or Mount Egypt or Mount Sudan.
Then we will have a sympathizer at the very heart of Samarian
society. We will learn all the 'holy' secrets—and we will find
the Alleluia Files, if they are there.''

''Not a bad plan,'' Jared said. ''But most of the acolytes are
chosen from the gentry. How would you pass off one of your
Jacobite children as a Manadavvi daughter or a river merchant's
heir?''

''We will think of a way,'' Jani said, raising her chin defiantly. ''And *without* the help of the angels.''

Jared laughed at her. ''Lest you forget,'' he said, ''your precious Alleluia was an angel, too.''

Jani looked angry enough to toss back an unforgivable insult,
but Conran intervened before she could speak. ''Manners, mikele, manners,'' he said. ''If you would be better than the allali,
you must start with your behavior. Besides, this angel has been
a friend to us. Why would you want to abuse him?''

''I'll see his friendship proved,'' Horace muttered, but no one
else dared to offer a retort.

''Back to the files,'' said someone in the back of the room.
Tamar thought it was Wyman. ''What if they're *not* at Mount
Sinai or one of the other sanctuaries? What then? We must have
an alternate plan. We must look in every possible hiding place.''

''I agree,'' said Conran, but before he could continue, voices
called out from around the room. ''The ruins of the Augustine
school!'' ''Luminaux!'' ''Hagar's Tooth!'' ''Semorrah! Well,

why not? You can buy anything else you want there." "The Plain of Sharon." "Breven—it's the last place anyone would look."

Conran held up his hand for order. "*Chahiela,* my friends! Chahiela! If anyone is to be heard, everyone else should be silent."

Tamar was as startled as everyone else to see Jared practically jump away from the wall. His wings swept back and he looked somehow taller, suddenly imposing. Actually, it was not at all difficult to see why some might want to name him Archangel.

"*What* did you just say?" he demanded of Conran.

The Jacobite leader lifted his eyebrow. "In the Edori tongue, I called for silence," he said. "I did not mean to be so rude as to exclude you from the conversation."

Jared shook his head impatiently. "No, no, not rude . . . The word you used—'chahiela'? Isn't that a place, as well as an Edori expression?"

Conran nodded. "Yes, it is a town on the very southern tip of Bethel. It was founded, oh, a century or so ago, as a school for the blind and the deaf." He smiled. "That is why it was named Chahiela. After the Edori word for silence."

Jared stood with his chin tilted slightly toward the ceiling, in a pose that made the skin tighten across his cheeks. Tamar was sure his stance looked like arrogance to some, but to her it looked like he was merely trying to contain excitement. Mystified as the others, she sat up straighter in her chair.

"Chahiela is where the oracle Jecoliah was raised," the angel said slowly. "She told me so herself. She is nearly blind and she was sent to that school to receive an education."

"Doesn't sound like *she* was the child of a Manadavvi lordling," Jani said with a little sniff.

Jared nodded absently. "You're right. She wasn't. And neither was the oracle before her, who was named Deborah—who also came from Chahiela. Or the oracle before *her*—who was born in Chahiela, at the school her mother founded."

"But the oracle before Deborah—" someone said, and there was a long, strained silence, as all the untutored Jacobites struggled to recall their sketchy history lessons.

Conran was the one who remembered it first. "Was Alleluia," he said.

•   •   •

After that, there was not enough *chahiela* for anyone to speak more than two sentences together before someone else interrupted. Almost before Jared could finish his next sentence ("Where better to hide something you wanted no one to find than in a place where no one can see?") there was a babble of voices raised in speculation and excitement. Tamar felt it, too, that curious melting flutter at the center of her abdomen, but in her case it was augmented by equal parts wonder, pride, and fear. *The angel is my friend, I brought him here,* she wanted to say, shaking her finger in the faces of all those who doubted him; but in fact she did not move a muscle. He might not be correct, of course, though his solution had that seamless sense of rightness that you would sometimes get when you fitted together two broken pieces of china after trying for half an hour to get the edges to match. Right or wrong, in any case, his was a better idea than any they had come up with in the past five years, and she felt rosy with his reflected glory.

But she was afraid, too. Afraid because, before the first person in the room yelled out the words, she knew what the next motion would be for: an immediate visit to Chahiela to look for the hidden files. Back to Samaria, back to the haunts of the angels and the lairs of the Jansai. And there was no way she could stay behind if all of her comrades were going.

"When can we set sail?" Duncan was saying. "Tomorrow? Is there a ship in port?"

"The Wayward," someone replied. "But it will only hold about ten of us."

"Ten is all we need."

"And who will volunteer to stay behind? Not me! We need a ship big enough to carry all of us."

"We need no such thing," Conran said firmly enough to grab everyone's attention. "I agree, we must get to Chahiela as quickly as possible, but there is no need to be stupid about it. Some of us must be left behind in case this mission somehow goes awry. Ten is plenty. Ten is more than enough."

"Who will go? Shall we have a lottery?"

"We shall choose based on need," Conran said.

"You need fighting men," Duncan said instantly. "So you must have me."

"And me," Horace chimed in.

"What we must have is a translator," Conran said. "Because

the oracles use the old language to communicate with *Jehovah*. And there's no reason Alleluia would not have made her memoirs hard to decipher if she would make them hard to find.''

''Does anyone in your group know the old language?'' Jared asked. ''I thought only the oracles were taught it.''

''Many of the Augustine engineers have learned it so that they can read manuals printed in that text,'' Conran said. ''A few of the Jacobites have also learned it, but most of them are dead. I myself could never master the words. At the moment there is only one linguist among us.''

Somehow he had guessed, for Jared looked straight at the Jacobite he had rescued from certain death. ''Who is it?'' he asked.

''Tamar.''

She met the angel's eyes as if that was the hardest thing she had ever done, as if his gaze had a weight and a pressure that she could not lift with all the strength in her body. If he only knew how much she wanted to recuperate here in Sahala, give up her place on that Edori boat, frolic here in the forgiving Ysral sunshine and let her mind graze absently over unimportant things. But. She was a Jacobite and this was the grail Jacobites had sought since before she was born. If it was within their grasp and only she had the key to decoding it, there was simply no choice.

''When do we sail?'' she asked.

Jared was shaking his head. He was still staring at her as if there was no one else in the room, no one else in the world. ''She can't go,'' he said.

Conran looked over at him in mild shock. ''And why not?''

''She just barely escaped from Samaria a few days ago! And she was half-dead then! Her picture is in the hands of every Jansai on the continent—''

''So is mine, so is Duncan's, so are the faces of half the people in this room,'' Conran said dismissively. ''Tamar is in no more danger than the rest of us. And if she is too sick to leave tomorrow, well, then we will wait until she is recovered. A week or more will not hurt us when we have waited decades.''

''She can't go,'' Jared said flatly.

Conran laughed at him. ''I don't know that you have too much to say about it,'' he said genially.

"I have a lot to say about it."

"I mean, that will do any good," Conran added gently.

Someone laughed, and then everyone was talking at once. No one paid attention anymore to the angel or Conran, still arguing over the rising tumult of voices—and they scarcely paid attention to each other, either, so eager were they to share their own opinions and excitement. Chahiela! But of course! They should have thought of that before, but it didn't matter now. The Alleluia Files were within their grasp, they were days away from hearing the words that would validate their lives and change the whole face of Samaria.

Tamar remembered similar times, similar epiphanies, when they had thought they had uncovered the miracle and then found that all their speculations were wrong. But that had not stopped them from trying, from hoping, from believing. And if they were wrong this time, so be it; that would not end their quest or make them lose their faith. *Till we find the Alleluia Files.* That had been their credo for so long that it was their only absolute. Nothing would keep them from Chahiela now—not angels, not Jansai, not Jovah himself, should he manifest himself before them at this very moment and claim to be a deity after all.

But Tamar was afraid to go. And although nothing—certainly not this furious angel even now engaged in a shouting match with the unyielding Conran—nothing would prevent her from boarding that ship whatever day they decided to sail, she could not shake off a cold sense of prescient dread. Whatever awaited them in Chahiela, she thought, would change them forever, unless it destroyed them utterly. And though she tried to join in the revelry of her ecstatic friends, she could not shake that conviction from her heart, and she could not truly rejoice.

Tamar successfully avoided Jared that night and the next day, but there was one angel she was anxious to say good-bye to before *The Wayward* sailed. Conran had met with the ship's captain (Mario? Tamar could not quite remember, but then, she had been hallucinating for most of her voyage on that vessel). They had determined not only that the Edori captain was willing to make the trip but that he could accommodate eight Jacobites as passengers. "Nine if Reuben agrees to stay behind," the captain had said with a smile. "And something tells me he'll be more than willing."

There was no true port at Chahiela, but there was a natural harbor not far from the town that smugglers and Edori and most ship captains in dire need knew how to find. *The Wayward* would drop anchor there, and the Jacobites would be able to find their way to Chahiela in a matter of hours.

Conran had chosen the seven Jacobites who would accompany him on this mission and high-handedly refused to listen to the petitions of those who would be left behind. Besides Tamar, he had selected Duncan, Horace, and Jani, as well as an eighteen-year-old girl named Loa and two young men named Sal and Wyman. It was clear to everyone that, except for himself, chosen for seniority, and Tamar, chosen for special abilities, his criteria had been health, strength, swiftness, and skill. If they really were overtaken by the Jansai, he wanted to give his little band a fighting chance.

As the captain had expected, Reuben had readily agreed to yield his place to a Jacobite passenger, but that ninth slot had been ferociously bespoken by Jared, and Conran had reluctantly ceded him the honor. Tamar's reaction to the news of Jared's inclusion was beginning to feel familiar: a mixture of elation, terror, and dread. In such cramped quarters, it would be hard to avoid the angel entirely, and she did not particularly want to hear what he had to say about the folly of young women who continually exposed themselves to danger.

On the other hand, it was hard to imagine returning to Samaria without him. Going anywhere without him. Existing without him. But of course, that day would come.

And she was finding it harder than she had imagined to leave another angel behind.

"But I have only just found you!" Lucinda wailed when she heard the news. It was the morning after the fateful meeting, and the Jacobites were engaged in a frenzy of packing. "Can't you stay behind? Can't someone else translate these stupid files?"

"Maybe. Maybe not. Not if they're in the old tongue."

"I can't bear to have you leave so soon."

"I'll come back as soon as I can. I promise."

Lucinda sighed and tried to shake away her blues. "I feel like I should give you a talisman for luck," she said. "I don't have—I know! My necklace. The perfect thing."

"I don't need any good-luck charms," Tamar said, but the

angel had already leapt up and crossed the room. They were sitting in her bedchamber in the Edori house (Tamar thought Jared was less likely to find her there), so all Lucinda's possessions were close at hand.

Lucinda returned to Tamar's side carrying a small silver box with a painted glass lid. "I keep the necklace here when I'm not wearing it," she said. To Tamar's amazement, the angel crooned a short wordless melody over the treasure box, and a tiny click sounded in her cupped hands.

"What in the world was that?"

Lucinda was holding out the silver casket. "See? The song unlocks the box. And the same song sung backward locks it again. Isn't that clever? Reuben gave it to me."

Tamar took it gingerly from her hand and peered inside. On the black velvet lining lay the emerald ring that Lucinda usually wore, a silver necklace coiled around a flat oval pendant, a blue wing feather from some Ysral bird, and a smooth quartz rock that looked to have been salvaged from a riverbed. A diverse array of treasures, indeed.

"That song you've heard me sing?" Lucinda went on. "In your head? That's really the backward version of one of the angels' prayers."

Tamar looked up with a grin. "So? Does that mean I can countermand a prayer if I sing that?"

"I suppose so, but it's not a prayer that's ever sung, as far as I know. Instead I could teach you the reverse version of the prayer for rain, and you might have some use for it."

"I don't care if it rains," Tamar said, and turned her attention back to the silver box.

"The necklace," Lucinda instructed. "Put it on. That's what I want you to have."

"I don't need your jewelry. I won't forget you."

With an impatient exclamation, Lucinda took the box from her sister and extracted the necklace from the pile. She looped the chain around her finger and held up her hand so the delicate woven strands glinted in the afternoon light. "The finest metal from the Luminaux silversmiths," she said softly. "When you run your finger down the chain, it's as if you're touching glass. Put it on."

Reluctantly, Tamar took it. She was not used to expensive gifts or tokens of affection; it was not something she felt she had a right to. "Did your aunt give this to you?"

"When I was old enough. It was our mother's, though Gretchen told me no one ever saw her wear it. It was around her neck when they discovered her body."

"Is there anything inside the locket?"

"Open it."

Tamar pried her fingernail between the tightly clasped halves of the oval, and silently they fell apart. Inside, each half of the locket was engraved with a single elaborate letter, a *D* on the left and an *R* on the right.

Lucinda was peering over her arm. "David and Rinalda," she said. "He must have given it to her while she was imprisoned in Cedar Hills. It's the only thing of value she had on her when she died."

Tamar felt a rush of sadness make all of her muscles turn inward as if to cocoon her heart. "I can't take this," she said in a choked voice. "If it's all you have of your mother—"

"Your mother, too," Lucinda said. "I want you to have it so you remember you're not alone in this world—you have a family, a history, a genealogy that goes back to the Archangel Delilah. You aren't alone now—and you weren't born alone. I was with you then, and I'm with you now."

Tamar nodded once, and then burst into tears. The angel instantly had her arms around her twin. It was strange to Tamar that, after only two days, this woman's touch would seem as familiar to her as Elinor's, as Dawn's, as the casual, absentminded hugs she had received now and then from all of the Jacobites. She allowed herself to be comforted, and then she allowed herself to be persuaded, and when she finally left the Edori house, she was wearing her mother's locket.

And when *The Wayward* set sail the next day, and the Jacobites on the shore waved good-bye to the lucky few embarking on the most glorious of all quests, Tamar clutched the pendant where it hung around her neck and waved good-bye in turn. There were forty Jacobites and maybe a dozen Edori gathered at the port to see them off, and Tamar cared deeply for most of them and knew them all by name; but it was Lucinda she waved to and Lucinda she hated to leave behind.

"Sing to me," she had whispered in her sister's ear as they hugged good-bye on the wharf. "I will listen for you."

"Be careful," Lucinda had whispered back. "Don't do anything too dangerous. And be kind to Jared."

That had made Tamar laugh shakily as she pulled away. "It is not in me to be kind to angels," she said loftily, though she spoiled the effect by scrubbing away a few undisciplined tears.

Lucinda held up two fingers. "Just me and Jared," she said. "The rest you can scorn your whole life long."

Tamar held up one finger, then touched it to Lucinda's cheek. "We'll be back in a little less than three weeks, is what I think Conran said. I'll see you then."

One more quick hug good-bye, then run up the gangplank onto the Edori ship. Then crowd along the railing with all the others, shouting out farewells and promises.

Then turn back toward the main deck of the ship to find herself face-to-face with the angel Jared.

CHAPTER EIGHTEEN

Jared had not realized he had such a deep capacity for anger. He could not remember ever in his life feeling more than a quick flare of irritation that evaporated in a minute or two, no matter what the provocation. Well, in general not much provoked him. People didn't go out of their way to throw obstacles in his path or show him small, annoying discourtesies. His hold was well run, and any minor problems that came up from time to time were things his mother and sister could deal with efficiently and gracefully. He was aware in a vague way that injustices existed in the world, and had he been present at any blatant example of one, he would have done what he could to correct it, but for the most part he was not a witness to suffering or cruelty or despair. And so, very little upset him.

But *this*. Tamar's incredible stupidity, ignorance, stubbornness, self-destructive willful *blindness*, had roused in him such a storm of fury that to contain it he had had to build an iron wall around his temper. He had had to construct an amiable mask and place it over his face; he had had to force himself to behave with all his normal charm and poise, or the anger would have swept over him like a typhoon and carried him away.

This was the first time he had seen Tamar in two full days. She had obviously been at some pains to keep clear of him, and he had not made much effort to track her down. They would be aboard this ship at least six days, as the captain kicked up its speed to full power, and Tamar would have to talk to him sooner or later. He could bide his time.

And the time had come.

"You've grown quite close to Lucinda in a few short days, I see," he began, civilly enough. "Have you thought how you will stay in touch with her once this adventure is over?''

"I haven't given much thought to anything beyond getting to Bethel and back," she said warily. She had edged as far from him as the railing would allow. They had barely pulled beyond shouting distance of the shore, but already the Jacobites had scattered to other parts of the ship; they were virtually alone here on the stern of the upper deck.

"You should not even be on this trip, you know," he said conversationally.

"I know nothing of the sort."

"Oh, I think you do," he said, and though he kept his voice calm, he could feel that anger rising, boiling up, flaming through him like exhilaration or fear. "If you didn't realize you had no business on this ship, you wouldn't have gone to such great lengths to avoid me in the past two days."

"I knew *you* thought I shouldn't go, and I didn't feel like having an argument about it," she said swiftly, in that tough, contemptuous voice he knew so well. "But *I* certainly consider my presence necessary."

"It's not and you know it," he said. "Even if they find these precious files—even if they are recorded in some arcane old language—even if you're the only Jacobite in the whole damn pack who can understand the oracles' words, you don't have to go to Samaria to do it. Won't they bring the files back to Ysral? Certainly Conran won't leave them behind in Chahiela."

Tamar shrugged and turned away. "Unless the files are inscribed on some tablet that can't be moved. Unless what we find in Chahiela is a map that leads us to the place where the files are really stored, and that map is written in the old tongue. There are dozens of reasons why I should go—but only one really matters. I want to go, and it's my life. What you think doesn't matter."

He had never in his life laid a finger on anyone in anger, but now he put a rough hand on her shoulder and jerked her around to face him. "It's your life, but I saved it, and I have some right to it now," he said grimly. "And I tell you at this moment that I refuse to see you waste it in some foolhardy stunt—"

Her laugh was really a gasp of sheer amazement; she yanked herself away and stood there staring. "Foolhardy—! The search for the *Alleluia Files*? It's the most important—and what do you mean, you won't see me waste my life? What do you think you can do about it? You can't stop me from going—you can't stop any of us from going—''

"I could, and I'm still thinking about it," he said, his voice even harder. "I could snatch you up right now and fly back to Ysral, and there would be nothing you or anybody else could do to stop me. I could—''

"You wouldn't dare."

"Why wouldn't I? Why shouldn't I? To keep you alive? What do I care if you hate me, as long as you're safe?"

"Who in this world is ever safe? Are you?" she broke out in a voice as passionate as his own. "I can't remember a day of my life that didn't pass in some kind of fear. Fear of starvation, fear of discovery, fear of capture. Fear of death. You think I've only been in danger since the Jansai got my picture, but I've been in danger since the day I was born. So have you— so have we all. You could die of disease or a misplaced thunderbolt. You could die if a big transport truck came roaring down and you couldn't get out of the way in time. You could die if a storm blew up unexpectedly when you were flying and you got thrown to the ground. Who is keeping *you* safe? And why do you think you have to guard *me*?"

He leaned close enough to make her eyes widen in alarm, close enough so that his wings, falling forward over his shoulders, made a white wall on either side of her, though not a single feather touched her skin. "Because I can," he said softly. "Make no mistake, you are only on this journey as long as I consider it relatively free of hazard. The instant a Jansai ship pulls into view, or a Jansai caravan heaves over the horizon, I will seize you and carry you back to Ysral. I don't care if every one of your comrades goes down in flames or dies with a Jansai dagger in his back. *You* will survive this quest."

"Just because you saved my life?" she said in that sarcastic, disbelieving voice. "You think you own me, because of that?"

"Because I love you," he said.

It was as if he had struck her a blow across the mouth. The words startled him almost as much as they had startled her, and the well of his anger in a single pulse transformed to an inferno of white-hot fear. *Because I love you and you could die.* The most primitive of all emotions, and the most powerful. He had used a smiling face to disguise his anger from the world, but he had used anger to hide his love even from his own heart.

He said it again, this time aloud. "Because I love you and you could die."

He was not surprised when she had no reply for that. Straight-armed, she shoved him in the chest and ducked outside the protective circle of his wings. In two running steps, she had reached the doorway that led belowdecks and disappeared. It seemed unlikely that she would speak to him again for the rest of the trip.

Jared spent the next six days in the air. Even though *The Wayward* was traveling at a rate about twice its usual pace, Jared was still faster; he could easily catch up after ranging twenty or thirty miles away to check for unwanted company. He spotted Jansai ships more than once, and returned to the Edori vessel to advise Maurice on how to avoid the raiders.

"Wish I had a lookout like you every time I sailed this ocean," the captain said the second time Jared came back with a warning. "If you ever get bored with your Gloria and your sacred masses and all your other angel duties, you just come on over to me and I'll sign you up as a member of my crew."

"Could happen," Jared said with a smile. "I'll let you know."

He would have patrolled the waters in any case, on this journey, with this frail human cargo, but since the argument with Tamar, the Edori boat seemed too small to comfortably hold both of them. For himself, he felt stifled and starved for breath during those few waking hours that he stayed on board the ship; and anytime his feet touched the deck, Tamar disappeared to the rooms below. He could only imagine how claustrophobic she was beginning to feel.

To make matters worse, it was a small ship, with nothing resembling privacy. All the crew and all the Edori had cabin mates, sometimes crowding three to a room, and no one could walk across the deck or down to the galley without tripping over half a dozen fellow passengers. Only when Jared was soaring above the ocean did he have a moment to himself.

Although, in one sense, he was never alone, since thoughts of Tamar were with him constantly. In his mind, he said it better, phrased it more romantically, explained to her how through impossibly small degrees she had become ingrained in his heart, part of its shape and rhythm. In these conversations, she listened sympathetically, shyly spoke of reciprocating sentiments, then melted into his arms and lifted her face to be kissed. Despite the fact that he had never yet seen Tamar in a tender moment (except possibly when she was hugging her sister farewell and even then she had seemed fairly fierce), this scene seemed quite realistic to Jared; he imagined it on an hourly basis for the whole six days of the trip.

How his friends would smile, if they could see him lovesick for a wild young Jacobite. How Isabella Cartera would stare, then laugh and laugh until she had to sink into a plush, over-stuffed chair, drained by hilarity. His mother—his sister—everyone who was used to treating his light romances with amusement and tolerance—all of them would gape with astonishment to see the careless and insouciant Jared snared by a rebel siren.

He couldn't think what to do about it. Impossible to imagine her tamely tending to hold matters back at Monteverde. Impossible to picture himself setting up household with her in some stone cottage on the edge of Sahala, debating religious philosophies with Conran and the other heathens.

Impossible to imagine life without her.

Well, he would finish out this adventure and then he would force a reckoning with Tamar, and then . . . well, Jovah alone knew what then. All Jared knew was that it would not end here.

They dropped anchor at midnight in a rocky cove that was no more a harbor than Conran was an angel. *The Wayward* was a small ship, but too big to ease close enough to the shoreline to throw down a gangplank, so Maurice and two indistinguishable crew members lowered a dinghy to the water by the light of three small lamps. Not enough light to see by, of course, but that was the point. They didn't want to draw attention from anyone on land or sea.

It took two trips to ferry everyone from the ship to the soil although Jared needed nobody's transport. He would have offered to carry one of the Jacobites to the shore except he was pretty sure they all would have declined with loathing. Well, Tamar would have, he knew, and she was the only one he really wished to carry in his arms. So he just took care of himself, and awaited the others on the dark beach.

Maurice had come briefly ashore with Conran. "We'll wait

a few miles off the coast for three days. Send the angel back to get us, and we can be here in an hour. If you're gone longer than three days, you'll have to find another ship home, because we can't hover in these waters too long without drawing attention.''

The Jacobite leader shook hands with the ship's captain. ''You've done a great deal for us already,'' he said, adding some phrase in a language Jared couldn't understand. Probably that godless Edori tongue again. ''Do not endanger yourselves. With any luck, we'll see you again in three days—or a few weeks, back in Sahala.''

When the little dinghy was once more in the water, moving soundlessly toward the ship, Conran gathered his band together. ''We'll camp here for the night and head for Chahiela first thing in the morning.''

''Here?'' Jani said with distaste, looking at the damp, shifting sand. Conran grinned.

''No, not in this precise spot, mikala. Half a mile inland on dry ground, I hope. We should be safe enough, but just to be sure, we'll all take a turn on watch. Anyone who's not sleepy can take first shift.''

Jared would have volunteered except, again, he didn't feel like anyone in this circle valued his skills. Damned if he was going to offer any service that they would reject with disdain. Although he would never forgive himself if he was snoring away when the Jansai arrived . . . He shivered slightly. Maybe he would just take care to sleep very, very lightly. Close enough to Tamar to smuggle her out of harm's way should it come roaring up in the middle of the night.

They trudged up from the beach and found flat, dry land almost immediately. They appeared to be in the middle of nowhere, miles from the trade road or any farming community; there weren't even any memorable features to the landscape around them, at least by the light of the half-moon. Not that any of them spent much time looking. They were all tired and a little cross. The hothead Duncan demanded the first watch. The rest of them dropped where they stood, made whatever pallets they could from their duffel bags and cloaks, and fell instantly asleep. Jared waited long enough to note Tamar's position, and then he closed his eyes.

Morning came far sooner than he had expected, beating down

on them with a merciless cheer that was infinitely irritating. Conran roused everyone by stalking through the camp and slapping his hands together briskly. "On your feet, time to get moving!" Even zealots, Jared observed from his own jaundiced eyes, found it hard to be enthusiastic after four hours' sleep on a wretched bed.

They ate fruit, dried meat, and bread rolls as they walked west, following the coast. Conran was in the lead, but Duncan, Horace, and Sal were only half a pace behind him. Wyman, who was probably the best built of the lot and could have outdistanced even Duncan had he put his mind to it, was loitering behind with the women to dally with Jani. Tamar made halfhearted conversation with Loa when she wasn't skipping ahead to chat with Conran. Jared brought up the rear.

What in Jovah's name was he doing on this enterprise? Looking for the Alleluia Files in the company of criminals who would be executed by the Archangel if Bael could ever catch up with them? And despite the fact that Jared had been the one to suggest this site as a hiding place, it seemed wildly unlikely to him that the secret documents would really be there. Since it seemed wildly unlikely that they even existed.

His mother and his friends wouldn't laugh at this quite so merrily. Only Christian, who had sent him on this bizarre chase, would take him by the hand and say, "Well done." Even Mercy, who had so reluctantly agreed to practice mild treason against Bael, would find this mad venture incomprehensible.

Though she might forgive him for love. If everyone else in the world laughed at him for that, Mercy would not. That thought gave him a little comfort and allowed him to tramp on behind the others, mile after weary mile.

Angels hated walking. Lucinda was the only angel he'd ever seen who would stroll down a city street rather than fly from end to end—but Lucinda, on so many counts, was hardly common. Most angels would rather forgo the most exquisite pleasure you could name than walk a block to see it. It was a game with them to compare the soles of their feet, tender and uncallused as a baby's cheek. Jared was no exception. But he walked with the Jacobites. He did not want to be even three wing spans away from Tamar if the Jansai suddenly appeared. He was here to keep her safe and, by the god's great grace, he would do it.

At noon, bowing to the pressure of many complaining voices,

Conran called a brief halt for lunch. It was more of the same and they ate quickly. The women disappeared for a few minutes behind a stand of trees, though Duncan called after them, "Hey, girls, what are you hiding?" When they came back, Loa threw a rock at him, and everybody laughed.

After this stop, they turned almost due north and walked about three more miles. They could see Chahiela half an hour before they actually crossed into it. It looked like any other small town on the edge of a trade route. There was a collection of squat new buildings lining the main road, and two distinct neighborhoods on either side of the highway, one belonging to the passably wealthy and the other devoted to the struggling poor. At the very western edge of the town stood a disorganized cluster of older buildings that had probably been there even before the road.

Where now? Jared wondered. He didn't think even Conran had the nerve to stroll up to total strangers and start inquiring after the Alleluia Files. For himself, he was stymied.

But Conran kept on walking and the others straggled behind. The Jacobite leader bypassed all the new homes, all the recent warehouses, and headed straight for the original buildings that must have housed the school when this little community was first haphazardly put together. Even now, Jared realized, the school still existed: As they approached the older outbuildings, he saw young children leading others by the hand and older youths navigating the streets with the aid of canes and deep concentration.

Conran came to a halt outside a large communal building and looked around indecisively. Jared, trying to reason like a Jacobite, wondered what he might say to the first person who approached and asked their business. The angel couldn't think how anyone could frame the essential questions.

He didn't have long to speculate. Within three minutes, as the Jacobites stood in an uneasy cluster, a middle-aged woman with a pleasant expression stopped in front of Conran.

"Can I help you?" she asked. "Are you looking for someone? Is someone in your group looking to become a student with us? I am Arla."

"Conran," the Jacobite replied with the big warm smile that most people found irresistible. "Actually, I'm looking for information. Perhaps you can supply it. Which of these houses is the one where the angel Alleluia grew up?''

"Oh, the Wellin house! But none of her family owns it anymore, you know. Alleluia never lived here after her mother died, and the house passed into the hands of one of Hope Wellin's closest friends. *Her* name was Mara Lanette, but of course she's been dead since before I was born. It's *her* granddaughter that lives there now, and I believe her granddaughter lives with her. She's quite old, you know. Can't hear a word. All the Lanettes have been born deaf—except this youngest granddaughter. Now, *she* can hear, though it's my belief she reads lips as much as hears the words. Sometimes if you call out to her when she's walking down the street, she passes on by as if you haven't said a word.''

A lot of stupid gossip that no one could care about, Jared thought. But Conran was nodding wisely, as if all this talk of deaf women and great-granddaughters was precisely what he had come to Chahiela to hear. Jared was amazed that the woman would volunteer so much information to a total stranger, but then again, maybe she was not used to having a listening audience. Not everyone in Chahiela was blind, after all; it had been named *silence* for another reason.

"This woman who lives in the Wellin house now," Conran said. "What's her name? Do you think she'd mind if we came by to visit?"

"No, she'd be delighted to have company. She's the nicest lady. If you want to talk to her, you'll have to ask her granddaughter to interpret, of course, but she's a good girl. She won't mind.''

"And their names?"

"Maretta Lanette—she was named after her grandmother—and Caley Boster. Caley's mother married that Boster boy, but it didn't really work out. But it worked out for Maretta, because now she's got Caley living with her and it's made everything so much easier for her.''

"And the house? Can you point it out to me?"

"Why, it's right over there." And she indicated a small, two-story stone house with a painted white fence and a meticulously maintained lawn. Maretta and her devoted granddaughter certainly spent a lot of time in their yard, Jared thought cynically. Of course, they didn't have to waste all day listening to the inane chatter of their neighbors, so no doubt they were able to accomplish more than most of the residents. He admired Conran for his undiminished cheerfulness and the seeming sincerity with which he thanked their informant. After two more interminable exchanges, they were on their way again, all nine of them, to the house where the oracle Alleluia had been born.

The woman who answered the door was slim, dark, exhausted, and young, so Jared assumed she was the long-suffering grand-daughter and not the elderly Maretta. She seemed startled to see so many strangers appearing on her doorstep at once, though she couldn't summon the energy for true astonishment. "Can I help you?" she asked doubtfully.

"My name's Conran. These are my friends. We wanted to ask your grandmother some questions."

"All of you? Who are you?"

"We are researchers looking for biographical information about the angel Alleluia. The oracle Alleluia. We understand this is the house she was born in, and we thought there might be some—artifacts—here that would be useful to us."

"Well, there are lots of old boxes and things in the cellar," Caley said without enthusiasm. "I suppose you could look through those."

"We were hoping to talk to your grandmother. She might know where to find what we're looking for."

"Oh. Well. I guess that would be all right." She surveyed their little group again, and some of their tension must have communicated itself to her, for a little briskness came to her voice. "Why don't you come into the parlor and I'll go fetch her?"

So they tumbled in after her into the narrow hallway, Jared wondering how any angel could have endured living in such close quarters. His own wings brushed the walls on either side. The parlor was clean but sparsely decorated with somewhat worn furnishings; Caley and her grandmother certainly did not live a lavish life. There were not enough places to sit, and none of the chairs would accommodate angel wings. Jared and the other young men stood; Conran and the women sat.

Five minutes later Caley returned, with a smiling old woman in tow. Maretta Lanette was everyone's vision of the perfect grandmother, with curly gray hair, rosy cheeks, a knitted shawl thrown over her shoulders to ward off whatever chill the air might hold.

Caley led the old woman straight to Conran, who got rather stiffly to his feet. "My name's Conran," he said. "My friends and I are researching the life of the oracle Alleluia."

Maretta continued smiling, but her eyes had gone to her granddaughter's hands. Caley was weaving her fingers in the air, repeating Conran's message in the silent language of the deaf. Jared watched with interest because, although he had heard of such communication, he had never seen it performed. When Caley was finished, Maretta asked her a question in the same language.

"My grandmother says, what do you want to know? What are you looking for?"

"Can she read lips?" Conran asked the girl.

"If you look straight at her and speak very slowly. But she usually likes to have me interpret anyway."

Conran nodded and stared at Maretta. "We are looking for memoirs that Alleluia may have left behind here when she was an old woman. Something she would have wanted your grandmother to keep for her safely. Something she would not want many people to see. We don't know what form these memoirs are in, but we think they were recorded somehow. They are very important to us."

Maretta watched him intently, nodding once or twice, then looked over at Caley, who quickly sketched in the details. Maretta's hands asked a question; Caley repeated it.

"But if she left them here to keep them safe, is there any reason I should give them to you now?"

Conran grinned broadly. "She has been dead sixty years," he said. "It cannot possibly matter to her now what we may learn about her."

"They say she was a secretive woman," Maretta said through Caley's mouth. "But my grandmother adored her."

"Learning some of her secrets now may save a number of lives," Conran said gently. "Do you know where we might find these memoirs I have described to you?"

"In her old room. There is something—I cannot describe it— a piece of equipment. It might hold the information you're looking for."

"A piece of equipment?"

"We found it eight or nine years ago when we had to do repairs to that room. It was behind a false wall. Caley guessed that it was meant to play music, but as I cannot hear it, I have never turned it on. It may have belonged to Alleya."

"Alleya?"

"That is what the people here called the angel Alleluia," Caley said.

"Charming," Conran said. He had spoken slowly and calmly till now, but Jared could sense his excitement building. "May we see this equipment? May we listen to any recordings that are there?"

Maretta gazed at Conran for a long time while Caley watched impassively. Had Jared been the one to undergo such a searching gaze, he would have tried to make his eyes limpid and his expression saintly, but Conran stared back at her with all the intensity at his command. It was as if he was willing her to acquiesce, winning her over by the strength of his desire.

Finally, Maretta nodded once, sharply, and everyone from Conran on back let out a sigh. "This way," Caley said, and everyone turned to follow her back into the cramped hallway. Maretta made no move to join them. Conran held out his hand to her.

"Won't you come with us?" he asked, but she shook her head.

"She can't hear what the machine says, so she sees no need to come," Caley said.

"You could interpret for her."

Caley smiled briefly, a pretty flash of mischief across her tired face. "She doesn't like secrets. She says no secret revealed ever did anybody good."

"This one will. That I am sure of."

Caley led the way upstairs and into a small, featureless room with a single window and drab decor. Faded wallpaper covered three walls; the fourth, once presumably hidden behind the false front, was of rough brick. There were really only three pieces of furniture in the room: a narrow bed covered with a thin coverlet, a rickety old chest of drawers with a cracked mirror leaned on top of it—and a bulky metal box studded with gauges and knobs.

A clench of unbearable excitement tightened Jared's stomach almost to the point of nausea. Recording equipment. It looked nothing at all like the sleek black transmitters he had seen in Luminaux and at Christian's, but in an odd way it resembled the machinery in the music rooms at the angel holds. And when Caleb Augustus built this piece of equipment—for who but that rogue engineer would have constructed such a thing?—the only recorders he had encountered had been those ancient, mysterious systems brought in by the original colonists.

Caley gestured at the metal box. "Is this what you're looking for?" she asked. "I have no idea how it works."

Conran was on his knees before it, and Duncan and Sal hovered behind him, but it was young Wyman who was the only mechanic of the group. Or so Jared surmised. When Wyman said, "Let me see," the others fell back. He bent over the box and studied the controls.

"Hunh," he said, and began touching dials and switches. Everyone tried to remember to breathe, but clearly the room was airless; they were all pale from lack of oxygen, from excitement, from fear. There might be nothing inside this old, bulky music box; there might be everything.

"Ah," was Wyman's next pronouncement, and the lid of the contraption flew open and almost struck him in the chin. Everyone jumped back a pace. Jani stepped on Jared's wings, which caused him to bite back a yelp of pain and move hurriedly to the back of the room. Strange clickings were emanating from the old equipment; it sounded like a piece of metal heating up to a sizzling pitch.

"Well. I see. If that . . . no, *that* one," Wyman said, and his voice was laced with satisfaction. "Okay. Hold tight. I think this may be the 'go' button."

He turned a knob, and the room was filled with the sound of a woman speaking. Jared was caught first by the utter sweetness of that voice, chime-sweet, child-sweet, beguiling as birdsong on the first day of spring. There was nothing this woman could have said to him that he would not have believed absolutely; nothing she would have asked from him that he would not have gladly done. He had heard of speakers blessed with hypnotic voices but he had never, till this moment, encountered one, and certainly would not have expected any recorded voice to have such power, divorced from the speaker's spirit by six decades of death.

It was therefore a few sentences into her speech before he

registered what she was saying—and the words were just as
astonishing as the voice.

"... Such knowledge, while important, has such calamitous
and far-reaching effects that I fear to share it with the rest of
Samaria. Our society lives by the rules set down by our god—
our world maintains its graces and its civilities primarily because
these have been ordained by Jovah. If the god were to be removed from our calculations, I do not know how our society
would continue to function. I do not know. I am afraid to find
out.

"And yet, having been taught to revere truth, I cannot in
conscience fail to correct a lie. I will tell only one living soul
what I have learned, but I will leave this record for future generations who may deal more hardily with knowledge than my
own. If Jovah has taught me one thing, it is that a truth will be
revealed when that truth is desperately needed, and so I hope
this secret becomes known when the time is right.

"The god Jovah is in reality a space-going vessel called the
Jehovah. It ferried us here from Eleison more than six hundred
years ago, and it still orbits above us today. It is built from
unimaginable technology and stocked with priceless commodi-
ties—seeds, chemicals, potions—that the ship can release to us
upon request. It is also armed with powerful weapons, weapons
so terrible and so precise that they can strike down a man standing in a crowd of men or destroy the whole world we call Samaria.

"It is voice-activated. It hears the angels' prayers and responds to the cadence of our songs. When we sing for rain, it
sprays chemicals into the clouds to make them gather overhead.
When we pray for medicine, it releases drugs that we do not
even know how to decode.

"When we gather every year to perform the Gloria, it counts
our voices and calculates our numbers. If we were to remain
silent, it would smite us with all the destructive power at its
command. It has no malice for us. It has no love for us. It is
programmed to act in this way. It is a machine.

"But it is a machine that controls our lives. One of the great
engineers of my time has said he cannot see a way to dismantle
it. Thus we cannot disregard it. We cannot, for instance, cease
singing the Gloria simply because we do not raise our prayers
to a god. In fact, a god might be more merciful than *Jehovah*.

"But *Jehovah* is also a wonderful, fabulous thing. It has stored in its memory banks all the knowledge of the universe. It has taught me more than I could ever record here, and I have not asked it one-one-thousandth of the questions it could answer. It can tell us how our bodies are formed, how our minds work, where our ancestors were born, and where people just like us live on other planets orbiting other stars. It can tell us how to build machines just like it, that would carry us elsewhere, to new worlds beneath different suns. It would tell us all this, but we are not yet ready to understand the answers. Or so I believe.

"How do I know all this? How can I be so sure? Because I have stood face-to-face with *Jehovah*. I have traveled to the interior of this ship, and heard the voice of its electronic brain speak to me as I am speaking to you now. I have touched its keyboards and controls—I have walked its vast white halls. I have stood there and despaired, because my god was a machine. And I have stood there and rejoiced, because I learned the truth.

"There is a way—a simple way—for any man or woman to transport himself to the interior of the spaceship as I have done. I have left those instructions elsewhere, in other trusted hands. Forgive me if I am being too careful. I have guarded this secret with my life, for so much of my life, that I am afraid to have said as much as I already have. But I believe that if you are meant to find the rest of the puzzle, you will find it. And if not, you can do very little harm.

"I have asked *Jehovah,* who is wiser than any human I know, when the time might be right for Samarians to learn the truth about their god. He gave, as he sometimes does, a cryptic reply. He said, 'That day will come when the twinned destinies of angel and mortal become one.' Perhaps that answer will mean more to you than it does to me.

"I have no more to say, but I beg you to use the knowledge you have gained only for the good of the world. I am the oracle Alleluia, and I bid you farewell and amen."

The recording ran for another full minute, making a quiet little whirring noise in the heart of the machine, but there was not another sound in the room. Jared felt heat at all the junctures of his body, a breathless pressure across his chest, and *he* had not spent his life looking for this very revelation. He could imagine how stunned the Jacobites were, how elated, how their very blood must be reveling in their veins and whirling their brains into ecstasy.

Caley was the first to speak, and her voice was amused and a little ironic. "She must have given quite a speech. I don't believe one of you has breathed since she started talking."

All the Jacobites looked at her, still too choked to reply, and Jared said, "You could not hear her?"

Caley shook her head. "Isn't that strange? They say almost everyone could hear Alleya, even those who had been born deaf and never heard another voice in their lives. But my great-great-grandmother Mara never heard Alleya's voice, and I cannot catch it either. I can hear you. I can hear most others. But not Alleluia."

"You have missed—an incredible performance."

"That's what he said, too."

"That's what—who said that?"

Jared saw Conran's head whip around, although the other Jacobites did not seem to be paying attention. They had begun to move now, in careful, fractional gestures, and to speak in voices scarcely above a whisper. They appeared to be shaking themselves loose from near-fatal comas and describing their experiences in awestruck tones.

But Conran stepped a pace closer to Caley and repeated Jared's question. "Who said that? Someone else has heard this recording?"

Caley nodded. She appeared surprised. "Oh, yes. About five years ago. It took him much longer to convince my grandmother to let him up to this room, though."

Conran and Jared shared glances of alarm. "Who was he? What was his name?"

"I don't remember his name," she said. "He was an angel, though. Older. With—" She fluttered her fingers around her head. "Silver hair, kind of wild. And a silver beard. He had the most beautiful voice. I could hear every word he said."

Jared felt his lips mouth the word but he could not say it aloud. Conran was staring at him, shaking his head very slightly. It was not possible. Was it possible? Had the Archangel been here five years ago, successfully solving the riddle the Jacobites had puzzled over for decades? Had he heard the oracle Alleluia proclaim that the god was a spaceship, swear it in a voice so calm and so convincing that no one could disbelieve it? Had he not believed her?

Had he believed her?

Was that why he had so venomously attacked the Jacobites? Had he, ruthlessly and with complete knowledge, set out to exterminate the reckless band of rebels who sought to shed a searing, terrible light on their entire world? Had he done it to save Samaria, to protect it from the confusion and turmoil that would overturn every law of their society once the truth was made public?

Or had he done it because he alone wanted the power that would come with knowledge? If there was no god, how could the god care who was Archangel? Why could Bael not remain Archangel for another year—another ten years—for the rest of his life? Who would stop him? Who would limit him? Who would challenge him?

The Jacobites . . .

Oh, Bael had known very well what he was doing. He had styled himself a prophet in the service of the god, but he was a cold-blooded killer eliminating any threat to his own bid for glory. Christian had said the Archangel was an evil man. He did not know the half of it.

"Was it who I think?" Conran asked in a very quiet voice. Everyone else in the room was still ignoring them.

"It was Bael," Jared said.

"Then we are in even more danger than we thought."

"I agree," Jared said. "I think we should get back to Ysral as soon as we can."

"We must bring the equipment with us."

Jared shook his head. "You can try. My guess is that it's immovable. Or why else is it still here?"

"Why does it still exist at all?" Conran shot back. "Why didn't he destroy it before we found it?"

Jared spread his hands. "Unfathomable. Unless he thought he might someday want proof, and this was the only proof he had. He must not have thought you would ever find it. He must have believed it was safe here. And that no one would be able to remove it."

Conran stared at him a moment and then, eyes still on the angel, barked out, "Wyman."

"Yo."

"This machine. Can you detach it? Take the recording out?"

"Just what I've been wondering," the young engineer said. Conran and the angel turned to find him still kneeling on the floor before Caleb Augustus's unique piece of equipment. "I can't figure out where it's connected or how to loosen the bolts. See, here's where it looks like it screws into the wall, but when you twist that—"

"Then the answer is no," Conran said impatiently, and Jared read a rising anxiety in his voice. "Everybody listen to me. We need to leave here. Now. Instantly. Make our way back to the rendezvous point. If something unforeseen happens, abandon the group, do you hear me? *Abandon the group.* Flee as fast as you can back to Ysral and take this information to the others."

There was a babble of questioning voices ("What's wrong?" "What did Wyman say?" "I'm not abandoning anybody!") but they all seemed to catch some of Conran's edginess. At any rate, when the Jacobite leader pointed a finger at the door and said "Go!," Jani, Loa, and Horace instantly ducked out and clattered downstairs. Caley went with them. Duncan, Sal, and Wyman followed less willingly, and Tamar lingered even after the others had left.

"What was that girl telling you, Conran?" she asked, but her eyes were on Jared.

"That we are not the first to seek this recording. Go. Downstairs. Run for it."

"But we—"

"Conran!" The frenzied shout came from downstairs, a heartbeat before someone shrieked. The air outside was suddenly alive with whoops of celebration and the small thunder of running feet. In the distance, but rapidly coming nearer, Jared heard the grumble of big transport trucks roaring down the quiet Chahiela road.

"Jansai!" Conran whispered, and grabbed Tamar by the arm when she would have hurtled downstairs after her friends. "No," he hissed. "Stay here and hide."

"But they—"

"*Hide!*" he repeated in that fierce undervoice. "What you know is more important than who you can save."

Below them was tumult: more screaming, the sound of a few solid blows landing across rebellious flesh, Caley's voice uselessly demanding, "Who are you? What do you want? Get out of my grandmother's house!'' Conran forced Tamar toward the small bed and jerked her to her knees when she still resisted, shoving her head toward the floor and under the rickety frame. Jared stood tense but indecisive. There was really no place for an angel to hide—in one of the other bedrooms? in some huge closet where he could draw close his wings?—and the window was far too narrow to allow him to escape.

And there was no time. Despite Caley's wild assurances— ''There is no one else in this house, I swear to you!''—booted feet were pounding up the stairway so quickly that Conran whirled to face his attackers before he had pushed Tamar all the way under the bed. She immediately sprang to her feet and so they all were standing there, stupid, empty-handed, when four Jansai burst through the door and yowled with triumph.

''Her! That's her!'' cried one of them, his vest spattered with the blue crescent moon that was Bael's emblem. ''And by the god's own grace, that's Atwell! Grab them—damn it, out of my way!''

Conran and Tamar closed with their enemies, fighting in fierce silence. Jared sprang toward Tamar, but two of the Jansai were upon him, muscling him back against the wall, pummeling him in the stomach, blinding him with blows to the head. He kicked out at them and writhed in their hold till he felt the cool, wicked tip of a knifepoint jammed under his right wing. He could help no one if he was crippled by a slashing blade. Violent despair washed through him, but he could not save her, could not save anyone, not trapped in this small room in this little house. He paused in his struggles, panting for breath, wildly trying to guess what he should try next.

And then a fifth man entered the room.

Jared stared, too breathless and too outraged to speak. It was the Archangel's son. He sauntered up to where Conran stood, his hands bound cruelly behind his back, and smiled in the Jacobite's face.

''That was really very stupid,'' Omar said in his rich voice, wearing his customary satiric smile. ''We have been watching this place for five years at least. We have always had guards outside of Chahiela. You were dead the minute you crossed the town border.''

''Kill me, then, and stop gloating about it,'' Conran said bluntly. Omar laughed.

"Oh, no, I think my father has something a little more—exemplary—planned for you. All of you. Something that will discourage the rest of the Jacobites from ever spouting their dreary doctrines again."

"Think again," Conran said. "We have seen death and betrayal before this, and it hasn't held us back. The more you try to destroy us, the stronger we will become."

Omar shrugged. "Boring doomed theatrics," he murmured, and turned his back on Conran. He stood for a long time gazing at Tamar, running his eyes with insolent familiarity over the contours of her face. "Well, well, well. So you are the missing child so long believed dead. You have no idea of the trouble you have caused us, my father and me, but it scarcely matters now."

Tamar said nothing, but stared stonily back at him. There was a bruise forming on her left cheek, and a trickle of blood pooling at the corner of her mouth. Like Conran, she had her hands tied behind her back. Jared could see her muscles working as if she was trying to free her wrists.

"You look very like your sister," Omar went on. "Although you do not quite have her sweetness of expression. She is very fond of me, you know."

"That's interesting," Tamar replied in a hard, steady voice. "She has told me about all her friends and lovers, and I don't believe your name ever once came up."

Omar laughed lightly. "Good try, my dear, but I would wager a great deal on the bet that you have never met your sister. You do not—forgive me—run in the same circles."

Not intending to, Jared let out a soft, amazed laugh. This piece of the puzzle, at least, had suddenly fallen into place. He said, quoting, "The day has come when the twinned destinies of angel and mortal are one."

Slowly, infinitely disdainful, Omar finally turned to confront Jared. With the same thoroughness he had used to examine Tamar, he let his glance wander over the angel, taking in his two assailants, the knife to his wing, the travel-weariness in his face and the defiance in his eyes.

"Jared," he said at last. "I hardly dare ask why I find you here."

"I couldn't figure out," Jared said, ignoring the question, "why it was so important to you to find Tamar. She was no more and no less valuable than any other Jacobite, yet she had somehow moved to the head of your list. Why could that be? Why did you want her?''

''Tamar,'' Omar repeated. ''We didn't have a name for her before. I hate to do an anonymous execution.''

''The prophecy,'' Jared said. ''Jovah told you. Jehovah—whoever. He said the knowledge would be revealed when the angel and mortal twins were reunited. And they have been. And if I know anything of Jovah's ways, once he has made a pronouncement like that, there's nothing any mortal or angel can do to change the course of events.''

Omar took a step closer to Jared, and in his eyes was the glittering conviction of madness so like his father's. ''Jovah is not a god,'' he purred in the angel's ear. ''Jovah is a machine, and he makes calculations based on the best available data. He may have foreseen the existence of your friend Tamar and her twin angelic sister, but he could not foresee what circumstances would separate them or what fate might await them. I am not afraid of a machine's proclamations. I know how to circumvent a prophecy. And this young woman—and all her friends—will die on the Plain of Sharon in two days' time.''

''No,'' Jared said.

''Oh, yes.''

''No.''

''And neither you, nor your heathen friends in Semorrah, nor any of the stupid Jacobites we have not yet managed to catch in our nets will be able to prevent that death.''

''Set her free,'' Jared said, offering a rash, unworkable bargain. ''Set her free—put her in my care. Take the others. I will watch over her. She will not trouble you or your father again.''

Omar actually laughed. What Conran and Tamar, tensely listening, might be thinking, Jared could not guess and had no time to wonder. ''She is dead, Jared, and no pleading on your part will change that fact. But you can still walk away. I am not overeager to send angels to their annihilation—and you, I think, could still have some value to us, if you wished. Your choice. Walk away now—or die with your questionable friends on the Plain of Sharon.''

There was a long moment of silence while Jared stared at Omar's handsome, fanatic face. If he left now, flew straight for Semorrah, he could rouse a force of merchants and angels, storm the Plain of Sharon, and prevent Bael's bloodthirsty demonstration. If he arrived in time, if the Jacobites weren't all murdered en route, if he and Christian and Mercy and the others could stop whatever dreadful vengeance Bael intended to put in motion . . .

He raised his eyes and looked straight at Tamar. Her unreadable gaze was fixed on him, but there was no emotion to be deciphered in her face. Not fear for her life, not contempt for him, not hope, not surrender. But her eyes did not waver and her body did not in the slightest degree tremble. He had never seen anyone so brave, so proud. Even Conran, growling beside her, could not compare to her. Nothing else in the whole world held an ounce of worth.

"Tell your man to withdraw his dagger," Jared said coolly, and Omar jerked his head. Reluctantly, the Jansai lowered his knife hand and retreated. Jared shook his wings back as a vain girl might toss back her gorgeous golden hair. Tamar's eyes dropped to the floor as if she could not bear to watch him defect.

Jared took two long strides to Conran's side, pushing aside the Jansai holding him. He felt Tamar's eyes follow him but he did not spare her a glance.

"I stand with the Jacobites," he said.

"Then you will die with the Jacobites."

Jared nodded. "So be it," he said, adding very softly Alleluia's benediction: "Amen."

CHAPTER NINETEEN

As delighted as Lucinda was to have Reuben to herself for as long as *The Wayward* was gone, she learned quickly enough that these next few weeks would not be simply a blissful lover's holiday. For one thing, she couldn't help fretting about Tamar, nearly every minute of the day—ridiculous, of course, to worry about a sister she had never even known she had until a few days ago, but the concern was there nonetheless. She kept her promise, and when no one else was around, she sang cheerful, hopeful melodies that might make a weary traveler smile as she pressed on in her uncertain adventure. And she watched the gliding colors in her Kiss, hoping to see—as Tamar had seen—evidence of her twin's existence in its capricious depths. But it yielded very few secrets. And she listened to the cadences of her own heart, and watched the pantomimes of her dreams, for by these signs if no others she was convinced she would be able to determine the state of Tamar's well-being.

So that was a preoccupation; and she was not the only one left behind who kept her attention focused on the voyage to Samaria. The Jacobites could talk of nothing else, and even the calm Edori seemed excited about the news that the travelers might bring back. Well, not excited. Interested. Intrigued. Willing to hear the details.

But all this might have been bearable if Reuben had not been so restless. Sleeping beside Lucinda in the stone Edori house, he tossed and turned and called out names every night, balling up the covers into one hopeless knot on the nights he did not throw them all to the floor. During the days he paced along the seashore, watching the incessant billowing of the waves, or begged his Edori brethren and Jacobite neighbors for some chore. He was, it turned out, a skilled enough mechanic to fix most anything that was broken—the axle of one of those small, sleek cars; the wires in some discarded piece of recording equipment; transmitters; receivers; unidentifiable objects. He had been trained at the Augustine school, he admitted to Lucinda, but wanderlust and a desire to see the world had lured him away before he had completed two years of study.

"And I was good! That's what they all told me," he said with a brief self-deprecating grin. "One of my professors said to me, 'If you stay two more years, I swear to you you'll be building boats instead of sailing them,' but that was hardly an incentive to me. Who wanted to stay behind building boats? I wanted to be out on the ocean, sailing from port to port, seeing everything. I still want to be."

Lucinda wondered if he had ever been on shore more than a week since the day he had first set sail. Clearly he could not stand the inactivity for long. She would remember this, if ever it crossed her mind to try to convince him to live with her, on Angel Rock or wherever she eventually made her home; she would remember that this man could not stay in one place for long without driving himself and everyone around him to the verge of lunacy.

Those first three days, she tried to come up with diversions, so they explored the nearby countryside and visited all the notable landmarks. It was breathtaking country, alive with color and scent, and Reuben was a knowledgeable and entertaining guide. But that palled on him quickly enough, and Lucinda had to admit that there were only so many lovely vistas and fields of exotic vegetation that she could admire with any sincerity, and so she racked her brains to come up with other excursions.

"You could take me traveling through Ysral," she suggested at the end of that third day. "We could meet up with your clan and I could see how Edori live on the road."

"Too far," he said briefly. "Take too long to get there and back."

He did not want to be a yard away from the harbor when *The Wayward* hove back into view, Lucinda knew. He was not going to let that ship set sail without him again. But: "If we fly," she said persuasively, "we could cross Ysral in a couple of days, don't you think? We wouldn't be gone more than five or six days."

"Some other time," he said. "When it's less risky."

She spread her hands, sighed softly, and turned aside, wondering what else she could suggest. She had never seen the sanguine Reuben so edgy—had never, as far as she could remember, seen any Edori out of temper. But even as she was frowning over her options, Reuben let out a small laugh and took her hand.

"Ah, and I should be apologizing for being such a crabby old bear," he said, smiling down at her, albeit with an effort. "It was I who volunteered to stay behind, not you who volunteered to entertain me, and I should be happy for the free days I have with you. And I *am* happy. It is just that I am not used to so many days of uncontested happiness in a row."

She could not help smiling at that. A sweet apology. "But I had an idea," she said. "Couldn't we go to this Augustine school? It's not too far, is it? Boyce said it took a day each way in one of those little cars. Or we could fly—it would take almost the same amount of time."

On the instant he brightened; the prospect of action always cheered him. "Yes, excellent thought!" he exclaimed. "I could introduce you to some of my old teachers, and you could see the campus. You won't believe some of the things they have there! Motors smaller than my hand and bigger than this house! And the whole building set aside for electrical experimentation—it's extraordinary, the lights and colors they produce in some of those rooms—"

He went on in this fashion for a few more minutes. Lucinda, glad to have hit on something that lit his enthusiasm, only listened closely enough to know when it was appropriate to nod or murmur her amazement. She was thinking about how much lunch she should pack and calculating exactly how long the trip would take and wondering what she should bring for a change of clothes.

"Let's leave first thing in the morning, then," she said, when Reuben finally paused for breath. "I think it will be fun."

And it was an enjoyable journey on one of those golden, serene days for which Ysral was famous. Reuben had elected to drive, which was fine with Lucinda since she thought he would enjoy the journey even more if he actually got a chance to feel each mile as it passed beneath him. They had borrowed a car from one of his Edori friends—a racy little two-seater with three wheels and incredible power—and Lucinda found herself wondering if she could, in fact, have kept pace with this vehicle. Technology would soon outdistance the angels, she realized, whether or not the god was revealed to be a machine. The thought made her a little frightened and a little sad.

As so much did these days.

They arrived at the Augustine school in early evening. It was not, Lucinda thought, the most beautiful collection of buildings she had ever seen. What appeared to be the main structure of the campus was a huge, two-story building that covered five acres at least and offered no interesting detail to break up the flat, honey-beige expanse of its stone exterior. Surrounding it in a somewhat haphazard array were a collection of smaller buildings, some of them sporting all manner of antennas, transmitting towers, and other odd features from their roofs and windows. One building was constructed entirely of some black, volcanic stone, and offered no windows and (from what Lucinda could see) only one door. At first she thought it was the burned hulk of some classroom destroyed by fire, but no, it was meant to look that way; she saw a handful of students exiting by that single door, talking and gesturing in great excitement.

Well, she hoped that they were, in fact, magnificent engineers, because as architects they were complete failures.

"What do you want to see first?" Reuben was asking. "The electrical engineering building? Or maybe we should save that for last. Those are the dorms, they aren't interesting, but you might like the transmitting stations. Or the music rooms. You could record something. The engineers would fall on their knees every day thanking you for such a service."

"Then let's go to the music rooms," she said.

Since the day was practically over, she expected most of the classrooms to be empty, but she was soon proved wrong. The engineering students, it seemed, were a dedicated breed, working on their theorems, their models, and their chemical combinations late into the night. Everywhere she and Reuben went, down each cluttered hallway filled with the peculiar mixed smells of electricity and alchemy, they encountered diligent students, arguing professors, excited interns, and abstracted technicians. Those who actually noticed the visitors nodded or smiled in the most desultory fashion imaginable.

"Is there anyone here you still know?"

"Oh, many. Once a teacher comes to the Augustine school, it's rare that he leaves for another place. Well, there's nothing like it, in Ysral or Samaria, so where else would he go? But it's been ten years and more since I've been here for more than a visit. They might not instantly remember my face."

"Your face?" she said, teasing. "Such a beautiful one! How could they forget it?"

He grinned, and pushed open a doorway that led to a large, high-ceilinged room. In a semicircle around the far end there were four smaller rooms, separated from the main chamber by panes of thick glass. Inside each room were banks of machinery that looked only vaguely familiar to Lucinda.

"Recording equipment?" she guessed.

Reuben nodded. "Looks upgraded from the last time I was here. Probably by now they've got the tones so rich they sound better than the singer performing live."

"Well, we think so, but most of our singers have been so wretched that it's hard to tell," said a cheerful voice nearby, and they turned to find a young woman standing behind them. She had wild hair pulled back in an inexpert bun, an array of tools and marking pens stuck in her pockets, and several unnoticed smudges across her smiling cheeks. Here was someone who loved her work more than she loved herself, Lucinda thought.

"I'm Alina," she introduced herself. "What can I do for you?"

"I'm Reuben, once a student in this marvelous institution but now fallen to the lowly career of seaman," the Edori introduced himself. Alina laughed. "And this is Lucinda. She's an angel."

"Really," Alina said. "If you hadn't told me, I could not possibly have guessed."

Reuben grinned. "I was just telling her how superb your recording equipment is, and how much you all would appreciate having a track or two laid down by someone who really *can* sing. Am I wrong?"

Alina became quite animated. "Not at all! We'd love to have an angel's voice on disk. In fact, I'm designing an experiment now that would compare the relative trueness of three different

recording media, but I haven't found anyone whose voice
seemed worth committing to posterity. Well, no, that's an ex-
aggeration, and I had just about decided to go with a speaking
voice, since after all it doesn't actually have to be a singing
voice—but if you'd be willing to make a recording for me—
three recordings—''

"Delighted," Lucinda said, interrupting because she didn't
particularly want to hear all the details. "The same song, three
times?"

Alina nodded. "Duplicating them as best you can."

"I can do that. Where do I go?"

The next half hour was fairly tedious for the angel as the
engineer set up her studios and explained to Reuben exactly
what she was doing. Lucinda hummed to herself to quickly
warm up her voice and mentally reviewed her repertoire. Well,
she had no idea exactly how these engineers might use her recording, so it seemed unwise to perform, for instance, masses
that called for rain or sunshine. Best would be a simple ballad,
easy to sing, easy to reproduce multiple times.

"All right, I'm ready for you," Alina called, and in a few
moments Lucinda was installed inside one of the small glass
chambers, looking out at Alina, Reuben, and a few students who
had drifted in to watch. She couldn't hear a word any of them
said, for apparently the room was soundproofed, but she assumed they would all be able to monitor her performance. She
watched Alina closely; when the woman gave her the signal to
begin, she launched into her chosen melody.

It was a pretty love song, one that the residents of Angel Rock
requested every time she gave a concert, so she knew it had the
power to please. Nonetheless, she was a little surprised to see
Alina stop her busy writing, the other students pause in their
chattering to stare at her, and Reuben close his eyes as if to
concentrate on every note. When she finished, there was a long
pause before anyone in the outer room moved or spoke. Then
there was a brief flurry of spontaneous applause, and a speaker
inside her chamber clicked on.

"That was unbelievable," Alina's voice said, sounding a little
tinny over the closed circuit. "Are you—I've never heard anything like that. Is that how all angels sing?"

"Pretty much," Lucinda said with a laugh. "Some much better."

"I can't believe it," Alina said. "Do you mind waiting while I play it back?"

"Not at all."

In less than a minute her own voice recycled through the chamber, and Lucinda listened critically. No, nothing special; it was how she always sounded, perhaps not as good, because she'd neglected her formal rehearsals since she'd been in Sahala. As her recorded voice dipped into the second verse, she began softly singing the high harmony, a dazzling counterpoint that Gretchen had sometimes sung with her, but only when she was in an approachable mood.

Alina abruptly shut off the music. Lucinda closed her mouth.

"What's that? Are you singing along?" the engineer asked.

"Sorry. Habit. I'll be quiet."

"No, it's beautiful. Would you be willing to record a second track?"

"What do you mean?"

"The harmony to this music. If I play this piece back, can you perform your own harmony?"

"Oh, certainly. Two or three different harmonies, if you like."

Even through the thick glass, Alina's face seemed to glaze over with awe. "Really? Oh, would you? You don't mind? Oh, this is wonderful."

So Lucinda spent the next half hour decorating the little ballad with descant, mezzo, and contralto lines. By the time she was done, the outer room was filled with more than thirty people, all listening as raptly as if they had never heard music in their lives. Well, mechanics. She had always heard that they were strange and unsocialized creatures, more tuned to their machines and their mathematics than to basic human interactions. Apparently it was true.

By the time she was done singing the final part, she was famished. "Would it be possible to take a break for dinner?" she asked before Alina could ask her to perform again. "We've been traveling all day and—"

"Oh! Of course! You'll eat with us, won't you, in the mess hall? And are you spending the night? Where are you staying?"

Reuben and Alina worked out the details while a student freed Lucinda from the glass studio. "You have a magnificent voice," he told her diffidently. "Maybe you'll sing for us again after supper."

"I believe I've already committed to that," she said with a laugh. "Something about recording the same song on different machines. I'm willing to do whatever she wants. But I'm really hungry."

A group of about twenty-five ultimately accompanied them to another one of those nondescript buildings which proved to be a cafeteria. The food smelled heavenly and proved to be excellent. Conversation at the table all around them was lively but mostly impenetrable to Lucinda, since it primarily revolved around scientific and experimental topics. She concentrated on her food.

The shy young man who had released her from the studio was sitting on her left. "What is an angel doing at the Augustine school?" he gathered the courage to say. "If you don't mind my asking."

She smiled at him to give him heart. "I've been visiting friends in Sahala," she said somewhat vaguely, not sure how much hard information she should give out.

His shaggy eyebrows went up. "Sahala. That's where the Jacobites are staying, isn't it?"

So perhaps it was not a secret after all. "Well, some of them," she said. "The ones who are still alive, apparently."

He nodded. "Two of them came here—oh, a month or two ago. Conran, I think his name was, and somebody else. Later Alina told me that Conran used to be a student here."

"So I understand. What were they looking for?"

Instead of answering, he asked a question of the girl sitting across the table from him. "Rhea? When those Jacobites came here, what were they looking for? What did they call it?"

"Oh, the Alleluia Files," she said.

Lucinda jumped, and her eyes flew to Reuben's. It had not occurred to her that anyone would seek the elusive papers here. "And why would the Alleluia Files be at the Augustine school?" she asked slowly. Nearly everyone at the table had stopped holding their individual conversations, it seemed, and all had started listening to this one.

"Because Caleb Augustus founded the school," Rhea replied. "And he was married to the angel Alleluia. And they haven't found the files anywhere else."

"And did you find them here?" Reuben asked quietly.

Rhea laughed. "Well, I didn't. I didn't even know where to begin looking! What is this precious file, anyway? A book? A recording? A cryptogram? A formula? Does it even exist? I poked around in a couple old books, but I didn't find anything, and I don't think anyone else did, either."

"Well," said the boy next to Lucinda, but he never had a chance to complete his sentence. Someone down the table called out another question, which everyone attempted to answer at once, and the student's voice was lost in the general commotion. In a few more bites, Lucinda had finished her food, and Alina led the way back to the recording studio.

It took another hour to complete the tasks that Alina requested, and Lucinda was starting to grow tired by the time they were done. It had been a long day, and she still was not sure *exactly* where they were sleeping although Alina had made a few references to "empty rooms in the dorm." Which sounded a little uncomfortable, but it was only one night, after all; and she was not used to luxury in any case.

"Great. That was perfect. You can come out now, and I'll play everything back tonight. Maybe tomorrow you can rerecord if there's anything that didn't turn out right."

"Gladly," Lucinda said, and waited for the door to be opened. She was just as surprised as Alina was when the same shy young man appeared to set her free.

"George. I didn't know you were still here," Alina said.

"Well, I—"

"Good. You can show them to the room where they'll be staying tonight. I've got a lot to finish here," Alina said, and turned her back on them to begin consulting her notes. Reuben grinned.

"Very single-minded, the engineers," he said in a low voice. "George, my friend, do you care if we stop at the car and pick up our baggage? It will just take a minute."

In a few moments they were back outside in the perfumed night air, under a sky so black that the stars looked humble. Lucinda took a deep breath and rolled her shoulders back.

"It never smells this sweet on Angel Rock," she observed. "Not even in spring."

"I was thinking," George said, and stopped.

Inwardly, Lucinda sighed, but Reuben spoke in a kind voice. "Yes? Something you wanted to tell us?"

"Well. After those Jacobites came. All of us did a little looking, but no one found anything. Not really. But I was going through some of Caleb Augustus's old papers."

He halted again, as if his speech was complete, as if he had told them all he had to say. But Lucinda felt a rising excitement prickle along her spine, and she could tell by Reuben's sudden stillness that he, too, was intensely interested.

But his voice was still soft, unalarming. "Yes?" he encouraged. "And you found something? Something that might lead us to the Alleluia Files?"

"Well. I'm not sure. It was a very old piece of paper. But I'm pretty sure it's Caleb's handwriting. We have plenty of examples of that," he added. "Old manuals. Old notebooks. Things like that."

"I'm sure you do," Reuben said soothingly. "But this paper you found. It must have been very unusual. What was on it?"

"Well, I'm not certain," George confessed. "I couldn't read it. No one could. It's not the old language, because there are about a dozen people here who can read that. It wasn't a language any of us knew. I thought it might be a code, you know, and I tried to crack it, but I never could come up with the key." He fell silent again.

"Well, I think I'd like to look at this mysterious piece of paper," Reuben said pleasantly. "Lucinda? Wouldn't you?"

"Indeed I would," she said. All her exhaustion had evaporated, and she felt as nervous as a child before her birthday. "Could we go now or must we wait until morning?"

"Oh, no reason to wait," George said. "I can take you there right now."

They carried their suitcases with them to a long, narrow building that huddled close to the ground as if for warmth or comfort. "Archives," George explained briefly. The outer door was dense and heavy, and he struggled with it until Reuben added his considerable strength. Inside, the air seemed rarefied, unscented, filtered of all personality. Temperature and humidity controls, Lucinda guessed. She was almost afraid to exhale and poison the perfectly balanced atmosphere.

"Where did you find this paper?" Reuben asked in a low voice.

George pointed, then led the way down the main hall. "You don't have to whisper," he said in equally subdued tones, "but everybody does. There's something so . . . quelling about this place."

In a few minutes they had found the storage room he was seeking. Lucinda and Reuben seated themselves at a small table while George foraged through a file drawer constructed of some unfamiliar-looking metal. Although the light was perfectly adequate, the room felt shadowed; Lucinda kept looking over her shoulder for ghostly watchers. The strange excitement had not left her, though she scolded herself repeatedly. *An ancient piece of paper written in a made-up language. There must be hundreds of such documents in this place!* And yet hope and anxiety still played tag across her back. She was breathing too fast. It was the air; it was the late night; she was being ridiculous.

George sat across from them and handed Lucinda the paper. "You see? Makes no sense. But maybe if you know the code . . ."

His voice trailed off, but neither the angel nor the Edori was listening. Reuben had crowded closer to Lucinda, and she held the paper so they could both scan it simultaneously.

Nonsense, indeed. She felt the excitement receding from her toes and fingers, withdrawing along each nerve route to make a clump of disappointment in her stomach. Vowels and consonants in no particular order, grouped as if to form words, but there were no words. None she recognized, anyway. She pursed her lips and silently tried to formulate the sounds. *Mee . . . far . . . neeos . . . Hol . . . vetri . . . lamecks . . .*

Beside her, Reuben's body sagged from its taut posture. "No," he said, shaking his head and pulling back from Lucinda. "Nothing I recognize. And it couldn't be the Alleluia Files anyway. There's less than a page of text."

"Well," George said. "I thought I should show you."

"And we appreciate it," Reuben said. "But these aren't even words."

Lucinda spoke softly. "They're phonetic."

She didn't lift her eyes from the page, but she felt both George and Reuben quickly look her way. "What do you mean?" George asked.

"In what language?" Reuben said.

She shook her head. "I don't recognize it. But I think you're supposed to read the sounds aloud and they'll become words. They just don't look like words."

Reuben reached for the paper, but she held it away from him, turning it so he couldn't see the printed page. "No, you listen," she said. "See how it sounds."

And she read slowly, carefully, accenting nothing because she wasn't sure where the emphasis of any word would fall. *"Mi-farnios holve trilamex yovasita merlaske—"*

"That's Edori," Reuben said abruptly.

She felt the excitement punch through her again, but she kept her voice level. "That's promising," she said coolly. "Is it Edori that makes any sense?"

"Something about standing in the center of the great chamber—the god's chamber?—some of the words have more than one meaning. I'd have to study it for a while before I could translate it accurately."

Lucinda turned to George, who was watching them hopefully. "What do we need to do," she said, "to remove the paper from here? Is there something we must sign?"

Now he was shocked. "Oh, you can't *remove* it," he said. "This is the *archives*. Everything must stay."

"Well, then, I guess we're here for a long night," Reuben said.

George was shaking his head. "I could take a picture of it for you," he offered.

Lucinda and Reuben exchanged quick glances. "Copy it over, you mean?" the Edori asked cautiously.

The student shook his head. "No. It's a new process. It reproduces any visual medium in a matter of minutes. Sometimes the copies are a little distorted, but I don't think that should matter in this case. Do you? As long as you can read the words?"

"Shouldn't matter at all," Lucinda said with a smile, handing him the paper. "We'll wait right here."

As soon as George was out the door, Reuben leaped to his feet. Lucinda had never seen him so animated. Like all Edori, he usually moved with a slow, purposeful grace. Now he paced around the room as if his body could not contain its energy.

"I'm thinking these aren't exactly the files your friends have been searching for," he said, and even his looping, lilting speech was hurried. "*Part* of the files, maybe. A careful set of instructions."

Lucinda laughed at him, breathless though she was herself. "And you could tell that much from a few words?"

"Ah, but the words were formal, not conversational, which indicates that the speaker would be teaching or instructing the listener. And the word *yovasita*. It can mean so many things— a big room, even a big natural site, a cave, for instance. The root word is *yova*—Yovah, of course. Yovah's site, Yovah's chamber. Sometimes the Edori call the Plain of Sharon *yovasita,* because it is a huge place, and because it is where Samarians go to worship the god."

"So is this telling us to go to the Plain of Sharon?"

He shook his head. "I don't think so. As I said, I'll need to be studying the manuscript awhile before I can be certain of its meaning. But *yovasita* is also a word the Edori use to refer to the sanctuaries where the oracles commune with their god."

"Mount Sinai," Lucinda breathed. She had not spent weeks in Sahala without learning something from the Jacobites. "Isn't that where Alleluia was supposed to have been when she was taken up by the god?"

Reuben nodded. "So I have always heard the story told. And the words you were reading could be interpreted to say, 'Stand in the center room of Mount Sinai and—' "

"And what?"

He laughed. "Well, that's all you told me!"

She couldn't sit still another second. She jumped up to pace beside him, her wings flowing over the pristinely kept floor. "So what do you think?" she demanded. "These are Alleluia's directions on how to board the spaceship *Jehovah*?"

He shrugged. He seemed to be growing calmer just as she was growing more agitated. "Well, we won't know that until we've read the whole text," he said. "But Caleb Augustus and his angel wife had plenty of Edori friends who could have helped them prepare that paper." He laughed. "And there have been plenty of Edori in the past century who have passed through the gates of the Augustine school possessing both a good sense of humor and plenty of time on their hands."

Lucinda felt as if her whole body contracted, head, chest, and feathers deflating into husks. "A hoax?" she whispered. "But who would do such a thing?"

Reuben shrugged. "Alleluia herself, for all we know," he said. "Or anybody in the world who came after her and had a command of Edori. Alleluia may have been a madwoman. She may have believed she flew up to some great silver spaceship in the sky and conversed with Yovah, but she may have been completely lunatic. Or she never said it happened, but somebody, at some time, took the opportunity to ascribe the adventure to her. Who knows? We are dealing in pure speculation here. Even if we decipher the manuscript tonight, we will not be able to prove what it says is true."

"Unless we go to Mount Sinai—or wherever it tells us to go—and try the directions for ourselves."

He laughed. "Unless we do that. Yes, mikala, then we will know."

"Well," she began, but the door opened and George stepped back into the room.

"Sorry it took me so long," he apologized. "It took the machine a little while to heat to usable temperature. Everything gets turned off at night in the archives."

"Let's see this new technology," Reuben said, taking the original and the copy and studying both. "Very impressive, indeed! You can read every word on the reproduction."

George looked shyly pleased. Lucinda wondered if he'd had some hand in the invention of the machine. "We're hoping to find a market for such equipment in Samaria," he said. "Christian Avalone already has one, though it is still illegal there."

"It won't be for long," Reuben said absently. Most of his attention was on the page before him. He had laid aside the authentic paper and was poring over the copy.

"Really? Why do you think that?"

"Because Christian Avalone is a man who knows how to translate his desires into hard reality," Reuben said, looking up. He bestowed his warmest smile on the boy, and George beamed happily back. "Thank you. This is excellent. May we take this copy with us as we leave?"

"Oh, yes. It's yours. Will it be helpful? Does it have what you want?"

"Maybe yes, maybe no. I'll need to read the whole thing."

"Do we owe you any fee?" Lucinda asked.

"Oh, no!" George replied, shocked again. "Knowledge is meant to be shared! Otherwise, how can we all learn?"

"The credo of the Augustine school," Reuben observed. "As always, it simplifies our lives. George, my friend, you have been of great help to us. If you would now see us to our rooms, we would be happy to release you for the night."

"Oh—yes—certainly! But I—" He hesitated.

"We don't know yet," Reuben said gently. "If we discover anything, we will let you know in the morning. You can be the one to tell the others."

George blushed, smiled, looked away, and smiled again. "You must be tired," he said at last. "Let me take you to the dorm."

It was well past midnight before Reuben had finally completed his translation. By this time, despite everything, Lucinda was nearly asleep on one of the narrow dormitory beds that seemed unlikely to accommodate one person comfortably, let alone two. She had at first perched upright on the edge of the mattress, but as the next two hours passed, her body had gradually angled down toward a horizontal position until she finally gave up and stretched out on the bed. She had even hiked up one of her wings to cover her face and block out some of the harsh overhead light.

So she was actually dozing when Reuben said "Done!" in a cheery voice and laid aside his pencil. She sat up, blinking rapidly and fighting off the dizziness she always experienced when she was woken too suddenly. "Yes? The Alleluia Files? Yes?"

He laughed at her. "Should this wait till morning?" he teased. "Are you too sleepy to hear the greatest news of your generation? It has kept for a hundred years, it can wait one more night."

"No, I'm awake, I'm awake, tell me what it says." She yawned mightily, clapped her hand across her mouth, and begged him with her eyes. "*Please*. I swear I'm awake."

"Well, some of it's a little rough, but this is how I think the words are meant to go. 'Stand in the center of Mount Sinai and look for the—' I think the word is 'pentagon' but I'm not sure. The Edori don't have a word for pentagon, but this says five-sided star. Pentagram? 'Look for the pentagon on the floor. Go to the—' I'm guessing again here. 'Go to the blue—window? screen? blue screen?—in the middle of the wall. Spell the word—' and here there's just a series of symbols written very carefully. Must be a word in the oracle's language, and she didn't even try to find an Edori word to match. 'Push the green button. Go quickly back to the pentagon and stand there. You will be covered in a golden light. You will feel your body—' I think she says 'evaporate'? Could that be right? 'When the light fades, you will be in a room of white and silver. This is the place where *Jehovah* resides.' "

"She says that? *Jehovah*?"

He nodded. "Phonetically. Hard to miss."

"And then what?"

" 'If you speak to *Jehovah* in your language, he will reply. He will answer any question you put to him. When you wish to return to Mount Sinai, simply ask for teleport.' "

"For what?"

Reuben shook his head. "I'm just reading syllables here. Teleport. I don't know what it means."

"Then what?"

"That's all it says."

She fixed her gaze on him, a visual reference point to occupy her eyes while her mind tried to assimilate the information. Well, it sounded simple enough; but then, Edori was a simple language, with very few scientific terms. The Edori who loved the new technology (and they were many) had to discuss it in the Samarian tongue. Alleluia had deliberately used a very unsophisticated language to convey an extremely complex process. Another way to disguise her information, to throw off her pursuers? Or a way of saying, "This is not difficult. Stand here, push this, say that. There is nothing to alarm you"?

Or was it even Alleluia who had left this message behind?

"We have to go there," Lucinda heard herself saying.

"To Mount Sinai?" Reuben asked.

She shook her head. "To *Jehovah*."

Reuben stared at her, and then burst out laughing. "What?" she demanded, instantly defensive. "Someone has to. We have to see if these directions are accurate. Conran and Tamar are gone, or we could send them. They'd love a chance to come face-to-face with *Jehovah*."

"And I'm thinking they're going to be just as welcome on the gracious continent of Samaria as you'd be. Even more so," he replied. His voice, which had been cool and clipped while he attempted to translate the paper, now resumed its customary lazy cadence. "Aren't you here in Ysral specifically because your admirable aunt Gretchen did not believe you were safe near the other angels and their kin?"

"Yes, but we can be careful for a day or two," Lucinda said impatiently. "We'll be safe enough once we're in Mount Sinai. I don't think Jecoliah is about to turn us over to the Jansai."

"Who?"

"Jecoliah. The oracle at Mount Sinai."

"Yes, but will she allow us to draw pentagons on her floor and call down great blazes of golden light? I'm thinking that sounds like an odd request from anyone, let alone a rogue angel and an Edori!"

"We'll think of something to tell her."

"And what then? We stand in the middle of Mount Sinai and wait for *Jehovah* to sweep us up to his famous white chamber? And nothing happens? What do we say then to this very unhappy oracle?"

"Well, she'd probably be even more unhappy if we *were* swept up to *Jehovah*," Lucinda said practically. "She'd much prefer it if we remained standing there, looking stupid."

He shook his head. "I'm thinking it's too much of a risk."

"And *I'm* thinking," she said, mimicking him, "that you don't have to come with me. I can fly to Samaria on my own, thank you very much."

"But you would not do so, would you, to prove a very tenuous theory?"

"I thought you wanted to know. Just as much as I did. I thought you wanted to prove the existence of the Alleluia Files—or expose the lie. I thought you were excited about this. Am I wrong?"

"You're right, mikala, and you know it. I am just not certain that we are the ones who should be doing the proving. It is not our quest, after all. And I am not joyful at the prospect of putting you again at risk."

She smiled at him, teasing him, deliberately provoking him. "And I thought you were Reuben sia Havita, great Edori adventurer. You've crossed oceans in a boat smaller than this bedroom. And you're afraid to take one more journey, travel to a place no one living now has ever seen? Were your Edori ancestors afraid to sail for Ysral, never having laid eyes on it? Would you have been afraid to make that trip?"

Reluctantly he smiled back. "It is not the same thing," he said.

"It is exactly the same thing."

"I think we should wait till Conran returns."

"You wait. I'll go without you."

"You are a very stubborn mikala. And you appear to be such a docile, even-tempered girl."

"My aunt Gretchen always says much the same thing," she replied serenely. " 'How anyone with a face as sweet as yours could be such an intractable child will be a mystery to me till I die.' Her very words. Come with me or stay behind."

"I'll go with you. When do you want to leave?"

"As soon as we've returned the car to Sahala."

A day later they took off for Samaria. They had left the Augustine school early in the morning, despite the fact that neither of them had gotten much sleep. They paused only to make a brief farewell to George, telling him honestly what they believed the paper said. He had listened with his mouth agape and his eyes bleached with disbelief.

"And this is true? It's genuine?" he had demanded, choking the words out with some difficulty.

"As to that, neither of us can say," Reuben had replied. "These are the words the documents contain. We cannot verify more than that."

As they sped away in their little car, south toward Sahala, Lucinda had asked, "Do you think that was wise? Shouldn't this secret have been kept a little longer? Or at least until we've proved it?"

"Not if it's the truth," Reuben had replied. "What if Conran and all his band are taken prisoner in Samaria? What if you and I perish in our flight across the ocean? Enough people have died for the Alleluia Files. If they exist, it is time the secret was revealed."

"And if it's a hoax after all?"

Reuben shrugged. "No harm done. A few engineering students make their way to Mount Sinai and cause the oracle great annoyance. And the watching god laughs. And the world spins on."

However, they did not, in Sahala, tell the Jacobites exactly where they planned to go. It would be too unwieldy, Lucinda thought, to try to discipline a horde of fanatic rebels who would all want to cram into Mount Sinai at once to watch the miracle. No, best to send a small party first, and wait for news.

So they packed, slept, and took off early the next morning, giving only the vaguest information about their destination. The skies were clear, and Lucinda settled quickly into her most efficient pace. Reuben was one of the few men she had ever encountered who seemed to enjoy being carried by a woman, who took the opportunity to gaze around at the world from this unique vantage point, who did not worry that he was too heavy or too dependent.

Flying at top speed and barring any battering head winds, an angel could cross the ocean in two days. With a two-hundred-pound man in her arms and a couple of packs strapped around her waist, Lucinda wasn't sure she could meet that goal, so she planned to attempt the trip in two and a half. Which meant they would have to find two friendly ships to shelter them overnight, which meant they had to look for Edori vessels, which meant they had to follow a more northerly course than the direct one between Ysral and Breven.

"And of course we can't stop at Angel Rock for the night," she murmured in Reuben's ear. "That *would* create a furor. Aunt Gretchen would never let me leave the island."

"Not a bad idea, perhaps," he replied, but she merely laughed.

They were lucky the first night: They spotted an Edori ship almost the instant they decided to start looking. Lucinda was not surprised, upon landing, to discover that Reuben was somehow related to the captain and one of the crew members. Even had that not been the case, she was sure they would have been welcomed just as warmly.

"Flying on to Breven, is that it?" the captain asked them over dinner. "We'd be glad to take you the whole distance, if that would suit your plans. No trouble at all."

"Actually, I like the flying," Reuben said with a grin. "I wouldn't have believed such a thing was possible, but it's even better than gusting through the ocean at top speed just a mile ahead of a storm."

Plainly the Edori disbelieved him but, before the angel, hesitated to mock him. "Well, then," one of the sailors replied, "that's the favor I'll ask from the god next."

The next morning, they were on their way again before the
first fragile light of dawn skittered across the horizon to their
backs. And for the first few hours of the flight, the day passed
much as the one before it had. The heavy heat of the sun was
brushed away by the incessant spiral of wind rising from the
restless sea; above them and below, there were only shades of
turquoise, cobalt, and celestine. The rush of wind, the call of
seabirds, the slap of water, and the beat of angel wings were
the only sounds in a vast, immobile, empty world. The serenity
was deeper than death.

And yet, as the afternoon advanced, painting both air and
water with an overlay of gold, Lucinda felt her arms grow tired
and her breath pull more laboriously into her lungs. She felt the
steady rhythm of her heartbeat skip and falter, and dread washed
across her like a blush. She ceased replying to Reuben's idle
comments and put all her energy into gaining another mile, and
another, without dropping her burden into the ocean and sinking
after him like so much blond-and-alabaster stone.

It was not even sunset before she started searching the horizon
for a ship that could take them in for the night, but it was another
half hour before she spotted something suitable. And even then
it was not ideal: an independent freighter out of Lisle, flying the
green Gaza flag under the standard of its merchant owner. But
as long as the sailors weren't Jansai, Lucinda had little fear. No
respectable tradesman would refuse to take in an angel.

And she was right, though the welcome here was civil as
opposed to genuine, and there was a lengthy wait before the
captain was able to clear out a cabin for their use.

"We ask a berth for just one night," Lucinda assured him.
"And we can pay you."

"No, no, no payment is required," he replied stiffly. "Of
course, we would be happy to have you join us for dinner."

"We have our own food, thank you," she replied, earning a
quick sideways glance from Reuben and a look of relief from
the captain. "We will attempt not to trouble you again at all."

In a few moments they had been shown to their room, a
meticulously clean if astonishingly small chamber that probably
belonged to the first mate or some other officer. Lucinda went
straight toward the bed, stripping off the packs around her waist
and letting them fall to the floor. She sat on the edge of the
bunk and stared sightlessly at the porthole.

Reuben stood with his back against the door, gravely watching her. "Are you ill?" he asked. "Is the strain of the long flight too much? They will not like it, of course, but we could stay another day aboard this vessel, until you have recovered your strength."

But she shook her head. The tumult in her head was so raucous that she almost could not hear his words, only the gray cacophony of panic and fear. Her whole body felt small, taut, braced for impact. She had never been so frightened in her life.

"Something's happened to Tamar," she whispered.

CHAPTER TWENTY

They jounced along the worst roads in Bethel in the worst trucks ever soldered together, and not a single Jacobite uttered a complaint or a curse. All nine of them had been shoved inside the back of one of the big transport vehicles, which consisted of a metal base enclosed by an iron cage high enough for even Jared to stand upright. They were sharing a space about as big as a reasonably sized bedroom— but there were nine of them, and there was no padding, and there was no privacy, and there was death at the end of the road. Tamar, who had traveled a good deal, considered this the worst journey of her life.

The last journey of her life.

She could not quite believe it, although it was plain the others did. Jani and Loa huddled together in one corner of the cage, crying quietly, their arms wrapped around each other and even their hair wet with their tears. Horace, whose arm had been broken in a fast fight with one of their attackers, lay in a trance-like state on the floor of the truck, refusing water or comfort. Duncan, Sal, and Wyman spent all their energy examining every last joint of the bars and the truck, looking for loose connections, looking for paths to escape. When the vehicle careened around a particularly bad corner and sent them flying to the hard floor, they merely waited till they had caught their breath or their balance, and climbed back to their feet, searching, testing, hoping.

Not that it would do them a damn bit of good to pry the whole cage from the shell of the truck, since their prison car was being followed by two truckloads of Jansai, no doubt watching for just such an event. But that was a Jacobite for you: never any idea of when to give up and go home.

Of course, they couldn't exactly go home. They could give up. But they wouldn't.

Conran divided his time between all of them, exhorting Horace to attempt to sit up, cajoling the girls into weak smiles, slapping the men on the back and telling them they would solve it yet, he had faith in them. Supreme faith.

Tamar sat with her back to the pursuing Jansai trucks, and watched Jared.

He sat in the corner across from her, knees updrawn, hands linked around his ankles, wings considerably curled tight to his body so that he took up no more than his allotted space in these very small quarters. He seemed to be completely at ease, fully relaxed, concealing neither chagrin nor alarm. Certainly, he did not appear to be contemplating a gruesome death in two days' time or ruing all the actions of his life that had led him to this regrettable end. So perhaps he did not believe they would all be killed, either—or at least, he felt certain he would be spared.

But Tamar had her doubts about that. The smiling Omar had said flat out that the angel could abandon the Jacobites or die beside them. He had made no provisions for people who suddenly recanted at the last minute.

Why had Jared passed up his chance to leave? Tamar could not get the question out of her head, and she toyed with her mother's locket while her mind worried over the problem. Why had he crossed to her side, defiant but calm, and stared back at the Archangel's son with absolutely no moue of remorse? He did not believe in their cause, did not care if the Alleluia Files were hidden for the next century or recited over broadcast wires to every ear in Samaria. Why had he joined them? Why would he sacrifice his life?

Well, she would die before she asked him those questions—die within the next two days, if Bael's son told the truth. But she could not stop herself from staring at Jared and wondering.

The caravan stopped twice during that first afternoon to give the prisoners and their guards a chance to attend to personal needs. However, it appeared they were not to be offered food, even though the Jansai and Omar made a great show of eating their dinner in full view of the Jacobites. That was not a great concern; they had all gone hungry before. What was worse was the thirst, which, on this hot southern day, grew more and more unbearable as the hours rolled on. Between them, the Jacobites had five canteens that had been slung over various shoulders while they prowled through Maretta's house—but only three of them held any water, and that supply was low.

But then, if you were going to die anyway, what did it matter what you died of? Tamar ran her tongue across her lips and tried not to think of water.

After the second break, at what she judged to be about six in the evening, Omar approached their truck at a languid pace. He ran his eyes comprehensively over the occupants of the truck, noting who was weeping and who was scheming, and came to a halt just outside the bars where Jared sat.

"Are you enjoying your trip so far?" asked the Archangel's son.

Jared turned his head slowly to look at him, examining Omar as thoroughly as Omar had examined them. "It would be more pleasant if you would offer us a few gallons of water," he said.

Omar raised his eyebrows. "And why would I go to any extra trouble to make a few miserable Jacobites comfortable? Jacobites who are as good as dead where they lie?"

"Well, they are not dead now," Jared replied coolly. "And any living creature in your care should be treated with decency, no matter how much you despise it."

Omar laughed disbelievingly. "I'd water a dog before I'd water a Jacobite," he said. "I hope you suffer the torments of the damned." And he turned on his heel and stalked off. A few minutes later the trucks rumbled to life again, and they continued on their way.

North, to the Plain of Sharon.

Tamar forced herself to sit in her place for the next two miles, but after that she could stand it no longer. She pushed herself to her hands and knees, and crawled past Horace and Conran to Jared's side. He looked at her with the same undecipherable gaze he had turned on Omar.

"There's a little water," she said. "In Horace's canteen. And in some of the others. If you're thirsty."

"There's not enough for us all," he said.

"Well, we're all sharing. No one would begrudge you a mouthful."

He smiled at her strangely, almost kindly. Not an expression of regret or hatred, but she still could not read his face. "More will be provided," he said.

She doubted it, but she did not want to say so. Having made the effort to come to his side, after days of avoiding him, she found she could neither speak casually nor bring herself to move away. She could not talk to him and she could not leave him.

Just as well, then, that she would die in two days. She would not be able to endure this agony for long.

"Do you think he will really kill us all?" was the only thing she could think to ask. "Bael? Do you think so?"

Jared nodded. "Oh, yes. He would, if he could, destroy every last Jacobite on the planet."

Tamar nodded once, but she still didn't believe it. Oh, she *knew* it, the way she knew the sun would rise in the morning and no prayer of hers could prevent it, but she didn't *believe* it. She could not imagine it happening. "How? Do you know?"

Again, that odd smile, distant and a little pitying. "I have my theories," he said, but did not elaborate.

"And why the Plain of Sharon? Why not just do us all in right there in Chahiela?"

"The Archangel wants an audience. He wants to show anyone who might not realize how serious he is just how much he dislikes Jacobites—and anyone else who questions the existence of the god."

"But will there be an audience? On the Plain of Sharon, I mean?"

Jared nodded again. "There's a big fair going on this week. A cattle show, I think, or maybe pigs. Farm animals. But it's not just your credulous yokels who show up for these fairs. Half the Manadavvi landowners are competitive breeders, and of course all the big farm conglomerates in Bethel are run by rich landowners. Most of the gentry of Samaria will be present. And all of them, I assure you, will get the message."

"Are you afraid?" she asked before she could stop herself.

For the first time he appeared to look at her fully, and the depth and brilliance of his gray eyes momentarily made her forgetful. "A little," he admitted. "It is no pleasant thing to face your own death and feel absolutely helpless."

"They'll let you go," she said, the words again coming without her volition. "If you ask them to. If you tell them it was a mistake. Omar will let you go. Or Bael."

He watched her a long time before he replied. "I stand with the Jacobites," he said.

"But why?" she whispered. Now her body, like her mouth, moved of its own independent will. She had laid her hand on his arm before she was conscious of wanting to touch him. "Why did you not step aside?"

"You tell me," he said.

She shook her head wildly. "Because I told you once—something I don't even remember saying!—because I said there was nothing in your life worth dying for! But you are not a Jacobite—this is not a cause you have lived for your whole life. It should be not be something you die for, either."

"Oh, I am not dying for the Alleluia Files," he said lightly.

"Then why are you on this truck? Why did you come with us and follow us when you could have run?"

"I came for you," he said, and his voice was completely steady. "You are the thing I will die for."

The shock went through her like electricity, like violence. Every muscle in her body burned, every vein ran with acid. He had told her before that he loved her, but she had managed to hate him for saying it. She had not had much luck explaining that alchemy to herself, but she had used a great deal of energy believing it. But you could not even pretend to hate a man who would lay down his life for you.

"I wish you would not," she whispered. "I don't want you to die."

He smiled, a little more cheerfully this time. "Well, to tell the truth, I don't want to, either. And when darkness falls and I can be reasonably certain none of the Jansai can see me, I'll attempt to contact some of my friends. Maybe they will be able to effect a rescue."

"Contact—?" she repeated blankly. "Contact them *how*?"

"It's a communications device. I believe the Edori invented it. It transmits sound to a designated receiver over a great distance. At least I hope it does. It's been a while since I tried to use it."

She felt suddenly eager. "Is there anything I can do to help?"

He regarded her again with that mysterious expression. "Yes. One thing."

"Gladly."

"Sit with me and wait for night to fall."

That caught her by surprise, and she gazed at him doubtfully. She could not love an angel; he could not love her. The truth was so self-evident that there was no need to explain it, to herself, to him. Yet his face haunted her dreams and his voice spun through her mind during every waking hour; to him, though not aloud, she had explained every action of her life, recounted every adventure. If he was anywhere near her—in the same house, on the same ship, in the same city—she knew exactly where he was at every hour of the day. It was as if some magnetic core smelted within his bones exerted a powerful draw on her eyes and brain and heart. Were she to live a hundred years longer, she would not be able to escape the insistent drag of his presence, no matter how far away she ran, no matter if she never laid eyes on him again.

And yet, they would die in two days, and she did not even know what it was like to feel the weight and shape of his mouth against hers.

He smiled at her again as if he could read the thoughts like signposts in her head, and the kindness of that smile did her in. She crept closer and he stretched out his arm; she crawled beneath it as if it were the only haven in the world. His wing wrapped around her, light and silken as a kiss, and he took one of her hands in his.

Oh, no, she could not die now. Not if the angel loved her.

The trucks traveled on for another hour, until the light had completely failed. Once more, the prisoners were allowed briefly out, then shepherded back inside the truck, apparently to bed down for the night. With sunset, the air had cooled considerably, and the Jacobites watched with envy as the Jansai and the Archangel's son gathered around a flickering fire.

"Lie together," Conran instructed the Jacobites, moving carefully between the sprawled bodies and outspread limbs to check on everyone's condition. "Find someone to sleep by and share your heat. It will be a cool night."

Duncan grunted. "There will be no sleeping."

"There had better be," Conran replied soberly. "For you will need all your strength and all your cunning if you are to survive more than another day."

Tamar, of course, had already found the body she intended to sleep beside. Jared, she had learned during the past hour, was nowhere near as relaxed as he seemed; every muscle in the chest she leaned against was corded with watchful anticipation, and his arm was strung with tension.

"Now would be a good time," she whispered. "While the Jansai are still laughing over dinner and will not hear you speaking."

He nodded. "I agree. Sit so you block me from view."

So she straightened her back and set her arms akimbo, while Jared slouched beside her and fumbled for something in a pack at his waist. A few minutes later she heard a series of sharp beeps, which drew the attention of every occupant of the truck. Of course, none of them was so indiscreet as to call out, "What's that you're fooling with, Jared?" Long before this, they had learned to rely on unlikely eventualities. But every head turned slowly their way.

Jared ignored them all. He seemed to be having some trouble getting his communicator to work, for the beeping sounds repeated several times, and twice he swore under his breath. "All right, then, Christian, let us see if another friend is home," she heard him say, and the little chirps sounded again.

And, seconds later, Tamar heard a tinny, astonished woman's voice float through thin air as if drifting down from a mountaintop. "Hello? Hello? Which one of you is calling me at this hour?"

Jared spoke in a hard, rapid voice. "Mercy. It's Jared. Don't ask questions. Omar and a band of Jansai have taken hold of me and a truckload of Jacobites—"

"Jacobites! Jared, what in the god's name—"

"Listen to me! And they're hauling us to the Plain of Sharon. I'd judge we're in the vicinity of the Corinni Mountains right about now. We'll be at the Plain of Sharon the day after tomorrow. Mercy, he plans to murder the lot of us. You have to—"

"*Murder!* Jared, stop, you have to explain to me—"

"There's no time! You have to go to Christian, now, this instant. Tell him what I've told you. Tell him there's to be an execution in two days—me and all the Jacobites—go to him. Bring your angels. Bring the angels from the Eyrie and Monteverde, if they can be reached. Do not fail me. Mercy, my life depends on this. He will kill us all, he truly will."

"I'll leave now. What can we do to stop him?"

"I don't know. My dependence is on Christian. Jovah guard you, Mercy. My life is in your hands."

Abruptly, the connection clicked off; there was a sudden humming silence, so faint that it would have been unnoticeable to someone who had not been listening to the previous conversation. Jared snapped some switch, and even the humming ceased. The angel slipped the communicator back in his pouch. The Jacobites, who had all frozen in place, gradually relaxed.

"And do you think your friends will meet us on the Plain in time to do us any good?" Conran finally voiced the question in everybody's head.

"I don't know," Jared admitted. "They'll be there. That I can guarantee."

"So if nothing else, they will witness our murders."

"There is something to be said for an observed death," Jared replied lightly.

"There is more to be said for a lived life," Conran growled.

"I have done what I can for now. Let us all try to sleep."

Jared stretched out, slowly and carefully, trying to avoid kicking Horace in the head. Tamar waited until he seemed completely arranged, and then she uncurled beside him, fitting her body to his. Again, his arm wrapped around her waist, comforting and warm; his wing settled lightly over her body, like lacy mist. She butted her head against the join of his shoulder and chest, just to feel those two inches of skin moving across her temple, gliding under the tangled silk of her hair. He bent his head, brushed his mouth across her cheek. She felt herself unknotting, disintegrating, in his arms. She could not remember the last time she had trusted someone else enough to sleep beside him.

She could not remember the last time she had felt so safe.

The next day was hotter. Unseasonable for this time of year, especially as they traveled north through Bethel, but miserable all the same.

"We need water," Jared had said imperiously to the Jansai who let them out a few hours after they had resumed their trip. The gypsy had laughed at him.

"You got no need for water, nor food, neither." He had sneered, and just for emphasis he punched Wyman as he staggered down from the truck. Duncan made a sudden movement, as if to leap for the Jansai and strike his own blow, but Conran caught his arm.

"Let it be," the Jacobite leader croaked. Tamar had not seen him take a swallow of water since they were first thrown aboard the truck. Not Conran, not Jared. "Save your strength for battles you can win."

Within fifteen minutes they were back in the cage, back on the road north. Now everyone but Conran, Tamar, and Jared lay prone on the floor of the truck, too hot, too weary, and too thirsty to waste energy in sitting or speaking. Bael would not need to tie them to stakes and torch them, if that was his plan; they would die wretchedly on their own.

The truck picked up speed, rocking a little wildly from side to side and causing Jani to spread her arms to keep from rolling across the floor. That was the moment that Jared chose to come to his feet. He steadied himself with a hand wrapped around one of the bars of the cage, and he tilted his head back to watch the merciless sky brighten above them.

And he began to sing.

The Jacobites all stared at him as if he had gone mad, even Tamar, crouching at his feet like a starving beggar. He had closed his eyes but kept his face pointing upward, sightlessly watching the hard blue heaven. He seemed to sing to the sky itself, to the sun, pleading with them to soften and darken and take pity on the poor traveling refugees. His voice, despite hunger, thirst, and fear, was untroubled and unfaltering, rolling through the heated air of the prison like a scented breeze.

Or perhaps the air itself was cooling. The vapors of the wind seemed to be imperceptibly coalescing even as the Jacobites watched. First the sky grew dimmer, as if the sun covered its face with a thin gray veil, and then an unexpected cloud boiled up from nowhere, directly overhead. Another cloud raced up beside it, angrier and darker, and suddenly the sky was nothing but clouds, nothing but temper. A streak of lightning sizzled to the ground, and the clouds exploded with applause.

Jared continued to sing, not once opening his eyes.

His voice sounded in Tamar's head much as Lucinda's had; she heard him not so much with her ears as with some receivers buried in her brain. She could not have said if his voice was rich or thin, powerful or pitiful, gorgeous or mistuned. But it shaped itself to her thoughts and desires; it snuggled into her cortex and her vertebrae. Her heart molded its rhythm to his beat, and she turned over her existence to him.

And then the rain came, falling like jewels tossed from a king's hand. Duncan yelped and scrambled to his feet. Sal yanked Horace's canteen from his limp hand, unscrewed the lid, and held it out between the bars to catch the glittering water. The other Jacobites copied him. The tempo and force of the storm increased; within minutes they were all drenched, and still the rain poured down. Now the Jacobites (all but Horace) were on their feet, arms flung out for balance, heads thrown back, trapping the delicious water in their open mouths. The rain sluiced down, plastered their hair to their heads and their clothes to their skins, and washed away everything—thirst, dust, fear, despair.

As quickly as the storm had swept up, it dissipated. The clouds flattened out, wrung of all their water; the fractious wind skipped once more around the caravan, then sighed and lay down to rest. The furious sun, throwing a tantrum of its own, shoved aside the bleached clouds and glared at the sodden earth below. Slowly, sullenly, the air submitted itself again to that tyrant's will.

But they were cooled, and they had water. When Jared, seeming almost disoriented, opened his eyes at last, he swayed once with the skidding motion of the truck and almost fell. Tamar caught his hand and drew him down beside her. He put his arm around her shoulders as if, even this low to the ground, he could not keep his balance. She leaned in and kissed him on the mouth. The whole universe paused in its eternal spinning; the very earth shook perceptibly with surprise. Jared's arms closed around her, drawing her wet body tightly against his. If she had not been soaked to the bone, she would have sworn she had been set on fire.

Another night, another morning, traveling so many hours that the minutes jumbled together, uncountable and indistinguishable. Now that their thirst had been appeased, all the Jacobites could think of was their hunger. It was better than contemplating their deaths. Another day of this and they would grow too weak even to care.

The land had changed slowly around them, from the lush emerald farmlands of southern Bethel to the mountainous terrain

that bisected the province, to the flatter, browner land farther
north. They had followed a northeasterly route until they neared
the Galilee River, and then they headed due north. Past Semorrah, on and on till they breached the ring of mountains that
guarded the Plain of Sharon.

As the trucks grumbled and clawed their way up those rocky
slopes, all the Jacobites began to stir. This was the end, of
course, their final destination. Anxiety and adrenaline gave them
back what two days of starvation had drained away: a restless,
unhappy energy that put them back on their feet and had them
clinging to the bars, looking once more for escape.

What they saw before them on the Plain of Sharon was not
promising. None of the Jacobites, Tamar surmised, had ever
been at this site when a Gloria was being staged, so none of
them was prepared for the commotion of a grand event. Tents,
pavilions, booths, and pens were spread over the level plain with
as much precision and variety as a small city, and the makeshift
aisles were crowded with more pedestrians than Semorrah on a
market day. The arrival of three additional trucks caused no
shopper to do more than turn an incurious gaze their way before
returning to his bargaining. They could have roared right
through the fair, silent or shouting, and caused no furor at all.
No one would have known, or cared, that the Jacobites had been
brought here to die.

But Omar was crafty. Tamar would grant him that. He halted
the trucks in what looked like the very center of the fairgrounds,
and then he hopped out and took a leisurely look around. Some
of the browsers knew him, that was evident from the murmur
of surprise that went up from many of the bystanders. Others
turned their attention to the trucks themselves, in particular the
traveling prison crammed to the edges with silent, defiant cap-
tives. As if unable to help themselves—drawn by the mystery
or the misery—the fairgoers drew closer, slowly at first, and
then in droves, until there were fifty of them, a hundred, two
hundred, gathered around the Jansai caravan and wondering
aloud what was afoot.

"Is my father here?" Omar asked finally in a carrying voice.
"Is the Archangel present?"

"He's at the inn where he usually stays for the Gloria,"
someone volunteered.

"Will someone fetch him?"

"I'll go!" came from a dozen voices, and suddenly the foot-race was on. Ten fled toward the hotels, half a mile away; others ran for their friends, still obliviously shopping the fair. No one knew what was going on, but clearly a drama was about to unfold; this would be something too rare to miss.

The Jacobites waited in tense silence. Bael, it seemed, was in no hurry to come to them, and the minutes edged by at an excruciating pace. Now the crowd around the trucks was five hundred strong, maybe more, men and women and bright-eyed children, staring in at them and wondering what crime they could have committed to land them here in such ignominy on such a beautiful day. They munched their candied apples, these watchers, and guzzled back their pints of ale, as if prepared to settle in for the exhibition of their lives, and Tamar hated every single one of them.

Finally, slowly, rolling back like a multicolored wave, those who had raced off to find the Archangel returned. With them came a couple dozen others, roused from their afternoon naps or called from their noisy recreation in the taproom. In their midst, walking with a slow, stately dignity, strode a silver-haired old angel dressed in flowing purple robes and looking, even from a distance, as if the fate of the world was his primary concern.

"That's Bael," Jared said, as if aware that few of the Jacobites would know the Archangel by sight. "With the silver hair and the long beard."

"He looks sure of himself, that one," Conran said. Jared gave a short laugh.

"That he is. Has always been."

The crowd made way for the Archangel, wordlessly opening up a passage all the way to the prison truck. All murmuring had ceased; even the noises of crunching and slurping had died away. The Archangel's measured footfalls were the only sounds to be heard.

And they came to a halt three feet from the bars of the Jansai truck, and Bael stared straight at the captured rebels.

"So," he said, and his booming voice was mellow and beautiful. "So, these are the Jacobites who have for so long troubled the realm."

Now the crowd briefly woke to astonishment ("Jacobites!" "*That's* who they are!" "I knew it! Didn't I say it as soon as the truck stopped? Jacobites!'') but quickly fell silent again to hear the rest of Bael's words. He had extended his right hand so that the embroidered purple sleeve fell back to reveal a white silk cuff, and he pointed at the occupants of the truck.

"You! Conran Atwell, who have spread dissent and trouble throughout Samaria for the last thirty years."

"Truth and knowledge," Conran replied cockily. "That's me."

"And you. And you. Duncan, Horace, Wyman, Jani. We know your faces and we know your names. We know the heresies you have spouted across the three provinces."

Duncan spit at him through the bars, but none of the others made a movement. Bael did not step back or even react. His accusing finger had swung toward Tamar.

"And you. The daughter of an angel. How you could have fallen so low, been so easily seduced by evil companions, I will never understand. Your blood, your heritage, should have shown you the shining light of truth."

"Perhaps if you hadn't sent me out to die with my mother on the coldest night of the year, you might have seen to it that I was properly raised," Tamar said loudly. A gasp went up from the crowd; the Jacobites around her burst into low laughter. "So I blame you for my being here. Actually I blame you for everything—"

"*Silence!*" the Archangel roared, and such was the power of his voice that, against her will, Tamar shut her mouth. "You will not speak lies and treachery to my very face!"

"And why should she not?" Jared said coolly. "You have spoken nothing else for the whole of your life."

"*Silence!*" Bael cried again, and this time he addressed not only the Jacobites, but the murmuring crowd as well. For what accusations were these? From despicable, heathen Jacobites, such words could be discounted, but from an angel? Accusing the Archangel of treachery? The mob could not be entirely quieted.

Bael now stabbed his finger in Jared's direction. "And you—you whom I have loved almost as a son, welcomed into my home and my life. You, to have joined this band of heretical liars, the very people that threaten to tear Samaria in two—"

"You are the one destroying Samaria," Jared said. "*You* are the one who has known for five years that the Alleluia Files actually exist. *You* are the one who has hidden the truth, who has lied, who has murdered, all because you did not want to give up the power you love so dearly—''

"Silence him!" the Archangel screamed, and the Jansai leaped forward, beating the metal bars of the prison with pots and sticks and shovels. Inside the cage, the din was so loud that they all shrieked and covered their ears to drown it; outside, the surging assembly shouted and questioned in their own riot of noise. In the commotion, it was impossible to hear what commands Bael gave to the Jansai warrior he motioned over. Two minutes later the truck rumbled to life and slowly inched its way free of the encircling mob.

''Where is he taking us?'' Tamar called to Jared.

''To the middle of the plain! Clear of the fairgrounds!''

''Why?''

But the angel did not answer.

They traveled perhaps half a mile from the booths and tents to a level, empty section of land toward the middle of the plain. There they stopped. They had moved so slowly that the entire crowd was able to follow on foot, still shouting out inquiries and insults and seeming to grow more frenzied by the moment. Yet for all its agitation, the whole mob grew still as once again Bael approached the prisoners and spread his arms for attention.

''Jacobites, pray, if you have any remnants of faith left in your god,'' the Archangel intoned. ''For you are about to die at that god's hands.''

Conran leaped forward, almost flinging himself against the bars. ''We may die at your hands, but it is a machine you call to, and not a god! Whatever kind of destructive power you can cause it to unleash, it is still a machine, a *thing* to whom you send a prayer, and not a god! Never a god!''

''Wait,'' Jared spoke, and for the first time his voice was strained, uncertain. His eyes desperately scanned the skies to the south, but he did not see what he was looking for. His friends, Tamar guessed, arriving too late or not at all. ''You cannot so summarily convict and execute us. Give us a day—give us till sundown. Let our arguments be heard.''

''Your arguments are worthless,'' Bael said contemptuously. ''I will not listen to them.''

''Wait till sundown. Wait even another hour.''

''Why should I?'' Bael demanded.

"You owe me that much for the life I have spent in service to you and the god you say you love."

"You forfeited your life when you turned your back on your god. I will not give you even a minute more. Move back!" he cried, raising his voice so suddenly that even the Jacobites jumped away, tumbling over each other in the narrow confines of the truck. They scrambled to their feet in time to see the roiling crowd also stumble backward, forced away from the truck by the power in that voice. "Move back! For the god will strike down any who stand too close to the unbelievers."

Now the fairgoers were tripping over each other in their haste to put room between themselves and the Jansai truck. Even so, their faces looked mutinous, appalled, disbelieving, and more than one man shouted out, "Wait! We should listen to what the angel says!" But the Jansai had moved quickly, forming a menacing, impenetrable ring all around the transport, shoving the crowd back, widening the circle more and more.

Only Bael now stood anywhere near the truck, oblivious alike to the shouts of the throng behind him and the Jacobites before. Again, he swept his arms out, and this time he threw his head back, and he seemed as rapt and ensorcelled as a madman in a seizure. The sun shimmered along his silver hair, his silver beard, his silver wings; he seemed haloed with its munificent light.

And then he shook his fists twice at the listening sky, spread his fingers as wide as they would go, and began to serenade the god.

For the past day and a half Lucinda had flown as far as her wings would carry them both, and still they had not reached Sinai as quickly as she had hoped. They had left the Gaza ship half an hour before dawn and continued on to Samaria, finally making their way to land a few hours after noon. And still she had flown on, another fifty miles and then another, before Reuben finally insisted they stop. She was so worn out with exertion and worry that she could barely stand once they came to rest outside a modest hotel in a town neither of them had heard of. Reuben negotiated with the innkeeper, led Lucinda to their room, went downstairs to fetch a dinner tray, and returned to find the angel sprawled facedown on the bed. He forced her to eat before allowing her to sleep.

And even when she slept, her dreams were haunted by terrors. The pressure of Tamar's fear weighted her own heart and made it hard to breathe. But there was something there besides the dread, a fugitive sweetness, a joy so remote but so bright that Lucinda turned from side to side in her bed, trying to glimpse it more fully. Wherever Tamar was, whatever was happening to her, she was not alone and she was not completely without hope. Only that realization allowed Lucinda to sleep at all.

In the morning when she woke, she felt heavy and unrefreshed. Reuben looked exhausted, as though her tossing and turning had kept him from sleep as well. He had already risen and washed himself before she opened her eyes, and he had brought up another tray for breakfast.

"Any better?" he asked, coming to sit beside her on the bed. Briefly she leaned against him, drawing some strength from the heat and structure of his body, then she pulled away.

"I can't tell what's wrong. I don't know what to do," she said, anxiety creeping back into her voice.

"Shall we return to Ysral? Shall we fly down to Chahiela to look for her? We do not have to journey on to Mount Sinai now."

"She is not in Chahiela," Lucinda said tersely.

"How do you know?"

"I can tell. She is—moving. Traveling. But I cannot sense a direction. She could be back on the ship. She could be heading for Breven. I don't know."

"We can look for her."

Lucinda shook her head. "We must go to Mount Sinai. To ask Jovah. Perhaps he will be able to track her Kiss and tell us where she is."

"Can he do that?"

"We'll find out." She abruptly pushed him away and leaped to her feet. "There is no time to waste."

"Enough time to eat breakfast, mikala," he said firmly, and so she sighed and made herself swallow a few bites. All she wanted to do was fling herself into the air and fly as hard and as fast as her wings would take her. To Sinai, to wherever Tamar was being tortured, to the god's back door, if necessary. The need for action was a fever in her veins.

"All right," she said, cramming a last piece of bread in her mouth. "Are you ready? Time to go."

They took off again, flying straight west. They were less than two hundred miles from Sinai, for they had flown farther than she thought yesterday; they were almost at the Galilee River. Good. Another three hours and they would be there, bursting in on Jecoliah and her acolytes with an impossibly lunatic demand. . . . Well, she would worry about that when they arrived. Now there was nothing to occupy her but the disciplined sweep of her wings, the weight of Reuben's body in her arms, the play of sunlight along her cheeks, the machinations of the trickster wind beneath her feathers. Flying toward a mountain range was always challenging, for the currents could shift so rapidly; if nothing else, she must pay attention to them. She must shut her mind to her fear for Tamar. There was nothing she could do now for her sister.

But terror drew a tighter and tighter string around her heart. Whatever doom awaited her twin crept closer even as the miles flashed past.

"There," Reuben said suddenly, pointing. "That's the range that houses Sinai."

Lucinda straightened her wings and coasted downward toward the clustered mountains. She was so unfamiliar with Samarian topography; she could have flown right by. "Are you sure?"

Reuben smiled. "I did not waste all my life crossing the sea between Samaria and Ysral, mikala," he said. "Like most Edori, I have spent some time traveling through the mainland just to satisfy my curiosity. And have you not learned by now that an Edori has a flawless sense of direction? That's Sinai. Drop closer to the ground."

She obliged, losing altitude slowly as they approached the gray peaks. "And which of these mountains holds Sinai?" she asked. "For they all look impassable to me."

"I was never inside it," he said. "I would guess there's a path up the mountain to lead the petitioners to the oracle's doorway. Look for some kind of road, though I imagine it's a bad one."

"I don't see—yes, wait, there it is! Do you see it? It looks like a dirt road and it's winding upward—"

She followed the track around the curve of the mountain, dropping even farther to meet the path as it climbed. Thus she was almost at the proper level when they finally spotted a wide open door carved into the mountain itself.

"The portal to Mount Sinai," Reuben said grandly. "Just where I thought it would be."

Lucinda laughed shakily. She slowed her wingbeat even more, barely above hover speed, to position herself just so for the landing on the narrow ledge before the door. It would almost be easier to climb the rough road than to attempt this maneuver. She waited till the wind was absolutely still, then dropped to her feet. A moment of heaviness, as her body accustomed itself to gravity, and then she released Reuben and stepped away.

"Now the hard part," she said, heading inside. "Explaining to the oracle why we have come."

But no one was there.

At first they thought they just had not penetrated far enough down the gaslit hallways, had not peered into enough big, empty waiting rooms, looking for visitors and acolytes. But soon it became clear—by the echoing, untenanted quality of silence, by the absence of any noise they did not make themselves—that there was nobody at Mount Sinai at all. Not petitioners, not servants, not acolytes, not the oracle herself.

"Where could they all be?" Reuben wondered aloud. "Is this some holiday that we do not know?"

"Some emergency, more like," Lucinda replied, thinking again of Tamar. Had whatever disaster befallen her sister also laid low half of Samaria? Had the oracles and all the angels been called together to soothe whatever crisis had arisen? Earthquake—plague—storm? It was hard to imagine a catastrophe so great.

"Well, whatever it is, it makes our task easier," Reuben said practically. "Now. Where do you suppose this blue window is? The one we are supposed to write on?"

"In the center of the god's chamber, right? So, I guess we go to the middle of the sanctuary. Perhaps it will seem obvious when we find it."

She didn't really think so when she said it, but as it happened, she was right. They made their way slowly through the whispering silence; even empty, Mount Sinai seemed so full of wisdom and experience that the stony walls exhaled their murmured memories. Clearly, they did not seek the kitchens or the dormitory rooms, so they need not go all the way down that corridor; and here was just another series of waiting rooms, more luxuriously appointed, designed no doubt for the more exalted of the oracle's visitors. But here was a room that even from the hallway looked bigger than the others—and once they stepped inside, they knew at once they had found what they were looking for.

It was a spacious chamber, well lit with a soft, pleasing light, and it was sparsely furnished with a few chairs, bookshelves, and tapestries. But its central feature, the item that instantly drew their eyes and then their bodies across the floor, was a glowing blue glass plate set into the very wall on the far side of the room. It was surrounded by a wholly mysterious set of buttons, and it pulsed with an eerie, alien light, but it was built into a shape that resembled a desk, and there was a rolling chair set right before it.

"A workstation of some sort," Reuben said to himself. "But what its purpose might be I could only guess."

"I have heard that the oracles use amazing equipment to commune directly with the god," Lucinda said in a low voice. "Perhaps this is it. It has a holy appearance to it."

"It looks like a kind of console," Reuben replied. "Something that might transmit or receive signals."

They had walked slowly as they spoke, and now they were standing directly in front of it. The unvarying blue light was somehow seductive. Lucinda could not keep herself from putting her palm to the glass itself. She expected to burn her fingers, but the screen remained cool beneath her hand.

"What kind of signals?" she asked.

Reuben shook his head. "I have not even the faintest idea. But this is encouraging, don't you think?" He pointed to an arrangement of keys on a shelf below the glass. "These are the same letters as those written in the Edori manuscript. The ones we are supposed to write on the screen."

"Then we have found the right place," Lucinda said, looking around. "I don't see any star on the floor, though, do you?"

"In the center of the room, it said," Reuben replied. "A pentagon. I suppose it is not visible to the casual eye. We must seek it out."

Lucinda moved away from him, bent half over, searching through the dust and scuffs on the floor for anything resembling a pattern. Reuben followed her, dropping to his knees and searching the floor with his fingertips.

"Here! Maybe. There's a groove in the floor just here, and it seems to continue in a straight line—"

She hurried over to stand beside him, tracing with her eyes the route his fingers traveled along the floor. "I can see it," she said suddenly. "There—and there—there! Yes—it's a *star*, a pentagram, I guess, bigger than you'd think. There, Reuben, do you see the edges?"

He climbed to his feet and looked where she pointed. "You're right, I see it. So we're supposed to stand here and wait for the golden light—"

"We have to write that word first," she reminded him. "On the blue screen. Then the light comes down."

He looked at her seriously, silent for so long that she felt the excited race of her heart slow a little in response to his contemplation. "What?" she asked.

"Are you sure this is what you wish to do?" he asked. "You don't know what that golden light will do to us—dissolve us, maybe, in a vitriolic haze. Blind us, make us mad. No one knows that we are here and what we are attempting. Should we wait a day and think it over?"

"No," she said without a moment's pause for thought. "Now. We must find out. We must take the chance. A day from now will be too late."

"Too late for what?" he said, but she could not answer him. She just shook her head and crossed her arms like an intractable child. The Edori sighed.

"Very well," he said. "You stand within the pentagram. I will address the blue screen and see if I can make it accept the letters I indicate. And then together we will wait for the golden light to waft us away into the arms of *Jehovah*."

She stood where he had left her, too determined to allow herself a moment of doubt, even a brief speculation as to what they might find once that iridescent light around them dissipated. If it dissipated; if it came. Reuben, who had been bending over the blue screen, straightened and sprinted to her side. Absently, he put his arms around her.

"How long do we wait?" Lucinda asked.

He shook his head. "No idea. Not long, I would think, or the time would have been specified in the document."

"Perhaps we should count, to pass the time," she said nervously. "Or sing."

He grinned at her, that slow, sleepy Edori smile that no crisis ever seemed to completely chase away. "Not so wise, do you think," he said, "to be singing as you approach the god's ear? He might misinterpret and think you were singing to him."

"Well, not a prayer, then, perhaps a lullaby or—"

The rest of the words scattered in her throat. The world was a well of burnished light; she could not see, or speak, or think. One by one, the molecules of her skin broke apart, drifted away; her flesh turned to whispering static. She felt her lungs flatten and her brain melt. She forgot her name.

And seconds later—or years later—opened her eyes to find herself reassembled, whole, animate, and in a wildly unfamiliar place.

She had somehow remained on her feet, though Reuben, beside her, had fallen to a crouch. She spoke his name urgently, and he stirred and looked up at her, his face blank, his mouth opened as if to speak. He did not utter a word.

"Reuben," she repeated, tugging on his arm. "Are you all right? Can you talk to me?"

"Dead I would indeed have to be if I were unable to talk," he wheezed out, and she laughed. "Give me a moment, mikala. That was a difficult journey."

She slackened her grip and looked around. They were, as the document had forewarned them, in a room of white and silver—but such a room as Lucinda would never have been able to imagine. All around them were a series of consoles similar to the one they had found in Jecoliah's chamber, an array of brightly lit screens and mysterious activating switches. The air was alive with a punctuated buzzing, interrupted and undercut by faint whistles, clicks, and chirrups. The air was completely unscented but somehow it felt very old. It was paper-dry against her cheek and stirred faintly around her as if surprised by the motion of her breathing.

"Where *are* we?" she asked in a low voice. "Reuben, do get up and take a look. Is this a spaceship? It looks like—it looks a little like one of the rooms at the Augustine school."

Laboriously Reuben hauled himself to his feet and took a long, slow look around him. "Indeed it does, and no surprise, if Caleb Augustus modeled his school after what he viewed up here," the Edori said.

"Caleb Augustus visited *Jehovah*? I have never heard that."

"Only a guess that he, like I, followed an angel lover to this place." His voice sounded stronger with each word; curiosity was rapidly restoring him. "These are monitoring devices of some sort, I would wager, and this—this looks much like the blue window we left at Mount Sinai. A communication console, it would appear."

So far, neither of them had ventured to move one inch from the place where the great light had deposited them, but now Lucinda sidled forward a pace. As she was not struck dead, she stepped forward twice more. "Well, let's explore! We must find some way to communicate with the ship."

Reuben caught her hand to hold her in place. "Try introducing yourself," he advised. "The document did say you could speak to *Jehovah* and it would answer back."

She took a deep breath, keeping her eyes on Reuben. She had not really believed that part, and so she had allowed herself to forget it. Feeling half-foolish and half-afraid, she said politely, "Hello, *Jehovah*. Are you listening? I am the angel Lucinda from Angel Rock and this is my friend Reuben sia Havita, an Edori sailor."

The voice, when it instantly replied, was so unexpected that she almost tumbled over. "Ah, an Edori," it said in deep, rolling tones that reminded her a little of Bael's. But even more powerful, even more resonant. "I could not identify him because he does not wear a Kiss. It is unexpected to be visited by an Edori."

There were so many questions to ask following that short speech that for a moment Lucinda stood silent. *Have you been visited by many others, Edori or no? Can you identify anyone who wears a Kiss? Can you track them? Who are you? What is this place we have come to?* "Are you really *Jehovah*?" she asked instead, her voice scarcely above a whisper. "And are you indeed a spaceship?"

"I am an interplanetary space cruiser designed to provide life support for no more than seven hundred individuals for as long as my systems survive," the melodious voice replied. "I was christened *Jehovah* many centuries ago, when I first ferried your ancestors to this planet from the world known as Eleison. You may refer to me as a spaceship if you like.''

"Amazing," Reuben said under his breath. "Simply amazing." He had lost most of his fear and was beginning to circle through the equipment, examining the knobs and buttons and putting his hands briefly to each glass monitor. "What does this—ah, yes, I can see that. And then this must be a navigational—but how does it—or is this where—ah, there. Amazing."

"Feel free to examine any chamber you like," the voice invited them. "There is much to see. This room, as you may have guessed, is the bridge, where most of the functions of the ship are centered and monitored. Elsewhere, you will find living quarters, self-contained greenhouses which produce crops and grain, storage facilities, the energy crystals that power the ship as well as the basic circuitry—"

"Yes, we'll look at all that later," Lucinda said somewhat sharply as Reuben eagerly turned toward what appeared to be the exit. "First, I have some questions to ask you."

"Yes, Lucinda?"

"My sister, Tamar, appears to be in some kind of trouble. Can you tell me where she is and what's happening to her?"

"It is not in my power with accuracy to determine where any individual is located. I can tell you that she is in Samaria and she is alive. More details are not at my disposal."

Lucinda felt a crushing weight of disappointment settle across her shoulders. Reuben turned to show her a sympathetic expression. She waited a moment, till the leap of panic subsided, and then began asking all the other questions she knew should be addressed to *Jehovah.*

"Is it true that the angel Alleluia came here to visit you a hundred years ago?"

"It was, more precisely, one hundred and three years ago, but yes, she was here several times. The engineer Caleb Augustus was also here during that time period."

"And others before them?"

"From time to time. Not often, once the planet was colonized."

"And is it true that you control the weather? And that you can dispense seeds and drugs when they are asked for? Is it true that you can track the lives of all Samarians by the Kisses that we wear in our arms?"

"I cannot precisely control the weather, but I have the capability of altering weather patterns if the angels sing a certain combination of notes that signal me to perform functions that will affect air temperature and wind formations on the planet below us. It is true that, again when my reactors are triggered by specific sound patterns, I can release my accumulated stores of grain and medicine. It is also true that I use the Kisses to follow the numbers of mortals and angels being bred on Samaria, and they are a useful source of data to me."

She took a long, shaky breath. "Is it true you will destroy the world if the Gloria is not sung?"

"I am so programmed."

"And what does *that* mean?"

"Certain functions have been laid down unalterably in my circuits. If this occurs, I must react in this way. I have no independent will. If an angel prays for a particular kind of rain, I respond with a prescribed combination of chemicals. If the Gloria is not sung, I respond with a blast of destructive energy. I cannot control these functions. Only you and the other angels can do so."

"Well, maybe, but it's nothing like control if we have to go along with what you've already been programmed to do," said Reuben in his most colloquial voice. "What if the angels and the mortals living on Samaria today decided they no longer wanted to come together to sing the Gloria? Could your circuits be altered? Could those commands be undone?"

"That is not a piece of knowledge I am equipped with," the spaceship replied, sounding almost prim. "As my circuits were programmed by men, I assume those instructions can be reworked by other men. But perhaps there is a fail-safe device built in which would prohibit the circuits from ever being tampered with. I do not know. I was not informed."

"Fail-safe. That's just what you'd expect from the sort of men who would design the likes of you in the first place," Reuben muttered. "I wonder where I might look to find that information? Just for curiosity's sake, you understand."

"In a minute," Lucinda said. She was not through with her interrogation of the spaceship. "You can hear angels from any point on Samaria, can you not? For instance, you could hear me when I sang from Angel Rock."

"Yes," *Jehovah* acknowledged.

"Then why must the Gloria be sung from the Plain of Sharon?"

"In point of fact, it could be sung from anywhere on the planet and I would hear it. But there are special receptors buried under the Plain that carry voices to me most clearly, and your ancestors wanted to be sure that, if I heard no other music, I heard the Gloria as it was sung every year."

"And it sounds like music? Like words? Like the conversation we are having now? It is that distinct?"

"Yes. If you like, I can open my receivers and allow you to overhear what is transpiring on the Plain even now, so you can experience exactly what I hear."

"But there's nobody on the Plain right now, is there?"

"Indeed, some kind of commercial event is being held there this entire week. A farmer's fair, I believe. There are many voices upraised, though most of it is unimportant chatter."

"Yes, I would like to hear this," Lucinda decided. "Just so I can say I stood beside the god and heard the talk of mortals."

Almost before she had finished speaking, the chamber around them was filled with an unbridled commotion. For an agricultural fair, Lucinda thought, the event seemed to have stirred a lot of tempers. The noises were so clear and so perfectly translated that she could catch the sounds of running footfalls, squealing horses, and rumbling motors over the confusion of angry discussion. Lost in amazement, it took her a moment to sort out individual voices, their words—and their meanings.

"That's Bael," she said suddenly. "Can't miss that voice. And he's—sounds like he's threatening somebody."

For over the ship's invisible speakers came the proclamation: *Jacobites, pray, if you have any remnants of faith left in your god. For you are about to die at that god's hands.*

"Wait—what is he saying?" Lucinda demanded, aghast and disbelieving. "Reuben, did he say—"

"Hush," said the Edori, listening intently. Both of them heard Conran's defiant reply. *We may die at your hands, but it is a machine you call to, and not a god!*

Lucinda stared at Reuben, stark terror in her eyes. "What's

happening? Why are they all on the Plain of Sharon? What is Bael going to do?''

"He's caught them," Reuben said, speaking more soberly than she had ever heard him. "I'd guess he's planning to kill them all now. Right there on the Plain of Sharon."

A sob caught in Lucinda's throat. She felt as if her body was being scorched, her brain seared. "Tamar," she gulped. "Sweet Jovah singing, Tamar is with them—''

Another voice filled the chamber around them, rising over the muttering of whatever crowd had gathered to witness the Jacobites' destruction. *You cannot so summarily convict and execute us. Give us a day—give us till sundown. Let our arguments be heard.*

"It's Jared," Reuben said suddenly. "He's with them."

Lucinda felt a spasm of hope, so brutal it left her lungs bruised. "Can he help them? Can he save them?"

"I don't know, mikala," Reuben said very gently. "It doesn't sound like Jared is arguing from a position of power."

"But then—but—he can't kill them! Reuben, he—dear god, dear god, and Tamar is with them—''

Reuben stepped forward to put his arms around her, but she tore herself away. No comfort, not now, not ever again. She had to hear every last word, every plea, every pardon. Surely there would be a pardon.

"Jovah," she whispered, for how could there not be a god, now when she needed one most? "Spare them, save them, Jovah teach me how to protect them. . . .''

But of course there was no god. She stood at the very heart of the spaceship *Jehovah*, solid proof that the god she had always loved had never existed. If there was no god to intervene, Bael would kill them all. Beat them, burn them, run them through with bayonets, and she could not say a word that would save them.

And then, eerie and magnificent in this sleek echoing chamber, the Archangel's voice came pouring in, raised in song, raised in prayer. Lucinda felt her heart stutter to a halt.

"What is that?" Reuben demanded. "What is he singing?"

"The prayer for destruction. Thunderbolts—lightning. The end of the world . . .''

"Can't he be stopped? *Jehovah*, can he be stopped?" Reuben called out. "Can we countermand him? *Jehovah*, tell us!''

But the ship did not reply. And its fussy, murmurous silence went on and on.

Jared had believed till this very moment that something would save them. That Christian and Mercy would swoop down, snatch Bael away; that the heavens would erupt with angels, vengeful and furious. He had believed he could reason with Bael, stall him, charm him. He had chosen death, but he had not believed he would die.

Until Bael began singing the prayer for annihilation. Then his body flooded with adrenaline, then his brain rioted with fear. "Get down!" he shouted at the Jacobites, and they all fell to the floor, hands covering their ears, cowering before the awful might of that song, that simple prayer. Bael's rich, magnificent voice filled their cage, liquefied their brains, ran through their arteries like silver flame. Jared flung his body across Tamar's, covered her from head to toe with the frail shield of his wings. Not that it would save her, not that anything could save her, Bael would murder her and every last one of them. Yet he clung to her for all that. If the god miscalculated, if the thunderbolt fell an inch too short, perhaps Jared's bones would deflect just enough of Jovah's rage so that Tamar would survive, scarred and witless, perhaps, but alive, alive. . . .

And he had never, at any point in his life, been so astonished as when she shoved him away with all her strength and pushed herself to a sitting position.

"Sing," she said fiercely, and began to do so herself.

Jared stared at her.

It was the wordless, repetitive little tune she had taught him that day in the Marquet hotel, the music she had said she could hear in her head. Even here, even now, the pure, untrained sweetness of her voice caught at his heart and made him silly with wonder. He felt the erratic flicker in his Kiss and knew without looking that it trembled with fire.

She had closed her eyes, as if she was listening, as if she matched her voice, her tempo, to the unseen metronome of someone else's performance. For a moment Jared could only watch her helplessly, marveling at the clean, devout contours of that upraised face, thinking she looked like a priestess, a holy woman, an angel, on her knees in supplication to her god.

And then, because he could not bear to do otherwise, he lifted his voice and laid it alongside hers. Instantly, she skipped upward an interval, twining her harmony around his melody, decorating his voice with her own. They wove the notes back and forth, warp and weft, embroidering the air with jeweled threads and fringes of gold. He drew strength from their braided voices and poured that power back into the song. Almost without his volition, he rose to his feet, pulling Tamar with him, and the song ascended with them. He felt his lungs filling over and over with each separate, momentous note; he felt each one rush through his throat, burst from his mouth, explode in the air with a shower of sparks. Choirs filled his head. The heavens chorused back. They would die singing this paean to a careless god, but they would be gloriously extinguished.

But the thunderbolt did not fall.

Jared could not hear Bael's voice anymore, though he could see the Archangel furiously delivering his prayer. The god could hear Bael's song, no doubt, and was even now shaping the lightning he would hurl to the earth below. Jared sucked in another great gust of air and plunged into his melody again.

And still the thunderbolt did not fall.

The air was so still it seemed to have evaporated, drained pantingly into the vacuum of the sky. Jared's skin crackled as if he stood before a fire; the hair on his arms was polarized with electricity. The world seemed breathless with portent as if the skies overhead prepared to convulse into destruction.

But the thunderbolt did not fall. As if Jared's song had made the god reconsider, as if Tamar's lilting harmony had pleased Jovah more than the Archangel's malevolent request. Nothing moved, nothing breathed, the world did not even spin as the angels sang and the god weighed their motley prayers.

Then suddenly the heavens were split with a great light, an opalescent fireball swirling with amber and saffron. Through this maelstrom an angel burst forth as if born of that crystal blaze. Her white wings were tipped with crimson; a vivid scarlet nimbus flared around her head. Her outstretched hands dripped coins of flame, and her feet were shod in fire.

Shock made Jared mute, and the Archangel fell to his knees with a single heartbroken cry. The fairgoers and the Jacobites all gaped upward, struck dumb. Into that eerie silence two voices continued to rise and fall, twinned, inseparable, singing the beseeching, haunting melody that Jared and Tamar had offered to

the god. It was Tamar's voice, even now, joined with the voice
of that avenging angel who hovered above the plain in a slowly
dimming sphere of light. Two voices, so similar they could have
been one, descant against melody, a harmony so perfect the
brain could not divide it, and the god could not help but prefer
it.

Tamar . . . and Lucinda.

Lucinda, whom they had left behind in Ysral, had appeared
from nowhere out of a golden cloud. Singing a strange, unartic-
ulated prayer that had forced the Archangel to the ground and
persuaded the god not to strike. Jared himself dropped slowly
to his knees, speechless with wonder, while the women repeated
the song another time, and another. Perhaps they would sing till
the world ended. He would not mind listening for just that long.

But now fresh trouble was boiling up on the plain, for he
could hear the growl of high-powered motors and the shouts of
new arrivals. Above them, the air was suddenly alive with angels, maybe a hundred of them, crowding together in a kalei-
doscope of overlapping wings and gesticulating arms. Lucinda
and Tamar fell silent, but these fresh spectators created enough
noise to drown out any prayer Bael might make, should he dare
to raise his voice again. Jared stared at them, trying to make out
familiar figures. Was that Mercy? Were those the angels of
Monteverde?

Before he had identified more than three faces, there was a
sudden tumult much closer to hand. Raised voices, angry shouting, an invasion of bodies pushing through the crowd of farmers
and Jansai ringing the Jacobite truck. There was the smash of
wood against metal, fist against flesh, as fierce fighting broke
out between the watchers, the guards, and the rescuers. More
furious voices joined in the general chaos. Jared had thrown
himself against the walls of his prison and was clinging to the
bars of the cage, straining to see who had arrived. Bael had
jumped up and whipped around to face this new onslaught, calling out to his son and his Jansai raiders to form a circle of safety
around him.

But it was useless. Five minutes later a band of rivermen
wearing Christian Avalone's livery broke through the mob of
farmers and Jansai, wielding clubs and knives. Three of them
descended on the Archangel and forced him back to the ground,
hands behind his back, face almost in the dirt. Two of them had

captured Omar and dragged him, swearing and screaming, around the side of the truck. It was a coup so rapid, ruthless, and effective that Jared had a moment's grave misgiving. If the prestige of the Archangel could be so swiftly overcome, could Samaria ever return to faith in Jovah and his angels?

But so much of the world was overturned already. How would it be possible to put any of it to rights?

In a very few moments Christian himself came striding through the milling throng, intense, focused, in control. *And if we have just changed governments, here is the man we have no doubt elected,* Jared found himself thinking as his friend shouldered his way past the cornered Jansai and came directly over to the truck.

"I see you were serious when you told Mercy she must contact me instantly," were Christian's first words.

Jared could not help smiling. "A few minutes sooner would have been fine with me."

"You have news? You have found the Alleluia Files?"

"We have. Although we have not yet found a way to travel to the ship, we believe those instructions are elsewhere."

"But you have proof? Where did you find it?"

"Proof. In Chahiela. Where, I believe, Bael also found the same proof five years ago."

"Bael . . . Ah," Christian said on a soft, evil sigh. "Then all his fanatic behavior in the past few years . . ."

"Exactly. We must ask him, of course," Jared added dryly. "For he has been scrupulous with the truth so far."

"There are many things we must ask the Archangel," Christian began, but before he could enumerate, a voice rang out that silenced every buzz of conversation on the plain.

"People of Samaria," the voice cried, and every eye turned upward to stare at Lucinda. Even the angels who clustered in the air a few meters below her twisted their heads and batted their wings to achieve a better view. "I have come to you directly from Jovah. I have been flung here by the god's hands. And I tell you—your god is not who you think. People of Samaria, open your minds and prepare to hear the truth."

CHAPTER TWENTY-ONE

They held the first of what Conran referred to as the "postapocalyptic conferences" right there on the Plain of Sharon in one of the hotels that the wealthy used during the Gloria. Tamar thought Conran's mocking title was very apt, for indeed, the Samarians she encountered at the hotel looked shell-shocked, dumbfounded, heads knocked askew with wonder. No surprise; she and the Jacobites might have looked just as stupefied and foundering if all their questing had resulted in just the opposite revelation, that the god existed after all. She blamed no one for being bewildered.

There was not much decided at this first conference, anyway, except that a second, more comprehensive gathering must be set up to discuss the implications of their discoveries and to determine how to proceed. In point of fact, people had only a handful of questions, but these they desperately wanted answered. Among them were: How did the angel Lucinda manage to appear so dramatically overhead, materializing out of nowhere at the most crucial moment? and what was the song that froze Bael's prayer in his throat, that caused the spaceship to reconsider its thunderbolt and saved the Jacobites from destruction?

Tamar could have answered the second one but she did not bother, because the person whom everyone wanted to ask was Lucinda. She watched with an odd, completely unenvious pride as her sister patiently and lucidly explained the same events over and over again. Lucinda did not grow flustered or sullen, as Tamar would have; she did not become angry at the constant expressions of incredulity and denial. She was poised, serene, gracious, and absolutely sure of herself, and everyone who heard her walked away a believer.

Jared, who had listened politely to Lucinda's tale, later pressed Reuben for more details. "So you were aboard the spaceship, exploring, and you just happened to ask *Jehovah* to let you overhear whatever was occurring down on the Plain of Sharon—"

"Strange but true," the Edori replied with a smile. He, Jared, and Tamar had found a quiet spot on an outdoor patio in the rear of the hotel, and they were drinking some wine Jared had fetched. Tamar sipped hers. It was very potent.

"And you heard Bael threatening us, and he started singing— and then what? Lucinda burst into song herself? Did you think she'd gone mad?"

Reuben laughed comfortably. "Well, the thought did take a moment to meander across my mind, for she was distraught enough to be making little sense. But I was the one who had taught her how the same melody, sung in reverse, can undo the effects of the original song. I quickly decided that she was singing the Archangel's song backward, negating his prayer. As it happened, I was right."

"And *Jehovah* could hear her? Her voice was that much stronger because she was right there on the ship?"

Reuben shook his head. "I don't believe so. As I understand the technology, his cues must come from Samaria. She could have sung her heart out, and he would not have heeded her."

Jared glanced at Tamar, but she had already decided she was not taking part in this conversation. She was going to drink her wine, and she was going to keep on drinking it until she got pleasantly intoxicated. It had been longer than she remembered since she had felt safe enough to entrust herself to liquor.

"So until Tamar and I began singing . . ."

"Exactly."

"And because harmony is more powerful than a solo voice . . ."

"As I understand it."

Jared returned his gaze to Tamar. "Did you know when you started singing what you were trying to accomplish?"

She shook her head, then nodded, then sighed. She must explain after all. "No. Well, in a way. Lucinda had explained the concept to me before we left Ysral, but it didn't really make sense. But when I heard her singing—"

"*Heard* her singing?" Reuben interrupted.

Jared nodded. "She hears Lucinda's voice in her head. So she says."

Tamar gave him a minatory glance before addressing the Edori again. "When I heard her, I guessed what she was doing. So I started singing, too." She shrugged. *Simple, really.* Though she had not thought it would work. They had been so close to death right then; she had been able to smell the acrid, sulfurous buildup in the air. She had sung more from defiance than from hope, as she had done most things in her life. And won, this time. She took another sip of wine.

"So our song stopped the thunderbolt," Jared said slowly. "That part I almost understand. But then—from nowhere—Lucinda came exploding through the heavens in this sort of golden mist—"

Reuben nodded wisely. "She teleported," he said.

"She *what*?"

"Teleported. It's the word *Jehovah* uses to describe the way he instantly transports someone from one location to another. It's how we were brought aboard the spaceship from Mount Sinai. It occurred to me to ask him, while Lucinda was singing, if he could transport her to someplace other than Sinai. He said he could. And so we attempted it."

Jared was shaking his head. "But—sweet Jovah singing!— the risk! She could have plummeted to her death, you know. To suddenly find herself in midair, with no momentum or wingbeat to sustain her—she could have dropped like a stone."

"Yes, I did think of that, and I tried to explain it all to her while she continued to sing and continued to listen to all the clamor on the plain. Believe me, I was far from certain she would survive the transfer. But here we all are, safe and happy, so the story has a bright ending after all."

Jared waggled his head from side to side, as if he was not sure about that. "I think the turmoil is just beginning. We are about to tell millions of people that the god they have believed in all their lives does not exist. We have just shoved angels from the seat of power they have occupied for seven centuries. What do we do with Bael? What about Omar? What about the Jansai? How will we deal with them?

"We are about to create a new government and a new religion all at once—and you have a more blithe picture of human nature than I do if you think all that will be accomplished without heartache," Jared summed up. "We have survived the crisis, yes, but that is all we have done. There is far more trouble ahead."

"Well, you are alive to confront it," Reuben said cheerfully. "Which you wouldn't have gambled on a day ago. Pass the wine, that's what I say. Pass the wine and your troubles will miraculously melt away."

Tamar laughed out loud. Reuben filled his glass again and raised it to her in a toast of admiration. Jared was still shaking his head, but Tamar and Reuben clinked their glasses together and swallowed every last drop.

Two days before the second, more decisive conference was held at Christian Avalone's mansion on the River Walk, Lucinda's aunt Gretchen arrived in Semorrah. *My aunt Gretchen, too,* Tamar had to remind herself; but she had had nobody, no blood relatives, for so much of her life that even now she could scarcely credit the existence of a sister, let alone a more distant connection. And this Gretchen (as described kindly by Lucinda and humorously by Reuben) sounded like such a difficult, contrary, domineering woman that Tamar viewed her arrival with a mixture of reluctance and dread.

She was alone in the lovely, airy bedroom Christian had assigned to her and Jared when she heard voices in the hall. "Where is she? Where is that child? Is this the room?"

"Here, let me knock and see if—"

But Lucinda had no time to put her knuckles to the door before it was swept open and a hurricane swirled in. Tamar jumped to her feet, fingers automatically closing around her mother's locket, feeling an absurd leap of panic in her chest. The woman who entered was thin, graying, sharp-faced, and crammed with so much restless vitality that it snapped around her as visibly as an aura. Nonetheless, she came to a dead halt just across the threshold, and stared at Tamar as though at an apparition.

"Dearest, sweetest god, it is indeed you," she whispered. "And you did not die, after all. He could not kill you. Oh, child, if I had known you were alive, I would have searched the earth and heavens for you. I would have taken you with me to safety. Tell me you believe that, for it is the god's own truth."

Tamar smiled with some difficulty. "I believe you. From the

story I was told, you could never have thought I was alive.''

Gretchen came closer, still staring, still marveling. ''And the
life you have led. It makes my blood go cold. I will curse that
devil Conran till the day he dies for not telling me the truth,
when for twenty-eight years he knew it—''

''Don't curse Conran,'' Tamar said, smiling a little more naturally now. ''He did very well by me. He kept me alive, and
you must thank him for that at least.''

Another step closer, the faded eyes still searching every plane
and angle of Tamar's face. ''Well, the face is well enough, and
of course you've got fine eyes just like your sister, but your
hair! Child, couldn't you have found a better cut? And you may
have thought that dye was attractive once, but it's nowhere near
as pretty as your natural color. I think it's time to put a little
more thought into your appearance, especially with everyone
arriving for this big important meeting.''

Lucinda burst into uncontainable laughter, sagging against the
door frame and cramming a hand across her mouth. Tamar felt
her own laughter bubble up, more and more uncontrollably as
Gretchen's face began to simmer with irritation.

''Well, I don't think I said anything so funny, and you've got
just as much work to do with *your* hair and clothing.'' Gretchen
fumed, rounding on Lucinda and shaking her finger. ''Running
wild the way you have! I would never have sent you to Ysral
if I thought you would forget everything I'd taught you about
manners and decorum, every single thing—''

''Aunt Gretchen, I adore you,'' Lucinda said, stopping the
older woman's diatribe by enclosing her in a comprehensive
embrace. ''Don't you ever change. Come. Let's sit down and
get to know Tamar.''

So that had been much less alarming than Tamar had feared,
though she thought it would take her years to grow accustomed
to Gretchen's close, personal attention and forthright criticism.
Nonetheless, in an instant she had been added to Gretchen's
short list of people for whom she would fight till the death. It
was strange, oppressive, and wonderful to mean so much to
another human being. Something else it would take years to
grow used to.

Gretchen liked Jared, though. She fussed over him as she
would a wealthy guest come to spend the summer at the Manor,

or at least so Lucinda said. She looked after his comfort, deferred to his opinion, and never lost an opportunity to tell her nieces how handsome he was ("in looks *and* behavior, because one means nothing without the other"). Jared accepted her homage with his usual flawless courtesy, and laughed about it privately but never unkindly.

Gretchen was less pleased with Reuben, and Lucinda's news that she planned to marry the Edori. "Except that Edori don't marry, so perhaps I just mean that I will be spending the rest of my life with him. Or at least, what portion of his life he isn't away at sea. I don't have the details worked out yet. But he's the man I love."

"He's well enough for an Edori, but you'd be wasting your life to be throwing it away on such a man," was Gretchen's reply, and the two of them argued about it obliquely for the next several days. Lucinda remained completely unruffled about her aunt's disapproval, and confided her suspicions to Tamar later.

"I think she was in love with Conran once, but he wasn't faithful," she said sunnily. "You can see it even now when she looks at him, that she remembers this sort of bone-deep despair. It's turned her against all Edori forever, I think."

"Well, I don't think it's turned her against Conran, because I saw them holding hands on the rooftop garden the other day," Tamar replied.

Lucinda bubbled over with laughter. "Did you really? I can't imagine—but you know him better that I do. Can you *picture* him with Aunt Gretchen?"

Tamar thought. "Well, all the Jacobite women are strongwilled, as a rule, but he always seemed to be involved with the most hardheaded ones of the group. If you'd ever met Elinor . . . Actually, Gretchen reminds me a little of Elinor, and she was the love of Conran's life."

"What happened to her?"

"Died at the Jansai's hands, six or seven years ago."

"I'm sorry."

Tamar shrugged to avoid a direct reply. "Anyway, I can't see him mending his ways at this age and becoming a tame old house cat. I can't see him settling down on Angel Rock and helping Gretchen run the hotel."

"No," said Lucinda, a bit regretfully. "But however it turns out, I think she's enjoying herself now."

But Gretchen was one of the few guests at Christian Avalone's house who had come merely for personal reasons. As the days passed and the house filled up, it became clear that the other visitors had arrived charged with sober purpose: to decide the fate of the world.

Representatives from almost every group on Samaria had been invited: river merchants, Manadavvi, Luminauzi, Edori, farmers, Jansai, oracles, priests, angels. They had constituted themselves a parliament of sorts, and every member would need to vote on any referendums that they drafted. But the real work of mapping out a plan for the future lay with a select group that met one day in Christian's elegant conference room. Christian was there, of course, and the Manadavvi Ben Harth. Jared and Mercy spoke for the angels, Jecoliah for the oracles. Conran was the only Jacobite allowed in the room, if you didn't count Tamar, who was only there because Jared insisted. Reuben and Lucinda had been invited because, as Christian said, "they can speak for *Jehovah* better than the rest of us." Everyone else was barred from the room.

"First order of business," Christian said once the group had been called to order, "what do we do with Bael? And what do we do with Omar?"

"Kill them both," Conran growled, but Mercy hushed him impatiently, and everyone else tried to ignore him. "Kill them," the Jacobite repeated, raising his voice. "Between them, they've murdered hundreds of innocent men and women. They're criminals and assassins, and they need to be tried as such."

"This is not a society that has ever condoned execution for any crime, and we are not about to institute it as a punishment now," Mercy said, swinging on him and speaking hotly. "I understand your own life has been full of brutality, and I regret that for your sake, but you will not bring your bankrupt ethics into this meeting and expect us to sympathize. If you cannot say something constructive, then please do not speak."

Well, that was almost entertainment enough to make Tamar glad she had come to the meeting. She had never seen Conran so wrathful or so silenced. She turned her head away to hide her grin.

"If we are to leave them living," Christian said dryly, "what are we to do with them? We could exile them to Ysral—"

"Poor Edori," Jared murmured.

"Ah, the Edori are very forgiving," said Reuben. "They will welcome the Archangel and his son and try to teach them the simpler joys of life."

But Mercy was shaking her head. "Bael has a powerful voice, and I understand that Jovah—*Jehovah*—can hear all of us from any point on the planet. If Bael were to raise his voice in song and ask for thunderbolts, for instance—"

"I agree," Jared said, speaking more soberly this time. "I think he must be incarcerated, and in a soundproofed chamber, much like the music rooms we have at the angel holds. There are engineers at the Augustine school who could construct a comfortable prison for him."

"Comfortable!" Conran exclaimed. "Is this a man who deserves comfort? Is this a man who—"

"I agree," Christian said, ignoring Conran. "And what of Omar?"

"I would incarcerate him alongside his father," Jared said. "I sometimes think, even now, that Bael acted from belief—he had heard the recording of the Alleluia Files, yes, but he could not credit its veracity. Or, if he did, he was afraid the truth would destroy Samaria—a fear all of us must face right now. But Omar acted out of sheer power lust, and for that I do not think he can be forgiven."

Jared looked over at Mercy, as if expecting her to challenge him, but she was nodding slowly. "Much as it pains me to say it," she said, "I agree with Jared. Neither of them can be allowed to run free, or they will harm us in some manner."

"Then we will have a place built for them," Christian said. "And may it be far from here. Next item. As we all know by now, the so-called god is a ferociously powerful spaceship programmed to destroy Samaria if certain events do not occur. Must we live the rest of our lives, and must our children and their children also live, in fear of the destructive force of this machine? Is there any way to reprogram it so that it will *not* listen for the Gloria? So that we can be free of that annual requirement and the doom that hangs over us?"

Everyone in the room turned to look at Reuben, whose face had assumed a thoughtful expression. "I asked much the same question while we were aboard," he said. "And was not surprised when the ship replied that it did not believe its circuits could be altered. But we could not expect it to help us out with that particular chore. Can it be reprogrammed? Not by me. Perhaps some of your Augustine engineers can work the magic. But I would guess that feat would be a generation or two away."

"Very well, then," said Ben Harth. "Say we are required to produce a Gloria every year. Can we not record it ahead of time and play it back from the Plain of Sharon on the appointed day?"

"I wouldn't think so," Lucinda said, speaking for the first time. "The mass has to be different every year, doesn't it? And it has to contain the voices of people from all over Samaria, right? And if you go to the trouble to gather them all together to *record* the music, wouldn't it be just as simple to gather them together to sing the Gloria?"

"And doesn't Jovah track the Kisses we wear in our arms?" asked Jecoliah, glancing around the table with her milky eyes. "Wouldn't he sense it if we were not actually on the Plain, performing our required song? Would he not consider that a breach of contract and respond in kind?"

"It's a risk," Christian admitted. "I am not eager to run it very soon."

Mercy was glancing around the table and bridling in indignation. "And how does it hurt you—any of you!—to join together once a year and prove that you can live in harmony? If you were able to make these recordings and trick Jovah, would you want to do so? Would you *want* to live in a world where Edori and Jansai did not have to try to live in peace? I think the Gloria keeps us civil—and even so, we are not a peaceful people. Without the threat of the world's destruction, would we be able to live as harmoniously as we do?"

No one answered for a long moment, though Tamar heard Conran mutter a few observations on how civil *his* life had been for the past thirty years. At last Jared lifted his eyes from contemplation of the polished table, and he smiled somewhat crookedly at Mercy.

"You're right, of course," he said. "But I find I am curiously reluctant to sing my *prayers* to an entity that I know is only so much metal and electricity. I can sing mathematically calculated melodies that will produce the desired physical response, but I cannot pray to such a thing. I cannot worship it. I cannot give my heart to the god when there is no god."

Mercy gazed back at him a long time, searching his face with her eyes. "Jovah is not a god, we know that now," she said slowly. "But I do not believe that means there is no divine presence watching over us at all. When our ancestors came to Samaria, they brought some divinity with them—they taught us our words for worship and piety. They believed in a power stronger than themselves, which they could not outrun by crossing millions of miles of space. We have misinterpreted their god, perhaps, but they had one, and it was not *Jehovah*.

"And even if they had founded Samaria, cynical and athe-istic, I would still believe there was a god," she said, her voice growing stronger. "Who drew the patterns of the stars, if not a god? Who designed the marvelous cycle of cloud and rain and river, if not a god? Who made you—and you—and you—if not some god whose name we have forgotten?"

"Science could answer every single one of those questions," Conran snorted. "And has already begun to do so. We can take apart your flesh fiber by fiber and tell you why you have every bone in your body and every mineral in your blood. As for the dance of the stars, mass and gravity will give you those for-mulas, and there is nothing easier to explain than how the sea turns into storm."

"You are missing the point," she said to him calmly. "If there is no god, what is left but science? What is left to endow us with any grace? You can tell me the chemical makeup of my skin and my brain, but how can you explain away my soul? And if there is no god to watch over me, chastise me, grieve for me, rejoice with me, make me fear, and make me wonder, what am I but a collection of metals and liquids with nothing to celebrate about my daily living?"

"You have your friends for that!" he exclaimed. "They love you when you're good and despise you when you're not. Who needs more than that?"

Mercy regarded him fixedly. "Do you truly want to live in a universe where you, Conran Atwell, are the highest achieve-ment, the only moral arbiter and the final judge? I do not trust to your goodness enough. I do not trust to any man's. If we do not have a god, we have no limits. And a race without limits will become savage in a generation."

"I am not a savage," he muttered. "And I need no god to keep me moral."

"But if there is a god, how do we find him? Where do we

look?'' Jecoliah asked. ''Do we create him ourselves, from our hopes and our desires? We have been down that road before, and it was a blind alley. We do not want to delude ourselves again.''

''Alleluia said that *Jehovah* has great stores of information about our ancestors and their society,'' said Jared. ''Perhaps we could turn to it for guidance, for it may hold the knowledge we seek. And if not—''

''We can all live as the Edori do,'' Reuben interposed. ''Believing in one great nameless god who watches over the entire universe, who is everywhere at once but nowhere reveals himself. He hears every prayer, though he does not always answer—''

''Because he does not exist!'' Conran shouted.

''No, I believe he does,'' Tamar said, speaking suddenly when she had had no intention of even opening her mouth. She was embarrassed to find all eyes upon her, but she plunged ahead anyway. ''I have been raised to deny the existence of Jovah—of any god. And yet, when I was at my most desperate and most afraid, I prayed. The words rose to my mouth before I knew I was thinking them. And help came. I think we need a god so greatly because some god has created us, and he left behind that deep desire. I don't believe in Jovah, but I believe in something.''

''That's because you're a credulous, uneducated fool!'' Conran roared, practically leaping across the table as if he would take her by the throat and shake her. Jared shoved him back with more force than the Jacobite expected, and every other voice was raised simultaneously. Christian had to call repeatedly for silence before the room reluctantly quieted down.

''Among other things, it would seem that we need to form a commission on the study of religion,'' the merchant observed when he finally had at least half the attention of everyone in the room. ''And we can decide who should head that commission after we have decided a few more key questions. Namely, do we still require an Archangel to lead Samaria? And if so, who will it be? And if not, how shall we run this country?''

''We have had enough of Archangels, and angels, too,'' Ben Harth said at once, clearly expecting Christian's instant agreement. But the river merchant surprised Tamar by cocking his head to one side and looking extremely thoughtful.

"You and I may have—our friend Conran certainly has—but I am not so sure the rest of Samaria is ready to be done with Archangels," Christian said slowly. "Jared is right. We have such a huge transition ahead of us that I view the coming months with a certain trepidation. And how will the common people of Samaria feel to be stripped of everything in a single blow—their god, their government, their system of redress? Even if the Archangel no longer serves the god, don't we still need an Archangel to mediate between *Jehovah* and Samaria? Don't we still need an Archangel to lead the Gloria? To direct the angels? To inspire the people of Samaria? To serve a civil, if not a divine, function?"

"*I* don't," Conran said, but most of the others in the room were nodding. Ben Harth looked coldly furious and spoke almost before Conran had finished.

"I do not believe I need the intervention of an angel to tell me which taxes are fair and how to administer justice to my tenants," he said in measured tones. "And many of the other Manadavvi will echo my opinion. As long as we are threatened by the spaceship *Jehovah,* we may need the skills of the angels, but we don't have to treat them like deities themselves. We don't have to honor them, or go to them in their mountain holds like penitents and beggars—"

"You should honor the angels because you should honor every living being," Mercy said in a steely voice. "And that does not change because the god has changed."

"Yes, but there may be a kernel of truth in what he says, Mercy," Christian said in a gentle voice. "Perhaps it is time to take the Archangel out of the hold and put him somewhere more accessible. Luminaux, maybe, or Semorrah. Make him—or her— part of a council of officials who debate and decide policy. For surely you would not exclude angels entirely from our future system of government?" he added, turning back to Ben Harth.

"No, perhaps not," the Manadavvi said stiffly.

"But if we are to keep the institution of Archangel," Jared said, "how shall that person be chosen? By the god's—by the spaceship's—recommendation? He did not choose so well last time. Yet I am not sure we would choose any better."

"Surely we cannot leave *Jehovah* out of the process entirely," Lucinda said. "Bael may not have been a good choice, but for centuries *Jehovah* selected wise leaders who have guided us well. We must at least ask for his advice, don't you agree?''

"I think so, yes," Christian said slowly, eyeing her intently. "But I have my own theories about who should be selected. And among other things, I believe that our next Archangel should be flexible enough to break with tradition but sensible enough to avoid foolhardy crazes. Someone who has managed to steer clear of the cliques and alliances that have shaped Samaria for the past forty years. Someone sympathetic to Jacobites and Edori, who values the knowledge they have to offer. And it would not hurt, I believe, if this Archangel had a personal familiarity with the workings of *Jehovah*."

Now everyone in the room was looking at Lucinda. Her eyes had widened with disbelief; shock had blanked her face. Before she could speak, Conran muttered, "Yes, well, she's the only one of the lot with a soul, so you may as well have her if you've got to have someone," and Ben Harth had said, "Acceptable, but barely."

"Jecoliah?" Christian asked, still watching Lucinda. "Do you think you could propose Lucinda's name to *Jehovah* and receive a coherent reply?"

"Actually," Jecoliah said, "I asked him the day before I left for this conference if he had yet determined the name of the next Archangel."

"And he said?"

"That Lucinda should be given the office in one year's time."

"But—" Lucinda said, but other voices drowned her out. "One year!" "We cannot wait so long!" "And in the meantime?" Christian raised his hands to call for silence.

"So we must find an interim Archangel to finish out Bael's term, is that what *Jehovah* has suggested?"

"Not a bad idea," Mercy said. "That will give us time to train Lucinda in the ways of Samaria—for you may want her innocent, but you don't want her ignorant, or there will be no end of trouble!"

"But," Lucinda said.

"And for interim Archangel," Jared said with a smile, "there can be only one choice. I think we are all agreed on that."

"Yes," Christian said softly. "Mercy? Are you prepared to move to Semorrah for a year? I will gladly house you here, or help you find whatever accommodations suit you better."

Now Mercy looked as startled and uncertain as Lucinda.

"Me?" she exclaimed. "Well, I'll serve any way I can, of course, but I don't think I—"

"You're the only one," Jared told her. "We have a rough year ahead of us, and we will need someone with bottomless resources of civility and grace. You are our old order. Lucinda"—and he stretched a hand across the table toward the other angel—"is our new. If you cannot keep us all in harmony for the next year, then no one can, and we will have no world to turn over to Lucinda for safekeeping."

"But I—well, certainly you can put it up for a vote, and if this is what the grand council wants—and I'll do what I can—but—"

"But I don't know why you think I should be the Archangel after Mercy," Lucinda finally managed to say. "I know nothing about your politics or your way of life. And I have no interest in power, religious or temporal. I've never given it a thought in my life."

"Yes, and that's why it must be you," Jared said gravely. "For nearly twenty years Samaria has been in the hands of a man who *did* care greatly for power. And now we need someone who does not. Someone who can see clearly, eyes unclouded by prejudice, and mind unfettered by fear. If there is something you are afraid of, I have yet to see it. And if there is someone you cannot tolerate, I have not met that man. You are our fresh hope, Lucinda, as we enter a perilous new course. Won't you agree to help us? We will all be there to help you."

There was another moment of taut silence, which Conran broke with a snort and a scowl. "Well, *I* won't be," he said. "You just damn well better count me out."

And this time Tamar could not help herself. That tense and respectful silence was broken by the sound of her smothered laughter, which she could not restrain and could not entirely muffle. At first everyone around the table tried to quell her with looks of reproof and indignation, but one by one they gradually succumbed to the contagion of her merriment. First Jared, then Christian, then Mercy began to smile, and soon everyone else grinned or chuckled along. Lucinda was the last to give in, for she still seemed more stupefied than gratified, but finally she, too, began to smile shyly. The room seemed full of it, Tamar thought a few minutes later as she finally managed to choke down her last giggles—not laughter, after all, but hope.

• • •

It was late that evening before Tamar had a chance to apologize for that outburst to anyone, and when she did, it was to Jared. He had pried himself free from the formal dinner much later than he had promised he would (but she had expected that; she had refused to accompany him to the meal, since she simply could not bear another discussion on the future of Samaria) and joined her on Christian Avalone's rooftop garden. They stood with their arms crossed on the brick wall that formed the outer boundary of the building, and looked down at the fantastical lights of the city.

"Sorry," she said, though she did not, even now, feel particularly sorry. "About laughing like that. But it was funny, you know, everyone so serious about the fate of the world and Conran, as usual, thinking only of himself—"

Jared patted her absently on the back as if to accept her apology. "I like Conran, though," the angel said. "Old bastard that he is."

"So do I," Tamar replied. They observed a brief moment of silence before she ventured a cautious question. "And do you mind?"

"Mind what?"

"Being left out like that. Not being named Archangel. I know it's something you wanted."

Eyes still fixed on the lights below, Jared said slowly, "No, I never did want to be Archangel. My name was brought up often enough as a possibility, though, and I was never sure why. Oh, I'm the right age and I look the part, I suppose, and people like me, but—Archangel? I've always been something of a dilettante. I've never even carried out the duties at my own hold with much fervor. I would have made a very bad Archangel."

"So what do you do now?"

"Now . . . I think I will start to become the sort of man who *would* have made a good Archangel. Pay more attention to Monteverde and Gaza. Take up my responsibilities. Become an ally to Mercy, and then to Lucinda—a smart, well-informed, cunning ally. I need to be more deeply involved in the changing world around me, and to do that, I need to be more anchored to my own home."

His words took him farther and farther from a vagabond Jacobite who, suddenly, had no purpose in her own world. Tamar felt an unaccountable depression steal over her, a hopelessness she hadn't felt since that day in the Jansai truck when this very same angel lifted his voice to pray to the god for rain.

No god, of course; but there had been rain. And since that day, she had felt secure in the belief that the angel loved her. But that was on the verge of death and in the euphoria of reprieve. She could not imagine there was a place for her back in his very real world. Not a place for her anywhere. To prevent him from asking the question she had no idea how to answer— *And what do you plan to do now?*—she spoke quickly and almost at random.

"Home. That's something I haven't ever had. Maybe now that all the Jacobites are safe, I can return to Luminaux. Or maybe go back to Ysral. I suppose that's where Conran's going."

But now Jared had turned to look at her, had shifted his body so that his hip rested against the brick wall and he had a hand free to hold out to her. As he did.

"You have a home with me, Tamar," he said quietly. "Even if the walls of my hold tumbled down around us and all the other angels turned me out, you would still have a home with me. In my heart. Anywhere I happened to be. I love you. Come to Monteverde with me and be my wife."

Her ears were ringing; her blood was shouting; this was delirium, or this was joy. But through the pandemonium, she managed to reply with a sort of calm derision. "Your angels and your family certainly would turn you out of Monteverde if you came home with me as your bride. A Jacobite? A heathen? I don't think I would be very welcome."

"Nonsense," Jared replied, and a teasing note crept into his voice. "You come from very honorable angel stock, after all. And do you forget that your sister will be Archangel in less than a year's time? A fancy enough pedigree for anyone, I should think."

"That's my sister," she argued. "I'm much less presentable."

"Well, it's true that you're evil-tempered and unpredictable," Jared said thoughtfully. "And if I had to entertain your aunt Gretchen more than once every six months, I'd consider gruesome forms of murder. And when your sister comes to visit, she'll no doubt bring along her outlandish Edori lover, who's far less presentable than you. But I think I can bear all those trials. Far more easily than I could bear losing you.''

He had dropped his hand on her shoulder and now he drew her nearer, though she stubbornly resisted falling into his arms. One more time in that winged embrace and she would never be able to wrench herself free. ''Well,'' she said, her eyes on her feet and her voice very low, ''I could come for a while. Stay for a little bit. See how I liked it. And leave if you—when you— if you got tired of having me around—''

''Splendid!'' Jared exclaimed, and pulled her emphatically against his chest. Her heart bounced against her ribs like a ball thrown down a stairwell. ''Then you'll stay forever! We'll set the wedding date as soon as you've had a chance to meet my mother.''

''But—'' she said, but, like Lucinda, got no chance to finish her protest. Jared closed her mouth with a kiss and all her racing thoughts, all her jumbled arguments, grew tame and docile witn that pressure. Everything ended here, or everything began; the world was made new. She put her hands tentatively up to his shoulders, felt the marvelous interplay of muscle and bone, re- siliency and strength. His wings settled around her like so much tangible starlight, ice-white and glowing in the dark, and for her, for the rest of her life, those would always be the colors and textures of home.

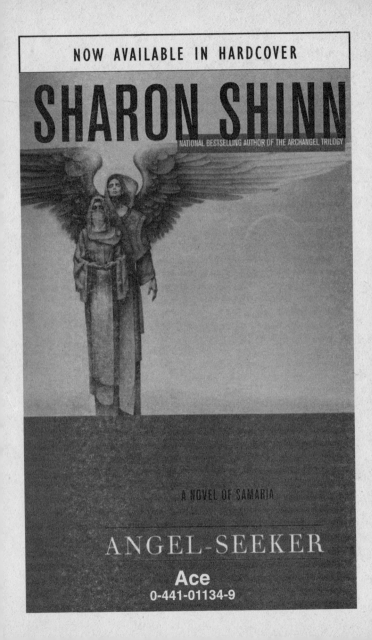

NOW AVAILABLE IN HARDCOVER

SHARON SHINN

NATIONAL BESTSELLING AUTHOR OF THE ARCHANGEL TRILOGY

A NOVEL OF SAMARIA

ANGEL-SEEKER

Ace
0-441-01134-9